W9-ARP-100

CAROLE MORTIMER is one of Harlequin's most popular and prolific authors. Since her first novel was published in 1979, she has shown no signs of slowing her pace. In fact, she has published more than 150 novels! Her strong, traditional romances, with their distinct style, brilliantly developed characters and romantic plot twists, have earned her an enthusiastic audience worldwide.

Carole was born in a small English village, and had early ambitions to become a nurse. When an injury interrupted her training, she went to work in the computer department of a well-known stationery company.

During her time there, Carole made her first attempt at writing a novel for Harlequin Books, and while it was rejected, her second manuscript was accepted, beginning a long and fruitful career that she has thoroughly enjoyed.

Carole lives "in a most beautiful part of Britain" with her husband and children.

USA TODAY Bestselling Author

CAROLE MORTIMER

The Yuletide Engagement

A Yuletide Seduction

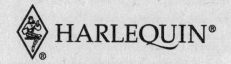

TORONTO • NEW YORK • LONDON
AMSTERDAM • PARIS • SYDNEY • HAMBURG
STOCKHOLM • ATHENS • TOKYO • MILAN • MADRID
PRAGUE • WARSAW • BUDAPEST • AUCKLAND

Recycling programs
for this product may
not exist in your area.

ISBN-13: 978-0-373-68815-9

THE YULETIDE ENGAGEMENT & A YULETIDE SEDUCTION

Copyright © 2010 by Harlequin Books S.A.

The publisher acknowledges the copyright holder of the individual works
as follows:

THE YULETIDE ENGAGEMENT
Copyright © 2003 by Carole Mortimer

A YULETIDE SEDUCTION
Copyright © 1999 by Carole Mortimer

CONTENTS

To Peter

THE YULETIDE ENGAGEMENT

CHAPTER ONE

"CINDERS shall go to the ball!" Toby announced as he stood poised in the kitchen doorway, a look of triumph on his boyishly handsome face. "Although the first person to call me the Fairy Godmother is going to get slapped!"

Ellie looked up from the newspaper she had been reading where she sat at the kitchen table, blue gaze narrowing as she took in the pleased flush on her brother's cheeks. "Toby, did you call into the pub again on your way home from work?" she prompted suspiciously. His eyes looked overbright, and he wasn't making much sense, either!

"That's all the thanks I get for getting you out of a difficult situation—accusations of inebriation!" He grinned widely as he came fully into the kitchen, leaving the door open behind him, despite the fact that snow was forecast for later this evening.

Ellie gave an involuntary shiver as a cold blast of air followed her brother into the room. "At least shut the door, Toby," she reasoned with indulgent affection. "You—"

"Didn't you hear me, Ellie?" He pulled her easily to her feet, swinging her round in the close confines of the kitchen.

"Something about Cinders and a ball." She nodded,

starting to feel slightly dizzy as the kitchen became a giddy blur; maybe intoxication was infectious? "Toby, will you please stop?" she gasped weakly.

He did, holding onto her hands as she swayed slightly. "Ellie, I asked him and he said yes. Can you believe that?" he exclaimed happily. "Didn't I tell you he's one of the good guys? He's even coming round later this evening to sort out the details," he announced triumphantly. "Isn't that just—?"

"Toby, will you just slow down and tell me who you have asked to do what?" Ellie cut in impatiently, but she already felt a terrible sense of foreboding as it slowly started to dawn on her exactly what Toby might have done. Surely he hadn't—he wouldn't have—? She had been joking, for goodness' sake!

Toby let go of her hands, grinning at her victoriously as he reached for an apple from the bowl in the middle of the kitchen table, biting down on its crispness with complete enjoyment.

"Toby!" Ellie said warningly. "Will you just tell me exactly what it is you've done?" Although she had a feeling she already knew the answer to that!

Her brother returned her gaze with guileless blue eyes. "I've asked Patrick to escort you to your company Christmas dinner, of course," he dismissed with satisfaction.

"Patrick…?" she echoed faintly.

"Patrick McGrath. My boss." her brother enlarged impatiently as she just stared at him. "Remember? We were discussing the problem at the weekend and you said that what you really needed was someone high-powered like Patrick to accompany you. That way—"

"But I wasn't being serious, Toby," she cut in incredulously, sinking back down onto the kitchen chair, staring disbelievingly at her brother. He was the younger by only a year, but sometimes—like now—it could feel like ten!

The company Christmas dinner was quickly looming, and this year, after Ellie's recent break-up with Gareth, a junior partner in the law firm they both worked for, it promised to be something of an ordeal for her. Not to go would give the impression she was too much of a coward to face Gareth and his new girlfriend, but to go on her own would make it look as if she were still pining for him. Which she most certainly was not!

Which was why, over the weekend, as she and Toby had lingered over their meal together on Sunday evening, she had drunk one glass of wine too many and suggested that she needed someone like Patrick McGrath, Toby's wealthy entrepreneurial boss, to go with her to the dinner—no one could possibly think she was still interested in Gareth when she was in the company of such a man.

Tall, dark, handsome and extremely successful, Patrick McGrath was the ideal man to allay any doubts anyone might have as to her having any lingering feelings for Gareth.

But she had thought Toby knew that it had only been that third glass of wine talking, that she hadn't really meant for it to happen!

She closed her eyes now in pained disbelief. "Toby, please, please tell me you haven't really asked Patrick McGrath to take me out next week," she groaned desperately.

Her brother paused in the act of taking another bite of his apple. "I haven't?" he said uncertainly, some of the look of triumph starting to fade from his face as he finally noticed Ellie's marked lack of enthusiasm.

"You haven't!" she repeated firmly.

She had met Toby's boss only once, five months ago. It had been enough. There was no doubting that Patrick McGrath was very rich, very self-assured, and very eligible. In fact, the very last person Ellie would ever want to ask her out!

Toby looked puzzled. "But on Sunday night you said—"

"I had drunk too much wine, for goodness' sake," Ellie stood up to pace the confines of the room. "I wasn't being serious—I just thought of the most unlikely person ever to—I didn't really *mean* it when I said—"

"Patrick would make the perfect escort for your dinner a week on Friday," Toby finished obligingly.

She winced as she remembered saying exactly that. But it was a situation that required an extreme solution for unusual circumstances. On Sunday evening she had run the gamut of them, and had suggested Patrick McGrath being the perfect escort as the most extreme of those extremes. She certainly hadn't expected Toby to act on it!

"Exactly," she confirmed weakly. "Toby, please tell me you didn't—"

"But I did," Toby told her impatiently. "I asked Patrick to accompany you. And as he said yes I can't see what your problem is." He shook his head.

He couldn't see—! The problem was that Ellie felt totally ridiculous and completely humiliated. She had no intention of—of—

"Toby, you can just call the man right now and tell him not to come here this evening—that you made a mistake, that your sister doesn't need an escort next Friday or any other time, and that if or when I do need an escort I'll find one of my own, thank you very much!" She glared her indignation at her irresponsible brother.

Blue eyes blazed at the thought of her humiliation if she should ever meet Patrick McGrath again. Her dark, shoulder-length hair seemed to crackle with the force of her anger, every inch of her five-foot-two-inch frame seeming to bristle with indignation.

"But—"

"Call him, Toby," she repeated with cold fury. "Call Patrick McGrath right now and tell him!"

"But—"

"Now, Toby!" she ground out forcefully.

"I think what your brother is trying to tell you—Ellie, isn't it?—is that there's no need for him to call and tell me anything—I'm already standing right here," drawled a lazily amused voice from directly behind her.

Ellie had spun round at the first sound of that drawling voice, having to arch her neck back in order to look up into the confident face of Patrick McGrath.

If ever she had wanted the ground to open and swallow her up it was right now.

Patrick McGrath!

Tall—well over six feet. Dark—hair kept deliberately short as it looked inclined to curl. Handsome—grey eyes beneath arched dark brows, an arrogant slash of a nose, chiselled lips that were curved into a smile at the moment, an out-of-season tan darkening those distinctive features. Successful—even the casual clothes he was wearing this evening—a black silk shirt and faded denims—obviously bore a designer label, and the black leather shoes were no doubt hand-made.

"So, Ellie," he drawled softly. "What was it you wanted Toby to tell me?"

She was trying to speak, really she was; she just couldn't seem to get any words to come out of her throat!

"The details for next Friday, perhaps?" Patrick McGrath prompted interestedly, grey gaze lightly mocking.

How Ellie remembered that mocking gaze. How could she ever forget it? Toby still had no idea what had actually happened at her one and only other meeting with this man; Ellie hadn't told him, and as the days and weeks had passed, without Toby making any reference to it, it had eventually become obvious that Patrick McGrath wasn't going to tell her brother all the details of that meeting, either.

But Ellie was unlikely to ever forget them!

It had been an unusually hot summer this year, with everyone wearing the minimum of clothing, and Ellie, conscious of her impending summer holiday abroad and with a wish not to stand out like a sore thumb on the Majorcan beaches, had decided to spend one Saturday afternoon sunbathing in their secluded back garden.

Topless.

How could she have known that Patrick McGrath had been telephoning for over an hour, urgently trying to contact Toby? That he had decided to come over to the house in person when he'd received no reply? Or that he would stroll out into the garden when he found the house unlocked but seemingly deserted?

Ellie had made a mad scramble for her top when she'd realised she was no longer alone, but it hadn't been quick enough to prevent that piercing gaze from having a full view of her naked breasts.

Damn it, she was sure she could see the knowledge of that memory now, clearly gleaming in those mocking grey eyes.

Despite what she might have said on Sunday evening, warmed by the unaccustomed wine, Patrick McGrath was the last man she wanted to accompany her anywhere!

She drew in a deep breath. "Toby has— He was mistaken when he asked—I'm sorry you've been troubled, Mr McGrath." She spoke dismissively, her gaze fixed on the second button of his black silk shirt. "I never meant—"

"Toby, why don't you make us all some coffee?" Patrick McGrath turned to the younger man authoritatively. "While Ellie and I sort out whether or not I'm being stood up a week on Friday," he added derisively.

Toby set about making the pot of coffee and Ellie looked up at Patrick McGrath reprovingly. He might find all this funny, but she certainly didn't. As if any woman would ever stand this man up!

But they did need to sort this mess out, and she would rather do it out of earshot of her well-meaning but unthinking younger brother.

"Let's go through to the sitting room, Mr McGrath," she suggested briskly, some of her normal self confidence returning as she led the way down the hallway to their lounge.

She was twenty-seven years old, had cared for Toby since their parents were killed in a car crash eight years ago, taking over the running of the family home as well as continuing her full-time job as secretary, eventually to one of the senior partners in a prestigious law firm. She was more than up to dealing with this situation.

Well…ordinarily she could be up to dealing with it, she conceded as Patrick McGrath stood in the middle of the sitting room, looking at her with his laughing steely eyes.

How on earth did Toby cope with working for this man every day? she wondered frowningly. He had such presence, such confidence, that just being in the same room with him was a little overpowering. But she knew Toby thought the other man was wonderful, that her brother thoroughly enjoyed his job as this man's personal assistant.

Maybe it was only women who found Patrick McGrath overpowering…?

Well…one woman, Ellie conceded self-derisively. Maybe if she weren't so completely aware of the fact that this man had seen her sunbathing topless—

Stop that right now, Ellie, she told herself firmly. If she was going to sort this situation out at all then she had to put that embarrassing memory completely from her mind. Although it would help if Patrick McGrath were to do the same…

His next words didn't seem to imply that was the case!

"I don't believe the two of us have ever been formally introduced," he drawled softly, with an emphasis on the "formally", it seemed to a slightly flustered Ellie. How could she possibly have formally introduced herself while at the same time clutching a top in front of her naked breasts?

"Probably not," she conceded abruptly. "But I'm sure you're aware that I'm Ellie Fairfax, Toby's older sister, and I am aware you're Patrick T. McGrath—Toby's boss."

He gave an acknowledging inclination of his head. "The T stands for Timothy, by the way. And Ellie is short for...?"

"Elizabeth," she supplied dismissively. "Although what—?"

"It may come up in conversation a week on Friday." He shrugged broad shoulders.

"Mr McGrath, there isn't going to be any 'a week on Friday'."

She sighed frustratedly. "I have no idea what my irresponsible brother may have told you, but—"

"He adores you, you know," Patrick McGrath cut in softly.

She felt the warmth in her cheeks at this completely unexpected comment. "I love him too." She nodded. "Although I don't really think that's relevant to our conversation." She frowned.

"Ellie, do you think we could both sit down?" Patrick McGrath suggested gently. "At the moment we look like two opponents about to face each other in the ring," he added dryly.

Maybe because that was exactly how he made her feel—totally on the defensive! "Please—do sit down," she invited abruptly.

"After you," he drawled politely.

Ellie looked at him impatiently, finding herself the focus of Patrick McGrath's cool grey gaze as he waited for her to be seated before he would sit down himself.

Old-fashioned good manners, as well as all those other attributes!

Ellie sat down abruptly, determinedly putting those "other attributes" firmly from her mind. "I accept that

Toby meant well when he—when he spoke to you today—" she began huskily, stopping to look enquiringly at Patrick McGrath when he began to smile.

"Sorry." He continued to smile. "Toby is—he's one of the least selfish people I've ever met. As well as being completely honest, utterly trustworthy and totally candid." He sobered slightly. "You've done a lot for him, Ellie," he told her admiringly.

The warmth deepened in her cheeks at this even more unexpected compliment. "I'm pleased he's working out so well as your assistant."

"I wasn't just talking about him as my assistant, Ellie," Patrick McGrath cut in impatiently. "Toby is an exceptional young man. And it's all thanks to you," he added firmly.

She gave a rueful smile. "I think my parents may have had something to do with it."

"Your parents were killed when Toby was eighteen." He shook his head. "A very dangerous time for a young man to be left without guidance."

Ellie frowned. "You were right about Toby being candid!" It made her wonder exactly what else Toby had confided to Patrick McGrath about their private family affairs.

He looked at her quizzically. "You should be proud of him, Ellie, not—"

"Here we are." Toby was grinning widely as he kicked the door open with his foot and came in with the tray of coffee things.

Ellie looked up at him affectionately; she *was* proud of him—of the way he had carried on with his plans to go to university to study law after the accident that had killed their parents, of the way he had obtained a first-

class degree, of the way he had worked doggedly in a
law firm for the two years following, before applying and
succeeding in getting this position with Patrick McGrath.
Yes, she was very proud of him—she just wished that
she had taught him to be a little less candid when it came
to their own private affairs!

"All settled?" He sat back on his heels to look at them
both expectantly after placing the tray down on the low
table.

"Almost." Patrick McGrath was the one to answer
him dryly.

Almost nothing! Ellie was grateful to him for his
praise of Toby and of the part she had played in helping
to form him into the likeable young man he was—but
that did not mean she was going to agree to this ridiculous plan for Patrick McGrath to accompany her to the
company Christmas dinner!

"We just have to dot the *i*'s and cross the *t*'s," Patrick
McGrath assured the younger man.

"Really?" Toby looked pleased by the prospect as he
stood up. "I have a date later, so if neither of you mind
I'll just go upstairs and change while you two chat. Be
back in a couple of minutes," he added, before leaving
the room.

"You see what I mean," Patrick McGrath murmured
softly. "He's like a puppy, or a little brother that you don't
want to disappoint."

"He happens to *be* a little brother," Ellie reminded
him frustratedly. "And I'm afraid this time he's going
to be very disappointed!"

"Why?" Patrick McGrath regarded her with cool eyes.

"Because—because, Mr McGrath—" she began impatiently.

"Patrick," he invited smoothly.

"Very well—Patrick," she bit out decisively.

"Has something changed since Toby spoke to me this afternoon?" he prompted interestedly. "Have you and the ex-boyfriend managed to patch things up after all? Because if you have—"

"No, we haven't managed to 'patch things up'," she cut in evenly, her frustration increasing by the minute as she felt this situation slipping more and more out of her grasp. "And we never will," she added firmly. "But that does not mean—"

"You have to go to the dinner with me instead," Patrick McGrath finished slowly. "Do you have someone else in mind?"

"No. But—"

"Then where's your problem? I was asked; I said yes—"

"You're starting to sound like Toby now," she interrupted weakly. "Mr—Patrick," she corrected as he raised his brows in silent rebuke, "you can't seriously want to come to a boring company dinner as my escort!"

"Why can't I?"

"Because it will be *boring*!" she assured him heatedly. What was wrong with the man? Couldn't he see she didn't want him to go with her?

His mouth twisted into the semblance of a smile. "Ellie, I think you underestimate yourself," he drawled huskily.

"I wasn't—" She broke off, her cheeks fiery red. "Look, Patrick, Toby shouldn't have told you any of those things about my personal life. Because they are personal. And, quite frankly—"

"A little embarassing?" he finished calmly, obviously having taken note of her red cheeks.

A little? This had to be the worst thing Toby had ever done to her. Honest and trustworthy were fine, candid she really needed to discuss with him!

"Yes, it's embarrassing." Ellie sighed heavily. "And, apart from the fact that you value Toby as your employee, I have no idea why you should even have listened to his suggestion, let alone actually contemplated going through with it." She was totally exasperated with both men, and she didn't mind Patrick McGrath knowing it.

His eyes met her gaze unwaveringly for long seconds. "Can't you?" he finally murmured softly.

Ellie frowned at him. Was that a smile she saw lurking on the edges of those sculptured lips? And was that a faint knowing gleam she detected in the depths of those grey eyes?

She had an instant flashback to that scene in the garden five months ago, of her panicked grab for her top when she realized she was no longer alone, her eyes wide with dismay as she stared across the garden at the stranger standing there watching her with amused grey eyes.

The same amused grey eyes that were looking across the sitting room at her right now!

"Besides, Ellie," Patrick drawled huskily, "why should you be the one to feel embarrassed because some man was too much of an idiot to appreciate what he had?"

There was a compliment in there somewhere—if she could only find it.

"That isn't the reason I feel embarrassed," she assured

him dismissively. "My broken relationship is—was private. I just can't believe Toby has been so indiscreet as to ask you to be my dinner partner next week." She shook her head disgustedly.

"You were going to ask me yourself?"

"Of course not," she answered impatiently.

What was wrong with these two men? Couldn't they see that it was humiliating that either of them had thought she was incapable of finding a dinner partner for herself?

"Well, as I had no idea of the dinner until Toby told me about it, I could hardly have been the one to do the asking," Patrick reasoned lightly.

As if he would have asked her anyway; it was obvious he had only agreed to the suggestion now for Toby's sake.

"Look, Toby meant well," Patrick insisted when he could see she was about to protest once again. "He's—just concerned for your happiness," he added evenly.

"But he has no reason to be," she protested. "I'm twenty-seven, not twelve."

His mouth quirked into a teasing smile. "I don't think anyone is disputing your maturity, Ellie," he murmured tauntingly.

So he did remember that afternoon in the garden as well as she did!

"If anything," he continued frowningly, "it's the opposite, I think."

Now it was Ellie's turn to frown. "What do you mean?"

"Nothing," he dismissed abruptly, standing up. "And if you're absolutely sure about not needing an escort next Friday...?"

"I'm sure," she said firmly.

Much as she would have enjoyed sweeping into the restaurant on the arm of this attractive and successful man, if only to see the stunned look on Gareth's face, she knew that she really couldn't do it under these circumstances.

"It isn't that I'm not grateful." She grimaced.

"Just thanks but no thanks?" Patrick mused.

"Yes," she sighed.

He nodded. "Then I'm obviously wasting our time," he added briskly. "I trust you'll explain the situation to Toby when he comes down? Tell him that at least I tried, hmm?"

"The coffee…" she reminded him lamely, belatedly realizing she had made no effort to offer to pour him a cup.

He smiled humourlessly. "We both know that was just a ploy to keep Toby busy while the two of us talked."

"Yes." Ellie sighed again, moving to accompany him from the room.

Patrick paused in the open doorway. "Don't be too hard on Toby, hmm?" he encouraged softly. "He feels a certain—responsibility where your happiness is concerned."

"I'll try to bear that in mind," she assured him dryly.

"Ellie…?"

She looked up, her breath catching in her throat as she found herself the focus of Patrick's McGrath's enigmatic grey gaze.

He really was the most gorgeous-looking man, she acknowledged weakly. All six foot two inches of him!

"You know where I am if you should change your mind..." he told her pointedly.

Yes, he was gorgeous, and there was no doubt that having him as her escort would have salvaged her damaged pride—just as there was no doubt she had no intention of taking him up on his offer!

'I won't,' she assured him with finality.

How could Ellie have known, how could she possibly have guessed, that something disastrous would occur during the following week—something that would necessitate her not only changing her mind, but having to go to Patrick McGrath herself and ask him if he would consider coming to the company dinner with her after all?

CHAPTER TWO

"How do I look?" She grimaced at Toby questioningly as she entered the kitchen where her brother sat eating the dinner she had prepared for him before getting ready for her evening out.

"You look great," he assured her enthusiastically. "New dress?" he observed teasingly.

Of course it was a new dress; she couldn't go out with Patrick McGrath wearing the old trusty little-black-dress that she had worn to last year's company Christmas dinner. No, as Patrick's dinner date she wanted to wear something much more stylish. And noticeable.

She had known as soon as she saw the knee-length figure-hugging red dress in the shop that it would ensure, once and for all, that Gareth was no longer under any misapprehension concerning her having fully got over him. Especially with Patrick McGrath as her dinner partner!

"Do you like it?" she asked her brother uncertainly.

Trying the dress on in the shop and actually putting it on at home were two different things, she had realised a few minutes ago. Seen in this homely setting, the dress was much more revealing than anything Ellie had ever worn before, clinging to her slenderness in a bright red swathe, the low neckline and sleeveless style showing arms and throat still lightly tanned from her holiday in the summer.

Her hair was swept up loosely from the slenderness of her neck and secured with two gold combs. The change in hairstyle seemed to enlarge her eyes and the dark sweep of her lashes. Blusher highlighted her cheeks, and the bright red gloss on her lips was the same colour as the dress.

Ellie had noted all of this in her bedroom mirror a few minutes ago, sweeping out of the room and down the stairs before she had time for second thoughts and settled for the familiar black dress after all.

"You look wonderful, sis," Toby told her, sitting back to look at her admiringly. "You're going to knock him off his feet!"

She frowned. "Toby, the idea isn't for me to attract Patrick McGrath—"

"I was referring to Gareth," he murmured pointedly.

"Oh…Gareth," she acknowledged weakly, feeling the colour warming her cheeks at her mistake. In all honesty she had totally forgotten about Gareth as she prepared for her evening out. Which was ridiculous when he was the reason she had gone to all this trouble in the first place.

The reason she had swallowed her pride and gone to Patrick, and told him she had changed her mind after all!

To give the man his due, he hadn't batted an eyelid when she had turned up at his office three days ago— without an appointment—and asked him if he was still agreeable to going out with her on Friday evening.

She had acted instinctively, knowing that if she gave herself time to think about whether or not she should go and see him she would change her mind. Although she had been a little thrown by his opening comment!

"I'VE been expecting you." He put his gold pen down on top of the papers on his desk before smiling across at her as she stood just inside his office, his secretary having closed the door behind her as she left.

"You have?" Ellie frowned; how could he possibly have been expecting her when until half an hour ago she hadn't expected to be here herself?

"Call it a hunch." He nodded. "You can sit down, you know, Ellie," he added mockingly. "There's no charge!"

He seemed different today, Ellie realized, more the thirty-eight-year-old successful businessman that he was. He was dressed formally too, in a dark grey suit with a white silk shirt, a light grey tie knotted meticulously at his throat.

She made no move to sit in the chair he indicated, knowing that she had made a mistake in coming here today, that she should have taken the time to think after all, that—

"I still have Friday evening free, if you're interested," he told her huskily.

Her eyes widened. "You do?"

He nodded. "Are you interested?"

She swallowed hard, wishing she could say no but knowing that, after what she had learnt today, she badly needed this man's presence at her side on Friday evening—for moral support if nothing else.

"Ellie...?" he prompted at her continued silence.

"I'm interested," she admitted abruptly.

"Has something happened?" he asked shrewdly.

Had something happened! Gareth, that selfish, unthinking, uncaring—

"Something's happened," Patrick acknowledged ruefully, standing up to pour her a cup of coffee from the hot percolator that stood on the side. "I'm sorry it's nothing stronger," he apologised dryly as he handed her the cup and saucer. "You look as if you could do with a double whisky!"

"I don't drink whisky," she said vaguely, taking a sip of the hot coffee. Not because she thought it would make her feel any better, more for something to do with her shaking hands.

Cold hands, she realised belatedly as she wrapped them about the cup; the snow that had been threatening to fall all week had finally come tumbling down this morning. And in her agitation Ellie had completely forgotten to collect her outer coat and gloves before leaving the office earlier.

"Is it anything I should know about?" Patrick gently urged.

"Anything...? It isn't Toby, if that's what you're worried about," she hastened to reassure him.

"I didn't think for a moment that it was; as far as I'm aware Toby is in York today, with—with another of my employees," Patrick dismissed lightly. "I wish you would sit down, Ellie," he said softly.

Of course. He wouldn't sit down if she didn't. Ellie sat, the cup rattling precariously in the saucer as she did so.

Patrick moved back to sit behind his desk. "Take your time," he invited. "I don't have any appointments for a couple of hours."

"It isn't going to take me that long to—!" She broke

off, her face pale as she brought herself under control. "My ex-boyfriend intends announcing his engagement at the dinner on Friday evening," she bit out reluctantly.

"Ah," Patrick murmured comprehendingly.

Ellie looked across at him sharply. "It doesn't bother me," she assured him.

He raised dark brows. "It doesn't?"

"Look, Mr—Patrick," she amended as he raised those brows even higher. "I don't know what Toby told you about the end of my relationship with Gareth, but—"

"Nothing at all, as it happens," he assured her dryly. "Toby can be discreet when he needs to be," he added at her sceptical look. "He wouldn't have lasted long as my assistant if he couldn't!"

"Yes. Well." Ellie grimaced. "I was the one to end my relationship with Gareth."

Patrick frowned. "Then why—?"

"He told everyone at the office that *he* was the one to end it," Ellie recalled disgustedly. "And when he was seen with someone else only a few days later...!" She shook her head. "If I had tried to contradict his story then I would have just looked like 'a woman scorned'," she reasoned heavily.

"Hmm. Just out of interest—why *did* you stop seeing him?" Patrick asked interestedly.

"Because—" She drew in a deep breath, shaking her head. "I think that also comes under the heading of 'Private'," she told him stiffly.

"Okay," he conceded reluctantly. "But if you aren't bothered by his engagement...?"

"I'm really not," she insisted firmly. "At least, only so far as... I have to work with all these people, Patrick."

She grimaced. "Gareth informed me a couple of hours ago about the engagement announcement."

"Big of him," Patrick bit out scathingly.

It had been more out of spite, actually, but she was way past caring about anything Gareth did or said to her. "If I turn up alone on Friday evening and the announcement is made—"

"All your work colleagues are going to end up feeling sorry for you," Patrick acknowledged hardly.

Her eyes flashed deeply blue. "Yes!" And the pity of people she worked with on a daily basis—even misplaced pity—was something she just couldn't bear to think about.

Even if it meant coming to this man and admitting she had made a mistake in so arbitrarily refusing his offer to act as her escort at the dinner!

"If you agree—if you're still willing—it will be a purely business arrangement if you consent to accompany me on Friday evening," she told him coolly. "I will, of course, be paying any expenses you may incur—including the petrol to get us there, any drinks we have to buy, the—"

"Stop right there, Ellie," Patrick cut in firmly. "When I take a woman out for the evening I do the paying. Okay?"

"No, it is not okay," she came back, just as determinedly. "I'm taking you out. That means I pay. What do you mean, no?" She frowned as he shook his head.

"I'll only agree to go if I take you. Otherwise the deal is off, Ellie," he added decisively.

"But this isn't one of your business deals—" she broke off as she realised *she* had been the one to say Friday evening was to be treated on a businesslike footing.

Patrick laughed softly. "Ellie, isn't the important thing here to show this Gareth that you're more than capable of attracting a man other than him? Which, of course, you obviously are," he continued, his grey gaze sweeping over her with slow appreciation.

Ellie was dressed in one of the suits she wore to work, a fitted black one today, teamed with a blue blouse. Slightly damp from the snow still falling outside!

Ellie was under no illusions as regarded her looks; at best they could be called pleasant. She was neither fat nor too thin, and her hair—her one good feature as far as she was concerned—was always kept clean and well-styled. Her eyes were a clear blue, her lashes thick and dark, her skin smooth and creamy, but other than that her features were nondescript.

Which was why, when Gareth had joined the company six months ago—a blond Adonis with warm blue eyes and a charm that drew women to him like bees around honey—Ellie had been completely bowled over by his marked interest in her.

But she had definitely learnt her lesson where that sort of flattery and attention were concerned, which was why she knew that Patrick McGrath was just being polite now.

He was watching her with narrowed eyes. "How long is it since the two of you broke up?"

"What does that have to do with anything?" she came back stiffly.

Patrick shrugged. "I was merely wondering why you don't already have a new boyfriend."

She gave a humourless smile. "Because after my experience with Gareth I have no interest at the moment in finding myself a new boyfriend!"

"This gets more and more intriguing by the minute," Patrick murmured interestedly.

Ellie shot him a reproving look. "Believe me, it really isn't," she assured him dismissively.

"So it's easier to ask me, a complete stranger, to go to your company dinner with you than it is to complicate matters with a genuine new boyfriend?" Patrick murmured consideringly. "It makes a certain sense, I suppose." He shrugged.

Ellie frowned. "It does?" It sounded rather cold and contrived to her, but other than not going to the dinner at all—which was impossible now that Gareth had told her of the pending announcement of his engagement; she simply wouldn't give him the satisfaction of just not turning up!—she couldn't see any other way round the problem.

"It does," he assured her enigmatically. "Well, as I've already said, Ellie, I still have the evening free on Friday."

She drew in a deep breath. "Then you'll go to the Delacorte dinner with me?"

He gave a sudden grin, looking years younger, his grey eyes warm. "I thought you would never ask!"

She wouldn't have done ordinarily, and they both knew it. But nothing about this situation was ordinary.

WHICH was why she was standing here, wearing a revealing red dress and more make-up than she had ever worn before, feeling decidedly like the overdressed Christmas tree that adorned their sitting room—waiting for Patrick McGrath to arrive...

He was late.

It was already seven forty-five, and before Ellie had

left his office three days ago they had agreed that he would pick her up at seven-thirty, in order for them to drive to the restaurant and arrive a polite ten or fifteen minutes late for pre-dinner drinks. At this rate they would be lucky to arrive in time for the serving of the first course!

"Is he always this unpunctual?" She frowned at Toby as he cleared away his dinner things, before getting ready to go out himself.

"He'll be here, sis," Toby dismissed assuredly. "But I have to leave now." He glanced up at the kitchen clock. "I told Tess I would pick her up just after eight," he added apologetically. He was going to the cinema this evening with his girlfriend of the last two months. "Do you want me to try reaching Patrick on his mobile before I leave? Maybe the car broke down or something."

"Do Mercedes break down?" Ellie came back dryly, wondering if she was going to get to "the ball", after all!

"Mine doesn't," drawled a familiar voice.

Ellie gasped, spinning round to face Patrick as he stood in the doorway. She was glad she had already gasped—otherwise she would have done so now; he looked absolutely breathtaking in a dinner suit!

"I wish you wouldn't keep creeping up on me like that," she complained, to cover up the confusion she felt at his appearance.

Was anyone supposed to be this handsome? This suavely sophisticated? This—this breathtaking? There really was no other word for Patrick's appearance this evening.

"Will I·do?" He arched mocking brows at her as she continued to stare at him.

Would he do as what? As a more than adequate replacement for Gareth? Certainly. As a means for making every other woman in the room jealous of her good fortune in having him as her partner for the evening? Assuredly. As a calm and soothing balm to her already battered emotions? Definitely not!

He was a one-evening-only companion—just a shield for what promised to be a very difficult evening for her. He wasn't supposed to make her pulse flutter, her knees feel weak, her insides as if they were turning to jelly!

"Ellie is feeling a little—tense this evening, Patrick," Toby excused her lightly, picking up his jacket from the back of the chair before walking over to the door. "Have a good evening. Want me to wait up for you, Ellie?" he added mischievously, dark brows raised teasingly.

"No, thank you!" She shot him a reproving look as he ducked out of the doorway, grinning widely as he raised a hand in farewell before disappearing into the darkness.

"We aren't going to be late back this evening, are we, Ellie?" Patrick looked down at her mockingly. "Only I'm usually in bed by ten-thirty."

Ellie would hazard a guess that the only reason this man would be in bed by ten-thirty at night would be because he wasn't there alone!

"You're late," she told him sharply, more flustered that she had just had such a thought about Patrick's nocturnal habits than she actually was by his tardiness.

"Only a few minutes," he dismissed unconcernedly. "I stopped along the way to buy you this."

"This" was a corsage, a single red rose, newly in bud, made even more beautiful by the melted snowflakes clinging to the dewy petals.

Ellie blinked hard before looking up at Patrick, hastily looking down again as he returned her gaze with slightly challenging eyes. Bringing her a rose, red or otherwise, was not very businesslike. And they both knew it. But then Patrick had warned her three days ago that he intended doing this his way...

"Thank you," she accepted huskily, taking the rose and the pin he held out to her.

"Would you like me to—?"

"No! No, thank you." She tried to refuse his offer of help less abruptly, at the same time giving him a sceptical glance. "I can manage." And to prove it she attached the rose to her dress at the first try.

"I thought you might," he murmured ruefully. "I suppose we should be on our way, then."

"I suppose we should," she echoed dryly, inwardly chiding herself for the fact that she was a little disappointed he hadn't mentioned her new dress, or anything else about her appearance.

Not that she had mentioned how gorgeous he looked either; it simply wasn't in keeping, she accepted, with their arrangement.

"What a pity," Patrick murmured as he watched her pull on her long black winter coat. "You look absolutely stunning in that dress; it's a shame to hide it beneath that coat," he explained as Ellie looked up at him questioningly.

"Thank you." She felt an inner glow now rather than the outer warmth of the coat.

"Hmm." Patrick nodded as they went out to the car, opening the door for her to get in. "Gareth can just eat his heart out," he added with satisfaction.

"That's what Toby said!" She laughed to cover her flushed pleasure at his compliment.

"And, as we both know, Toby wouldn't tell you a lie," he reminded her teasingly.

No, Toby wouldn't tell her a lie—at least, not a major one—but she had a feeling this man was more than capable of practising the subtle art of subterfuge if he thought the occasion warranted it. There was a steely edge to Patrick McGrath, a ruthlessness that obviously made him such a success in business.

But Ellie dismissed both Patrick's compliments and thoughts of that steely edge as they neared the restaurant where all the other Delacorte, Delacorte and Delacorte staff would already be gathered. No doubt all believing, with the lateness of the hour, that she had decided not to attend after all.

"Everything is going to be just fine, Ellie." Patrick reached out in the warm confines of the car and gave her restless hands a reassuring squeeze before returning his own hand to the steering wheel of his Mercedes sports car. "Trust me, hmm?" he encouraged as she glanced at him with troubled eyes.

She wasn't sure, after Gareth's duplicity, that she would ever completely trust another man again. But Patrick wasn't asking her to trust him in that way...

"I don't believe I've ever thanked you for agreeing to help me out like this," she murmured ruefully. Mainly because she had been too embarrassed by her need for him to be here to actually get around to thanking him!

"I believe you did mention the word gratitude once," he drawled. "But that was last week—when you were turning me down."

Before she'd had to go back and tell him the situation had indeed changed!

"Ellie, why don't we wait until the end of the evening and see if you still want to thank me then, hmm?"

Ellie shot him a sharp look; that sounded a little ominous.

"Don't look so worried, Ellie." He chuckled after a brief glance in her direction. "I promise to be the soul of discretion this evening."

"You do?" She eyed him doubtfully.

After all, what did she really know about this man? Only what Toby had told her. Which, now that she thought about it, really wasn't much. Maybe Toby *could* be discreet if he needed to be! At least as far as Patrick McGrath was concerned...

Thirty-eight. Extremely successful. Single—which was probably all she really needed to know. Except... For all she knew the man might be a terrible flirt, or become terribly loud after a couple of drinks. In which case having him as her escort could prove more of a liability than a plus!

"Of course, Ellie," he answered blandly. "I'll try very hard not to mention to anyone that you occasionally like to sunbathe topless in the back garden—weather permitting!" He grimaced as snow slowly began to fall on the windscreen.

"You—!" Ellie gasped, feeling the sudden heat in her cheeks as she turned to stare at him. "Patrick—"

"Ah, here we are," he informed her lightly, turning the Mercedes into the car park of the restaurant, parking it beside the green Rolls Royce owned by Ellie's boss before getting out of the car and coming round to open Ellie's door for her. "Was it something I said?" he prompted innocently as she made no move to get out of the car.

He knew very well that it was!

"Come on, Ellie. I'm getting wet out here," he encouraged briskly.

Of course he was; the snow was coming down in earnest now. Ellie wrapped her coat around her and pulled up the collar about her neck as they hurried over to the entrance to the restaurant.

"We'll leave this here, I think," Patrick said firmly as they entered the foyer, removing Ellie's coat and handing it to the receptionist before Ellie even had time to realise what he was doing.

She suddenly felt self-conscious again as she looked down at the eye-catching red dress. Maybe it was too much. After all, this was only a company Christmas dinner. Instead of looking eye-catching, as she had hoped, was she going to look ridiculously overdressed?

"Ellie, you look beautiful," Patrick told her firmly— before his lips came down gently on hers and his arms moved about her waist to mould her body against the hardness of his.

The kiss was so unexpected that Ellie responded, her lips parting beneath his even as her arms moved up about his shoulders.

She totally forgot where they were, why they were there—who she was, even—as those warmly sensual lips continued to explore the softness of her own. The tip of Patrick's tongue was now moving erotically against her lower lip, turning her body to liquid fire, her legs to jelly.

His eyes were dark with query as he finally lifted his head to look into the flushed beauty of her face. "Better." He nodded, his thumb running lightly across her slightly swollen lips. "Now you actually look like a woman out for the evening with her lover!" he added with satisfaction.

Of course. That was the reason Patrick had kissed her. The only reason.

"Perhaps next time you could give me some warning of what you're about to do," she bit out abruptly, covering her confusion—and her blushes!—by opening her evening bag and searching through its contents. "Lipstick," she told him abruptly, and held out a tissue for him to wipe his mouth.

"You do it," Patrick encouraged huskily. "I can't see what I'm doing," he reasoned before she protested.

She swallowed hard, willing her heart to stop pounding, her hand not to shake as she reached up to wipe the smears of lipstick that he now had on his mouth.

So engrossed was she in not betraying how shaken she felt that she didn't even see the man walking past, a dark scowl on his handsome features as he stopped to stare at the two of them.

"Ellie...?" he questioned uncertainly—as if he couldn't quite believe the woman in the red dress, a woman who had obviously just been very thoroughly kissed, was actually her.

She stiffened before looking at him. "Gareth," she greeted him distantly, feeling rather than seeing Patrick as he moved to stand beside her, his arm curving possessively about her waist. She glanced up at him, a shiver running down her spine as she saw the narrow-eyed look he was giving the younger man. "Patrick, this is a work colleague—Gareth Davies," she dismissed with deliberate lightness, glad of that lightness as she saw Gareth's scowl deepen. "Gareth—Patrick McGrath," she added economically, still too shaken by that kiss to think how to describe him to the other man.

"*The* Patrick McGrath?" Gareth questioned abruptly as he looked frowningly at the other man.

Patrick smiled—a smile that didn't reach the cold grey of his eyes. "I very much doubt there's only one Patrick McGrath in the world," he answered the other man tauntingly.

"We really should be going in, Patrick," Ellie put in determinedly as she saw the light of challenge that had now appeared in both men's eyes. "If you'll excuse us, Gareth?" she added dismissively, not giving him a second glance as she turned and walked in the direction of the main restaurant, Patrick at her side, his arm still firmly about her waist.

Not quite the way she had envisaged the evening beginning!

But then she hadn't expected Patrick to kiss her either...

Why on earth *had* he kissed her? Just for effect, as his words afterwards had seemed to imply? Well, he couldn't even begin to imagine the effect his unexpected behaviour had had on her!

She could still feel the sensuous touch of his lips against hers, still feel the hardness of his body as she moulded perfectly against him, the warmth that had coursed through her, that totally not-knowing-where-she-was-and-not-caring-either feeling.

As for Gareth! Amazingly, she had felt absolutely nothing as she'd looked at him just now. Except perhaps a vague disbelief that she had ever been taken in by his overt good looks and charm...

What did it all mean...?

But as they walked into the restaurant and Patrick was greeted effusively by her boss, George Delacorte, Senior Partner at Delacorte, Delacorte and Delacorte, Ellie knew she would have to get back to that particularly puzzling question later!

CHAPTER THREE

"I HAD no idea you were going to be here with Ellie this evening, Patrick." The older man greeted him warmly and the two men shook hands. George Delacorte was a tall, distinguished-looking man with iron-grey hair and twinkling brown eyes that belied the shrewd trial lawyer he actually was. "You should have told me, Ellie," he chided teasingly.

Told him what? Until a few seconds ago she hadn't even known that he and Patrick were acquainted! Patrick certainly hadn't mentioned that he knew the older man.

"How are Anne and Thomas?" George smiled.

"Very well, thank you, sir," Patrick replied smoothly, his arm still lightly about Ellie's waist, almost as if he weren't aware that she was staring up at him in amazement.

Why hadn't he told her he knew George Delacorte? It was obvious from the easy way he was talking with the older man that Patrick had been perfectly well aware that he would be seeing the other man this evening! In fact, she knew that he had; she had told him herself that it was the Delacorte Christmas dinner!

"And Teresa?" the older man continued lightly. "Breaking hearts, as usual?"

Patrick shrugged. "I think she might finally have met 'the one'," he answered indulgently.

"Good for her." George chuckled.

Who on earth were Anne and Thomas—let alone Teresa? Ellie realised she really should have asked Patrick for a few more personal details. And maybe she would have done if she had known they would be relevant to this evening!

"I must just go and tell Mary you're here; she'll be so pleased to see you," George said happily. "Sarah is here too—somewhere." He frowned. "You're coming to the family party tomorrow?" he prompted abruptly.

"Of course," Patrick assured him.

"Bring Ellie, too," George went on with a smile in her direction. "If you would like to come, my dear?" he added gently.

She had no idea what party either of these two men were talking about!

"I'm not sure what Ellie's plans are for tomorrow." Patrick was the one to answer smoothly. "We'll let you know."

"Of course," George accepted briskly. "I'll just go and find Mary." He gave them another smile before going off in search of his wife.

"So that was the infamous Gareth," Patrick murmured thoughtfully once the two of them were alone. "I have to say, Ellie, I wasn't very impressed." He shrugged.

"Never mind Gareth for now—who are Anne, Thomas and Teresa?" Ellie hissed explosively. "And how is it that you know George Delacorte?"

"He's my uncle," Patrick told her dismissively, at

the same time looking interestedly at the forty or so other Delacorte staff in the room. "As for Anne, Thomas and—"

"Your uncle?" Ellie spluttered incredulously, gaping up at him unbelievingly.

"By marriage." Patrick nodded. "Mary Delacorte is my father's sister."

"Why on earth didn't you tell me?" she demanded indignantly.

Patrick turned to look at her, dark brows raised over slightly mocking grey eyes. "I didn't think it was relevant."

"You-didn't-think-it-was-relevant!" she repeated disgustedly.

"Ellie, why do you keep repeating everything I say?" he taunted derisively.

"Because I just can't believe this!" The colour was high in her cheeks, blue eyes sparkling. "Is Toby aware that my boss is your uncle?" she asked suspiciously as that idea suddenly occurred to her.

"I'm really not sure." Patrick shrugged. "But I would have thought so. Do you think we ought to mingle?" he added consideringly. "Several of your work colleagues have looked curiously across at us in the last few minutes."

She didn't care who had looked at them in the last few minutes; she intended getting to the bottom of this if it took all night. If Toby knew that Patrick was related to George Delacorte, then he must also be aware—

"Patrick!"

Ellie turned just in time to see Sarah Delacorte, George's daughter and only child, throw herself into Patrick's arms, kissing him enthusiastically.

Ellie felt her heart plummet as she looked at the beautiful young woman laughing up into Patrick's face, her pleasure at his presence obvious.

Sarah Delacorte was beautiful, there was no doubt about that, with her tall, slender figure—shown off to advantage now in a slinky black knee-length dress—her long silky blonde hair and delicate child-like features.

Unfortunately she was also the woman Gareth had been dating for the last six weeks and was about to announce his engagement to!

And she was, Ellie realised with dismay, Patrick's young cousin...

"What are you doing here?" Sarah demanded, still holding onto Patrick's hands as she gazed up at him in obvious delight.

Patrick looked no less pleased to see his cousin, grinning broadly. "Ellie brought me," he explained lightly, releasing one of his hands to turn and firmly clasp one of Ellie's, to bring her forward to stand at his side.

"Goodness, Ellie, I haven't seen you for ages!" Sarah greeted her warmly. "You look wonderful!" she added with genuine warmth.

It was true the two women hadn't met for some time. Sarah had been in Paris for the last year, initially working with one of the fashion designers over there. But her career in modelling had taken a meteoric rise over the last six months, with her photograph appearing on the front page of all the popular women's magazines.

Sarah's absence abroad was also the reason she had no idea Ellie had still been dating Gareth until six weeks ago!

Ellie very much doubted that Gareth had told the other woman anything about her, or the fact that they had still been dating after he and Sarah met. And Ellie certainly had no intention of telling the other woman any of that either. Although the fact that she now knew Patrick was the other woman's cousin certainly made things more than a little awkward in that direction!

"I understand congratulations are in order?" Patrick looked down teasingly at his young cousin.

Ellie noted that the warmth was no longer in his eyes, and his smile lacked some of its earlier spontaneity...

"Isn't it wonderful?" Sarah said dreamily, suddenly looking a very young twenty-one-year-old. "One moment I was young and fancy-free, and the next—I was just swept off my feet the moment I looked at him!" She laughed self-consciously.

Patrick's hand tightened about Ellie's fingers as he felt her stiffen beside him, although his narrowed gaze remained fixed on his cousin's glowingly lovely face. "Love at first sight, hmm?" he prompted dryly.

"Something like that." Sarah gave another happy laugh. "Wait until you meet him," she enthused. "You're going to love him!"

Considering what Patrick had said to Ellie about Gareth a few minutes earlier, she somehow doubted that very much!

Although how much of Patrick's opinion had been formed by what Ellie might have said or implied about the other man and what Patrick had actually decided for himself she had no idea!

Not that it mattered; this was just a very awkward situation all round.

What on earth had Toby been playing at when he originally organised this date for her with Patrick? Because Toby, of all of them, was well aware of the connection of all the key players in what was turning out to be a fiasco!

Patrick gave a slight inclination of his head. "I'm sure you'll have a chance to introduce the two of us later. For the moment, I think Ellie wants to introduce me to some of her friends," he added lightly.

"Of course," Sarah instantly accepted. "It really is lovely to see you again, Ellie," she added warmly. "We must go out and have coffee together some time, like we used to."

When Sarah, no doubt, would want to wax lyrical about Gareth! No, thank you!

It was true the two women had occasionally had coffee together before Sarah's departure for Paris, but they had lost touch with each other during the last year. In the present circumstances Ellie thought it better if it remained that way!

"We must," Ellie agreed non-committally.

"Catch up with you later, Sarah," Patrick told his cousin, before strolling away, Ellie very firmly pinned to his side. "Save it for later, hmm?" he told her between barely moving lips.

"But—"

"Ellie, this is not the place to discuss it. Okay?" he prompted as she came to an abrupt halt in the middle of the crowded room.

No, it was not okay. She had no idea what was going on—how could she when the whole evening had been turned upside down by Patrick's family connection to the Delacortes?

He sighed at the mutinous expression on her face. "I know how this must look to you—"

"You can have no *idea* how this looks to me," she assured him derisively.

"Probably not," Patrick conceded with a grimace. "But we do have the rest of this evening to get through," he reasoned. "And your ex-boyfriend's engagement is still going to be announced before the end of it."

"Gareth's engagement to *your cousin*," Ellie bit out pointedly.

"Yes," he acknowledged heavily. "It probably escaped your notice earlier, but George isn't exactly thrilled at the prospect of having Gareth Davies as his son-in-law!"

Ellie blinked. "He isn't?"

Of course George had known that Ellie was dating Gareth until a couple of months ago—everyone at Delacorte, Delacorte and Delacorte had been aware of it. But when the older man had approached the subject of Sarah's involvement with the other man with Ellie she had dismissed her own relationship with him as a mere friendship. After all, she did have her pride...

She hadn't realised that George was talking to her about Gareth because he didn't exactly trust the younger man's motives regarding his daughter!

"No," Patrick confirmed grimly.

She frowned. "Then why doesn't he do something about it?"

Patrick smile derisively. "Such as what? Tell Sarah he's nothing but a fortune-hunter? Because he is, isn't he?" he drawled scathingly. "A man with an eye to the main chance. A man who fancies the name Davies being added to the end of Delacorte, Delacorte and Delacorte!"

Yes, that was exactly what Gareth was. Handsome, charming—but totally mercenary. Ellie, as George's much-valued secretary, had seemed like a good prospect to him six months ago. But Gareth had dropped her like a hot coal when Sarah had returned from Paris and he'd realised George had a marriageable daughter.

"Yes," Ellie confirmed miserably, feeling totally humiliated by her own past gullibility.

Patrick nodded abruptly. "And how do you think Sarah is likely to react if anyone should tell her that about the man she believes herself madly in love with?"

How would Ellie have reacted if someone had told her those things about Gareth three months ago? Even two months ago? Would she have believed them if she weren't now the one with the knowledge of just how mercenary Gareth could be?

She gave a derisive grimace. "She'll tell them to mind their own business!"

"In one." Patrick nodded in mocking confirmation.

Ellie shook her head dismissively. "But if George really distrusts his motives—"

"He does," Patrick bit out grimly.

"Then why doesn't he just sack him?"

"For the same reason, wouldn't you think?" Patrick derided.

Yes, Ellie *did* think. It was obvious from Sarah's behaviour earlier, from the things she had said about Gareth, that the other woman was completely taken in by him.

As Ellie had once been...

But, as Ellie had learnt only too well—and obviously Patrick and his uncle knew too—Gareth's charm was all a front for his calculating brain, to create Delacorte, Delacorte, Delacorte, and Davies!

At only thirty-two Gareth had ambitions that he had no intention of working at if they could be achieved by a simpler route—such as marrying the senior partner's daughter!

It had taken Ellie almost two weeks to realise that

Gareth was dating someone else besides herself—he hadn't wanted to give up on one option before making absolutely sure of the second one! Once she had realised what he was doing she had told him precisely what she thought of him. And what he could do with the relationship he had tried to offer her as consolation prize.

If she had thought he was genuinely in love with Sarah then it would have been a different matter; she would have just accepted the inevitable. But by that time her eyes had been wide open where Gareth was concerned, her illusions shattered.

But she still had no idea what Patrick was up to...

Because he was up to something. She was sure of it!

"So, Ellie, what do you think?" Patrick looked at her consideringly now. "Do you want to help us prove to Sarah what an absolute bas—What a calculating mercenary her new fiancé actually is?" he amended harshly.

Ellie glanced across the room to where she could see Gareth, now talking to Sarah, a superior smile curving his lips as she looked up at him with absolute adoration, obviously enthralled by his every word.

A shudder ran down Ellie's spine. Had she once looked and felt as Sarah so obviously did? She had been attracted to Gareth, of that she had no doubt—just as she had no doubt that she had been meant to feel attracted to him! She had been flattered by his interest too— what woman wouldn't be when he was so handsome and charming? But she was relieved to realise that if she had ever believed herself in love with him it had been short lived, because she felt nothing but disgust as she looked at him now.

She turned back to Patrick, her shoulders straightening

with resolve. "I have absolutely no idea how you intend going about that, but, yes, I'm willing to help. If I can," she added uncertainly.

If Patrick and George, two very capable men, had no idea how to go about revealing Gareth in his true colours to the besotted Sarah, what could she possibly do to achieve that?

Simply telling Sarah what she thought of Gareth would do no good. She had thought of that once she'd become aware that Sarah was Gareth's latest target—her concern and liking for Sarah were completely genuine—but she had concluded that Sarah was very unlikely to believe anything she had to say about Gareth once he had told Sarah the "woman scorned" story. Pity was the more probable emotion Sarah would feel on hearing it—for Ellie!

Patrick gave her hand a triumphant squeeze. "I hoped my instinct about you was right, Ellie," he told her warmly.

She eyed him uncertainly. "What instinct?"

He grinned. "I knew you were a fighter," he said with satisfaction. "You had to be, to have chosen and suc-ceeded in taking on the responsibilities you did eight years ago. Any woman who could do that isn't going to let a man like Gareth Davies get away with anything—least of all gulling some other poor woman in the same way you were!"

Again, Ellie was sure there was a compliment in there somewhere—it was just buried beneath the insult that had followed it!

CHAPTER FOUR

"WHAT on earth do you think you're playing at?"

Ellie turned slowly to face Gareth, already knowing by the aggressive tone of his voice that his mood was ugly. She had briefly left the dinner table after dessert to go to the ladies' room. Gareth must have deliberately followed her.

Yes, she was right about Gareth's mood. He looked less than handsome in his anger, blue eyes glittering furiously as he strode purposefully towards her.

"I'm sorry?" she answered coolly, very aware of the fact they were completely alone in the foyer. The receptionist was inside, helping to serve drinks now, the Delacorte party having taken over the whole restaurant for the evening.

"You heard me, Ellie," he snapped impatiently. "What are you doing here with George's nephew?"

"Eating dinner, the same as everyone else," she dismissed with a lightness she was far from feeling. She knew that physically there was nothing Gareth could do to her here—even if he did look as if he would like to wring her neck—but verbally he could rip her to shreds!

Gareth's mouth twisted frustratedly. "Don't get clever with me, Ellie," he scorned. "Moving in rather exalted company nowadays, aren't you?" he added insultingly.

Deliberately so, Ellie knew. Although she refused to become angry. Or at least only with herself—that she could ever have been taken in by such a man. In fact, it was a pity Sarah couldn't see him in this mood—the younger woman would have no doubts about his duplicitous charms then!

But Ellie knew what he was referring to with that remark about "exalted company"; ordinarily she would have been seated at one of the tables with other secretaries and their partners, but as the nephew of the senior partner was her guest for the evening, she and Patrick had been moved onto the top table with the other senior members of staff.

The same table as Gareth and Sarah…

Ellie coolly met Gareth's accusing gaze. "Do you have some sort of problem with that?"

He gave a scornful laugh. "Not at all. So if you were hoping to make me jealous—"

"Don't flatter yourself, Gareth!" she cut in derisively, feeling her anger starting to rise. Really, the conceit of the man…! "The fact that Patrick and I are—friends has absolutely nothing to do with you."

"Have you said anything to him about me?" Gareth rasped nastily, taking a painful grip of her arm. "Because if you have—"

"Gareth, believe me, when I'm with Patrick I have better things to do with my time than discuss you," she assured him hardly. "Now, would you kindly let go of my arm?" she asked coldly.

He looked down at her with hard blue eyes, a humourless smile now curving his lips. "No, I don't think I will," he murmured slowly. "You're looking rather beautiful tonight, Ellie," he told her huskily. "Rather sexy, in fact."

Nausea welled up in her throat at this completely unwelcome compliment from a man she now despised, but the coldness of her gaze didn't waver from his. "Patrick happens to like me in red," she told him challengingly.

The angry glitter intensified in Gareth's eyes. "Why, you little—"

"Everything all right, darling?" Patrick's voice suddenly interrupted pleasantly. "You've been gone so long I thought there must be something wrong?" he added questioningly, and he strolled over to join them, much to Ellie's relief. She instantly felt the reassurance of his presence.

Gareth slowly released her arm, and Ellie resisted the impulse she had to wipe his touch from her flesh. Instead she shot Gareth a look of intense dislike before turning to smile her gratitude at Patrick. "I was just directing Gareth to the men's room," she dismissed lightly.

"Really?" Patrick turned cold grey eyes on the younger man. "But I thought that was where you were going when we met earlier this evening?"

Gareth pulled himself together with obvious effort, even managing to give the other man a rueful smile. "Actually, I was collecting Sarah's wrap that time," he explained pleasantly.

No doubt Gareth was making an effort to be pleasant because he was very aware that Patrick was George's nephew, Ellie guessed shrewdly.

"Ah, yes. My cousin Sarah." Patrick murmured coldly. "I'm very fond of Sarah," he added softly.

"She's a marvellous girl," Gareth agreed heartily.

"That she is," Patrick acknowledged evenly. "I would

hate to see her hurt in any way," he added softly, a dangerous stillness surrounding him.

Ellie was watching Gareth as Patrick made this remark. The handsome face remained pleasantly smiling, but there was a certain wariness in the younger man's eyes.

She wasn't sure it was absolutely wise for Patrick to challenge the other man, even in this mild way—not when his cousin's happiness was at stake. But, as she was quickly learning, Patrick really did like to do things his own way.

Gareth gave an inclination of his head. "We really should be getting back; George is going to announce our engagement as soon as the coffee has been served."

"So I believe," Patrick rasped, once again holding tightly to Ellie's arm as he felt her stiffen. "You go ahead," he encouraged the other man. "I just want to—have a few minutes alone with Ellie," he drawled dryly.

"I was just telling Ellie that she's a bit of a dark horse," Gareth drawled teasingly. "Who knows, Ellie? We may even be related to each other one day!" he added mockingly.

How Ellie wanted to smack that confident smile off his handsome face!

But instead she felt cold common sense come over her as she answered him. "Somehow I doubt that very much," she told him scathingly.

"I do hope your intentions are honourable, Patrick." Gareth's smile didn't reach the hard glitter of his eyes. "I should warn you George is extremely fond of Ellie— treats her almost like another daughter. He will not be happy if he thinks you're trifling with her affections!"

She really would hit him in a minute, common sense notwithstanding!

George Delacorte *was* fond of her, and had taken her slightly under his parental wing after her parents had died. Which was what made this situation so difficult now; she would hate any inaction on her part to contribute to the unhappiness of George's only child. But at the same time, as Patrick had already pointed out, what could any of them do about it?

Patrick gave a confident smile as he released Ellie's arm and put his own arm about the slenderness of her waist. "I don't think Ellie was referring to our own relationship when she cast doubt on the two of you ever being related," he assured the other man derisively.

Gareth's gaze narrowed assessingly on the older man. "I really wouldn't pay too much attention to second-hand opinions, if I were you, Patrick—especially when those opinions are biased, as Ellie's undoubtedly are," he added, with a pitying glance in her direction.

Ellie would have hit him then, if Patrick's hand hadn't moved from her waist to take a firm grip of her arm once more. Gareth was making her sound like some twisted, lovesick, scorned woman, out to hurt him in any way that she could!

"I make a point of always forming my own opinions concerning other people," Patrick told the other man smoothly. "Which is why I'm here with Ellie this evening," he added softly.

Gareth nodded. "I know how much Ellie hated the thought of coming here on her own tonight."

Why, the condescending—

"I can assure you, that was never an option," Patrick told the other man derisively, turning to smile at Ellie, the hard glitter in his eyes telling her of his own—controlled—anger. "There are plenty of other men who would willingly have taken my place tonight," he assured Gareth hardly.

"Of course," Gareth agreed sceptically. "Well, I really should be getting back," he added lightly. "It wouldn't do for one half of the engaged couple not to be in the room when the announcement is made, now, would it?" He smiled before walking confidently back into the restaurant.

Ellie let out a deep breath, unaware until that moment that she had actually been holding it. The last few minutes had told her that Gareth was even more dangerous than she had thought he was. His vindictiveness where she was concerned was more than obvious—to the point that he had deliberately tried to belittle her in front of Patrick, to make her sound like a—

"Don't let him get to you, Ellie." Patrick was looking down at her concernedly. "He only behaved in the way he did because he's still not quite sure how much you've told me about him," he added hardly.

Her main emotion at this moment was embarrassment. That she had been fooled by Gareth in the first place. That Patrick knew she had been fooled by him!

Because Patrick's opinion was important to her. And that had nothing to do with that pride she had been so desperately trying to hang onto for the last six weeks and everything to do with the fact that she did not want Patrick to think of her as some poor, wounded woman, still in love with Gareth Davies.

Which, in turn, led her to wonder *why* Patrick's opinion of her was so important...

She gave a dismissive shake of her head; she couldn't think about that right now—had other things to deal with. "I think Gareth could be a very dangerous man," she said slowly.

"Not dangerous," Patrick dismissed confidently. "Irritating, yes. Extremely so as far as George is concerned. But I was watching Gareth Davies through dinner—and whenever he thought no one else was taking any notice he was watching you. The fact that he saw you go out of the room and followed you shows that he isn't quite as confident of the situation as he would like us to think he is," he added shrewdly.

Ellie eyed him uncertainly. "He isn't?" Gareth had seemed extremely confident to her! She hadn't been aware of the other man watching her as they all ate dinner either. But obviously Patrick had...

Patrick gave a slow shake of his head. "You obviously bother Gareth Davies very much."

"Somehow I doubt that," she scorned disbelievingly.

"Oh, yes, you bother him, Ellie. At least, your being with me, Sarah's cousin, bothers him," Patrick muttered, obviously deep in thought. "In fact, we may not have to do anything other than produce you on a regular basis," he added shrewdly.

Her eyes widened. "What do you mean?"

Patrick grinned. "You have him rattled, Ellie!" he said with satisfaction. "All we have to do is keep up the pressure."

Ellie wasn't sure she liked the sound of that! In exactly what way was Patrick proposing they "keep up the pressure"...?

"Do you remember George mentioning a party earlier?" he reminded her.

"Tomorrow." Ellie nodded slowly, eyeing him warily.

As far as she was concerned this evening was a one-off situation. Especially as it had turned out to be so much more complicated than she could ever have realised.

But Patrick seemed to have other ideas...

He nodded. "The official engagement party." He grimaced. "I think it would be a good idea if you were to—"

"No," Ellie cut in firmly, at the same time shaking her head in protest. "The answer is no, Patrick," she insisted determinedly as his expression turned cajoling. "As far as I've been able to ascertain you accompanied me this evening under false pretences," she told him accusingly. "Admittedly you were doing me a favour, but as circumstances have turned out I think that favour has more than been returned. After all, George is your uncle; you knew that the engagement announcement I told you about was actually between Gareth and your cousin— that's why you weren't surprised when I arrived in your office earlier in the week!" Her eyes sparkled accusingly as that realisation finally dawned on her too.

"Ellie—"

"No, Patrick." She firmly resisted his teasing tone. "This evening has been awful. I have no wish to repeat it."

"Awful, Ellie?" Patrick repeated softly, suddenly standing much closer than was comfortable. For her peace of mind! "All of it?" he prompted huskily.

No, as it happened, not all of it. The kiss the two of them had shared earlier had been more pleasurable than she cared to think about. Certainly more disturbing than she cared to admit!

"All of it," she insisted forcefully. "I am absolutely, definitely not going to the party with you tomorrow!"

He looked at her consideringly. "Not even for Sarah's sake?"

"Not even for— That's emotional blackmail, Patrick!" she snapped irritably as her resolve began to sway at the mention of Sarah.

She and Sarah had been good friends in the past, and she knew the other girl to be bubbly, loving, completely carefree. Marriage to Gareth, once Gareth had shown just how ruthless he could be—and there was no doubting that he *would* show himself in his true colours one day—promised to ruin all that.

"I don't want to go to this party with you, Patrick," she protested.

And it sounded weak, even to her own ears.

"I have nothing to wear!" she added inconsequentially when he made no reply.

Which sounded even weaker!

As evidenced by the fact that Patrick laughed, eyes twinkling warmly, his teeth showing whitely in his mouth—that mouth that only two hours ago, on this very spot, had very thoroughly kissed hers!

It was a mistake to think of that kiss...

Because she wanted very badly for Patrick to repeat it!

Something of that desire must have shown in her face, because Patrick took her very firmly by the shoulders and held her away from him at arm's length. "No, Ellie," he murmured regretfully. "I'm not going to be accused of seduction as well as emotional blackmail!" He grimaced.

Ellie felt warmth enter her cheeks at her emotions

being that transparent. Maybe it was the way her gaze had gone to his mouth—and stayed there. Or maybe it was just an expression of longing on her face. Either way, it wasn't very sophisticated of her to allow her emotions to be so easily gauged.

"Very well, Patrick," she bit out abruptly. "I'll come to the party with you—"

"I knew you wouldn't let me down!" Patrick beamed, seeming to forget his resolve as he pulled her into his arms to hug her.

Ellie pulled back, looking up at him warningly. "I'm not doing this for you," she reminded him firmly.

"No, of course you aren't," he accepted lightly, but he still grinned broadly, looking far too attractive for Ellie's peace of mind. For the sudden rapid beat of her heart. For the heated longing that coursed through her body. For the way she wanted to just throw caution to the winds and kiss him if he wasn't about to kiss her!

She really would have to get a grip on her emotions where Patrick McGrath was concerned. Because to fall in love with him wouldn't only be ill-advised—it would be pure madness!

CHAPTER FIVE

"Not a word," Ellie cautioned Toby when he looked up from reading the Saturday newspaper as she came into the kitchen, dressed warmly for going out, needing only to pull her coat on when the time came. "Not one word, Toby," she repeated as he continued to look at her. "You aren't my favourite person at the moment," she added, and dropped down onto one of the kitchen chairs to wait.

Toby returned her gaze with too-innocent blue eyes. "I can't imagine why you're in such a bad mood, sis." He shrugged unconcernedly. "You know how you love shopping."

Ordinarily she did. But today wasn't ordinary. As Toby very well knew.

She glared across the table at her brother. "I think working for Patrick is having a bad effect on you," she muttered bad-temperedly. "You're becoming as sneaky as he is!"

Toby chuckled softly. "You forgot 'underhand', 'secretive', and—'manipulative', wasn't it?" he prompted lightly.

They were all the names she had called her brother this morning, after he had asked her how the previous evening had gone!

"You forgot 'too clever for your own good'," she reminded him heavily, but her mood began to thaw slightly.

"You really should have told me, Toby." She shook her head disgustedly.

"But then you wouldn't have gone to the dinner last night. At least, not with Patrick," he reasoned. "And that would have been a pity."

Ellie eyed him suspiciously. "Why?"

"Hey, look, Ellie, in case you've forgotten Patrick and I are two of the good guys," Toby pointed out protestingly. "Gareth is the bad guy—remember?"

Oh, yes, she remembered. She also remembered that look of triumph on Gareth's face the previous evening when George had stood up to announce the younger man's engagement to his daughter, Sarah.

"He doesn't deserve Sarah, Ellie—let alone you!" Patrick had muttered disgustedly at her side.

Which was why, when the Delacorte family—and Ellie—had all been chatting together at the end of the evening, Patrick had been only to happy to suggest that Ellie accompany Sarah the following day, when she shopped for a new dress to wear to the party tomorrow evening!

"Ellie has just been complaining that she has nothing to wear either," Patrick had told his young cousin happily.

Ellie glared up at him; she might have said something along those lines, but as Patrick must know only too well Sarah was the last person she wanted to go shopping with.

"I don't mind coming with you, Sarah," Gareth put in—rather hastily, it seemed to Ellie. A brief glance at Patrick, his expression knowingly satisfied, showed her that he thought so too.

"It's very sweet of you, darling." Sarah gave her new

fiancé's arm a grateful hug, the emerald and diamond engagement ring twinkling brightly on her left hand. "But you know how you hate shopping. Besides, I want the dress I'm wearing tomorrow evening to be a surprise."

"I thought it was the wedding dress I wasn't supposed to see until the day?" Gareth frowned.

"It is, silly." Sarah laughed huskily. "I just—wait and see," she dismissed excitedly, before turning to Ellie. "I think it would be lovely for the two of us to go shopping together tomorrow, don't you?"

It was obvious from Sarah's completely confident expression that she didn't expect Ellie to refuse. And, with Patrick looking at Ellie with the same expectation, what choice did she have? Absolutely none.

Which was why she was sitting here now, dressed warmly in jeans and a thick sweater, waiting for Sarah to pick her up so they could drive into town together.

"I remember," she answered Toby heavily. "Until Patrick told me last night I had no idea how worried George and Mary are by the relationship." She shook her head.

"Strange how these things come around in circles, isn't it?" Toby said ruefully. "Your dastardly ex-boyfriend engaged to Patrick's cousin," he explained, at Ellie's questioning look.

Ellie winced at having Gareth described as her ex-boyfriend; she just wanted to forget she had ever known him. Which was impossible in the present situation.

Although she had felt slightly warmed by Patrick's comment last night— "He doesn't deserve Sarah, Ellie— let alone you!" Quite what he had meant by that she wasn't sure, but again it had sounded as if there might be a compliment in there somewhere.

A compliment she would be wise to ignore, if she had any sense. And, after her recent disappointment over Gareth, she ought to have a lot of sense!

Except...

She had felt quite shy as Patrick had driven her home last night, wondering exactly how they were going to say goodnight to each other. Not that they had been out on a genuine date or anything—even less so than she had initially realised!—but Patrick *had* kissed her earlier in the evening.

She hadn't known whether to be disappointed or relieved when, having walked her to the door, he'd bent to kiss her lightly on the cheek before telling her he would call for her at eight o'clock the following evening.

"There's no point in getting there too early," he had added grimly.

"None at all," she agreed with a grimace.

"And don't worry about the shopping expedition with Sarah tomorrow," he told her with a grin. "Just be yourself and nothing can go wrong."

Which was okay for Patrick to say—but Ellie did not relish the thought of having to listen to several hours of Sarah telling her how wonderful Gareth was. It promised to be a very trying afternoon.

"Buy something blue, Ellie," Patrick had added huskily. "The same blue as your eyes."

Once again Ellie felt warmed by the fact that he had even noticed what colour her eyes were!

"Oh, and by the way—" he turned before getting into his car "—Anne and Thomas are my parents; Teresa's my younger sister."

Oh, great. She was going to meet all of Patrick's family tomorrow evening, too.

"THAT dress is perfect on you, Ellie," Sarah told her admiringly as Ellie came out of the changing room.

It might be, but a brief glance at the label whilst in the changing room had shown Ellie that the price was perfect too—for bankrupting her!

She should have known the other woman would want to go to a designer shop for her own outfit. In fact, Sarah had already picked out a gown—an emerald-green sheath that perfectly matched the emerald in her engagement ring—and had only returned to try the dress on after alterations.

The dress she had persuaded Ellie to try on was indeed the blue that Patrick had suggested, its material pure silk, with a fitted, mandarin-style collar and short sleeves.

"With your dark hair swept up like it was last night, and some kohl around your eyes, you'll look positively exotic, Ellie," Sarah enthused.

The gown was beautiful, it was also more glamorous than anything Ellie had ever worn before. Dared she buy it?

"Patrick is going to be bowled over when he sees you in this," Sarah added encouragingly.

She wasn't sure she wanted Patrick "bowled over" when he saw her. Where could any relationship between the two of them ever go? Nowhere, came the resounding answer. And yet a part of her so wanted the dress—if only to see if she *could* bowl Patrick over...!

"Why don't you think about it while the two of us have a cup of coffee?" Sarah proposed as she saw Ellie's uncertainty.

"Good idea," Ellie accepted with a certain amount of relief.

Although she wasn't so sure it *had* been a good idea once the two women were seated in a coffee-shop further down the street and the conversation naturally turned to Sarah's engagement!

"It was all a bit—sudden, wasn't it?" Ellie suggested lightly as she stirred sweetener into her coffee.

"Mmm," Sarah acknowledged thoughtfully. "I've quite enjoyed this last year—the modelling and having my photograph on the cover of magazines but you know, Ellie, it's a very lonely sort of life too. I missed my friends, the family," she added wistfully. "Most of all the family. Marriage, the possibility of having my own family, suddenly seemed the right option."

But, as Ellie knew only too well, Gareth most certainly wasn't the right man to share that option!

"You're only twenty-one, Sarah," she teased. "There's plenty of time for that once you've done all the other things you want to do with your life. Didn't you once mention that you wanted to do some fashion designing of your own?"

"I've already done some," Sarah told her excitedly. "I had totally forgotten in the excitement of the last few weeks," she went on ruefully, "but I'm waiting for Jacques, the designer I worked with in Paris, to tell me what he thinks of them."

Ah. So Sarah hadn't completely given up on her life in Paris after all...

"That sounds interesting," Ellie encouraged. "Do you think that will affect your engagement to Gareth?"

Sarah looked startled. "I must admit I hadn't given that much thought." She grimaced. "This being engaged and having to think of another person is all new to me," she added self-derisively. "But I would really like to follow it through if Jacques thinks I have any talent at all."

Again, this was encouraging, Ellie thought; it showed the other woman wasn't yet quite so tied up in her relationship with Gareth that she had given up on her own ambitions.

"I'm sure Gareth will understand if we have to wait a while before getting married," Sarah added dismissively.

Ellie thought the other woman was being slightly optimistic concerning Gareth's patience in that direction—after all, the sooner Sarah was his wife, the sooner his position at Delacorte, Delacorte and Delacorte was secured—but wisely she didn't voice any of those doubts to Sarah.

She did, however, relay the conversation to Patrick when he arrived to collect her that evening.

"You look wonderful, Ellie." He stood back to look at her appreciatively.

Ellie felt warmth in her cheeks at his praise. "Patrick, didn't you hear what I said? Sarah—"

"Still has plans to become a fashion designer," he finished dismissively. "That's great. But—"

"Just 'great'?" Ellie persisted frowningly. "Don't you realise this could be the way to drive a rift between her and Gareth?"

"Well, of course I realise that," he confirmed lightly. "He isn't going to like the idea of a delayed marriage at all."

"Exactly," Ellie said with satisfaction. "Which is good—isn't it…?" she added uncertainly when Patrick didn't look as thrilled by the news as she had been earlier.

"Very good." He nodded. "But at the moment I'm more interested in the way you look, Ellie. That dress is—you look wonderful," he said again.

Ellie had given in to impulse and gone back to the shop to buy the blue silk gown, aware that it was costing a small fortune but for the moment not caring. She had also swept up her hair and applied kohl to her eyes, as Sarah had suggested. The finished effect was pretty good, even if she did say so herself. And it was also good that Patrick liked the way she looked this evening. Wasn't it…?

That was the particular problem she had at the moment. There was no denying that she was attracted to Patrick, that she more than liked being in his company, but at the same time she was still very much aware that their relationship was nothing but a sham. It certainly wouldn't do for either of them to forget that. Because once this situation had been sorted out she and Patrick would go back to being strangers—perhaps occasionally mentioned to each other by Toby, but other than that strangers.

The fact that Patrick was once again dressed in evening clothes, and it made her heart flutter just to look at him, was not something Ellie could allow herself to dwell on!

There was also the matter of the large flat white box he had carried in under his arm…

"You told me off yesterday evening for repeating things," she reminded him dryly.

"Telling you how beautiful you look in that dress deserves to be repeated," he said unrepentantly, his gaze still appreciative. "It's blue too," he added with satisfaction.

"Shouldn't we be going?" Ellie prompted sharply, after a glance at her wristwatch, not particularly wanting to get into a conversation about why she had chosen this particular gown. "After all, there's politely late and then there's just bad manners!"

Patrick laughed softly. "You sound like my mother!"

Great! Just the person she wanted to be likened to!

"Oh, no, you don't." Patrick removed the heavy winter coat from her hand as she would have put it on, throwing it back over a chair before laying the white box on the kitchen table and removing the lid. "I bought you a present today," he told her lightly, folding back the tissue paper in the box.

"A present?" Ellie gaped. "For me? But—"

"For you," Patrick repeated firmly, taking something black and woollen out of the box. "It's a pashmina. It's made from the soft wool of goats in Northern India—"

"I know what it's made from," Ellie cut in dazedly, staring at the soft woollen shawl. She also knew that it was very expensive! "Patrick, you really shouldn't have—"

"I really should," he told her firmly, shaking out the long shawl to drape it decorously about her shoulders. "You deserve something in the way of thanks for what you're doing. Think of it as an early Christmas present. Besides," he added as she would have protested again, "that black coat does absolutely nothing for you," he told her dryly.

Or for the image of the woman who was to be his partner for the evening, Ellie realized ruefully.

Not that he wasn't right about her long black winter coat; it had been bought more for warmth rather than

as any sort of fashion statement. It was just the fact of
Patrick having bought her a gift—an expensive one at
that—that was so disturbing. And it might be Christmas
in just over a week's time, but Patrick wouldn't have been
buying her a present anyway...

But the shawl did feel so warm, and it had such pa-
nache—its front drape fell to just above her knees; the
other drape was thrown stylishly across one shoulder by
Patrick. She didn't want to refuse it!

Patrick's hands moved up to cradle either side of her
face as he looked down at her intently. "Just say, 'Thank
you, Patrick', politely," he told her dryly. "Give me a kiss
for good measure. And then we'll be on our way."

She tried to swallow, knowing which part of those
instructions had suddenly caused this obstruction in her
throat. Verbally thanking him would be no problem—

"Too difficult?" he teased mockingly. "Okay, just kiss
me and we'll forget all about saying thank you!"

That was the part that was bothering her! And Patrick knew it too. The light of challenge burned in those
otherwise enigmatic grey eyes.

The problem was, if she "just" kissed him, as he suggested, would either of them be able to forget about that?
Ellie knew that she wouldn't!

"Don't take too long deciding, Ellie," Patrick told
her dryly. "Or the party will be over before we even get
there!"

Which, to Ellie's mind, wouldn't be a bad thing!

But she was prevaricating. She knew she was. Patrick
knew she was, too. Why not just kiss him and get it over
with?

"Thank you for my present, Patrick." She stood on

tiptoe and kissed him lightly on the mouth. "But you shouldn't have—"

Patrick put silencing fingertips over her lips. "Don't ruin it, Ellie," he told her huskily. "And do you call that a kiss?" he added derisively. "Sarah shows me more enthusiasm than you just did!"

Sarah was his cousin, and perfectly free to kiss him as enthusiastically as she chose. Ellie—who wasn't quite sure what she was to him—felt rather more constrained.

"How about you try again, hmm?" Patrick encouraged throatily.

He was suddenly very close. Ellie was able to feel the warmth of his body, smell his spicy aftershave, and as she looked up into his eyes she could see that his pupils were dilated, so that only a ring of grey showed about the eyes.

"Patrick...!" She groaned huskily, before she once again rose on tiptoe, her mouth soft and pliant against his as she kissed him with all the pent-up longing inside her.

Patrick's arms moved about her waist as he pulled her in against his body, although he let Ellie continue to control the kiss.

If you could call it control when she just wanted to melt against him and give in to the languorous yearning of her body!

"Wow!" he breathed slowly when Ellie broke the kiss, lightly resting his forehead against hers. "Now, that's what I call a kiss. You have hidden talents, Miss Fairfax," he added warmly.

Ellie swallowed hard. "I—"

"Will I do?" Toby burst unceremoniously into the

kitchen, coming to an abrupt halt as he saw how close
Ellie and Patrick were standing to each other. "Sorry."
He grimaced self-consciously. "I had no idea— I
mean—"

"You'll do, Toby," the older man told him dryly as he
stepped away from Ellie. "I was just telling your sister
how beautiful she looks this evening," he prompted
pointedly.

"Er—yes, sis, you look great," Toby said, a perplexed
frown on his brow. He still sounded slightly flustered—
as well he might; the last thing he had expected was to
see Ellie and Patrick in what must have looked like a
clinch!

Ellie was a little puzzled as to why Toby was dressed
in a black dinner suit and white shirt...

Patrick shot the younger man a searching look, and
whatever he saw there in Toby's face caused him to give
an impatient shake of his head. "Did I forget to mention that Toby is coming with us this evening?" he said
blandly, turning to pick up his car keys from where he
had left them on the table earlier.

Not only had he forgotten to mention it—but so
had Toby!

CHAPTER SIX

ELLIE still had no idea, seated beside Patrick in the front of the car as he drove competently through the busy streets, why her brother should be accompanying them.

Obviously he was Patrick's assistant, but this was a family party, to celebrate—or commiserate!—with Sarah on her engagement to Gareth. Admittedly, Toby obviously knew much more of the Delacorte family than Ellie had at first realised, but what possible place did he have amongst such a gathering?

She gave a dismissive shake of her head, giving up on trying to work that one out; she already had enough to think about this evening without worrying about why her brother should have been invited too.

Patrick's present, for one thing...

Even now Ellie snuggled down into the warmth of the shawl, loving the feel of the soft wool against her arms. And Patrick had obviously been out and bought the gift himself. Which made it doubly precious.

That kiss, for another thing...

Given enough opportunity, she could quite get used to kissing Patrick. In fact, she couldn't think of anything she enjoyed more, could still feel the sensuous warmth of his lips against hers...

Stop it, she instantly ordered herself exasperatedly.

There was no point in getting used to Patrick kissing her. In fact, it might never happen again, so she had better get used to that!

The Delacorte house was ablaze with lights as Patrick parked the car outside. Over twenty cars were already parked in the long driveway—Jaguars, Mercedes, Rolls Royces and the occasional Range Rover, Ellie noted with a self-conscious grimace.

As Gareth had quickly realized when he'd come to work for Delacorte, Delacorte and Delacorte, Ellie was quite a favourite with George Delacorte, but she had never actually been to George and Mary's house before. She now found a butler opening the door to their ring, a maid taking their coats and wraps. The luxurious décor and furnishings of the house were all a bit overwhelming.

Did Patrick's parents have a house like this one too?

Probably, she acknowledged heavily. Even if, as she vaguely remembered Toby once telling her, as a bachelor of thirty-eight Patrick lived in an apartment of his own in town.

All this luxury made their own little house seem positively minute in comparison!

But then there was no point in comparison; the obvious wealth of Patrick's relatives only served to emphasise the differences between the two of them. Differences she would do well to remember.

There was the sound of voices and laughter coming from a sitting room that led off to the right of the huge reception hall, and it was to this room that Patrick took them, his hand lightly under Ellie's elbow. Almost as if he knew that what she really wanted to do was turn tail and run!

"My family doesn't bite, Ellie," Patrick told her mockingly now. "At least not on first acquaintance!" he added tauntingly.

"How reassuring," Ellie drawled, taking a glass of champagne from the circulating waiter.

"If the two of you will excuse me...?" Toby muttered distractedly, before disappearing into the throng of people already crowded into the room.

Ellie watched his departure with puzzlement. "What—?"

"Let's go and say hello to George and Mary," Patrick suggested lightly. "You had better hold my hand." He held it out to her. "I would hate to lose you in the crush."

Ellie would hate to lose him too; she hadn't recognised a single face in the room so far, apart from George and Mary Delacorte where they stood over by the huge fireplace, chatting to another middle-aged couple.

It was undoubtedly a large room, seeming to run the entire width of the house, with a huge bay window at one end and doors out into the garden at the other, but with fifty or so people in it there was barely room to move.

"We have a large family," Patrick told Ellie ruefully as he managed to push his way through in the direction of the fireplace.

Ellie and Toby had several aunts, uncles and cousins too, but they would be hard pushed to fill even their small sitting room with the dozen or so that made up their family.

It didn't help her nervousness when she instantly saw the likeness between Mary Delacorte and the tall dark-haired man who made up half of the other couple the Delacortes were chatting to. She knew she was right in the conclusion she had come to as the man gave a light laugh; his likeness to Patrick was unmistakeable.

Saying good evening to George and Mary was one thing, meeting Patrick's parents was something else entirely!

Ellie came to an abrupt halt before they reached the foursome, giving Patrick an accusing glare when he looked down at her questioningly. "I don't think that's a good idea, Patrick," she bit out tautly.

He gave her a considering look. "Ellie, introducing you to my parents is not tantamount to making a declaration about our relationship," he finally drawled teasingly.

"No, Patrick." She gave a firm shake of her head. "Helping out with this situation concerning Gareth is one thing, but I won't complicate things by meeting your parents." She determinedly released her hand from his. "You go and say hello to them. I'll go and find the ladies' room."

He frowned darkly. "But—"

"I said no, Patrick." Her gaze met his unwaveringly. "I'll be standing over by the bay window when you've finished talking to them."

"Wearing a pink carnation in your lapel?" he returned, with obvious impatience at her determination.

She gave the ghost of a smile. "I don't have a lapel."

Patrick shook his head as he looked down at her frustratedly. "You are undoubtedly the most stubborn woman I've ever met!"

Her smile was more genuine this time. "Nice to know

I have the distinction of being something," she returned unconcernedly.

His expression lightened. "Oh, you're a lot more than that, Ellie," he assured her dryly, before sighing resignedly. "Okay, no introduction to my parents. But try not to get lost, hmm?" he encouraged.

As it happened, despite directions from the busy maid in the hallway, she did get lost—several times—and it was almost fifteen minutes later when she came back down the stairs. Only to walk straight into Gareth—literally—as he began walking up them.

The words of apology died on his lips as he looked up and recognised her. The boyish smile turned to one of derision. "I thought you had decided not to come to the party after all when I saw your boyfriend was in there alone," he bit out caustically.

Ellie straightened her shoulders, her hand tightly gripping her evening bag; Gareth was the last person she'd wanted to find herself alone with! "Obviously you thought wrong," she returned, non-committal—about the "boyfriend" or the fact that she was there!

"Obviously," Gareth acknowledged hardly. "I don't know what you're hoping to achieve by all this, Ellie, but—"

"I have no idea what you're talking about," she interrupted firmly, glancing over his shoulder in the hope that Patrick or Toby might see her predicament and come to her rescue; neither of them was in sight.

He grimaced. "I realise that you're in love with me, Ellie, but—"

"You realise no such thing!" Ellie interrupted heatedly, knowing that briefly she might have thought herself in love with this man. But it had only been briefly. She was most certainly over whatever she had once felt for him! "If I'm in love with anyone, it most certainly isn't you," she added scathingly.

Gareth's gaze narrowed. "McGrath?"

She didn't know what she felt for Patrick—had spent most of the last twenty-four hours determinedly not giving herself time to even think along those lines.

Her chin rose challengingly. "And what if it is?"

He gave a pitying shake of his head. "Then you're wasting your time there more than you were with me," he scorned. "Delusions of grandeur!" he added nastily.

"And what about you?" Ellie flushed angrily—more so because she knew what he said was true. "Isn't Sarah Delacorte just as much out of your league as Patrick is out of mine?"

"Ah, but I've already succeeded with Sarah," he reminded her confidently.

"Not for long, if I have my way," Ellie snapped furiously. "You— Let go of my arm, Gareth!" she gasped as he grasped her painfully on exactly the same spot he had the previous evening. And she had the bruises to prove it!

He ignored her, maintaining his grip, his face very close to hers now, his eyes glittering angrily. "Don't try and mess this up for me, Ellie," he warned softly. "Because if you do—"

"Everything all right, Ellie?"

It was Toby who came to Ellie's rescue this time. Gareth released her in time for her to turn and see her brother strolling across the hallway to join them.

"Davies," he greeted the other man coolly before turning to look at Ellie concernedly.

Ellie had a good idea what he would see too; she was

both shocked and dismayed by Gareth's verbal attack on her, and the bruises on her arm were hurting.

"Ellie, Patrick was looking for you so that you can go into the buffet together," Toby said softly. "I think you should go and join him," he added firmly.

She didn't want to rejoin Patrick; she just wanted to leave, to go home and lick her wounds—literally. Her arm really was throbbing, adding to the discomfort of the bruises already there.

"I'll just stay here and have a few quiet words with Gareth," Toby continued lightly, before turning to the other man. "I don't think I've congratulated you on your engagement yet, have I?"

Ellie left them to it. These confrontations with Gareth were unpleasant as well as nerve-shattering. Although Patrick seemed to be right in his surmise that she only needed to appear in order to upset Gareth's self-confidence. She just wasn't sure she was up to the effect these meetings were having on her own self-confidence!

Patrick was frowning darkly as she joined him by the window. "Where on earth have you been?" he snapped. "I finished talking to my parents long ago. I— What is it?" he probed concernedly when Ellie's eyes misted over with tears. "Ellie…?" He lightly clasped her arm.

Ellie gasped at this added pressure on a spot that already felt black and blue, biting her bottom lip as her tears became tears of pain.

Patrick instantly released her when he realised he was hurting her. "Ellie, where have you been?" he asked slowly. "And why does your arm hurt?"

She shook her head, desperately blinking back the tears; she didn't want to make a complete fool of herself—and Patrick—in front of his family. "I bumped into Gareth in the hallway—"

"That's how you hurt your arm?" he ground out suspiciously, eyes narrowed to steely slits.

"Not exactly," she conceded awkwardly. "You see, I still have bruises there from last night, when he grabbed me, and—"

"Davies hurt you?" Patrick bit out, dangerously soft.

"I don't suppose he meant to," she lied—knowing from the expression on Gareth's face earlier that he would greatly enjoy strangling her for what he saw as her interference! "You see—"

"Yes, I do see, Ellie," Patrick ground out harshly, his narrowed gaze searching as he looked across the room towards the door. "Here's Toby," he rasped. "I want you to stay here with him—while I go and have a few words with my so-called future cousin-in-law!"

"Patrick, no—" But she was too late. He had already left her side, muttering a few words to her brother in passing before going out into the hallway himself.

This was awful! She deplored Sarah's choice of future husband, knew Gareth for exactly what he was, but the last thing Ellie wanted was to cause trouble at Sarah's engagement party. And she was pretty sure, from the grim expression on Patrick's face as he'd left her side, that there was going to be trouble!

Toby smiled as he reached her. "Patrick wants me to take you in to the buffet; he's going to join us in a few minutes."

Maybe this was the reason Toby had accompanied them to the party—this way Patrick had ensured that she was never left alone. Except she had been...

"Toby, Patrick is going to find Gareth and, from the looks of him, hit him," she said agitatedly, staring anxiously towards the direction in which Patrick had so recently disappeared.

"So?" Toby prompted unconcernedly.

"Toby—"

"Ellie," he cut in firmly. "I would have hit the man myself if I hadn't thought the bruises might show, but I had to settle for a few choice words instead. And talking of bruises…" He looked down at her searchingly. "Patrick said something about Gareth having hurt you just now?"

She sighed her impatience, wishing she hadn't given away the fact that her arm was bruised beneath the sleeve of her dress. "It doesn't matter," she dismissed. "What matters is that Patrick is going to make a scene." Her eyes were wide with distress at the thought.

Toby gave a confident shake of his head. "Patrick never makes a scene," her brother assured her dryly.

No, he probably didn't—could probably get his point over by talking in that softly dangerous voice she had heard him use just now. But, nevertheless, she doubted Gareth would just meekly stand there and take whatever Patrick had to say to him.

"Come on, sis," Toby encouraged lightly. "Let's go through to the other room and get some food."

The last thing Ellie felt like doing was eating! How could she even think about food when Patrick and Gareth might even now be at each other's throats?

She hung back. "I just want to go home, Toby." She sighed. "In fact, after tonight I need to rethink my whole life," she added frowningly.

After tonight she wasn't even sure she could go on

working in the same building with Gareth, let alone anything else. If Gareth could be this threatening in the
midst of his future in-laws, what possible chance did
she stand of avoiding his wrath at the office?

She had worked for Delacorte, Delacorte and Delacorte since leaving school at eighteen, had been steadily
promoted through the firm, until she'd become George's
personal secretary four years ago. It was a job she greatly
enjoyed. At least, she had. The last couple of months,
with the chance of bumping into Gareth around every
corner, hadn't been quite so much fun. And after this
evening it promised to get worse!

Toby frowned. "I don't think you need to do anything
drastic just yet, Ellie," he cautioned. "Give Patrick a bit
more time to resolve the situation, hmm?"

She gave a wry smile. "You have great confidence in
your employer!"

Her brother gave a rueful shrug. "I've never seen Patrick at the losing end of a fight yet."

No, she could believe that; Patrick had the air of a
man completely confident in his own abilities. But this
situation was too personal, too close to home, to be dealt
with like the business deals he was usually involved
with.

"Hello, Ellie," Sarah greeted her brightly, looking
exceptionally beautiful in the green dress she had bought
earlier that afternoon. "You don't happen to have seen my
fiancé about anywhere, do you?" she added ruefully.

Ellie felt the colour drain from her cheeks. "Er—"

"He was outside talking to Patrick when I last saw
him." Toby was the one to answer. "I'm Ellie's brother
Toby, by the way," he added lightly, holding out his hand
in friendly greeting.

"Sarah Delacorte." She gave Toby a considering look as she shook his hand. "Yes, I can see the likeness." She smiled warmly. "You work with Patrick, don't you?"

"For him, actually," Toby corrected dryly.

Sarah's smile widened. "Of course. Well, it's very nice to meet you," she added sincerely. "I hope you'll both excuse me while I go and find Gareth?"

Ellie looked up impatiently at Toby once they were alone. "Shouldn't you go and warn Patrick?"

Her brother shrugged unconcernedly. "One thing I've learnt from working for Patrick—he's quite capable of taking care of himself. Now, let's go and get some food; I'm starving!" With his hand under her elbow he guided her through to the dining room.

Toby had learnt something else from working for Patrick, Ellie realized: how to take charge of a situation with the same arrogance!

Somewhere along the way, she realised dazedly as she put food on her plate without even noticing what she had chosen, her little brother had grown up...

She had spent so long thinking of him as her younger brother, that she just hadn't noticed him grow into a man almost as confident as the one he worked for.

He was a handsome man too, Ellie had to acknowledge as a girl of about twenty who stood helping herself to the buffet—probably yet another relative of Patrick's—gave him more than a cursory glance from beneath lowered dark lashes.

At twenty-six and over six feet tall, with short dark hair, laughing blue eyes, a pleasantly handsome face and a healthily fit body from his visits to the gym several times a week, her brother wasn't the boy she had always thought him; he was a man who was obviously attractive to women.

When had that happened? She—

"You aren't eating, Ellie."

She turned sharply to find Patrick standing at her side, and quickly checked his face for signs of a fight. Thankfully she didn't find any.

"How was I supposed to eat when for all I knew you might have been lying unconscious in the hallway?" she came back, her sharpness due to her worry concerning his welfare.

Like a mother when her child came back to her unharmed after doing something she considered dangerous? Or like a woman worried about the man she loved...?

Patrick's reply didn't exactly calm her impatient anger. "Not very likely," he drawled confidently.

Ellie's eyes sparkled angrily. "That's okay for you to say, but—"

"Ellie!" Toby cut in laughingly. "I told you that Patrick is more than capable of taking care of himself."

She glared at them both—Toby laughing, Patrick amused, one dark brow raised mockingly. "Men!" she finally muttered frustratedly, turning away to pile more food haphazardly onto her plate.

"Are you sure you're going to eat all that?" Patrick murmured close beside her. "Maybe we should just share the plate," he added teasingly.

Ellie turned to find that she and Patrick were alone. Toby had wandered off, was now standing across the dining room chatting to the dark-haired girl who had given him such an admiring look a few minutes ago. He hadn't wasted much time!

She looked up at Patrick, some of her anger abating

in the face of his teasing look. "I had visions of a brawl in the hallway," she admitted ruefully.

He shrugged. "I very rarely resort to violence, Ellie. Although in Davies's case," he added hardly, his expression becoming grim, "I could be willing to make an exception. As it is, I've made it very clear what I will do to him if he so much as comes near you again, let alone touches you."

Ellie raised dark brows. "Oh?"

Patrick nodded abruptly. "I think we need to discuss your continued involvement in all this."

Ellie felt her heart stop for a moment. What did he mean? Was he suggesting that it was no longer necessary for her to be involved?

She might have decided minutes ago that she needed to rethink her life, to perhaps consider giving up her position at Delacorte, Delacorte and Delacorte as a way of avoiding accidentally bumping into Gareth any more. But she hadn't included not seeing Patrick any more in that rethinking... The very thought of that filled her with desolation.

A week ago Patrick had just been her brother Toby's boss—a man she had once shared an embarrassing experience with—but he was now so much more than that. How much more she still didn't want to admit to herself. She just knew she couldn't bear the thought of not seeing Patrick again!

Her mouth tightened. "You can manage without me now—is that it?" She was waspish in her disappointment.

"I didn't say that." Patrick gave her a reproving look. "I just think that it might be better for you—"

"I'll decide what's best for me, if you don't mind,"

Ellie told him shortly. "And while I can still be of any help in preventing Sarah making a terrible mistake I intend staying very much in Gareth's face!" she announced firmly—in complete contradiction of what she had decided minutes ago!

But the only way she could continue to see Patrick was to remain a thorn in Gareth's side.

And she very much wanted to continue seeing Patrick...

CHAPTER SEVEN

"I'M SORRY, how did you say Toby was getting home?" Ellie yawned tiredly as Patrick drove her home a couple of hours later.

He shrugged dismissively. "Someone he met at the party is driving him back later, I believe."

Ellie would take a bet on it being that pretty dark-haired girl who had looked at him so interestedly as they stood at the buffet table; she certainly hadn't seen much of her brother during the rest of the evening.

Oh, well, good luck to him, Ellie thought slightly enviously. She had spent the whole evening with Patrick glued to her side—but for completely the wrong reason!

"I felt so sorry for George and Mary this evening." She sighed heavily. The older couple's unhappiness at their daughter's choice of future husband had been perfectly obvious to Ellie as they'd looked at Sarah so wistfully. She frowned. "Does Sarah really have no idea how they feel about Gareth?"

"George has voiced his—reservations concerning the speed of the engagement." Patrick grimaced. "Anything else is sure to just make her all the more determined to have her own way."

Ellie turned to smile at him in the semi-darkness of

the illuminated streets they were driving through. "Runs in the family, does it?" she teased.

He gave a slight smile. "Something like that."

She couldn't believe it. They were certainly an attractive family, but stubbornness seemed to be one of their less endearing characteristics.

"Gareth is going to cling like a leech," Ellie warned heavily.

Patrick's mouth tightened. "I agree. He's a parasite."

How embarrassing it was for her that she had been the previous woman taken in by Gareth's charm! In fact, she would rather not talk about Gareth at all.

"So what's the next move?" she prompted briskly.

"Dinner on Tuesday, I thought," Patrick came back lightly.

Ellie turned to him frowningly. "What's happening on Tuesday evening?"

"I just said—dinner," he dismissed.

"Yes, but—what's it for?"

He shot her a sideways glance. "So we don't starve?"

"Yes, but—"

"You're repeating yourself again, Ellie," he mused teasingly. "I'm inviting you out to dinner on Tuesday evening," he explained lightly.

Ellie's frown deepened. "But—"

"Ellie, will you or will you not have dinner with me on Tuesday evening?" Patrick cut in patiently.

"Well, of course. I've already told you I'll do everything I can to help—"

"This is dinner with me, Ellie." He parked the car in the driveway and turned in his seat to look at her. "No one else. Well…I suppose there will be other people in the restaurant. But they will have nothing to do with us. Have I made myself clear now?"

If she understood this correctly, Patrick had just invited her out on a date!

He gave a smile at her perplexed expression. "I believe it's usual to invite your escort in for coffee at the end of the evening."

Ellie was still so dazed by his invitation out to dinner on Tuesday that she did ask him in, getting out of the car to unlock the front door of the house and lead the way in to the kitchen.

"Leave that for a minute," Patrick murmured softly, and he took the coffee pot out of her hand, turning her to face him. "I want to see the bruises on your arms," he told her grimly as he removed the wrap from her shoulders.

She felt the colour warm her cheeks as he turned the sleeves back on her dress. There was a huge thumbprint-size bruise on the front of each arm, one already turning a sickly yellow, the new one a blue-black. Ellie stood still as Patrick walked around to look at the back of her arm, hearing the angry hiss that followed.

"I should have hit him while I had the chance," Patrick snapped angrily. "Damn it—I've a good mind to go back to the party right now and hit him anyway!" he bit out harshly.

Ellie shook her head as she pulled the sleeves back down over her arms. "He really isn't important."

"No, he isn't," Patrick agreed abruptly as he moved to stand beside her, his eyes gleaming metallic grey. "But I have no intention of just standing by while he hurts you."

She gave a self-derisive laugh. "You're a little late in the day to prevent him doing that!"

Patrick stepped back, watching her with hooded eyes as she prepared the coffee. "Did you love him very much?"

"Not at all," she answered with complete honesty. "Oh, I may have thought I did for a while. But I was just—flattered by his attention, I suppose. Believe it or not, he can be very charming when he wants to be." Besides, she already knew that the way Patrick made her feel, just by being in the same room as her, was far deeper than anything she might have thought she felt for Gareth!

"I'm sure he can," Patrick dismissed scathingly.

"No—really." She gave a self-conscious laugh.

It was strangely intimate in the quiet of the kitchen—the muted light under the kitchen cupboards the only illumination, the only sound the drip, drip of the coffee percolator.

Patrick's eyes were mesmerizing now as he looked down at her, obliquely black, ringed with silver. "Dinner on Tuesday?" he prompted huskily.

"Er—Well—Yes," she agreed awkwardly, still unsure as to the reason for his invitation. "Although—"

"Just a yes will do," Patrick assured her mockingly, his arms moving lightly about her waist. "I would like to see you relaxed and enjoying yourself for a change," he added frowningly.

If he thought she was going to be relaxed in his company then he was mistaken! Although she *would* enjoy spending the evening with him. If she knew the reason for it...

But he was standing so close now she couldn't even

think straight, let alone try to rationalise his dinner invitation. Her heart was beating erratically, her breathing shallow as she looked up into the handsome ruggedness of his face.

"You look extremely lovely tonight, Ellie," he told her huskily.

"You said that earlier," she reminded him breathlessly.

He smiled, his eyes crinkling warmly at the corners. "Some things need to be repeated." His hands linked at the base of her spine and he moulded her body lightly against his, his head bending slightly as his lips moved teasingly across hers.

She had forgotten to breathe again, felt as if time itself were standing still. Only her hands resting on the broadness of Patrick's shoulders prevented her from actually falling down.

"You have a very kissable mouth, Ellie Fairfax," Patrick murmured huskily as he took little sips from her lips. "A very sensuous neck," he whispered as his lips moved down the silky column of her throat. "Divine breasts—"

"I think perhaps you should stop there, Patrick, don't you?" Ellie moved awkwardly in his arms, very aware of the sudden pertness of those "divine breasts", the nipples hard against the silky material of her dress.

He straightened, his head tilted to one side as he regarded her quizzically. "Why do I get the impression you're an innocent?" he murmured ruefully.

"Probably because I am!" Ellie admitted uncomfortably as she extricated herself from his arms, at the same time looking up at him irritably. "There's nothing wrong with that," she added sharply.

Patrick's smile deepened. "Did I say there was?"

"You looked as if there was," she snapped defensively.

He shook his head, still smiling. "I don't think so, Ellie."

Well…okay, maybe he hadn't. But he certainly seemed surprised to meet a twenty-seven-year-old virgin!

Maybe it *was* odd at that; Ellie really wouldn't know. It wasn't something she had ever discussed with any of the women she worked with.

She had been out with several boys of her own age up to the age of nineteen, but after her parents had died she had been too busy trying to keep a home for Toby and herself—hadn't really had much time to think about relationships. Which was probably the reason she had fallen for Gareth's charm six months ago!

But in the face of Patrick's sophistication, his obvious experience when it came to women, she must seem rather gauche and naïve.

Well, tough! She had no intention of pretending an experience she just didn't have. And that included appearing sophisticated in the face of Patrick's appreciative comments on her body!

"Coffee, Ellie," he reminded her lightly, moving to sit down at the kitchen table.

"Of course." She moved economically about the kitchen, getting out the cups, cream and sugar, all the time avoiding Patrick's gaze, but knowing it followed her every movement.

"Did Davies—? Steady," Patrick soothed as a spoon landed on the floor with a clatter when Ellie just dropped it.

She bent to pick it up, her face averted so that he shouldn't see the heated colour in her cheeks.

"Ellie?"

Just that. Her name. Nothing else. But it was said compellingly enough for Ellie to know he wanted her to look across at him. And she did exactly that. The steadiness of his gaze as he looked at her wordlessly was as forceful as Ellie had known it would be.

"What do you want to know, Patrick?" she snapped impatiently, picking up the tray of coffee things only to put it down noisily on the kitchen table. "Whether Gareth and I came close to being lovers?" she bit out sarcastically. "What business is it of yours if we did?" she added challengingly, blue eyes bright with anger as she glared down at him.

"Black, no sugar," he told her economically. "My preference for coffee," he explained mildly at her blank look.

"Oh. Fine," she muttered, sitting down abruptly to concentrate all her attention on pouring the coffee. She didn't want to think about anything else!

"You're quite right, Ellie," Patrick began softly, "it is none of my business just how—intimate your relationship was with Davies. Except…"

She looked up sharply. "Yes?"

His gaze was intense on the paleness of her face. "Did he hurt you, Ellie?"

She felt the blood drain completely from her cheeks, her hand shook as she held the coffee pot poised over one of the cups.

"Ellie?"

She drew in a deep breath, swallowed hard, willing herself to carry on pouring the coffee without spilling it. No, Gareth hadn't hurt her, he had humiliated her. But it wasn't an incident she particularly wanted to relate to Patrick. It was the reason she knew she had meant absolutely nothing to Gareth—the reason she knew what sort of man he really was...

She gave an over-bright smile, her gaze not quite meeting Patrick's as she handed him his cup of coffee. "It isn't important, Patrick," she dismissed lightly. "We're all agreed that he isn't a nice person."

Patrick reached out, his hand covering hers as it rested on the tabletop. "Tell me what happened," he encouraged huskily.

She closed her eyes, wishing she could shut out the memory of that last time she had been with Gareth but at the same time knowing that she couldn't.

GARETH called into her office as she was finishing work, suggesting that he drive her home. Things had been rather strained between them the last couple of weeks—forgotten telephone calls, cancelled dates—and she had welcomed this chance to talk to him alone for a while.

Toby was still at work when they arrived back at the house, and almost before Ellie and Gareth were in the door, it seemed, Gareth began to kiss her. But as the kiss deepened, with Gareth's hands roaming more freely over her body than ever before, Ellie began to pull away from him.

"Don't," she told him frowningly, at the same time pushing ineffectually at his painful hold about her waist.

He smiled then—a smile like no other Ellie had seen him give, a smile so scornful it made her cringe. "That's always been the trouble with you, Ellie," he told her scathingly as he released her so abruptly she staggered slightly. "Maybe if you hadn't been so frigid I wouldn't have needed to find someone else. As it is…"

Ellie stared at him. She had suspected something; of course she had. Gareth had been far too elusive these last two weeks for her not to have realised that something had gone seriously wrong with their relationship.

Gareth raised blond brows at her stricken expression. "Of course, it isn't too late," he drawled suggestively. "I could still be persuaded into continuing our relationship. If you were to—"

"You conceited—!" Ellie broke off angrily, glaring up at him disgustedly. "Let me get this right, Gareth," she said evenly, eyes narrowed now. "If I'll agree to go to bed with you then you'll consider breaking off your other—relationship?"

The fact that he had another relationship had come as a complete shock to her. But she would think about that later. Once Gareth had left. Because he *was* leaving. Soon!

He smiled. "Well, I wouldn't go quite that far," he mocked.

Her eyes widened. "You're suggesting that I become part of some harem?"

"Of course not, Ellie." He chuckled. "If everything goes according to plan, I should be getting married soon. But that's no reason for us to break off our relationship. If things were different between us," he added pointedly.

If everything went according to plan! What plan?

She swallowed hard. "If the two of us were lovers, you mean?" she clarified icily.

Gareth shrugged. "Well, it would hardly be worth the risk otherwise, now, would it?"

"Get out," Ellie told him shakily, her hand on the table

beside her for support; her legs felt so shaky she thought she might fall over otherwise.

"Now, Ellie, there's no reason to be like that," he cajoled huskily, taking a step towards her.

She straightened, her chin raised challengingly. "I said, get out, Gareth, and I meant it. And God help the poor woman you're planning to marry," she added disgustedly.

He had come to a halt some distance away from her. "Frigid," he repeated scornfully.

Her eyes glazed coldly. "You'll never know," she bit out forcefully.

He smiled. "But I already do know, Ellie," he assured her derisively. "Oh, well." He shrugged in the face of her stony expression. "I made the offer. See you around." He raised a hand in farewell before letting himself out of the house.

SHE turned to Patrick now, having no intention of relating any of that conversation to him. It was bad enough that she still remembered every painfully humiliating word of it, without sharing it with anyone else. Least of all Patrick!

She gave him a dismissive smile. "It isn't important what happened, Patrick," she told him lightly. "Gareth hurt me with words, that's all. And as my mother always said, 'sticks and stones may break my bones, but words can never hurt me'," she quoted ruefully.

Patrick looked unconvinced. "Bones heal; words can never be forgotten."

How true that was. She hadn't forgotten a single word Gareth had said to her six weeks ago, whereas a broken finger or wrist would have healed and been dismissed by now.

"Surely it's Gareth's problem if he considers that any woman who doesn't want to sleep with him must be frigid." She shrugged.

Grey eyes widened. "He actually said that? To *you*?" Patrick sounded incredulous.

Ellie gave him a disgruntled frown. "Yes, he said that to me," she repeated irritably.

Patrick chuckled softly. "You're right, Ellie." He gave a rueful shake of his head. "He isn't important," he explained at her questioning look. "He obviously didn't get to know you very well at all, did he?" he added derisively.

"Exactly what do you mean by that remark?" she demanded defensively.

He looked at her consideringly before answering. "Ellie, you are one of the warmest, most responsive women I have ever had the pleasure to meet."

Her cheeks coloured hotly. It was no good denying what he said; her response to him whenever he touched her was undeniable.

"I'll tell you something else," Patrick added huskily as he stood up to move round the table and pull her unresistingly to her feet. "I'm glad Davies never got close enough to you to discover that for himself," he murmured throatily, before bending to lightly brush Ellie's lips with his own.

So was she.

She hadn't always felt that way, had wondered in the days and then weeks that had followed Gareth's abrupt departure from her life whether she could indeed be frigid. But she only had to be in the same room with

Patrick to be completely aware of him, and when she was actually in his arms like this...!

No, she wasn't frigid. She was just a woman who only responded to the right man. The right man for her. Because, although he was unsuitable in every other way—rich, powerful, successful, completely removed from her own lifestyle—she knew she had fallen in love with Patrick McGrath.

She had been fighting that knowledge for some time now, refusing to allow the thought to even enter her head. But alone here with him in the silence of her kitchen, held in his arms, their two bodies moulded perfectly together, she could no longer deny how she felt about him.

To herself, at least.

To Patrick it was another matter!

"Well, I'm relieved to hear it," she told him lightly, at the same time moving determinedly out of his arms. "Maybe there's hope for me after all," she added with deliberate self-derision.

Patrick's gaze followed her frowningly. "Ellie—"

"I just heard a car in the driveway, so I think Toby must be home," she told him with a certain amount of relief.

Her mother used to say something else to her, about "jumping from the frying pan into the fire". Well, she had certainly done that where Patrick was concerned; he was a more unsuitable man for her to have fallen in love with than Gareth had ever been!

CHAPTER EIGHT

"DID you enjoy yourself on Saturday?"

Ellie gave a startled glance towards the open door of her office, her gaze narrowing as she focused on Gareth standing in the doorway, looking incredibly cheerful. As well as self-confident.

The latter instantly made Ellie more wary than she would normally have been in his unwanted presence, and she glanced towards the door that connected hers to George's, to make sure it was firmly shut, before replying. "The Delacortes gave you and Sarah a wonderful engagement party," she answered non-committally.

Gareth grinned, coming fully into the room before closing the door behind him. "That didn't exactly answer my question, now, did it?" he reproved derisively, moving to sit on the edge of her desk as he looked down at her with mocking blue eyes.

Ellie sighed. "I didn't think it really needed an answer," she dismissed, still eyeing him warily, sure his pleasantness wouldn't last for long; nowadays it usually didn't.

Besides, she remembered all too well his nastiness on Saturday evening. Still had the bruises to prove how angry he had been then.

He shrugged. "Thanks for the cut-glass crystal vase, by the way. Sarah will be writing to everyone formally, of course, but I thought I would come and thank you personally."

Cut-glass crystal vase? Ellie had been aware that Patrick had carried a gift-wrapped present into the house on Saturday evening, of course, but even if it had been a cut-glass crystal vase, what did it have to do with her...?

"'Congratulations, love from Patrick and Ellie'," Gareth continued tauntingly. "You've been 'Patrick and Ellie' for how long?" he added scathingly.

A matter of days. Except they weren't "Patrick and Ellie" at all.

She'd had no idea that Patrick had put her name beside his on the gift card that had accompanied the engagement present he'd given to his cousin on Saturday. She realised why he had done it, of course, but he might have warned her!

She gave Gareth a stony look. "Gareth, I have no idea why you should be in the least interested," she scorned.

"I'm not. Not really." He still looked incredibly pleased with himself. "It will be quite a coup for the Fairfax family if you and Toby manage to pull this off." He gave her an admiring look. "I must say, Ellie, you're something of a surprise. Especially after your holier-than-thou attitude before." He shook his head. "Those people in glass houses shouldn't throw stones, you know."

Ellie gave him a suspicious look. Could he possibly have been drinking? Admittedly it was only eleven-thirty in the morning, but she couldn't think of any other explanation for the fact that what he was saying made absolutely no sense to her.

She shook her head, not wanting to prolong this

unwanted conversation any further by asking him for an explanation. "I'll bear your advice in mind, Gareth," she dismissed. "Now, if you wouldn't mind, I have some work to do…?" She gave a pointed look at where he sat on some of the papers on her desk.

Gareth grinned, making no effort to move. "Don't you see, Ellie? There's no longer any need to be all coy with me. The truth is, you and I are more alike than I would ever have guessed."

She stiffened defensively. "I don't think so!" she snapped distastefully.

"But of course we are," he contradicted happily. "It's a pity you came on so prim and proper six weeks ago; you and I would have made a great team. And Toby, of course."

He *had* been drinking; there was no other explanation for this completely puzzling conversation!

"What on earth does Toby have to do with any of this?" She looked at him impatiently.

The two men had met on several occasions, when Gareth had come to call for her at the house, but as far as she was aware Toby hadn't particularly taken to the other man then, and he certainly didn't like him now. As for Gareth, he hadn't seemed particularly interested in Toby either.

Gareth grinned. "You can stop the pretence now, Ellie," he teased. "The game is up, so to speak. Maybe the three of us should form some sort of club? We could call it—"

"Gareth, I have no idea what you're talking about." Ellie lost all patience with him. "Besides which, you're sitting on my desk when I want to get on with some work. Now, would you please go?" She glared at him.

He stood up slowly. But looked no less confident. "Okay, play it that way if you want to." He shrugged. "But just remember that if you keep my little secret then I'll keep yours. And Toby's, of course," he added enigmatically. "Fair's fair, after all."

"Gareth—"

"Ellie, I'm just going across to—"

"Gareth…?" George came to a halt in the doorway that connected his office to Ellie's, his gaze narrowing suspiciously on the younger man as he saw him standing there.

Gareth looked completely unconcerned by the interruption. "I just popped in to tell Ellie how much Sarah and I loved the crystal vase she and Patrick gave us for an engagement present," he told his future father-in-law lightly.

"Well, now you've told her might I suggest you leave her to get on with her work?" George nodded abruptly, continuing to look at the younger man with narrowed eyes.

"Of course," Gareth accepted smoothly, moving unhurriedly to the door. "I believe I'm seeing you and Mary for dinner this evening," he added with a smile.

"I believe you are," George acknowledged noncommittally.

"See you later, Ellie," came Gareth's parting shot.

Not if she saw him first! She had found him obnoxious enough before. Now she not only disliked him intensely, she didn't understand a word he said!

George gave a shuddering sigh. "No matter how hard I try, I simply can't bring myself to like that young man." He shook his head sadly.

Ellie gave a wan smile. "I wouldn't worry about it, George; you're in the majority rather than the minority!"

He grimaced. "I wouldn't worry about it at all if Sarah hadn't decided to marry the man! I had just about decided that he wasn't suitable for Delacorte, Delacorte and Delacorte when Sarah dropped the bombshell of her engagement to the man. Her mother and I simply don't know what to do for the best," he added heavily.

Ellie gave him a sympathetic smile. "I think the two of you are doing very well. Very often seeming to do nothing is the right thing to do," she added encouragingly.

George gave her a grateful smile. "A word of advice, Ellie. Never have daughters; it plays the very devil with your heart."

She felt so sorry for him. Especially as there was nothing she could say or do to make him feel any better.

He straightened, seeming to shake off his despondency as he glanced down at the file he held in his hand. "I'm just going across to Gerald's office for a few minutes. My next appointment is at twelve-thirty?"

Ellie nodded after a brief glimpse at the appointment book on her desk, breathing a sigh of relief when she was finally left alone in her office.

Gareth's conversation was still a complete puzzle to her. But then, the man himself was a complete enigma to her; how could he possibly be contemplating marrying someone he so obviously didn't love? As beautiful as Sarah was.

And how could she be in love with a man when she stood absolutely no chance of him ever feeling the same way about her?

Ellie had pondered that question several times over

the weekend, and she still had no answer. Only knew that she was counting the hours until she saw Patrick again!

"OH, GOOD, you got the message and aren't dressed up," Patrick said with relief as Ellie opened the door to him at eight o'clock on Tuesday evening.

She raised dark brows. "It would serve you right if I said that I was dressed up." She opened the door wider to let him in, wearing a fitted blue jumper with faded denims.

He shook his head, grinning. "I knew Toby wouldn't let me down!"

Her brother had dutifully passed on Patrick's message earlier that they were going to eat at a pizzeria, and Ellie had dressed accordingly. Although Patrick looked as ruggedly handsome as ever in the black sweater and black denims that he wore.

"We always seem to be going somewhere formal," Patrick dismissed. "I thought it would be nice if we could completely relax this evening."

There was also no possibility of them running into anyone Patrick knew in some out-of-the way pizzeria!

Ellie had had plenty of time to think once Toby had passed on Patrick's message to dress casually because they were going to eat informally. Patrick had never said, and she hadn't liked to ask Toby, but there was always the possibility that Patrick actually had a woman in his life at the moment. Perhaps not someone he had wanted to introduce to his family, as in accompanying him to the party on Saturday evening, but that didn't mean he wasn't involved in a relationship. She had never thought to ask…

But she wanted to ask now—wanted to know everything there was to know about Patrick McGrath. Especially if there was already a woman in his life!

Not that Ellie didn't already know she was wasting her time feeling about him as she did; she just didn't like the idea of Patrick having to explain these dates with her to another woman. In fact, she just didn't like the thought of there being another woman at all!

"I hope you like Italian food?" Patrick prompted ruefully.

"I like it fine." Ellie nodded, picking up her fleecy blue jacket from the kitchen chair—if only to show him that she didn't always wear the unattractive long black coat.

The beautiful pashmina Patrick had bought for her on Saturday was now carefully folded and placed back in its tissue paper inside the box, stashed away at the back of her wardrobe. Ellie knew she might never find the opportunity to wear such a glamorous item again.

"Shall we go?" she prompted lightly once she had shrugged into the jacket.

Patrick looked at her consideringly. "Is everything okay? Has Davies been bothering you again?" he added hardly.

Ellie frowned. "Apart from a very strange conversation with him yesterday morning, no."

"Tell me about it while we eat," Patrick suggested, opening the door for her. "Unless you think it will give us both indigestion?" He grimaced as he moved to unlock the car door.

It was warm and cosy as she settled inside the car, which smelt vaguely of the aftershave Patrick favoured.

"No more than any other subject would, I don't suppose," she answered Patrick dismissively as he got in beside her.

He gave her a sideways glance. "What's that supposed to mean?"

Ellie sighed. "I still don't know what this evening is about—"

Patrick shrugged. "How about it's a thank-you for all the—inconvenience you're having to go through on my family's behalf?"

"What about the inconvenience you're now having to go to on my behalf?" she came back dismissively.

He frowned his puzzlement as he drove. "What inconvenience would that be?"

She gave a self-derisive smile. "Taking me out."

He smiled ruefully. "I have no idea what you're talking about, Ellie."

She grimaced. "It must be the week for it!"

"Forget Davies for the moment," Patrick bit out impatiently. "I want to know what you meant by that remark just now."

Seeing the determination on his face, Ellie wished she had never made the remark in the first place. She was just feeling sorry for herself because she had fallen in love with a man who was completely unobtainable. Which was absolutely no reason to try and make life difficult for him on the rare occasions she saw him!

"Forget it," she advised self-derisively. "It's just pre-Christmas tension, I expect. It's very kind of you to take me out—"

"Ellie, I know you haven't known me very long," he interrupted evenly, his expression grim, "but when you do know me better you'll realise that, although I'm not a cruel man, neither am I someone who takes a woman out—namely you—because I am simply being kind!"

She had seen Patrick in many moods over the last couple of weeks—amused, attentive, charming, angry when it came to Gareth—but he had never been annoyed or angry with her before. At the moment he appeared to be both!

"I'm sorry if I've mistaken the situation—"

"And don't start apologising," he cut in impatiently. "You have done nothing to apologise for. I appear to be the one who hasn't made myself clear. A fact I am about to change right now," he assured her determinedly, and he turned the car into a deserted private car park on the edge of town.

"What are you doing?" Ellie looked about them dazedly as Patrick parked the car in the middle of the dimly lit area.

He released his seat belt before turning in his seat to face her. "I'm about to convince you that I asked you out this evening for one reason and one reason only. You can let me know afterwards if I've succeeded or not," he added firmly, before reaching out to pull her into his arms, his mouth coming down forcefully on hers.

Ellie was so stunned by the suddenness of the kiss that for a moment she lay acquiescent in his arms, but then the magical thrill of his lips thoroughly exploring hers warmed her body in that familiar way, and her arms moved up about his shoulders as she returned the kiss with all the pent-up longing inside her.

Patrick's hands moved caressingly along the length of her spine, sending ripples of pleasure through her whole body. Her neck arched as his lips moved from her mouth to her cheek, and then down the creamy column of her throat, his tongue doing amazing things to the tiny hollow he discovered there.

Ellie's eyes were closed, her head back against the car seat, her fingers entwined the thick darkness of Patrick's hair as she held him against her.

"Are you wearing anything underneath this jumper, Ellie Fairfax?" Patrick murmured throatily as his thumb moved across the tip of one hardened nipple.

"What do you think, Patrick McGrath?" she came back huskily.

"I think perhaps I should find out," he said softly.

Ellie gasped at the first touch of his hands on her nakedness. They were cool as they cupped the warmth of her breasts, the moistness of his tongue against the hardened tips causing her back to arch instinctively, and she moaned low in her throat at the pleasure that swept heatedly through her body.

She felt mindless, every bone in her body fluid as the warmth of Patrick's mouth closed erotically over one hardened nipple. Her own hands moved restlessly up and down the long length of his back as she wished the pleasure to go on for ever.

Patrick's hands encircled her waist as he held her against him, his lips travelling down the flat slope of her midriff now, pausing to explore the dip of her navel revealed by the low-waisted denims.

Even that felt wonderful, Ellie realised with a surprised gasp, leading her to wonder what other parts of her body would respond to Patrick's slightest touch.

Patrick raised his head to look at her, his eyes bright in the semi-darkness. "I'm not hurting you?"

"Oh, no," she breathed weakly, feeling as if she must have died and gone to heaven.

"And do you know now why I invited you out to dinner?" he prompted huskily.

"Er—yes, I think so." She nodded; it was a little disconcerting looking at him over her bared breasts!

"You only *think* so?" he murmured teasingly, eyes glinting with intent. "Perhaps I wasn't convincing enough—"

"Oh, yes—you were!" She reached down and raised his head as he would have commenced kissing her breasts again. "Patrick—"

"I know." He grimaced self-derisively as he gently pulled her jumper down to cover her nakedness. "This isn't the ideal place for lovemaking. In fact—" he straightened, running his hand restlessly through hair already tousled by Ellie's own hands "—I think I'm a little old to be making love in a car park. But later, Ellie, when I get you home…!"

"Promises, promises," she teased self-consciously.

"Be warned, Ellie," he told her decisively, "I always keep my promises."

Had Patrick really just made love to her? Had he really just paid homage to her body as if he found her beautiful and desirable?

He most certainly had!

And, what was more, he'd said he was going to do it all over again once they returned from their evening out!

The rest of the evening—the Italian restaurant, the delicious food they ate there, the easy flow of conversation—all passed in a dream for Ellie.

She learnt that Patrick had gone to university, eventually leaving with a first-class degree in Business Studies, and that instead of going into industry working for someone else had put his knowledge to use on a personal basis, building up a varied and successful business over the last fifteen years. It was a challenge he obviously still enjoyed.

She also learnt that his was a very close family, that his sister Teresa was fourteen years younger than his thirty-eight, also that she was the cherished baby of the family.

What Ellie still hadn't established by the time Patrick drove her home was whether or not he had a woman in his life; it didn't seem the sort of thing she should ask him after their intimacy earlier this evening!

"Damn," he muttered as they arrived at Ellie's home and saw Toby's car was already parked in the driveway.

Ellie felt warmth in her cheeks as she guessed the reason for his irritation: Toby's presence meant that they wouldn't be able to carry on where they had left off earlier after all.

Patrick turned to look at her ruefully after parking the car behind Toby's. "Have you never thought of getting a home of your own?" he said dryly.

Until this moment, quite honestly, no. It had always seemed the natural thing for her and Toby to continue living together after their parents' death. But at this moment Ellie had to admit she was disappointed that they weren't to be alone again, too.

"Never mind." She squeezed Patrick's arm lightly. "It can't be helped," she added ruefully.

"You're right. There will be other occasions." He nodded before getting agilely out of the car to come round and open her door for her.

Ellie felt as if she were floating on air as they walked

over to the house; Patrick had said there would be other occasions. That must mean he was going to ask to see her again.

To her surprise, Toby was nowhere to be found once they were inside the house.

"He must have gone to bed." Ellie shrugged dismissively.

Patrick moved so that he was standing very close to her. "Does that mean we're alone after all?"

"I suppose it must do. I—" Ellie broke off as she heard the sound of feet descending the stairs. "Perhaps not," she added ruefully, turning expectantly towards the doorway that led out into the hallway. Except it wasn't Toby who came into the kitchen!

But Ellie had no trouble placing the other woman as the one who had looked so interestedly at Toby at the party on Saturday evening. And if she had been upstairs with Toby...!

"Thank goodness you're here," the other woman burst out agitatedly.

Although it wasn't to Ellie that she spoke...

"What is it?" Patrick was instantly alert and left Ellie's side to go to the other woman, the languid intimacy that had existed between the two of them all evening instantly broken.

"Toby," the woman choked emotionally. "I think it must be something he's eaten—I had to drive him here. He felt too ill even to drive home." She looked distraught. "Oh, Patrick, I'm so worried about him!" She launched herself into Patrick's arms, the tears starting to fall down her creamy cheeks.

Ellie looked at the two of them in total stupefaction. The other woman appeared to have spent the evening with Toby, and yet she and Patrick obviously knew each other rather well too. Of course, this woman had been at the party on Saturday evening, so the two might be related. Even so...

But for the moment she was too concerned about Toby herself to try to puzzle this one out, turning wordlessly to hurriedly leave the room and run upstairs to her brother's bedroom.

Toby looked awful. He lay weakly back against the pillows, his face waxen, his eyes dull with discomfort and pain as he looked up at Ellie.

"I'm going to call the doctor," she told him decisively.

"Fine," he nodded. "Tell him to bring something with him to put me out of my misery!" he called after her as she hurried from the room.

Ellie turned to give a strained smile at his attempt to joke. At least, she hoped he was joking! "I'll tell him." She nodded before running down the stairs again. The fact that her brother hadn't argued about her calling in the doctor told her just how ill he must feel; Toby, like most men, absolutely hated the necessity of ever seeing a doctor.

"Food poisoning, do you think?" Patrick prompted economically as he came out into the hallway where she stood telephoning.

"I think so." She nodded, frowning as she waited for her call to be answered. "I—perhaps you could make some coffee for all of us?" she suggested distractedly.

"Teresa is already doing that," he informed her grimly. "Who are you calling?" he added frowningly.

Ellie stared him speechlessly. Teresa? The young woman who was at this very moment making coffee in the kitchen, the woman Toby had obviously spent the evening with, was Patrick's young *sister*, Teresa?

What—?

"Ellie, who are you telephoning?" Patrick repeated firmly.

"The doctor—" She broke off as Patrick shook his head grimly.

"I'll ring my own doctor and get him to come out." He took the receiver from her hand, disconnecting her call and putting through one of his own.

Ellie could only stand by dazedly as Patrick spoke decisively with whoever had answered his call, not *asking* the doctor to come out and see Toby, but giving him the directions to do so.

The young woman in the kitchen—the same woman who had looked so interestedly at Toby on Saturday evening—was Patrick's sister, Teresa. Teresa? Tess…? That was a shortened version of the name Teresa, wasn't it? Could Patrick's sister possibly be the Tess that Toby had told Ellie he'd been dating the last couple of months?

And, if she was, why hadn't Toby ever told her that it was Patrick's sister he was dating?

Why hadn't Patrick told her?

Because she was absolutely positive, from the fact that Patrick hadn't looked in the least surprised to see his sister here, that he had known about the relationship before this evening!

What did it all mean?

CHAPTER NINE

"WOULD you like one or both of us to stay with you for the rest of the night?" Patrick asked Ellie some time later. The doctor had been to see Toby, and diagnosed—as they had all suspected he might—that her brother had food poisoning.

It had been an extremely traumatic couple of hours for Ellie, worried about Toby and completely puzzled by his relationship with Teresa/Tess.

But the idea of either Patrick or his sister staying for the rest of the night did not appeal to her. It also wasn't necessary. The doctor had given Toby an injection to stop him vomiting, and although her brother was still pale, he was now fast asleep.

"That won't be necessary," Ellie answered Patrick distantly. None of the tension she had felt earlier, at discovering Toby's girlfriend Tess was in fact Patrick's sister Teresa, had evaporated.

In fact, if anything it was worse, all sorts of suspicions and conclusions having popped into Ellie's head over the last couple of hours. Most of them too depressing to contemplate for long!

"I'm very grateful for your help in getting a doctor here so promptly," she added as she realised she probably sounded less than polite.

"But now you want us to leave?" Patrick guessed ruefully.

It was almost one o'clock in the morning. She was incredibly weary from the worry over Toby, and her head ached from the circles her thoughts were going round and round in. So, yes, she wanted him—and his sister—to leave now.

She glanced at the younger woman, Teresa, sitting dejectedly at the kitchen table staring into a cup of cold coffee, her face pale.

Ellie could see a faint family resemblance between the brother and sister now—both were dark, with those magnetic grey eyes—but where Patrick's face was all ruggedly sharp angles Teresa's was softened into gamine beauty.

Why hadn't she seen that resemblance on Saturday evening?

Because she hadn't been looking for it! Because no one had told her that Toby's girlfriend Tess *was* Patrick's young sister!

That was what really bothered Ellie about all this; why had no one told her of the relationship?

Until she had the answer to that, she felt the more distance she put between Patrick and herself the better.

"If you don't mind," she answered Patrick evenly. "I wouldn't expect Toby in to work tomorrow either, if I were you," she added dryly; she doubted her brother would be strong enough to get out of bed in the morning, let alone anything else!

"I wasn't," Patrick dismissed impatiently, looking down at her frowningly. "Ellie—"

"Patrick, I don't think now is either the right time or place for the two of us to talk," she bit out abruptly, moving sharply away from him, at the same time giving a pointed look in the direction of his sister.

Not that Teresa looked as if she were taking any notice of their conversation. She was completely wrapped up in the misery of her worry over Toby. Which probably meant that the affection Toby obviously felt for "Tess" was reciprocated.

Why had no one told her that Toby was dating Patrick's sister?

But perhaps someone had, Ellie realised slowly, as she recalled Gareth's enigmatic conversation of yesterday...

Gareth had seemed to be under the impression that Toby, as well as herself, was no better than he was. Because he believed them both to be dating the McGrath brother and sister for the same reasons he had become engaged to Sarah—wealth and ambition? He was totally wrong, of course—on both counts. But—

"Ellie?"

She looked up to find Patrick watching her concernedly. "Perhaps you should take your sister home now," she suggested stiffly. "She looks as if she's had enough for one evening," she added, with a rueful glance at the younger woman.

"I think we all have." Patrick nodded grimly. "I'll call in tomorrow and see how Toby is."

And continue this conversation, his words seemed to imply. Well, Ellie needed time and space to form her tangled thoughts into some sort of order. She wasn't sure twelve hours was long enough for that!

"Of course," she accepted smoothly. "Now, it really is late..."

He gave her another searching look before turning abruptly to his sister. "It's time to go, Teresa," he told her briskly. "I'm sure Ellie will call us if she needs us," he added as Teresa looked about to protest.

Considering the only telephone number she had for Patrick was his business one, that wouldn't really do a lot of good. Although Toby would have Patrick's mobile number.

"Of course I will," Ellie assured the younger woman as Teresa gave her a distressed look.

Teresa stood up, very tall and slender. "I'm really sorry we've had to meet for the first time under these circumstances." She grimaced.

Yes, it might have been better—it definitely *would* have been better for Ellie!—if the two of them had met before now.

"I don't suppose Toby will feel like this for long, and then perhaps he can bring you here for a drink one evening," she consoled.

Once he had given Ellie an explanation as to exactly what was going on! Because something *was* going on—Ellie was just too tired at this moment to be able to make sense of it all.

"Maybe the four of us could go out to dinner together at the weekend," Patrick put in smoothly.

Ellie turned to give him a cool look. "I think it would be better if we took one step at a time. Besides," she added firmly as she saw Patrick was about to argue the point, "I doubt Toby will feel up to eating anything for several days." It was a valid point—one she could see Patrick would have a problem arguing with.

Thank goodness. She didn't want to tie herself down to a definite time for seeing Patrick again. Not until she had some answers to a few pertinent questions. Answers that only her brother could give her.

"I'll ring you in the morning, if that's okay," Teresa McGrath told her a few minutes later as she stood in the doorway preparing to leave.

"Of course," Ellie accepted, deliberately avoiding looking at Patrick as he stood at his sister's side. "Brr, it's cold out here." She shivered from the icy wind blowing around them.

"Yes, it does seem to have turned a little icy," Patrick murmured softly.

Ellie looked at him sharply as she sensed his double meaning, and those raised dark brows told her she hadn't been mistaken. "The forecast is for snow," she returned, deliberately meeting his gaze.

"Luckily it never settles for long in our climate," he came back, just as deliberately.

Ellie shrugged. "The forecast is for a long-term cold front." Two could play at this game. And, until she knew exactly what was going on, a cold front was exactly what she intended showing Patrick McGrath.

He shrugged broad shoulders. "Ice and snow eventually melt."

"Eventually," she echoed evenly.

"Patrick, you can discuss the weather another time; we really should go, and let Ellie get back inside out of this biting wind," Teresa prompted her brother, obviously having no idea of the double-edged conversation that had been taking place between her brother and Ellie.

To Ellie they had sounded like a couple of secret agents in a B-rated movie, talking in a code only the two of them understood!

"So we should." Patrick nodded abruptly before bending his head and lightly brushing Ellie's mouth with his own. "But I will be back in the morning, Ellie."

A threat if ever she had heard one, Ellie decided irritably. Well, if, as the doctor had implied, Toby was better by the morning, Patrick would arrive here to find Toby recovering on his own and Ellie at work!

But not before she had spoken to Toby herself...

"I HAVE no idea what you're talking about, sis." Toby shook his head, his face still very pale as he lay back on the pillows. He had slept well through what had been left of the night, and the nausea seemed to have completely abated, although he had been left with a severe headache.

Join the club, Ellie thought, and gave a deep sigh before sitting on the side of her brother's bed. "Okay, let's start this off simply: why did you omit to tell me that the Tess you have been dating the last few months is actually Teresa McGrath, Patrick's young sister?"

"I—"

"Please, don't tell me that you didn't think it was important," Ellie advised him dryly—she sensed he was about to tell her exactly that. "Because you know very well that it is. That it always was. That it still is," she concluded pointedly.

"I'm not sure you should be badgering a sick man in this overly strident way." Toby shook his head before lying back to close his eyes, having just risked consuming a cup of weak tea and a dry piece of toast, both of which seemed—so far—to have stayed down.

"It could get worse, Toby," she warned him. "If what I suspect is true, I could actually end up strangling this 'sick man'—and so put *everyone* out of their misery!" Her eyes glittered dangerously.

She had had plenty of time to think during a rather

sleepless night—and some of the conclusions she had come to had been less than reassuring!

Toby opened one eye to look at her with obvious reluctance. "Why don't you tell me what you suspect—and then I'll tell you if it's right or not?"

"There's little point in doing that if you aren't going to answer me honestly!" she bit out sharply.

Both Toby's eyes opened innocently wide now. "My big sister taught me to always tell the truth."

"Very funny!" Ellie gave a humourless smile, getting up from the side of the bed to move impatiently about the room, her narrowed gaze fixed on her brother the whole time she did so. Finally she gave a heavy sigh. "Are you and Teresa McGrath serious about each other?"

"Yes," Toby answered unhesitatingly.

Ellie nodded; it was the answer she had expected. "Why did Patrick McGrath agree to take me to the company Christmas dinner?"

Her brother frowned his puzzlement at this sudden change of subject. "I told you—"

"I know what you told me, Toby," she cut in impatiently. "But now I want the real reason."

He shook his head, wincing as it obviously caused him a certain amount of discomfort. "But that *was* the real reason. Wasn't it?" he added uncertainly as Ellie looked unconvinced.

To Ellie's relief, her brother's answer told her one thing at least; whatever Patrick McGrath had been up to this last couple of weeks, Toby had obviously played no part in it. Which meant it had all been Patrick McGrath's own doing!

She had thought about several of the puzzling remarks Patrick had made this last week, about how much Toby cared for her, how her young brother felt a responsibility towards her, and all those questions about why she didn't have someone else in her life after Gareth—questions that all seemed to lead to the same unpleasant conclusion.

She was even more convinced about it now she knew from Toby that his relationship with Teresa McGrath was a serious one: Patrick was desperately trying to clear the way—clear Ellie out of the way, if only temporarily—in order to secure his young sister's happiness with Toby.

"Toby, why didn't you just tell me about Tess?" she prompted gently.

"But I did tell you about her," he answered evasively.

Ellie shook her head. "Only when the two of you were going out. Nothing else about her. Certainly not that the two of you are in love with each other. Why was that?"

Toby drew in a ragged breath. "I'm sure that was just what you wanted to hear two months ago!" he bit out disgustedly.

Two months ago? When she had suspected that Gareth was seeing someone else behind her back—six weeks ago when she had finally found out the truth and stopped seeing him?

"Oh, Toby!" she cried emotionally, tears misting her eyes now. "I would be pleased to hear of your happiness at any time. Any time at all!" she repeated with affectionate exasperation.

Instead of which Toby had kept the seriousness of his relationship with Tess a secret in an effort not to hurt Ellie.

Patrick McGrath, it seemed, was the one who had taken it a step further than that!

She sat back on the side of the bed, taking her brother's hand in her own. "Are you and Tess going to get married?"

Toby gave a start at the directness of the question, his gaze not quite meeting Ellie's searching one. "Maybe— in time," he answered evasively.

It was just as she had thought!

Toby and Tess *were* serious about each other, and until six weeks ago it must have looked as if Ellie was in a serious relationship too. But that had all come crashing down around her ears, leaving Toby feeling the responsibility towards her that Patrick had mentioned.

She could see exactly what had happened now— knew that Toby, despite numerous protestations on her part, felt he owed her an emotional debt for taking care of him after their parents died. The fact that her relationship with Gareth had fallen apart under unpleasant circumstances had triggered Toby into putting his own relationship with Teresa McGrath on hold.

Except Patrick obviously had other ideas where his sister's happiness was concerned...

So much for what Ellie had thought—hoped—was developing between the two of them!

"No 'maybe', Toby," she told her brother firmly now, standing up. "No 'in time' either," she added decisively. "If you love the girl, and she loves you, then you should ask her to marry you."

Toby grimaced sheepishly. "I already have."

"When?" Ellie prompted sharply.

"Eight weeks ago," he admitted reluctantly.

Ellie raised dark brows. "And?"

The grimace turned to a self-conscious smile. "She said yes."

Ellie gave an emotional laugh. "You are an idiot, Toby," she told him affectionately. "You've asked her; she's said yes. The next move is to buy her a ring. Then arrange the wedding. I'll be there to dance at it," she promised. "Am I making myself clear, Toby?" she teased.

He grinned widely. "Very."

"Good." She nodded her satisfaction. "I'll just have to learn to cope with having the arrogant Patrick McGrath as some sort of relative." She frowned.

Toby frowned too. "But I thought you liked him?"

Too much!

She swallowed hard, straightening determinedly; after all, there was such a thing as pride involved here—her own! "He's your boss, Toby; of course I had to be pleasant to him. Now that he's going to be your brother-in-law too, I'll just have to continue being pleasant to him. It shouldn't be that difficult; with any luck I'll see very little of him," she dismissed scathingly, turning to leave the bedroom—and finding herself face to face with a stricken Teresa McGrath!

Ellie looked at the other woman searchingly, knowing by her unhappy expression that she had heard every word of Ellie's last statement...

CHAPTER TEN

"I KNOW I said I was going to telephone, but— I did knock on the kitchen door when I arrived, and when no one answered I let myself in," Teresa explained awkwardly. "I hope you don't mind?" she added with a self-conscious grimace.

Mind? Of course Ellie didn't mind the younger woman letting herself in—it was the remarks that Teresa had overheard her making about her brother that Ellie minded! It was one thing to say those things about Patrick to Toby—completely out of defence for her heart—quite another for a member of the McGrath family to have actually heard her saying them...

"Tess...?" Toby called hopefully from inside the bedroom.

Teresa's face visibly brightened. "He's feeling better?"

"Much," Ellie assured her warmly. "I'll go down and make some coffee and leave the two of you to have a chat." And, hopefully, regain some of her lost composure!

What she really wanted to happen was for the ground to open and swallow her up!

Ellie was shaking by the time she reached the sanctuary of the kitchen, sitting down weakly in one of the kitchen chairs before burying her face in her hands with a groan of self-disgust.

All she had wanted to do with those remarks she'd made to Toby was regain some of her damaged pride—and what she had succeeded in doing was probably alienating her future sister-in-law!

How could she explain that to Teresa without giving away the fact that she had fallen completely in love with Patrick?

Her groan of self-disgust turned to one of pain. She had fallen in love with Patrick, and all he had been doing was keeping her romantically occupied long enough to ensure that Toby announced his engagement to Teresa.

She was sure now that was all Patrick had been doing this last week or so. She was the one who had been stupid enough to take his attention seriously. To fall in love with him!

How to extricate herself without Patrick ever being aware of that fact, without completely losing her self-respect? That was the problem!

Out of the frying pan into the fire, once again sprang to mind.

She had thought her infatuation with the fickle Gareth was the worst thing she had ever done in her life, but falling in love with Patrick had to be so much worse. Because he wasn't fickle. The love she felt for him wouldn't be as easily shrugged off as her feelings for Gareth had been.

It was because she truly loved Patrick that she was now able to see her previous feelings for Gareth for exactly what they were!

But this time she would come out of it with at least

her pride intact, Ellie decided as she straightened deter-minedly. She had to!

The coffee was fresh in the pot, and cups, cream and sugar placed on the kitchen table by the time Teresa came downstairs ten minutes later. The smile on Ellie's face was warm and friendly.

"He's much better, isn't he?" she told Teresa lightly.

"Much." The younger woman nodded, her expression slightly reserved.

Was that so surprising, when minutes ago Teresa had walked in on a conversation where Ellie had been to-tally dismissing any need for her to like this woman's brother?

Ellie drew in a ragged breath, deciding it was probably better to jump in at the deep end. "Look, concerning what you overheard me saying about Patrick earlier—"

"Please," Teresa cut in with an awkward wave of her hand. "I know how—how Patrick can be sometimes. He really doesn't mean anything by it. He's just—well, he's used to being in charge." She grimaced. "Not that he's in the least arrogant about it." She hastened to defend her brother. "Usually he just charms people into submission!"

Ellie knew just how true that was!

She shook her head. "That was still no reason for me to—to—Well, I'm sorry you overheard my remarks," she concluded heavily.

Great, Ellie, she instantly chided herself. That was really apologising for being so rude earlier about Teresa's brother!

"Would you like some coffee?" she offered briskly.

Teresa turned to look at the things laid out on the

kitchen table before glancing back at Ellie. "That would be lovely, thank you." She smiled before sitting down.

Somehow Ellie very much doubted this young woman was any more used to sitting down in a kitchen drinking coffee than Patrick was; it would most likely be served to them in the drawing room, by staff as efficient as George's had been on Saturday evening.

Which posed the disheartening thought: where did Toby fit into all this?

No doubt he and Teresa were in love—that was only too easy to see after last night!—but how would the two of them fare being married to each other when their backgrounds were so different? Toby, as Patrick's assistant, earned a very good wage, but he certainly couldn't keep Teresa in the life to which she was accustomed...

"I'm an interior designer."

Ellie looked up from pouring the coffee to find Teresa McGrath smiling at her ruefully.

Had her thoughts been so obvious? Or was it just that Teresa had the same ability as Patrick to be able to read her thoughts in particular? After Ellie's earlier remarks about Patrick, that was a disquieting thought.

Ellie shook her head. "I didn't mean—"

"I know." The other woman reached out to give Ellie's hand a reassuring squeeze, giving a shake of her head as she chuckled huskily. "It's only that I've already had all those particular conversations with Toby," she admitted affectionately. "He has this terrible dread that people will think he's only interested in me for my money."

In the same way that Gareth was interested in Sarah!

"I know that he isn't," Ellie said firmly.

"Of course he isn't." Teresa's chuckle deepened. "If

you only knew the trouble I had getting Toby to go out with me in the first place...!" She gave a shake of her head, dark hair silky on her shoulders. "He seemed to think that as Patrick's sister I came under the heading of 'untouchable.''

Ellie could well imagine that he had. In the same way she thought that Patrick was unobtainable to her...

"But you obviously managed to charm him into submission?" Ellie returned lightly.

"Not exactly." Teresa smiled wistfully. "I told Patrick how I felt about Toby, and he—well, he arranged for me to be around rather a lot—redesigning the offices he has here, and some new ones he's acquired in York."

York...? Hadn't Patrick said something the other day about Toby being in York with another of his employees? Employee, indeed; his younger sister hardly came under that heading! And, no matter what Teresa might say to the contrary, the role of matchmaker that Patrick had adopted for himself was arrogance personified!

"I see." Ellie nodded.

"Ellie—may I call you, Ellie?" Teresa paused politely.

"Of course," she instantly acknowledged.

"Tess," the other woman invited lightly. "The family always calls me Teresa, but I prefer friends to call me Tess. And I do hope the two of us are going to be friends, Ellie...?"

For Toby's sake they would have to be. Although Ellie had to admit the McGrath family were very difficult to dislike, having a warm charm that drew like a magnet.

"Of course," Ellie said again, wondering exactly where this conversation was leading.

Tess nodded, her expression intent now. "I'm really

not some little-rich-girl who saw something she wanted and instantly had her wish granted by an over-indulgent older brother. I love Toby very much, and those differences between us that you were thinking of earlier are totally unimportant."

"Now," Ellie felt compelled to point out.

Tess gave a definite shake of her head. "Ever. Yes, my parents are rich. Yes, my brother is successful, and also rich. But we were both brought up with the belief that we had to make our own way in the world, to earn our own living. We were never going to just sit around waiting to inherit. I know how awful that sounds—" Tess grimaced as Ellie gave a surprised choking noise "—but it's exactly the way a lot of children of wealthy parents behave nowadays."

"I wouldn't know." Ellie laughed incredulously.

Once again Tess reached out and squeezed her hand. "You don't need to—the closeness you and Toby have makes you so much richer than a wealth of money could ever do. I hope you will allow me to become part of that closeness…?" She gave Ellie a wistful look.

How could she resist this charming young woman? How could Toby have resisted her? Obviously he couldn't!

And if Toby and Tess's marriage meant that she would have to see more of Patrick than was comfortable, then she would have to learn to live with that. Because she had no intention of taking anything away from the love Tess and Toby had found together.

Ellie gave the other woman a warm smile. "I can't wait to dance at your wedding," she assured her—and instantly wished she hadn't. That was exactly the remark she had made earlier—before coming out with her insulting remark about Patrick!

A remark Tess remembered all too well if her teasing smile was anything to go by. "So you said." She nodded.

Ellie felt the colour warm her cheeks. "I really wish you hadn't overheard those remarks." She grimaced.

Tess chuckled, grey eyes warm with humour. "I wouldn't worry about it, Ellie; I'm sure Patrick has had much worse said to his face!"

"But not from his future—I'm not quite sure what the relationship is between the brother and sister of the bride and groom!" Ellie frowned.

"Neither am I." Tess grinned. "But, as I said, don't worry about it; if need be, Patrick is perfectly capable of standing up for himself."

"And *do* I need to?"

Ellie swung round guiltily at the sound of Patrick's voice behind her, the colour in her cheeks fiery-red now as she saw the narrow-eyed way he was looking at her.

"I heard the two of you talking and decided not to disturb you by knocking on the door." He shrugged, coming fully into the kitchen to close the door behind him.

Not to disturb her! Patrick disturbed Ellie every time she so much as looked at him! Did no one in this family ever knock?

She stood up abruptly. "We were just having a cup of coffee. Would you like one?" she invited awkwardly.

"No, thanks," he dismissed. "What I would really like—"

"Toby is much better today," Tess cut in brightly. "He was asleep earlier, but I'm sure he will want to see you."

She stood up, a slight figure in fitted denims and a thick black sweater.

Patrick's gaze hadn't wavered from Ellie's stricken face. "You go up; I'll join you in a moment," he told his sister slowly.

"Oh, but—"

"I'll come upstairs once I've spoken to Ellie," Patrick told Tess firmly.

Tess gave Ellie a sympathetic glance before leaving the kitchen, both women knowing that when Patrick spoke in that tone of voice there was no point in arguing with him.

The very air seemed to crackle with tension once Ellie and Patrick had been left alone in the kitchen. Ellie busied herself clearing the used cups from the table to put them in the dishwasher. At least that way she didn't have to look at Patrick!

But she was very aware of him standing behind her, of every magnetic inch of him, his dark hair, that aristocratic face, the business suit, white shirt and grey tie that in no way detracted from the powerful body beneath.

Was it always going to be like this? Ellie wondered in dismay. Would she still feel this complete awareness of him, this love for him, in all the years to come? Years when he would probably marry and have children of his own? She hoped not!

"What's going on, Ellie?"

She drew in a controlling breath before turning to face him, a brightly meaningless smile curving her lips. "I have no idea what you mean." She kept her tone deliberately light. "I like Tess, by the way," she added— before he could tell her exactly what he had meant by that earlier remark! "I'm sure she and Toby are going to be very happy together."

"No doubt." He nodded uninterestedly, eyes still narrowed as he looked at her searchingly. "Look, I'm sorry you had to find out about the two of them in the way that you did—"

"Don't be silly, Patrick," she said derisively. "In fact, I have no idea what the big secret was in the first place," she continued hardly, her head back challengingly. "Toby is twenty-six and I'm twenty-seven; it's well past time one of us moved on."

She couldn't pretend—to herself, at least—that it wouldn't be a little strange, no longer having Toby's less than peaceful presence around the house—that she wouldn't miss the way he never shut a door behind him, left the bathroom in a shocking mess every morning and more often than not forgot to put his washing in the wash-basket, but she had never been under any illusion that the status quo would continue indefinitely. Her brother was a handsome young man, for goodness' sake; Ellie had never doubted that he would eventually find someone he loved and wanted to marry.

The fact that the woman Toby loved was the sister of the man Ellie had been stupid enough to fall in love with herself was just something she would have to learn to live with!

"Ellie—"

"Patrick," she cut in firmly, blue eyes flashing a warning now. "I'm aware that you've been acting as—as some sort of ambassador for Toby and Tess this last ten days or so, but there really was no need!"

Patrick's mouth tightened now, a nerve pulsing in his

jaw. "Is that really what you think has been happening this last week?"

"Of course," she dismissed scathingly, desperately hoping that none of the aching love she felt for him showed in her face or eyes. "Not that I don't appreciate the fact that you came to the company dinner with me. It's nice to finally know that it was actually an attempt on your part to further family relations."

Patrick took a step towards her. "You think that's the only reason I agreed to accompany you to that dinner?" he murmured huskily.

Ellie stood her ground, even though every particle of her cried out for her to move away from her complete physical awareness of him. "Of course," she said again. "Oh, I'm aware there was also a curiosity on your part to meet your cousin's fiancée on neutral territory, but other than that—" she shrugged "—it must have been quite a chore for you."

His eyes suddenly glittered silver. "Exactly what is going on, Ellie?" he rasped. "Last night—"

She gave a dismissive laugh. "Last night I think the two of us may have got a little carried away by the roles we've been playing—"

"Last night I didn't think we were playing any roles. I thought we went out to dinner together for no other reason than I asked you and you accepted!" Patrick insisted harshly.

And she shouldn't have done! Shouldn't ever have allowed herself the luxury of believing there was any future in a relationship between Patrick and herself. In fact, now that she was aware of the reason behind Patrick's attentions, she knew very well that there wasn't a future in it!

She forced another rueful laugh. "Then you thought wrong," she bit out derisively.

He took another step towards her, so close now Ellie could feel the heat of his body against her sensitised skin. "I didn't imagine your response to me last night." He spoke gruffly now.

"Or your own to me," she came back, with a defensive arch of her brows. "I'm not denying there's an attraction between us—it would be silly to even try. As I said, I think we both got a little carried away with the moment. But it really wouldn't do—in the circumstances," she continued, determined though Patrick would have interrupted once again, "for the two of us to indulge in a meaningless affair."

Patrick's mouth tightened. "Meaningless…?" he repeated softly. Dangerously, to Ellie's ears.

But what did he expect from her? What did he want from her? She had already had one disastrous relationship this last year—and a relationship with Patrick promised to be even more catastrophic than that had turned out to be!

She shook her head. "Patrick, I think, for Tess and Toby's sake, that we shouldn't pursue this attraction. After all," she continued brightly, "once the two of them are married, the two of us will be related too. Which could prove a little embarrassing if we've been silly enough to indulge in an affair."

Patrick looked down at her searchingly, the silver gaze seeming to see deep into her soul.

Ellie stood that probing gaze for as long as she could—precisely thirty seconds!—before giving a lightly dismissive laugh. "Patrick, isn't it already bad enough that I find going to work extremely uncomfortable, in case I have to see or speak to Gareth, without having that same discomfort concerning any necessity to see Toby's future in-laws?" She arched dark brows at him.

"You do care for him after all? Is that it?" Patrick rasped.

Care for Gareth? Absolutely not. Ellie could see him for exactly what he was now—and the knowledge was extremely unpleasant. As well as embarrassing.

But wasn't Patrick's suggestion giving her the perfect let-out for what promised to be an even more unacceptable situation…?

"I'm not sure what I feel any more." She shrugged, though actually claiming to feel anything but contempt for Gareth was lodging in her throat and staying there. "About anything," she added firmly.

"I see." Patrick's expression became unreadable and he moved away from her.

Did he? Somehow Ellie doubted that very much. But it was better this way, she told herself firmly. For all of them.

Except…the thought of not knowing when she would see Patrick again gave her a feeling of heaviness in her chest. She rushed into awkward speech. "Of course, I understand there's still a problem concerning Sarah's engagement to Gareth. And if there's anything more I can do to help—"

"Like winning Davies back yourself, for example?" Patrick rasped scathingly.

Ellie drew in a sharp breath at what she guessed was a deliberate insult. "Somehow I don't think so," she came back evenly; if she lost her temper she might just say things she would be better keeping to herself! Totally damning things, like how could she even *think* of looking at another man when she was desperately in love with Patrick?

"Then I think we've probably imposed on your good nature enough already," Patrick assured her distantly, every haughty inch the successful businessman he was.

That heaviness in Ellie's chest instantly got heavier. Well, she had wanted to distance herself from this man, to keep her pride intact, and it appeared she had succeeded. Only too well!

But there was nothing more she could say or do now, without backing down from the stand she had made concerning any sort of a relationship between Patrick and herself.

She glanced at her wristwatch. "If you'll excuse me? I really have to be going now. Toby is so much better, and I promised George I would try to get into the office before lunch," she explained briskly.

Patrick nodded tersely. "Teresa will probably want to stay with Toby for most of the day anyway."

"Of course," she accepted evenly, reluctant to go even after claiming that she had to. Reluctant to part from Patrick not knowing when she would see him again.

Oh, she knew she would see him again some time, at Toby and Tess's engagement and at their wedding, but they would be occasions crowded with lots of other people, when Patrick wouldn't even need to speak to her if he didn't want to. And after today she accepted he probably wouldn't want to.

Patrick gave her another searching glance before nodding abruptly. "I'll go up and see Toby now."

"Yes." Ellie looked up at him, hoping all the aching

longing she felt in her heart for him to hold her, to kiss her, wasn't evident in her eyes.

"I'll say goodbye, then." He turned sharply on his heels and left the room, his back stiff with disapproval.

Proving to Ellie she was a better actress than she would have given herself credit for!

Not that that helped in the least now that she was left alone with her feelings. Part of her wanted to run after Patrick, to tell him that she had made a mistake, that it hadn't been an act on her part at all, that she wanted him with a desperation that made her shake with longing, in any sort of relationship he cared to choose.

But she did none of those things. Slowly she collected her coat from the closet, able to hear the murmur of voices upstairs—Tess's lightly teasing one, Patrick deep baritone—as she let herself out of the house.

It was beginning already, she realised as she drove numbly through the busy streets, totally immune to the Christmas gaiety in the shops around her. Toby was moving away to become a part of the McGrath family, to be enveloped in their warmth.

Something that, after today, Ellie knew she would never be...

CHAPTER ELEVEN

"It's official, sis," Toby announced happily as he came into the house Friday evening, throwing his outer coat over a chair as usual. "Tess and I went out and bought the ring at lunchtime today," he explained brightly as Ellie turned from cooking their evening meal to give him a questioning look.

She had been expecting it, had thought she had prepared herself for it, but as the sinking feeling increased in her stomach Ellie knew that she hadn't been ready for it at all.

It was all happening so quickly now that the decision had been made. Toby had dined with Thomas and Anne McGrath the previous evening, in order to ask Tess's father's permission for the two of them to marry. In view of Patrick's favourable opinion of Toby, Ellie had known there would be no objection to the request, and there hadn't been. The McGraths were absolutely thrilled for their daughter, welcoming Toby into their family as if he were another son. Which, indeed, he would be.

Whereas Ellie still hadn't quite come to terms with the fact that she wasn't so much losing a brother as gaining the McGrath family. One member of the McGrath family in particular!

As she had expected, after their last conversation she had heard nothing from Patrick since they'd parted so abruptly on Wednesday morning. It had been a very long three days!

"The engagement party is going to be at the McGraths' on Christmas Eve," Toby continued chattily, as he uncorked the bottle of champagne he had brought in with him and took three glasses out of the cupboard.

The engagement party...!

Ellie was filled with a mass of contradictions at the thought of seeing Patrick again. Happiness, because she ached to see him, and despair, because seeing him again would do nothing to alleviate that ache. Besides, he might actually be at the party with someone!

"That's wonderful, Toby." She pushed aside her own feelings to give her brother a congratulatory hug. "I'm really pleased for you both," she added with total sincerity, taking the glass of pink champagne her brother handed her. "To you and Tess," she toasted warmly.

Toby took a sip of the champagne before lifting up his own glass. "To the best Christmas ever," he returned with feeling.

Ellie took another sip of her drink. Christmas. Despite knowing that it was quickly looming, she hadn't really given it much thought. But now that Toby was engaged to Tess it posed the problem of whether she and Toby would actually even celebrate Christmas together this year.

Christmas always tended to be rather a quiet affair for the two of them anyway, with them having no really close relatives. It promised to be even quieter than usual for Ellie this year!

"We're both invited to spend Christmas with the McGraths too," Toby informed her as he turned to pick up the bottle of champagne and replenish their glasses.

Ellie was relieved that her brother was actually turning away as he made this announcement, otherwise he wouldn't have failed to notice the look of complete dismay that she wasn't quick enough to hide.

Christmas with the McGraths. With Patrick.

Much as Ellie longed to see him, to be with him, she hated the thought of being invited to spend Christmas with his family as if she were some sort of charity case!

"It's very nice of them to ask me, Toby," she said slowly, at the same time shaking her head. "But I really don't think—"

"If you don't go, sis, then neither do I," her brother told her with a frown.

Blackmail. Of the emotional kind. But not deviously so; Ellie knew it was only that Toby just wouldn't be happy leaving her here on her own over the Christmas period. Even if she would have preferred it!

She drew in a controlling breath. "Perhaps for Christmas lunch," she conceded reluctantly.

"I understand the invitation is for the whole of the Christmas period," drawled an all too familiar voice from behind her.

Ellie turned sharply to look at Patrick as he stood in the doorway. She really would have to get a lock put on that door, one that came into effect automatically as it closed. In fact several of them, just to be sure!

"We were just drinking a toast to Tess and our engagement." Toby felt none of the dismay at Patrick's presence that Ellie did, turning to pour some of the bubbly champagne into the third glass he had put out on the work surface.

Three glasses. Which meant Toby had already been aware that the other man was about to join them…

"Cheers." Patrick toasted the younger man before sipping the champagne. But his gaze, enigmatic over the rim of his glass, remained firmly fixed on Ellie. Who just continued to stare back at him. Toby had obviously known the other man was coming here this evening, but for what reason?

Toby put his empty glass down on the worktop. "I'm just going upstairs to change; I won't be long."

"Not exactly subtle, is he?" Patrick drawled ruefully once Toby could be heard going up the stairs two at a time. Patrick was wearing a dark overcoat over the suit he had obviously worn to work, flecks of the gentle snow falling outside had settled on his shoulders and in the darkness of his hair.

Ellie had recovered from some of her shock at Patrick being here, although she was still slightly puzzled as to why he was there at all. "Does he need to be?" she said guardedly, feeling decidedly casual in her worn denims and sloppy old blue jumper. Patrick gave a shrug. "I thought I would come and add my—voice to my parents' invitation for you to spend Christmas with all of us."

His voice? What did that mean, exactly?

He sighed, putting down his glass, the champagne only half drunk. "Ellie, I realise that you probably don't want to spend Christmas with me, of all people, but if I try to keep my presence down to a minimum will you at least think about it?"

"There's really no need—" She swallowed hard, touched by his offer in spite of the fact that he had it all wrong—he was exactly the person she would love to spend Christmas with! Just not under these circumstances. "It's very kind of your parents to make the offer," she said non-committally.

His mouth twisted into a humourless smile. "They really do want to meet you, Ellie," he assured her dryly.

She shrugged. "I'm sure there will be plenty of opportunity for that at the engagement party."

"Hmm," Patrick conceded slowly. "Ellie, about the engagement party…"

She looked up at him sharply, tensing defensively as she guessed by his guarded expression that he was about to say something she wasn't going to like. "Yes?" she prompted warily.

"Look, would you mind if I took my coat off? It's very warm in here," he added, even as he shrugged out of the thick outer coat.

Ellie's wariness deepened. Obviously Patrick wasn't in any particular hurry to leave this evening, and dinner was quite obviously cooking away quite happily on top of the stove, a roast chicken was in the oven; the last thing she wanted was to feel compelled by good manners to ask him to join them for dinner. She would probably choke on the chicken!

"You were saying?" she prompted sharply.

Patrick picked up his champagne glass, emptying it in one swallow before looking across at her once more. "It's going to be a big family party." He grimaced. "Brothers, sisters, aunts, uncles—and cousins," he added pointedly.

Meaning Sarah and Gareth would undoubtedly be there…

"What I'm trying to say, Ellie," Patrick continued impatiently, "is do you think you could bury your hostility for one evening and come to the party as my partner?"

"Hostility...?" she echoed faintly, knowing exactly why he had made the invitation, but knowing a sense of inner excitement anyway. If he were inviting her to be his partner on Christmas Eve, then he obviously wasn't taking anyone else...

But did he really think she viewed him with hostility? When it was taking every ounce of will power she possessed not to throw herself into his arms and kiss him until they were both senseless? It was a weakness she had no intention of giving in to!

"I don't feel in the least hostile towards you, Patrick," she told him crisply, at the same time giving a firm shake of her head. "I have no idea why you should even think that I do." Unless...? Tess wouldn't have told her brother of those remarks of Ellie's she had overheard, would she? She knew that the brother and sister were close, but it would be rather silly of her future sister-in-law if she had; it certainly wasn't guaranteed to further the smooth running of inter-family relations.

Patrick's mouth twisted into a self-derisive grimace. "You were pretty—forceful in expressing your feelings towards me the other morning."

But surely not to the point where he'd thought she felt hostility towards him?

She frowned. "I believe I admitted to there being a certain—attraction between us—"

Patrick nodded. "At the same time as you told me you still have feelings for Davies!" he bit out harshly.

Well...yes, she had hinted at something like that. But what else could she have done, in the circumstances? She still felt battered and bruised from Gareth's totally mercenary betrayal two months ago; wasn't she allowed a little self-pride now?

"Let's leave Gareth out of this," she suggested abruptly.

"I would be pleased never even to hear the man's name again," Patrick assured her harshly, his face set in grim lines. "Unfortunately, that isn't yet possible. He and Sarah will be at the party on Christmas Eve; there's absolutely no doubt about that. In the circumstances, I think it would be—politically correct if you were there as my partner." His eyes was narrowed on her compellingly.

Politically correct. How Ellie hated the phrase that seemed to have become so popular over the last few years. But in this case she could see how adequately it described the situation they found themselves in.

Her mouth twisted ruefully. "Not the most gracious invitation I've ever received," she mocked lightly. "But if you think it will be of any help, of course I'll come as your partner." It wasn't a completely unselfish decision; she hadn't particularly relished the idea of being at the party on her own anyway.

The tension seemed to ease out of Patrick's shoulders, his expression relaxing into a self-derisive smile. "Not the most gracious acceptance of an invitation *I've* ever received either—but I suppose it will have to do," he added dryly.

Ellie eyed him uncertainly, not quite knowing what to say next. Patrick seemed to be having the same problem, and the air of tension deepened between the two of them, with only the sound of the saucepans boiling on the stove to breach the silence.

Pointedly so, it seemed to Ellie, and if it were anyone

else but Patrick she would already have invited them to stay to dinner…

Thankfully Toby chose that moment to come bouncing back into the kitchen, changed now into an Aran sweater and a pair of black denims. But he seemed to lose some of his bounce as he noticed the food cooking.

"Did I forget to mention that Tess and I are going out to dinner at a Chinese restaurant this evening?" He grimaced guiltily.

No, Ellie instantly realised with dismay, Toby hadn't forgotten to mention it at all—she was the one who was so muddle-headed at the moment that she had forgotten he had ever told her!

Going to work had become a nightmare, never knowing whether or not she might accidentally bump into Gareth and so be a victim of more of his veiled threats, and life at home didn't feel much better at the moment— she was either pining because she wasn't seeing Patrick, or a trembling mass of nerves when she did. Not a good inducement to remembering anything that was said to her.

Toby glanced at the bubbling saucepans. "Perhaps Patrick—"

"Go, Toby," his boss and future brother-in-law cut in decisively.

"But—"

"If your sister wants to invite me to share her evening meal, then I'm sure she will do so." Patrick sharply interrupted Toby once again. "Don't bully her into it, okay?" he added, more gently.

"Okay." Toby shrugged, as if he couldn't quite see what the problem was but didn't have the time right now to try and find out. "I'll see you later, then, sis."

He moved to kiss her lightly on the cheek. "I really am sorry about the meal." He grimaced again in apology, raising a hand in parting to Patrick before hurrying out of the house.

The silence after his departure was even more tense. Except for those bubbling saucepans, Ellie acknowledged impatiently.

"I had better—"

"Would you—?"

They both began talking at once, both breaking off at the same time too.

"After you," Ellie invited with a rueful shrug.

"Ladies first," Patrick insisted.

She didn't want to go first, positive that Patrick had been about to say he had better be leaving, whereas she—through sheer good manners—had been about to invite him to share her evening meal. Something she was sure Patrick was well aware of, which was why he was suggesting she go first! Although why on earth he should want to stay and have dinner with her Ellie had no idea...

She drew in a deep breath. "I was about to suggest that you join me for dinner. It seems a pity to waste the roast chicken," she added dismissively.

Patrick continued to look at her for several seconds. Then his mouth began to twitch, and finally he burst out laughing. He finally sobered enough to speak, eyes sparkling with humour. "You know, Ellie, you do absolutely nothing for my ego. 'It seems a pity to waste the roast chicken'," he repeated incredulously, before he began to laugh again. Ellie looked at him frowningly for several seconds, before she also saw the funny side of it. She had sounded distinctly uninterested in his answer, to the

point of rudeness. In fact, it was to Patrick's credit that
he could laugh about it.

"I'll try again, shall I?" she decided self-derisively.
"Patrick, I would like it very much if you would join me
for dinner," she amended ruefully.

Patrick sobered, but his eyes still laughed as he looked
across at her. "Truthfully?" he prompted sceptically.

"Truthfully," she echoed huskily.

It might be a mistake on her part, a self-indulgence
that she would later regret, but at this moment, after
several days of not seeing or hearing from him, she could
think of nothing she wanted more than to spend the
evening with Patrick. Anything to stop him leaving just
yet.

"Then I accept." He nodded teasingly. "The roast
chicken smells wonderful," he added. "Much better than
the frozen lasagna I was going to put in the microwave
when I got home!"

Ellie moved to take the vegetables off the cooker. "Do
you cater for yourself a lot?" she prompted interestedly,
relieved to have an innocuous subject to talk about. Although, no matter how hard she tried, she couldn't quite
see Patrick wandering round a supermarket buying his
weekly groceries!

"Sometimes." Patrick nodded. "Is there anything I can
do to help?" he offered as she began to serve the meal.

She opened her mouth to refuse, and then thought
better of it; a busy Patrick wouldn't be able to sit and
watch her as she carved the chicken and served the vegetables. "There's knives and forks in the drawer under
the table. Salt and pepper in the cupboard over there,"
she accepted lightly.

It was strangely intimate, moving about the kitchen

together, with Patrick pouring some more of the champagne to accompany their meal once he had set the kitchen table.

Something else Ellie was sure Patrick didn't normally do. No doubt he usually ate in the dining room in his own home. Well, they didn't have a dining room as such—the house wasn't big enough for such a luxury.

"This reminds me of when I was a child," Patrick told her happily as they sat down to eat their meal. "My nanny used to serve tea in the nursery when I was home from boarding school," he explained at Ellie's questioning look. "I was less than pleased when I reached the age of twelve and my parents decided I was grown up enough to eat in the formal dining room with them. No fun at all," he added with a grimace.

Ellie eyed him interestedly. "Did you enjoy going to boarding school?" Their lives, their upbringing, really had been so different.

"Not particularly," he dismissed. "It was just the done thing, I suppose." He shrugged. "My father and grandfather went there before me—that sort of thing." He frowned. "That particular tradition will end with my own children, I'm afraid; I have no intention of educating them away from home."

His children. He spoke about having them so easily that he must have given the subject some thought.

Whereas Ellie found the thought of Patrick's children—children he would have with some as yet unnamed other woman—highly displeasing!

"Mmm, Ellie, this food is delicious!" Patrick broke enthusiastically into her disturbing thoughts, having just tasted the roast chicken. "Where on earth did you learn to cook like this?" he complimented warmly.

Her cheeks became flushed with pleasure at the obvious sincerity of his compliments. "My mother and my grandmother before me, I suppose," she returned lightly.

"Thank you, Mother and Grandmother!" He raised his glass in a toast. "When Toby moves out, can I move in?" he added hopefully.

He was only joking, Ellie knew he was, and yet just the thought of it deepened the blush in her cheeks. What would it be like, living with Patrick all the time? Talking with him, laughing with him, making love with him? Heaven, she decided wistfully.

And just as quickly pushed the thought very firmly from her mind!

"Wouldn't it be easier to just hire yourself a cook?" she suggested derisively.

"It might," he conceded slowly. "But, again, not as much fun," he added with a smile.

Ellie eyed him interestedly. "You seem to put great store on having fun...?"

Patrick shrugged. "If you aren't enjoying what you're doing, or who you're with, there doesn't seem to be much point in pursuing it. Does there?" he reasoned huskily.

Did that mean he enjoyed being with her? That he wouldn't be here at all, wouldn't have accepted her invitation, if that weren't the case?

That did seem to be what he was saying. But Ellie knew she must try to keep remembering that Patrick's only interest in her lay in ensuring the happiness of his much younger sister...

Besides, he could just be warning her of how stupid she was to continue to have feelings for Gareth!

How she wished she had never made that claim! It

had seemed the only thing to do at the time, had been done completely out of self-defence. But a part of her still wished Patrick hadn't believed the outright lie...

"Not everyone has the luxury of such choices," she told him hardly.

Patrick gave her a considering look. "Is working at Delacorte, Delacorte and Delacorte still proving difficult?"

Impossible would probably better describe this last week. In fact, she was seriously thinking of changing her job. Maybe it was time she moved on anyway; she had worked for the same company for almost ten years now. Her home life would be changing radically when Toby and Tess were married and her brother moved away from home, so maybe it was time for her to move on too?

She turned away from Patrick's probing eyes. "I'm sure you can have no real interest in hearing about my problems," she dismissed lightly. "Your food is getting cold," she reminded him as he would have spoken.

Patrick continued to look at her wordlessly for several long seconds before giving an abrupt inclination of his head. "So it is."

The silence that followed as they began to eat— Patrick with obvious enjoyment, Ellie less than enthusiastically—was no more reassuring than his probing questions had been.

She could sense there was still so much Patrick would have liked to say to her, but didn't. And it was the content of what he had left unsaid that troubled her now.

"That was excellent, Ellie," Patrick told her warmly as he finished his meal.

She stood up to clear the plates; Patrick's was completely empty, her own food was only half eaten. "I'm afraid we don't usually bother with dessert," she explained with a grimace.

"I don't eat them, anyway." He sat back in his chair to look across at her. "Ellie, do you think—?" He broke off as a knock sounded on the back door, his body tensing, his eyes narrowing coldly as Gareth opened the door and entered the kitchen.

Ellie stared at the other man in total disbelief.

What on earth was Gareth doing here?

CHAPTER TWELVE

GARETH didn't look surprised to see the other man sitting in the kitchen with Ellie, and she quickly realised that was because he must have seen the Mercedes parked outside in the driveway and drawn his own conclusions as to its owner being Patrick.

Which posed the question: why had Gareth come here, knowing that Patrick was already there?

In fact, why had Gareth come here at all?

Not that the why really mattered; one look at the suspicion that now narrowed Patrick's eyes, the disgusted twist on his lips as he slowly stood up, was enough to tell Ellie that he had drawn his own conclusions as to the reason Gareth was here.

Ellie felt her heart plummet at the realisation. It was one thing for her to actually claim—falsely!—to have residual feelings towards Gareth, something else entirely for Gareth to come here and so give Patrick the impression that there might be more to it than that.

Gareth gave a confident smile. "Patrick," he greeted him lightly. "Ellie," he added warmly.

With Patrick's broodingly disapproving attention all focused on the other man, Ellie felt free to glare her resentment across the kitchen at Gareth. He looked so completely unconcerned at her obvious lack of welcome, so sure of himself, that a part of her just wanted to wipe that slightly mocking smile off his too-handsome face!

He raised mocking brows at her obviously glowering expression. "I didn't have a chance to see you before you left the office earlier, so I just popped in to wish you a merry Christmas," he told her with a challenging smile.

A merry—! What on earth was Gareth up to? With Christmas just under a week away, Delacorte, Delacorte and Delacorte had finished for a two-week Christmas holiday at five o'clock this evening. Ellie had decided to give the usual impromptu office party a miss this year, mainly in an effort to avoid seeing Gareth and so completely ruining her day. With his arrival here instead, she realised she might as well have saved herself the bother!

"You could have done that on Christmas Eve." Patrick was the one to answer the other man harshly. "My parents are having a party that evening to celebrate my sister Teresa's engagement to Ellie's brother Toby; you and Sarah are obviously invited," he explained scathingly.

Uncertainty flickered briefly in Gareth's eyes at what was obviously news to him, to be quickly masked as he once again smiled confidently. "Of course," he said smoothly. "But parties can be so impersonal, can't they? And Ellie and I used to be such close friends," he added pointedly.

Not *that* sort of "close friends"! Thank goodness. This situation would be even more humiliating if she and Gareth *had* ever been lovers!

"Champagne?" Gareth's gaze narrowed as he noticed the empty bottle standing on one of the worktops. "The two of *you* wouldn't have something to celebrate too, would you?" he added, with a conspiratorially knowing look in Ellie's direction.

He really believed that she and Toby were no better than he was, she realised angrily. "Only Toby and Teresa's engagement," she snapped coldly.

"Of course," Gareth acknowledged smoothly.

Too smoothly for Ellie's liking. Why didn't he just go? He had obviously succeeded in what he'd come here to do, namely create a difficult situation for Ellie where Patrick was concerned, so why didn't he just leave? Surely there wasn't more to come...?

"Looks like we're all going to be one big happy family, doesn't it," Gareth continued pleasantly.

"Two out of the three, perhaps," Patrick rasped icily. "And in your case I wouldn't be too sure about the third one either!" He gave the young man a scathing glance.

Gareth looked at Patrick consideringly. "I get the distinct feeling that you don't particularly like me..." he murmured slowly, at the same time somehow managing to sound like a hurt little boy.

Not that Patrick looked particularly impressed by the latter, Ellie noted ruefully.

What she really wanted now was for both men to just leave. Her nerves were stretched to breaking point after the last hour or so, and Gareth's arrival a few minutes ago was doing nothing to help that situation. In fact, she was starting to feel decidedly ill, not knowing from one moment to the next what Gareth was going to say. Patrick either, for that matter. The two men looked like a pair of gladiators, facing each other across the arena!

"I've never liked men who feel the need to beat up women," said Patrick disgustedly, hands clenched into fists at his sides as he glared at the other man.

"Beat—? Ellie?" Gareth scowled as he turned to look at her. "What on earth have you been telling Patrick about me?" He looked slightly less confident now.

"She didn't need to tell me anything," Patrick assured him coldly. "I've seen the bruises you inflicted on her the night of the company dinner, and at my aunt and uncle's house the following evening! Next time you feel like threatening someone, come and see me, hmm?" He looked challengingly at the younger man.

As far as Ellie was concerned, this situation was rapidly spiralling out of control; if she didn't put a stop to it right now she had a feeling the two of them might actually start fighting in the middle of her kitchen!

She stepped forward, effectively standing between the two men. "You've said what you came here to say, Gareth," she rasped—done what he wanted to do! "Now I suggest you leave."

He continued to hold Patrick's gaze for several more long seconds, before giving a slight inclination of his head. "I'll look forward to seeing you both on Christmas Eve, then." He shrugged dismissively.

"Don't hold your breath on that one either," Patrick bit out harshly as the other man left.

Gareth paused to turn in the doorway and look back at them. "Sarah and I have set our wedding date for Easter weekend," he drawled mockingly.

"A lot can happen in three and a half months," Patrick replied calmly.

Gareth gave a derisive grin. "Who knows? Maybe you and Ellie will decide to make it a double wedding!" he taunted, his smile one of satisfaction as he saw Ellie's embarrassed dismay at the outrageous suggestion. "See you," he added lightly, before letting himself out.

If she had thought the situation tense before Gareth's arrival, Ellie now felt as if she could cut the atmosphere with a knife. Gareth was nothing but an arrogant, troublemaking—

Patrick spoke forcefully into that tense silence. "I will never—never, *ever*," he continued with feeling, "understand what either Sarah or you see in that man!" His mouth twisted with distaste, his eyes still cold with the dislike he didn't even attempt to hide.

As far as Ellie was concerned, she saw Gareth exactly as Patrick did. But she knew she would just be wasting her time to try and tell him that now—could see by the scorn on his face that he wouldn't believe her.

Patrick gave an impatient shake of his head. "I think I should leave now," he rasped, taking his overcoat from the back of the chair. "Do you want me to collect you on Christmas Eve, or will you drive over with Toby?" he added uninterestedly.

What Ellie most wanted to do right now was sit down and have a good cry. And once Patrick had gone that was exactly what she was going to do. In fact, if he didn't soon leave she might just break down and cry in front of him!

"I'll come over with Toby," she answered quietly, looking down at the tiled floor in preference to Patrick's scornful expression.

"Fine," he snapped harshly. "I— Thanks for dinner," he added, with a slight softening of his tone.

That slight relenting on Patrick's part was her undoing. The tears started to fall hotly down her cheeks, a sob catching in the back of her throat as those tears threatened to choke her.

"Hey," Patrick murmured gently as he saw those tears, throwing his overcoat back down on the chair to come over stand in front of Ellie. "He isn't worth it, you know," he added dismissively, his hand moving to lift her chin and raise her face so that he could look at her.

The tears fell more rapidly because she knew he had misunderstood the reason for them, but also knew she couldn't correct him without losing all the ground she had gained in the last few days; it would be just too humiliating if Patrick were to realise her tears were because she was in love with him, and not Gareth, as he supposed!

"Why is it that nice women seem to fall in love with bastards?" Patrick rasped, with a disgusted shake of his head.

She shrugged. "Sarah is still very young—"

"I was referring to you!" Patrick cut in harshly, grey eyes glittering coldly.

Ellie blinked, looking up at him uncertainly. "Am I a nice woman...?"

"Of course you are," he confirmed impatiently. "One of the nicest I've ever met," he assured her hardly. "In fact, the only thing that's wrong with you is this tendency you have to be in love with the wrong man!"

She gave a choked laugh. "The only thing...?"

Patrick gave an impatient snort. "Ridiculous, isn't it?" he dismissed disgustedly. "But I'll tell you one thing, Ellie," he snapped decisively. "After speaking to the man this evening, I'm even more convinced that Gareth Davies marries Sarah over my dead body!"

Ellie looked up at him searchingly. What about her? How would he feel about *her* marrying Gareth? Not that it was even a possibility, but she couldn't help noticing Patrick's omission where she was concerned...

Patrick returned her gaze for several long minutes,

finally releasing her chin to take a step away from her. "Once I've sorted that particular situation out," he said grimly, pulling on his overcoat, "I'm going to do everything in my power to ensure *you* don't marry him either!"

She swallowed hard. "You are?"

"Most definitely," he assured her determinedly. "There is absolutely no way that man is going to become part of my family—even by marriage!"

Oh. Patrick's vehemence had nothing to do with her personally. He just wanted to ensure Gareth had nothing to do with the McGrath family.

She grimaced. "You'll have more trouble convincing Sarah of that than me!"

"We'll see," he came back enigmatically. "You're sure you don't want me to pick you up on Christmas Eve?"

"Positive," she assured him with feeling.

He nodded impatiently. "I'll see you in a few days, then?"

"Yes," she confirmed.

Why didn't he just go now? He had made it more than plain exactly what his interest was in her and her supposed feelings for Gareth, so why didn't he just leave?

Before she started to cry again!

Patrick shook his head frustratedly as he continued looked down at her tear-stained face. "I could kiss you until you're senseless!" he muttered harshly.

Ellie's eyes widened. "What would that achieve?" she finally murmured huskily.

"Absolutely nothing," he accepted impatiently. "But it would make me feel a whole lot better!"

And it would reduce her to a complete emotional puddle!

She straightened defensively. "I don't think so, thank you, Patrick," she told him evenly.

His mouth twisted humourlessly. "No, neither do I." He sighed, turning without another word and letting himself out of the house, closing the door gently behind him as he left.

Ellie's shoulders slumped once she was alone.

How much more of this would she have to take? How much more of this could she be expected to take?

CHAPTER THIRTEEN

"TOBY, could you zip me up—?" Ellie's words came to an abrupt halt as she entered the sitting room and found not Toby sitting there, as she had expected, but Patrick. She quickly turned fully to face him, clutching the front of her black dress to her chest. "I thought Toby was in here…" she murmured self-consciously.

When had Patrick arrived? She hadn't heard the doorbell ring. Although, come to think of it, he hadn't rung the doorbell the last few times he'd arrived here unexpectedly either!

"He was, but he had to leave early so that he can be at the house with Teresa when the first guests arrive." Patrick put down the magazine he had been idly flicking through when Ellie entered the room and stood up. "You mentioned you have a zip that needs fastening…?" he prompted expectantly, once again suave and sophisticated himself, in a black dinner suit and snowy white shirt.

That had been before she'd realised it was Patrick in the room and not Toby!

"I'll manage," she frowned. "Okay, I understand about Toby, but what exactly are you doing here?" If Toby had told her he had to be at the McGraths earlier than arranged then she could quite easily have been ready in time to go with him. She was also quite capable of calling herself a taxi.

Patrick shrugged dismissively. "I told you. It was decided that Toby should be with Teresa when the first guests arrive—"

"I understood that bit," Ellie dismissed impatiently. "I'm just not sure who decided you should be here." She frowned.

"Does it matter?" Patrick dismissed uninterestedly.

Ellie gave a puzzled shake of her head; this present arrangement really didn't make much sense.

"Turn around and let me do up your zip," Patrick instructed dryly.

Her hand tightened on the material she held up in front of her. It was yet another new dress, a figure-hugging black tube that seemed to cling to her body magnetically, having neither shoulder straps nor sleeves to keep it in place, leaving her legs long and shapely beneath its knee length.

"I said turn around, Ellie," he repeated encouragingly.

She wore neither bra nor slip beneath the dress, just a pair of black lace panties, the top of which would be clearly visible if she turned around, as the zip unfastened down the whole length of her spine.

But she could see by Patrick's face that he wasn't about to be fobbed off with an excuse, and sighed heavily as she slowly turned her back towards him.

Nothing happened for several long seconds. Ellie finally looked back over her shoulder to see what the problem was.

Patrick was looking across at her with dark eyes, his

expression remotely unreadable, but a nerve pulsing erratically in his tightly clenched jaw.

Ellie turned quickly away again. "We're going to be late ourselves if we don't leave soon," she encouraged huskily, finding she was trembling slightly now, unsure what to make of that look on Patrick's face. In any other man she would have said it was— But Patrick was like no other man she had ever met!

She gave a sensitive start as she felt the light touch of his fingers on the base of her spine, her back stiffening defensively at her unbidden response.

His fingertips slowly travelled the length of her spine, Ellie's skin seeming to burn where he touched, stopping as they reached the sensitised arch between her shoulderblades.

What was he doing? Ellie wondered with a mixture of pleasure and dismay. Pleasure because she liked his touch upon her naked flesh, dismay because the involuntary arching of her body must have told him how much she liked it!

His hands lightly gripped the tops of her shoulders, his thumbtips now moving in a slow caress against her spine and up the silky length of her neck.

Ellie swallowed hard, not sure how much more of this she could stand without turning in his arms and kissing him. Which would nullify everything she had done this last week to put a certain amount of distance between them.

"The zip, Patrick," she reminded him determinedly, her jaw clenched in tight control now.

"Your skin feels so wonderful to the touch," he murmured admiringly, seeming not to have heard her. Or, if he had, choosing to ignore her! "But then I always knew that it would," he continued gruffly. "When I saw you in the garden, that day in the summer—"

"Never mind. I'll do the zip up myself!" Ellie said sharply, and she moved abruptly away to turn and glare at him. "I think it's decidedly ungentlemanly of you to even mention seeing me that day in the garden!" she told him indignantly, eyes glowing deeply blue, her cheeks fiery-red with embarrassment.

Why, oh, why, couldn't Patrick just pretend not to remember seeing her sunbathing topless? It certainly wasn't the first time he had mentioned it!

She gave a low groan in her throat. "I'll be back down in a few minutes!" She turned and fled the room before Patrick could even think of preventing her.

This was awful. Just awful. And it was only the beginning of the Christmas holiday—a holiday she had finally allowed Toby to persuade her into spending with the McGrath family. What choice did she have when Toby had refused to go if she didn't?

But it was going to be three days of hell if Patrick didn't hold to his promise to keep his distance!

"Ready?" he prompted lightly when she rejoined him downstairs a few minutes later.

Ellie eyed him warily, the black pashmina he had bought for her now brought back out of its box at the back of her wardrobe, draped about the nakedness of her shoulders. "There's just my case and that bag to take with us," she answered slowly, nodding in the direction of the two pieces of luggage she had brought down with her and left in the hallway.

Patrick bent down and picked up Ellie's case and the bag containing the impersonal Christmas presents she had bought for the McGrath family, straightening to grin at her. "This feels almost indiscreet, don't you think?" He quirked dark brows. "Almost as if the two of us are sneaking off somewhere together for the weekend," he explained teasingly at her frowning look.

The warmth in her cheeks seemed to be becoming a permanent fixture! "I really wouldn't know anything about that," Ellie told him sharply; he probably had more experience with clandestine weekends away than she did. How could he not? Her own experience in that direction was precisely nil! "I just need to check round the house once more before I leave to make sure I've switched everything off." It really wouldn't do for the house to burn down in her three-day absence!

Patrick nodded. "I'll put your things in the car while you do that."

Ellie breathed more easily once he had left the room, moving slowly to double-check that she had switched off all the Christmas lights. As usual the tree looked starkly gaudy without its glittering lights. Ellie gazed up at it sadly as she accepted that by the time she returned to the house in three days' time Christmas would effectively be over.

It was strange to think—

What on earth was that?

She could hear raised voices outside, and they certainly didn't sound like the happy revellers she had been hearing the last few evenings; these voices sounded distinctly angry.

They also, she realised incredulously, sounded like Patrick and Gareth!

Ellie hurried from the sitting room, through the kitchen and out onto the driveway—arriving just in time to see Patrick punch Gareth on the chin!

She came to an abrupt halt, staring in horrified fascination as Gareth reeled from the blow but remained standing on his feet, only to swing his own fist up and land a punch in Patrick's right eye.

What on earth—?

Patrick also remained standing on his feet, his expression cold with fury as his arm swung once again.

"Patrick!" Ellie cried out in alarm. The sound of her voice caught both men off-guard and they turned to look at her.

But not quickly enough to stop Patrick's fist once again making contact with Gareth's chin. And this time he went down, falling heavily onto the concreted driveway, despite the thin layer of snow that still partially covered it.

"What do you think you're doing?" She hurried over to both men. The air seemed to pulse with their fury as she looked from one to the other of them.

Gareth still sat on the driveway, his hand raised to his bruised chin as he glared up balefully at the other man. Patrick was standing over him, his hands clenched into fists at his sides.

Ellie drew in a ragged breath, still not quite able to believe this was happening. "I said—"

"Don't try and pretend you aren't as much a part of this as your boyfriend!" Gareth scorned, getting slowly to his feet now, dusting the snow from his denims as he did so.

"Leave Ellie out of it," Patrick rasped harshly. "In fact, why don't you just leave?" he added scathingly.

Gareth shook his head, his eyes narrowed with dislike as he looked at the older man. "I'm not going anywhere," he said slowly.

"No, you're not, are you?" Patrick acknowledged with satisfaction.

Ellie looked at both men as she felt the tension rising between them once more; any minute now they were going to start hitting each other again! "Would someone please tell me exactly what is going on?" she demanded determinedly.

Gareth's mouth twisted derisively. "Did the two of you think I would just take this lying down? Because, if you did, I can assure you—"

"You seemed to be doing a fair imitation of doing exactly that a few seconds ago!"

Patrick was antagonizing him. Almost as if, Ellie realised dazedly, he *wanted* the other man to take another swing at him—just so that he had a good excuse to hit Gareth again!

An angry red tide of colour moved into Gareth's cheeks. "You—"

"Will you both stop this?" Ellie ordered impatiently. "This happens to be my home. And, if nothing else, you're giving my neighbours something to gossip about all over Christmas!"

She had already seen the curtains twitching in the house opposite, the couple that lived there no doubt alerted to the fight outside by the sound of raised voices. As she had been...

"If you really must continue this—argument," she bit out caustically, "then at least come inside and do it. But don't even think about hitting each other again once we're in the house," she warned as she turned to go inside. "I don't want anything of mine broken!"

Anything *else* of hers broken; her heart was already in pieces!

She still had no idea what had caused this flare-up in the ongoing dislike the two men had of each other, but she certainly intended getting an explanation—from one of them!—before the evening was over.

Thankfully the two men followed her into the house, and Ellie looked at them frowningly once they all stood in the sitting room. Gareth's expression was belligerent as he glared at the other man; Patrick's was one of quiet satisfaction. It was that latter expression that roused Ellie's curiosity the most... But it was to Gareth she expressed her next remark.

"What are you doing here?"

Even if she and Patrick left for the party right now they were going to arrive well past the given time of eight o'clock; Gareth, wearing denims and a thick Aran jumper, wasn't even dressed to go out for the evening yet.

"Letting your boyfriend know that as far as I'm concerned this is far from over," Gareth answered, his jaw clenched.

Ellie really wished he would stop referring to Patrick as her boyfriend...!

Patrick eyed the younger man derisively. "In what way is it not over, Davies?" he prompted challengingly. "Unless I'm mistaken, George has given you three months' notice at Delacorte, Delacorte and Delacorte. Notice he has waived in lieu of never having to set eyes on you again! I believe your engagement to Sarah is likewise terminated. Permanently!"

His satisfaction was no longer quiet!

Ellie's eyes widened. When on earth had all this happened? Four days ago Gareth had definitely still been a junior partner with Delacorte, Delacorte and Delacorte, and his engagement to Sarah had seemed unshakeable too...

But there was no mistaking the fact that Gareth certainly wasn't wearing the right sort of clothes to attend Toby and Teresa's engagement party this evening...

Gareth's mouth twisted contemptuously. "You both think you've been so clever, don't you? Did you really think I would just go quietly?" he scorned, shaking his head. "For one thing, George has no reason to dismiss me other than a personal one, which in a court of law—"

"He doesn't need one," Patrick cut in confidently. "I'm surprised at you, Davies; you really should have read the small print on your contract of employment," he taunted. "It clearly states that three months' notice can be given, on either side, without prejudice, during your first year of employment. You've been with Delacorte, Delacorte and Delacorte how long now...?" he prompted pointedly.

Ellie could see by Gareth's stunned expression that he really *hadn't* been aware of that particular clause in his contract of employment.

"As for your engagement to Sarah," Patrick continued derisively, "I believe it's a woman's prerogative to change her mind?"

Gareth's expression was ugly now. "With a lot of help from her interfering family!" he rasped.

"Maybe." Patrick shrugged unconcernedly. "It doesn't change the fact that Sarah *has* changed her mind."

The relief Ellie felt on hearing this completely dispelled any doubts she might have had about having the two men fighting in her driveway in full view of her neighbours. She didn't care how Patrick had achieved it. All that mattered was that Sarah had escaped Gareth's mercenary clutches!

But Gareth's feelings about the broken engagement were obviously different, and as he turned on the other man. "You self-satisfied—"

"I said there would be no fighting in here, Gareth!" Ellie told him firmly as he took a threatening step towards Patrick.

Gareth turned a furious blue gaze on her. "As for you—"

"I believe I told you to leave Ellie out of this," Patrick reminded him in a dangerously soft voice.

The younger man's hands were clenched into fists at his sides. "From what I can tell she's already in this up to her pretty neck!" Gareth rasped, his gaze raking over her scathingly. "I hope you realise he'll never marry you, Ellie," he taunted with hard derision. "The McGraths and the Delacortes believe themselves far too good for the likes of you and me!" he added bitterly.

Ellie swallowed hard as she felt the colour drain from her cheeks, at the same time desperately hoping that neither of these men had seen just how much Gareth's last remark had hurt her. Of course Patrick would never consider marrying her; it wasn't even a possibility. But she could well have done without having that fact thrown in her face. Especially by a man she so utterly despised.

"How do you work that one out, Davies?" Patrick was the one to answer the other man scornfully. "Tonight we're celebrating the engagement of Ellie's brother and my sister!"

"An engagement isn't a marriage," the other man came back derisively, before turning to look pityingly at Ellie once again. "An affair even less so," he warned her mockingly.

"Get out," she told Gareth shakily.

"Oh, I'm going," he assured her, raising a hand to his bruised jaw. "But I'll be back," he added softly.

"In that case, make sure it's me you come back at; come near Ellie again and you'll find out how it feels to be on the wrong side in a court of law," Patrick warned him coldly. "Which I don't think would do a great deal for the furtherance of your legal career," he added challengingly.

Gareth's cheeks flushed angrily. "Don't threaten me, McGrath," he rasped.

But his tone held little conviction, Ellie noted; the possibility of ending up as the defendant in a court of law rather than the prosecuting lawyer—for what charge was anybody's guess!—obviously didn't appeal to Gareth one little bit, if the suddenly wary expression on his face was anything to go by.

A fact which, by his next comment, Patrick had obviously noticed too. "Davies, I think the best thing for everyone is for you to just disappear back down whatever sewer you came out of," he advised dismissively.

The ugly flush deepened in Gareth's cheeks as he turned to direct his next insult at Ellie. "Give me a call when he's finished with you—you never know; I just might be interested in continuing where we left off!" With one last contemptuous glare in Patrick's direction he exited the room, the back door slamming noisily behind him seconds later as he left the house.

The awkward silence that followed his abrupt exit made Ellie squirm...!

What must Patrick think of her now?

CHAPTER FOURTEEN

"Is IT my imagination, or does Patrick have what looks to be the beginnings of a very black eye?"

Ellie turned sharply at the sound of Sarah's voice. She had been looking at Patrick herself until that moment, as he stood across the room talking with one of his numerous aunts; Ellie had quickly learnt, on their arrival at the party an hour ago, that the McGrath family was a large one, and Patrick a particular favourite with all of them.

She looked up warily at Sarah now. "Sorry?" she prompted guardedly.

Sarah's smile was a little strained, but other than that she looked as beautiful as ever in a short, figure-hugging red dress. "Don't look so apprehensive about seeing me, please, Ellie." She reached out and gave Ellie's arm a re-assuring squeeze. "After all, I believe we've both recently made a very lucky escape?" She quirked self-derisive brows.

Ellie grimaced. The problem was, she still didn't really have any idea what had happened to end Sarah's engagement to Gareth. It had been well after eight o'clock by the time Gareth made his furious exit from her house, and, other than pausing briefly to collect an ice-pack to place on Patrick's rapidly bruising eye, the two of them had come straight to the engagement party. Although, as

Sarah had so astutely noticed, the ice pack didn't seem to have worked too well; Patrick definitely had the start of bruising that would be a very black eye!

"Yes," she confirmed huskily. "And, yes, Patrick does have a black eye." She grimaced. In fact, by tomorrow, it would probably rival the bruises on her arm for all the colours of the rainbow! Gareth, when thwarted, really was a very violent man.

Sarah frowned across at her cousin. "I suppose it's too much to hope that Gareth had nothing to do with it?"

Ellie sighed. "I'm afraid it is." She nodded.

Sarah shook her head, her gaze troubled as she looked at Ellie. "How could two such accomplished women as us ever have been so stupid where Gareth was concerned?" she muttered disgustedly.

Ellie couldn't help it; she laughed. And, after several stunned seconds, so did Sarah, the two women falling weakly into each others arms as they laughed together.

"'Two such accomplished women as us'?" Ellie repeated as she finally straightened, aware that their laughter had a slightly hysterical edge to it. Also aware that they were attracting a certain amount of attention.

Sarah took two glasses of champagne from a passing waiter, handing one to Ellie. "To liberation," she toasted determinedly.

Whatever had happened to cause Sarah to break her engagement, Ellie was pleased to see that on the surface at least Sarah seemed to be recovering rapidly from the disappointment.

She couldn't help admiring the younger woman; it couldn't have been easy for Sarah to come here this evening. The announcement of her own engagement had only been made days ago—an engagement that had now been abruptly terminated.

"Liberation," Ellie echoed just as firmly, before taking a sip of the bubbly wine. "Sarah—"

"It really is all right, Ellie," Sarah assured her with a smile that didn't quite light up her eyes. "I'm still a little shell-shocked, obviously, but I'll get over it. How about you?"

Ellie shuddered. "I got over Gareth months ago!" Only to fall irrevocably in love with Patrick!

"Hmm." Sarah nodded ruefully. "I believe I was mostly to blame for what happened to you—for—for—"

"Gareth dumping me?" Ellie finished dismissively.

"Yes, you were—thank goodness." She gave a shake of her head. "Gareth didn't—he didn't hurt you in any way, did he?" She frowned her concern.

The younger woman gave a humourless laugh. "My pride," she grimaced. "I can't believe now that I ever thought he was so wonderful! Boy, did his true colours come out when I told him about the designs I had sent Jacques, and that I would like to delay the wedding for a while so that I could return to Paris for six months." She gave a disgusted shake of her head. "He seemed to think that you and Patrick had had a hand in it somewhere, which I found extremely puzzling to start with. But he kept going on about 'a woman scorned'—that you would say and do anything to try and break the two of us up. The penny finally dropped, and I realised that you and he must have been dating until I came back to England a couple of months ago. Why didn't you tell me, Ellie?" she chided gently. "In your shoes, I would have wanted to scratch the other woman's eyes out!"

Ellie gave a shake of her head. "I knew what Gareth

was really like by then, and if anything I wanted to try and warn you off him."

Sarah took a sip of her champagne. "So why didn't you?" she prompted curiously.

She glanced across to where Patrick was now in conversation with his parents. "Patrick convinced me that you probably wouldn't believe me." She grimaced.

"He did?" Sarah looked across at her cousin, blonde brows raised speculatively.

"Mmm." Ellie nodded. "So what did happen to—to change your mind about Gareth?"

Sarah gave another grimace. "Well, I wasn't too happy with the things he said about you and Patrick. As you've probably realized, Patrick is a particular favourite with me, and, although we haven't seen a lot of each other this last year, you and I have been friends for a long time too," she said. "The things he said about the two of you were bad enough, but it was when he started insulting my father that I took exception!"

Ellie looked up at her disbelievingly. "Your father?" Was Gareth completely stupid? Or, more to the point, so arrogant he didn't realise when he was stepping on dangerous ground?

Sarah gave a rueful smile. "Never, ever insult the girl's father ought to be the first rule any man should learn about courtship!" She gave a self-conscious shake of her head. "Ellie, I adore my father—"

"It's reciprocated," she confirmed affectionately.

Sarah nodded. "Gareth was obviously too stupid to realise that," she dismissed hardly. "And all because he couldn't have his own way about the wedding!"

"You do realize why now, though?" Ellie prompted cautiously.

"Oh, yes," Sarah acknowledged self-disgustedly. "Don't worry, Ellie, my eyes are wide open now where Gareth Davies is concerned!"

"I'm very glad to hear it!" Patrick announced with satisfaction as he joined the two of them.

Ellie gave a nervous start, having been completely unaware of his approach. She looked up at him as he came to stand beside her. Yes, his eye was now turning a rather nice shade of purple.

He returned her gaze unblinkingly. "How about you, Ellie, are your eyes wide open now too?"

About Gareth? Or did he mean something else...?

"I think we should put some raw steak on that eye," she answered instead.

Sarah winced as she looked at him. "Does it hurt?"

Patrick shrugged. "Not as much as Davies's jaw, I expect," he said with satisfaction.

His young cousin laughed. "I hope you gave him a punch from me!"

Patrick grimaced. "I think he may have a little trouble eating for a few days."

"Good," Sarah bit out firmly, before turning to Ellie and lightly squeezing her arm. "I'm really glad the two of us have had this little chat together. But now, if the two of you will excuse me, I think I'll go over and tell my father how wonderful he is!" She gave a glowing smile.

"I'm sure Uncle George will be pleased about that," Patrick encouraged huskily.

"I hope so." Sarah laughed softly. "I'll see you both later."

There was a silence after Sarah had left to weave her way through the crowd to where her father stood talking to Patrick's parents. Although it wasn't a particularly awkward silence. More, Ellie decided, an expectant one...

"I'm sure there will be something in the fridge in the kitchen that I can put on this eye." Patrick finally spoke huskily at Ellie's side. "Care to come with me?"

Why not? The engagement had already been announced, and Toby and Teresa were the centre of attention as everyone stood around laughing and talking. The buffet supper was to be served in an hour's time.

"If you think I can be of help," Ellie agreed.

Patrick gave her a considering look. "I'm not really sure you're ready to hear what I'm thinking right now, Ellie."

She looked up at him searchingly. Could she be mistaken, or had there been a wistful note in his voice just now?

She drew in a deep breath, swallowing hard before speaking. "Patrick, exactly why did you come to my house this evening?"

He shrugged. "Because I knew, once I was made aware that Sarah had finished things with Davies, that his next move would be to pay you a call."

She had already worked that part out for herself! "And?" she prompted huskily.

"Ellie, do you think we could get out of this crush of people before I answer that?" he asked impatiently, not waiting for her answer but taking a firm hold of her arm to guide her out of the sitting room, through the hallway—beautifully decorated with boughs of holly and red ribbons—into the kitchen at the back of the house.

As Ellie had expected, the McGrath house was equally as grand as the Delacortes'. The huge kitchen was of mellow oak, with a dozen or more copper sauce-pans hanging from the rack over the work table in the centre of the room, and a green Aga giving the room its warmth.

Patrick grimaced as he saw there were several members of the household staff bustling around the room, preparing the last of the buffet supper. "Is there nowhere in this house that we can be alone?"

He scowled his displeasure, whereas Ellie felt heartened by the fact that he wanted to talk to her alone!

"They've almost finished, Patrick," she soothed lightly, giving one of the maids a sympathetic look as she glanced at them curiously. "Why don't you see if there's any red meat in the fridge we can put on your eye?"

"Damn my eye!" he dismissed impatiently, grasping hold of her hand to pull her out of the room, back down the corridor and into another room off the hallway. "Ah," he said with satisfaction as he saw this room—probably his father's study, judging by the desk and book-lined walls—was empty. He closed the door behind them decisively, and the two of them were instantly surrounded by blessed silence.

Ellie eyed Patrick quizzically for several seconds. "And?" she finally reminded him huskily.

He grimaced. "I came over to your house this evening because—because—"

"Yes?" Ellie prompted breathlessly, a cautious excitement starting to build up inside her.

Patrick drew in a harsh breath. "Because if Davies had come over to see you with the intention of hurting you in any way I intended stopping him," he bit out determinedly, grimacing as Ellie continued to look at him wordlessly. "Because if he'd come to see you with any intention of persuading you into taking him back into your life I intended stopping him from doing that too! As I told you I would," he concluded impatiently, grey gaze challenging.

It was a challenge Ellie had no intention of answering. A hope was welling up inside her now, so intense that she could barely breathe, let alone speak.

"Ellie, don't you want to know the reason why?" Patrick finally asked harshly.

She thought—hoped!—she knew the reason why. But she wasn't sure...

"Ellie, will you please say something?" Patrick demanded at her continued silence.

Was there a time and place to lose that pride she had been trying so desperately to hang on to? And was this the time and place?

"For days now I've had trouble stopping you from saying things I *didn't* want to hear, and now I want you to say something—anything—you've been struck dumb!" he muttered frustratedly. "Ellie, I'm tired of waiting for you to come to your senses. And I swear, if you don't soon say something I'm going to pick up my father's favourite whisky decanter and throw it out the window!"

Once again Ellie couldn't help it; she laughed. "And what good will that do?" she finally sobered enough to ask. "Except break a perfectly beautiful decanter and let in all the frosty air from outside!"

"It's preferable to the overwhelming urge I have right now to wring your beautiful neck!" Patrick rasped.

Tears filled her eyes now. But they were tears of joy,

not sadness. "Patrick— Oh, Patrick—" It was no good. She couldn't talk through the emotion that choked her.

His expression softened slightly before he moved to wrap her fiercely in his arms. "Ellie, I can't stand this any more! I love you," he told her forcefully. "I've loved you for so long, it seems—since the moment I called at your house in the summer, walked round to the garden and saw you lying there—"

"Patrick!" she protested as once again he reminded her of the embarrassment of being caught out bathing topless. Only to become very still in his arms as his words fully penetrated her heightened emotions. "I— Patrick, did you just say that you love me?" She stared up at him unbelievingly.

He nodded, his mouth twisting into a smile as he looked down at her. "For all the good it's done me!" He sighed heavily. "I was always under the impression that falling in love would be a joyful experience—not make me feel as if I had been pole-axed!" he muttered disgustedly. "Of course it might have helped if the woman I fell in love with felt the same way about me, but as it is—"

"Oh, but she does," Ellie cut in eagerly, her hands tightly gripping his arms as she gazed up at him, a feeling of such joy welling up inside her she felt as if she might burst. "I mean—I do," she corrected awkwardly.

"You do?" Patrick repeated slowly.

She smiled shyly. "I do," she confirmed huskily.

He looked at her uncertainly now. "But the other night, when Davies left so abruptly, you were crying—"

"Because of the way he'd kept belittling me in front of you—making me sound like—! Patrick, I only told you that I still cared about Gareth to try and cover up the fact that I've fallen in love with you," she added softly.

"And all this time I've been going quietly insane with jealousy!" he groaned. "Ellie, do you love me enough to walk down the aisle to me with Toby at your side, to stand next to me in front of a vicar, with all our family and friends looking on and wishing us well as we make our vows to each other?" he said slowly.

Was Patrick asking her to marry him? It certainly sounded like it!

"A 'meaningless affair'," he muttered disgustedly, before Ellie could answer him. "As if that's what I ever wanted from you!" He moved back slightly, holding her away from him as he looked down at her. "I love you, Elizabeth Fairfax. Will you marry me?"

She swallowed the tears, gazing up at him adoringly. "Oh, yes!" she answered joyfully.

His eyes widened. "You will…?"

"I will," she confirmed emotionally.

He closed his eyes briefly, as if he couldn't quite believe what he had just heard, and then those eyes gleamed silver as he looked at her once again.

"Darling Patrick." Ellie raised a hand to gently touch the hardness of his cheek, making no effort to hide her love for him now, knowing by the sudden glow of emotion in his eyes how deeply affected he was just by the touch of her hand. "Why did you never tell me before—show me that you felt this way about me?" she choked.

"Because when I first began to feel this way about you I very quickly learnt from Toby that you were involved with Gareth Davies, and had been for several months." He scowled at the memory. "Not the best news I'd ever had in my life. Patience is not exactly one of my virtues," he admitted self-derisively, "but I decided, when it came to you, I didn't have much choice in the matter; no one else would do for me once I had seen you."

Ellie could hardly believe all this; Patrick had been in love with her for months and she had had no idea!

She frowned. "But I stopped seeing Gareth two months ago…"

Patrick nodded. "And I'm sure having me turn up on the doorstep with every intention of sweeping you off your feet would have been exactly what you wanted immediately after that!" he drawled. "No, I decided I had to leave things for a while, give you a chance to get over— whatever." He scowled again, just at the thought of her ever having felt anything for Gareth. "It was all I could do to stop myself getting up and hugging Toby when he came to me three weeks ago and asked if I would mind taking you to the Delacorte dinner!" he revealed happily. "Mind?" he repeated mockingly. "I 'minded' so much I followed Toby home that very evening just for the opportunity of seeing you again!"

Ellie winced as she remembered that evening. "At which time I said thanks, but no thanks. I'm so sorry, Patrick." She groaned in remorse. "I really had no idea."

No idea that he had loved her for months. No idea that all this time she had been fighting her feelings for him he had already been in love with her.

"It doesn't matter." He shook his head. "None of that matters if you really do love me." He still looked as if he couldn't quite believe it was true.

And no wonder, when she had been pushing him away at every opportunity, to the point where she had even claimed to still have feelings for Gareth!

"Patrick, I thought—" She gave a heavy sigh. "When

I found out about Toby and Teresa that evening we came back from dinner, I thought you had just been taking me out to give them enough of a breathing space to convince Toby into announcing their engagement. You were so—definite about Toby's sense of loyalty, how fond he was of me, how he felt a responsibility—"

"But not to the point of my deceiving you in that way!" he instantly protested. "Was that the reason you suddenly cooled towards me? Another reason you told me that you were still in love with Davies?" he added hopefully.

"Yes," she confirmed with a grimace.

"Ellie, by saying those things about Toby I was just letting you know that, when the time came I'd fully approve of Toby as my sister's future husband, listing the qualities he had that made me feel that way. I never—" Patrick broke off, shaking his head. "Ellie, I only ever went out with you because I'm so deeply in love with you I can't think straight half the time! Do you believe me?" He looked down at her intently.

She gave a tremulous smile. "As long as you tell me that the children you're going to educate from home will be my children too!"

The tension left him and he gathered her close in his arms. "They were never going to be anyone else's," he assured her huskily.

Her arms tightened about his waist as she told him fiercely, "I love you so much, Patrick."

"I love you, Ellie." His words were muffled in the dark thickness of her hair. "Would you mind very much if we were married as soon as it can be arranged? I really don't think I can wait too much longer to make you completely mine," he owned longingly.

She didn't want to wait either—wanted to be Patrick's wife as much as he wanted to be her husband.

"I don't mind at all," she assured him huskily. "But perhaps we should wait until you no longer have a black eye; at the moment you most resemble a panda bear!" she added teasingly.

"As long as you become *Mrs* Panda Bear, who the hell cares?" he dismissed happily.

Certainly not Ellie!

How different everything was now from her unhappiness when the evening had begun. She loved Patrick. He loved her in return. They were going to be married. To each other.

Toby was right; this was going to be the best Christmas ever.

And it was only the start of what promised to be the best years of her life.

Of their life together.

Patrick and Ellie.

How wonderful that sounded!

* * * * *

A YULETIDE SEDUCTION

To Peter

CHAPTER ONE

GOLD.

Bright, shiny, *tarnished* gold.

She didn't want to touch it any more than she needed to, didn't want it touching her either, the metal seeming to burn her flesh where it nestled on her left hand.

She pulled the gold from her finger. It wasn't difficult to do. She was so much slimmer than when the ring had first been placed on her finger. In fact, the ring had become so loose that it had spun loosely against her skin, only her knuckles stopping it from falling off by itself.

How she wished it had fallen off, fallen to the ground, never to be seen again. She should have pulled it off, wrenched it from her finger, weeks ago, months ago, but she had been consumed with other things. This tiny scrap of gold lying in the palm of her hand hadn't seemed important then.

But it was important now. It was the only physical reminder she had that she had ever—ever—

Her fingers closed around the small ring of metal, so tightly that her nails dug into her flesh, breaking through the skin. But she was immune to the pain. She even welcomed it. Because that slight stinging sensation in her hand, the show of blood, told her that she, at least, was still real. Everything around her seemed to have crumbled and fallen apart, until there was nothing left. She was the only reality, it seemed.

And this ring.

She unclenched her fingers, staring down at the ring, fighting back the memories just the sight of it evoked. Lies. All lies! And now he was dead, as dead as their marriage had been.

Oh, God, no! She wouldn't cry. Never that. Not again. Not ever again!

She quickly blinked back those tears before they could fall. Remember. She had to remember, to keep on remembering, before she would be allowed to forget! If she ever did...

But first she had to get rid of this ring. She never wanted it near her again, never wanted to set eyes on it again, or for anyone else to do so either.

Her fingers curled around it again, but lightly this time, and she lifted up her arm, swung it back as far as it would go, before launching it forward again. And as she did so she threw the ring as far as it would go, as far away from her as she could make it fly, watching as it spun through the air in what seemed like slow motion, making hardly a ripple in the water as it was swallowed up by the swiftly running river in front of her, falling down, to be sucked in by the mud and slime at the bottom of the river.

It took her several breath-holding seconds to realise it had gone. Finally. Irrevocably. And with its falling came release, freedom, a freedom she hadn't known for such a long, long time.

But freedom to do what...?

CHAPTER TWO

"TAKE the cups through to—" Jane abruptly broke off her calm instruction as one of those cups landed with a crash on the kitchen floor, its delicate china breaking into a dozen pieces. The three women in the room stared down at it, with the one who had dropped it looking absolutely horrified at what she had done.

"Oh, Jane, I'm so sorry." Paula groaned her dismay. "I don't know what happened. I'll pay for it, of course. I—"

"Don't be silly, Paula," Jane dismissed, still calmly.

Once upon a time—and not so long ago—an accident like this would have sent Jane into a panic, the money she would have to pay for the replacement cup cutting deeply into the profit she would make from catering a private dinner party. But those days were gone now, thank goodness. Now she could afford the odd loss without considering it a disaster. Besides, if this evening was the success Felicity Warner hoped it would be, then Jane doubted the other woman would be too concerned that one of the coffee cups in her twelve-place-setting dinner service had met with an accident.

"Take the cups through." Jane replaced the broken cup, putting it carefully beside the other seven already on the tray. "Rosemary will bring the coffee. I'll clear away the broken cup." She gave Paula's arm a reassuring squeeze before the two women left the high-tech kitchen to serve coffee to the Warners and their six dinner guests.

Jane almost laughed at herself as she bent down, dustpan and brush in her hand. In the last two years since she'd first begun this exclusive catering service to the rich and influential, she had moved from a one-woman band to being able to employ people like Paula and Rosemary to help with the serving, at least. But, nonetheless, she was back down on her hands and knees sweeping up! Some things just never changed!

"My dear Jane, I just had to— Darling...?" Felicity Warner herself had come out to the kitchen, coming to an abrupt halt as she spotted Jane on the floor behind the breakfast-bar. "What on earth—?"

Jane straightened, holding out the dustpan containing the broken cup. "You'll be reimbursed, of course—"

"Don't give it another thought, darling," her employer for the evening dismissed uninterestedly, the affectation sounding perfectly natural coming from this elegantly beautiful woman, slim in her short, figure-hugging dress, long red hair loose about her shoulders, beautiful face alight with pleasure. "After this evening I'm hoping to be able to buy a whole new dinner service and throw this old thing away!"

"This old thing" was a delicate china dinner service that would have cost thousands to buy rather than hundreds! "It's been a success, then?" Jane queried politely as she disposed of the broken cup, her movements as measured and controlled as they usually were.

"A success!" Felicity laughed happily, clapping her hands together in pleasure. "My dear Jane, after the wonderful meal you've served us this evening, Richard is likely to divorce me and marry you!"

Jane's professional smile didn't waver for a second, although inwardly the mere thought of being married to anyone, even someone as nice as Richard Warner appeared to be, filled her with revulsion. Although she knew Felicity was only joking; her husband obviously adored her and their two young daughters.

But she was pleased the evening seemed to be working out for this friendly couple. Cooking this evening's meal for the Warners had been a last-minute arrangement, aided by the fact that Jane had had a cancellation in her busy diary. And, from what Felicity had told her this afternoon, the last few months had been difficult ones for her husband's business. The couple could certainly do with a little good luck for a change!

Although it was the first time Jane had actually cooked for Felicity, she had found the other woman warm and friendly; in fact, the other woman had been chattering away to her all afternoon. Some of it through nervousness concerning the success of this evening, Jane was sure, and so she had just let Felicity talk as she continued to work.

Every morsel of food that had appeared on the table this evening had been personally prepared by Jane herself, even down to the chocolates now being served with the coffee, meaning that she'd spent a considerable time at her client's home before the meal was due to begin. Felicity, aware of how important this evening was—to her husband, to the whole family—had followed Jane about the kitchen most of the afternoon, talking endlessly. So much so that Jane now felt she knew the family—and their problems—intimately. Felicity obviously felt the same way!

"Nothing has actually been said, of course," Felicity

continued excitedly. "But Gabe has asked to meet Richard at his office tomorrow morning, so that they can "talk." She smiled her pleasure at this development. "A vast improvement on just buying Richard out and to hell with him! And I'm sure it's your wonderful meal that's mellowed him and tipped the balance!" She grinned conspiratorially. "He told me he doesn't usually eat dessert, but I persuaded him to just try a little of your wonderful white chocolate mousse—and there wasn't a word out of him while he ate every mouthful! He was so relaxed by the time he had eaten it that he readily agreed to talk with Richard in the morning!" she concluded gleefully.

So it wasn't the other man who had actually asked for the meeting, but Richard Warner who had instigated it. Oh, well, a little poetic licence was allowed on the other woman's part in the circumstances. Felicity's husband ran and owned an ailing computer company, and, from what Felicity had told Jane, this man Gabe was a shark: a great white, who ate up his own species as well as other fish, without thought or conscience for the devastation he left behind him. The fact that he had agreed to have dinner with them at all had, according to Felicity, been more than she had ever hoped for.

The man sounded like a first-class bastard to Jane, not a man anyone would particularly want to do business with. But the Warners didn't seem to have any choice in the matter!

"I'm really pleased for you, Felicity," she told the other woman warmly. "But shouldn't you be returning to your guests...?" And then Jane could begin the un-enviable task of clearing away. She never left a home without first doing this; it was part of the service that none of the mess from her catering would be left for the client to clean up. Paula and Rosemary would leave as soon as they had served coffee, but Jane would be here until the end of the evening.

But she didn't mind that. She would work an eighteen-hour day, as she had done a lot at the beginning, as long as she was independent. Free...

"Heavens, yes." Felicity giggled now at her own social gaffe. "I was just so thrilled, I had to come and tell you. I'll talk to you again later." She gave Jane's arm a grateful squeeze before hurrying back to rejoin her guests in the dining-room, leaving a trail of the aroma of her expensive perfume behind her.

Jane shook her head ruefully, turning her attention to the dessert dishes. Under other circumstances, she and Felicity might have become friends. As it was, no matter how friendly they might have become today, Jane knew she would leave here this evening and not see Felicity again until—or if—the other woman needed her professional services again.

She readily admitted that it was a strange life she had chosen for herself. Her refined speech and obvious education—an education that had included, thank goodness, a Cordon Bleu cookery course—set her apart from many people, and yet the fact that she was an employee of Felicity's, despite being the owner of the business, meant she didn't "belong" in that set of people, either.

A strange life, yes, but it was one that gave her great satisfaction. Although occasionally it was a lonely life.

"—really is an absolute treasure," Felicity could be heard gushing out in the hallway. "I don't know why she doesn't open up her own restaurant; there's no doubting it would be all the rage." Her voice became louder as she entered the kitchen. "Jane, I've brought someone to meet you," she announced happily, a thread of excitement underlying her voice. "I think he's fallen in love with your cooking," she added flirtatiously.

There was no warning. No sign. No alarm bells. Nothing to tell Jane that her life was about to be turned upside down for the second time in three years!

She picked up the towel to dry her hands before turning, fixing a smile on her lips as she did so, only to have that smile freeze into place as she looked at the man Felicity had brought into the kitchen to meet her.

No!

Not him!

It couldn't be!

She was successful. Independent. *Free*.

It couldn't be him. She couldn't bear it. Not when she had worked so hard.

"This is Gabriel Vaughan, Jane." Felicity introduced him innocently. "Gabe, our wonderful cook for the evening, Jane Smith." She beamed at the two of them.

The Gabe Felicity had been chattering on about all afternoon had been Gabriel Vaughan? *The* Gabriel Vaughan?

Of course it was—he was standing across the kitchen from where Jane stood as if she had been turned to stone. He was older, of course—but then, so was she!—but the granite-like features of his face still looked as if they had been hewn from solid rock, despite the fact that he was smiling at her.

Smiling at her? It was the last thing he would be doing if he had recognised her in return!

"Jane Smith," he greeted in a voice that perfectly matched the unyielding hardness of him.

He would be thirty-nine now. His dark hair was slightly overlong, easily brushing the collar of his dinner jacket, and he had a firmly set jaw, sculptured lips, a long, aristocratic nose jutting out arrogantly beneath the only redeeming feature in that hard face—eyes so blue they were almost aquamarine, like the clear, warm sea Jane had once swum in off the Bahamas, long, long ago.

"Or may I call you Jane?" he added charmingly, his American accent softening that harshness.

The black evening suit and snowy white shirt that Gabriel Vaughan wore with such disregard for their elegance did little to hide the power of the body beneath. His wide shoulders rippled with muscle; his height, at least six feet four inches, meant that he would easily tower over most men he would meet. At only five feet two inches tall herself, Jane had to bend her neck backwards to look up into that harshly carved face, a face that seemed to have become grimmer in the last few years, despite the fact that he was directing a charming smile in her direction at this moment.

Oh, Paul, Jane cried inwardly, how could you ever have thought to come up against this man and win?

But then, Paul hadn't won, had he? she acknowledged dully. No one ever had against Gabe, if the past newspaper reports about this man were to be believed. In fact, now that she knew who Felicity and Richard Warner were dealing with, she believed Felicity might be rather premature in her earlier feelings of celebration!

"Jane will be fine," she answered him in the soft, calm voice she had learnt to use in every contingency over the last three years—although she was inwardly surprised she had managed to do so on this occasion!

This was Gabriel Vaughan she was talking to, the man who had ripped through the fabric of her life as if he were a tornado. She was damn sure he had never looked back to see what destruction he had left behind him!

"I'm pleased you enjoyed your meal, Mr Vaughan," she added dismissively, hoping he would now return to the dining-room with his hostess. Outwardly she might appear calm, but her legs were already starting to shake, and it was only a matter of time before they would no longer support her!

He gave an inclination of his head, the overhead light making his dark hair almost appear black, although there were touches of grey now visible amongst that darkness. "Your husband is a very lucky man," he drawled softly.

Questioningly, it seemed to Jane. She resisted the impulse to glance down at her now bare left hand, knowing that not even an indentation now remained to show she had once worn a gold band there. "I'm not married, Mr Vaughan," she returned distantly.

He looked at her steadily for long, timeless seconds, taking in everything about her as he did so. And Jane was aware of everything he would see: nondescript brown hair restrained from her face with a black velvet band at her nape, pale, make-up-less features dominated by huge brown eyes, her figure obviously slender, but her businesslike cream blouse and black skirt doing nothing to emphasise her shapeliness.

What Jane didn't see when she looked at her own reflection in the mirror—and would have been horrified if she had!—were the red highlights in the abundance of the shoulder-length hair she was at such pains to keep confined, or the stark contrast between that dark curling hair and the pale magnolia of her face, those huge brown eyes often taking on the same deep sherry colour of her hair. Her nose was small, her mouth having a sensual fullness she could do little to hide—despite not wearing lipgloss. In fact, she deliberately wore no make-up, but her face was peaches and cream anyway, adding to the hugeness of her captivating brown eyes. And, for all she believed her clothes to be businesslike, the cream blouse was a perfect foil for her colouring, and the knee-length of her skirt could do little to hide the curvaceousness of her long, silky legs.

"May I say," Gabriel Vaughan murmured huskily, his bright blue gaze easily holding hers, "that fact is to one poor man's detriment—and every other man's delight?"

"My dear Gabe," Felicity teased, "I do believe you're flirting with Jane." She was obviously deeply amused by the fact.

He gave the other woman a mocking glance. "My dear Felicity," he drawled dryly, "I do believe I am!" He turned back challengingly to Jane.

Flirting? With her? Impossible. If only he knew—

But he didn't know. He didn't recognise her. There was no way he would be looking at her with such warm admiration if he did!

Was she so changed? Facially, more mature, yes. But the main change, she readily accepted, was in her hair. Deliberately so. Once her hair had reached down to her waist, a straight curtain the golden colour of ripe corn—a stark contrast to the shoulder-length chestnut-brown it now was. She had been amazed herself at the difference the change of colour and style made to her whole appearance, seeming to change even the shape of her face. And eyes she had always believed were just brown had taken on the rich colour of her hair, the pale skin that was natural to her blonde hair becoming magnolia against the rich chestnut.

Yes, she had changed, and deliberately so, but until this moment, with Gabriel Vaughan looking at her with a complete lack of recognition, she hadn't realised just how successful she had been in effecting that change!

"Mr Vaughan..." She finally found her voice to answer him, her shocked surprise under control, if not eliminated. She was Jane Smith, personal chef to the beautiful and affluent, and this man was just another guest at one of those dinner parties she catered for. He shouldn't even be out here in the kitchen! "I do believe—" she spoke slowly but firmly "—that you're wasting your time!"

His smile didn't waver for a second, but that brilliant blue gaze sharpened with interest. "My dear Jane—" he lingered over the deliberate use of her first name, well aware of her own formality "—I make a point of never doing that."

Outwardly she again remained calm, but inwardly she felt a shiver of apprehension down her spine. And it was a feeling she hadn't known for three years...

"Now, Gabe," Felicity cut in laughingly, linking her arm through his, "I can't have you upsetting Jane," she scolded lightly. "Let's go back to the dining-room and have a liqueur, and let's leave poor Jane in peace." She slanted an apologetic smile towards Jane. "I'm sure she would like to get home some time before morning. Come on, Gabe," she encouraged firmly as he still made no effort to move. "Or Richard will think we've run away together!"

Gabriel Vaughan didn't join in her throaty laughter. "Richard need have no worries like that on my account. You're a beautiful woman, Felicity," he added to take the sting out of his initial remark, "but other men's wives have never held any appeal for me."

Jane drew in a sharp breath, swallowing hard. Because she knew the reason "other men's wives never held any appeal" for Gabriel Vaughan. Oh, yes, she knew only too well.

"I'm sure Richard will be pleased to hear that," Jane dismissed with a calmness that had now become second nature to her. "But Felicity is quite right; I do still have a lot to do. And your coffee will be going cold." She turned to smile at Paula and Rosemary as they returned from serving coffee and liqueurs. Their timing couldn't have been more perfect!

She willed Gabriel Vaughan to leave the kitchen now, before her calm shattered and her legs collapsed beneath her.

She had believed she had succeeded in pushing the past to the back of her mind, but at this moment she had a vivid image of three years ago when her own photograph had appeared side by side with this man's for days on end in all the national newspapers.

She had wanted to run away and hide then, and to all intents and purposes she had done so. And although he wasn't aware of it—and she hoped he never would be—the man who had once haunted her every nightmare, waking as well as asleep, had finally caught up with her!

He was still watching her, that intent blue gaze unwavering, despite the urgings of his hostess to return to the dining-room. His behaviour, Jane knew, was bordering on rudeness, but, as she was also aware, he was very conscious of the fact that he had the upper hand here this evening. In the process of buying out Richard Warner's ailing company, backed up by the millions of pounds that was his own personal fortune, he had no reason to do any other than what he pleased. And at this particular moment he wanted to look at Jane...!

Finally—when Jane was on the point of wondering just how much longer she could withstand that stare!— he visibly relaxed, smiling that lazily charming smile, his eyes once more that brilliant shining aqua. "It was a pleasure meeting you, Jane Smith," he murmured huskily, holding out his hand to her in parting.

Paula and Rosemary, after one wide-eyed glance in her direction at finding their hostess and one of her guests in the kitchen chatting away to Jane, had busied themselves washing up the dessert dishes Jane hadn't been able to deal with because of the interruption. And Felicity was smiling happily, still filled with what she considered the success of the evening. Only Jane, it seemed, was aware that she viewed that hand being held out to her—a long, ringless hand, filled with strength— as if it were a viper about to strike!

"Thank you," she returned coolly, not about to return the pleasantry. If there were any "pleasure" attached to this meeting then it was definitely all on his side!

But she knew she had no choice but to shake the hand held out to her. Not to do so would be inexplicable. At least, to everyone else in the room. She knew exactly why she didn't want to touch this man—his hand or any other part of him. And if he knew, if he realised, he wouldn't be holding out that hand of friendship either!

His hand was cool and dry, his grip firm. Not that Jane gave him much chance to do the latter, her hand against his only fleetingly.

Those startling blue eyes narrowed once again, his hand falling lightly to his side. "Perhaps we'll meet again," he said huskily.

"Perhaps," she nodded noncommittally.

And perhaps they wouldn't! She had managed to get through three years without bumping into this man, and if she had her way it would be another three years— or longer!—before it happened again. And as Gabriel Vaughan spent most of his time in his native America, with only the occasional swim into English waters in his search for fresh prey, that shouldn't be too difficult to achieve!

"I should be in England for several months." He seemed to read at least some of her thoughts, instantly squashing them. "In fact," he added softly, "I've rented an apartment for three months; I can't stand the impersonality of hotels."

Three months! They could be as long, or short, as he made them!

"I hope you enjoy your stay," she returned dismissively, turning away now, no longer able to even look at him. She needed to sit down, her legs shaking very badly now. Why didn't he just go?

She moved to put the clean dessert dishes back on the pine dresser across the room, and by the time she turned back again, he had gone.

Jane swayed weakly on her feet, moving to sit heavily on one of the pine chairs that stood around the kitchen table. In reality, Gabriel Vaughan could only have been in the kitchen a matter of minutes—it just seemed much, much longer!

"Gosh, he was handsome, wasn't he?" Rosemary sighed longingly as she finished drying her hands, seeming unaware of Jane's distress.

Handsome? She supposed he was. She just had more reason to fear him—fear him realising who she was—than she had to find him attractive. Although it was obvious from Paula's appreciative grin that she too had found Gabriel Vaughan "handsome".

"Looks are only skin-deep," Jane dismissed sharply, feeling her strength slowly returning. "And underneath those trappings of civilisation—" there was no denying how dazzlingly attractive Gabriel Vaughan had looked in his dinner suit, or the charm of his manner "—Gabriel Vaughan is a piranha!"

Paula made a face at her vehemence. "He seemed rather taken with you," she said speculatively.

Jane gave a derisive smile. "Men like him are not 'taken' with the hired help! Now, it's time you two went off home to your husbands," she added teasingly as she stood up. "I can deal with what's left here."

In fact, she was glad of the time alone once the two women had left for home. She could almost convince herself, as she pottered about the kitchen putting dishes away, that everything was once again back to normal, that the encounter with Gabriel Vaughan had never happened. Almost...

But there was absolutely no reason for their paths to cross again. Lightning really didn't strike twice in the same place, did it? Of course it didn't! Just as having Gabriel Vaughan enter her life once again wouldn't happen...

EVERYTHING was cleared away, the last guest having taken their leave, when Felicity came back into the kitchen half an hour later. And she looked so happy, so vastly different from the worried woman Jane had spent the afternoon with, that Jane didn't have the heart to tell her of her earlier misgivings about the evening having been quite the success Felicity obviously considered it had been. The other woman would no doubt find that out for herself soon enough. After Gabriel Vaughan's meeting with Richard, no doubt!

"I can't thank you enough, Jane." She smiled, looking tired, the evening obviously having been more of a strain than it had earlier appeared. "I don't know how I would have managed without you."

"You would have been just fine," Jane said with certainty; Richard Warner obviously had a treasure in his young wife.

"I'm not so sure." The other woman grimaced. "But tomorrow will tell if it was all worth it!"

It certainly would! And Jane really hoped this nice couple weren't in for a deep disappointment. Although, given what she knew of Gabriel Vaughan, it didn't auger well...

Felicity yawned tiredly. "I think I'll go up to bed. Richard's just bringing through the last of the glasses. But leave them, Jane," she insisted firmly. "You must be much more tired than I am—and I'm staggering!" She walked to the kitchen door. "Please go home, Jane," she added with another yawn, turning before leaving the room. "By the way, you made a definite hit this evening." She raised auburn brows pointedly. "Gabe was very interested."

Jane forced herself to once again remain outwardly

composed, revealing none of her inner panic. "How interested?" she drawled lightly.

"Very." Felicity smiled knowingly. "I shouldn't be at all surprised if you and he meet again."

She drew her breath in sharply. "And what makes you think that?" she prompted tautly, still managing to keep a tight control over her nerves. Although it was becoming increasingly difficult to do so, the longer they discussed Gabriel Vaughan!

Surely he hadn't continued to be curious about her once he and Felicity had returned to the dinner party? There had been two other couples present, and Richard's recently divorced sister had been included to make up the eight; and Jane certainly didn't think any of them would have been interested in listening to a conversation about the caterer!

"Well, he— Ah, Richard," Felicity moved aside so that her husband could enter the kitchen to put down the glasses. "I was just telling Jane that I'm sure she and Gabe are going to meet again," she said archly.

Richard shot an affectionate smile at his wife. He was in his early thirties, tall and blond, with young Robert Redford good looks, and had a perfect partner in his vivacious wife. "Stop your matchmaking, darling. I'm sure Jane and Gabe are more than capable of making their own arrangements. If necessary," he added with a rueful glance at Jane.

"It never hurts to give these things a helping hand." Felicity gave another tired yawn.

"Will you please go to bed, Fliss?" her husband said firmly. "I'll just see Jane out, and then I'll join you," he promised.

And Jane wanted to leave; of that there was no doubt.

But she had felt a chill inside her at Felicity's last statement. What had the other woman done to give a "helping hand"?

"Okay," Felicity concurred sleepily. "And I do thank you so much for doing this for us at such short notice, Jane. You've been wonderful!"

"My pleasure," she dismissed lightly. "But I can't help but feel curious as to why you should think Mr Vaughan and myself will meet again," she persisted.

"Because he asked for your business card, darling," the other woman supplied happily. "He said it was so that he could call you when he gave his next dinner party, but I have a feeling you'll hear from him much sooner than that! Don't be too long, darling." She smiled glowingly at her husband before finally going upstairs to their bedroom.

"I'm sorry about all that nonsense, Jane," Richard said distractedly, running agitated fingers through the thickness of his blond hair. "Fliss has been so worried these last few weeks, and that isn't good for her in early pregnancy. But take it from me: Gabe Vaughan is the last man you should become involved with," he added grimly. "He would gobble you up and spit you out again before you had a chance to say no!"

Gabriel Vaughan was the last man she ever *would* become involved with!

She had been frozen into immobility since Felicity's announcement of having given Gabriel Vaughan her business card, but she moved now, hurriedly putting on her jacket. "I didn't realise Felicity was pregnant," she said slowly. The other woman was so slim and elegant, the pregnancy certainly couldn't be very far along yet, and Felicity hadn't mentioned it. She had no doubt this happily married couple were pleased about the baby, but at the same time she realised it had probably happened at a bad time for them, what with the uncertainty about Richard's business.

"Only just." Richard gave what looked like a strained smile. "Felicity is longing to give me a son. Although at this rate there will be no business for him to grow up and take over!" he added bleakly. He shook his head self-derisively. "Much as I also appreciate all that you've done this evening, Jane, unlike Felicity I think it's going to take a little more than an exceptional meal to convince Gabriel Vaughan that my company is worth saving rather than being gathered up into his vast, faceless business pool!"

Jane was inclined to agree with him. From what she knew of the ruthless American, he wasn't into "saving" companies, only taking them over completely!

She certainly didn't envy Richard Warner his meeting with the older man tomorrow!

She reached out to squeeze his arm understandingly. "I'll keep my fingers crossed for you," she told him softly before straightening. "Now I have to be on my way—and I think you should go upstairs and give your lovely wife a hug! There's a lot to be said for having a loyal wife and a beautiful family like you have, you know," she added gently, having no doubts that Felicity would stand by her husband, no matter what the outcome of his meeting with Gabriel Vaughan.

Richard looked at her blankly for several seconds, and then he laughed softly. "How right you are, Jane," he agreed lightly. "How right you are!"

She was well aware that it sometimes took someone outside the situation to remind one of how fortunate one was. And, no matter what happened tomorrow, this man would still have his beautiful wife and daughters, and their unborn child. And that was certainly a lot more than very many other people had.

And sometimes, Jane remembered bleakly as she left the house, all the positive things you thought you had in your life could be wiped out or simply taken away from you.

And a prime example of that had been this evening when Gabriel Vaughan had turned out to be the guest of honour at the Warners' dinner party! She had worked so hard to build up this business, to build something for herself—she would not allow it all to be wiped out a second time!

It had not been a good evening for Jane. First that broken cup—which she would replace, despite Felicity's protests that it wasn't necessary—then Gabriel Vaughan coming into the kitchen: the very last man she'd ever wanted to see again! Ever! And Felicity, poor romantic Felicity, had given him Jane's business card!

What else could possibly go wrong tonight?

She found that out a few minutes later—when her van wouldn't start!

CHAPTER THREE

JANE almost choked over her morning mug of coffee!
As it was, her hand shook so badly that she spilt some
of that coffee onto the newspaper that lay open on the
breakfast-bar in front of her, the liquid splashing onto the
smiling countenance of the man's face that had caused
her to choke in the first place!

Gabriel Vaughan!

But then, nothing seemed to have gone right for her
since meeting the man the evening before. It had been
past one o'clock in the morning when she'd discovered
her van wouldn't start, and a glance towards the Warners' house had shown her that it was in darkness. And,
in the circumstances, Jane had been loath to disturb the
already troubled couple. Besides, she had decided, if
Richard Warner had any sense, he would be making
love to his wife at this very moment—and she certainly
had no inclination to interrupt that!

But it had been too late to contact a garage, and there
had been no taxis cruising by in the exclusive suburb,
and finding a public telephone to call for a taxi hadn't
proved all that easy to do, either. And when she'd come
to leave the call box after making the call it was to find
it had begun to rain. Not gentle, barely discernible rain,
but torrents of it, as if the sky itself had opened up and
dropped the deluge.

Tired, wet and extremely disgruntled, she had finally arrived back at her apartment at almost two-thirty in the morning. And opening her newspapers at nine o'clock the following morning, and being confronted by a photograph of a smiling Gabriel Vaughan, was positively the last thing she needed!

This was the time of day when she allowed herself a few hours' relaxation. First she would go for her morning run, collecting her newspaper, and freshly baked croissants from her favourite patisserie on the way back. She had made a career out of cooking for other people, but she wasn't averse to sampling—and enjoying—other people's cooking in the privacy of her own home. And François's croissants, liberally spread with butter and honey, melted in the mouth.

But not this morning. She hadn't even got as far as taking her first mouthful, and now she had totally lost her appetite. And all because of Gabriel Vaughan!

She would never see him again, she had assured herself in the park earlier as her feet pounded on the pathway as she ran, slender in her running shorts and sweatshirt, her hair tied back with a black ribbon. As far as she was aware, the man had only paid brief visits to England over the last three years, and just because he had rented an apartment for three months that didn't mean he would actually stay that long. Once his business with Richard Warner had reached a suitable conclusion— to Gabriel Vaughan's benefit, of course!—he would no doubt be returning to America. And staying there, Jane hoped!

But this photograph in this morning's newspaper—of Gabriel with a dazzling blonde clinging to his arm—had been taken while at a weekend party given by a popular politician. It seemed to imply that his rare visits to this country in recent years had in no way affected his social popularity when he was here.

Jane stood up impatiently, her relaxation totally ruined for this morning. Damn the man! He had helped ruin her life once—she couldn't allow him to do it again, not when she had worked so hard to make a life and career for Jane Smith.

Jane Smith.

Yes, that was who she was now.

She drew in a deeply controlling breath, forcing back the panic and anger, bringing back the calm that had become such a necessary part of her for the last few years, reaching out as she did so to close the newspaper, not taking so much as another glance at the photograph that had so disturbed her minutes ago.

She had a job to do, another dinner party to arrange for this evening, and the first thing on her list of things to do was to check with the garage she had called earlier, and see if they had had any luck in starting her van. If it wasn't yet fixed she would have to hire alternative transport for the next few days.

Yes, she had a business to run, and she intended running it!

Despite Gabriel Vaughan.

Or in spite of him!

"HELL, I hate these damned things! If you're there, Jane Smith, pick up the damned receiver!"

Jane reached out with trembling fingers and switched off the recorded messages on her answer machine, quickly, as if the machine itself were capable of doing her harm. Which, of course, it wasn't. But the recorded message of that impatient male voice—even though the man hadn't given his name but had slammed the receiver down when he received no reply to his impatience—was easily recognisable as being that of Gabriel Vaughan.

She had telephoned the garage before taking her shower, had been informed that it would be ready for collection in half an hours' time, once they had replaced the old and worn battery. Then she'd showered quickly before switching on her answer machine as she usually did when she had to go out.

She had only been out of her apartment for an hour, but the flashing light on the answer machine had told her she had five messages. The first two had been innocuous enough—enquiries about bookings, which she would deal with before she went out to collect her supplies for this evening's dinner party. But the third call—! He didn't even need to say who it was—she could recognise that transatlantic drawl anywhere!

It wasn't even twelve hours since she had left the Warners' home; the damned man had left no time at all before trying to contact her again!

What did he want?

Whatever it was, she wasn't interested. Not on a personal or professional level. On a personal level, he was the last man she wanted anything to do with, and the same applied on a professional level. For the same reason. The less contact she had with Gabriel Vaughan—on any level—the better she would like it.

That decision made, she decided to totally ignore the call, pretend it never happened. After all, he hadn't left a name or contact number, just those few words of angry impatience.

Having so decided, she reached out to switch the machine back on. After all, she had a business to run.

"Jane! Oh, Jane…!" There was a short pause in the fourth message, before the woman continued. "It's Felicity Warner here. Give me a call as soon as you come in. Please!" Felicity had sounded tearful enough at the beginning of the message, but that last word sounded like a pleading sob!

And Jane didn't need two guesses as to why the other woman had sounded so different on the recording from the happily excited one she had left the evening before; no doubt Richard had been to his meeting with Gabriel Vaughan!

Maybe she should have tried to warn the other woman last night, after all, once she had realised who Richard was dealing with? But if she had done that Felicity would only have wanted to know how she knew so much about the man. And it had taken her almost three years to shake off the how and why she had ever known a man like Gabriel Vaughan.

But Felicity sounded desperately upset, so unhappy. Which really couldn't be good for her in her condition—

"Don't you ever switch this damned thing off, Jane Smith?" The fifth message began to play, Gabriel Vaughan's voice sounding mockingly amused this time—and just as instantly recognisable to Jane as on the previous message. "Well, I refuse to talk to a machine," he continued dismissively. "I'll try you again later." He rang off abruptly, again without actually saying who the caller had been.

But Jane was in no doubt whatsoever who the caller had been, remembered all too well from last night when he had called her "Jane Smith" in that mocking drawl. Two calls in a hour! What did the man want?

Some time in the last hour—if Felicity's cry for help was anything to go by—he had also spoken to Richard Warner!

The man was a machine. An automaton. He bought and sold, ruined people's lives, without a thought for the consequences. And the consequences, in this case, could be Felicity's pregnancy...!

Once again Jane switched off the answer machine. She didn't want to get involved in this, not from any angle. And if she returned Felicity's call she would become involved. If she wasn't already!

She didn't really know the Warners that well. She understood they had been guests at several other dinner parties she had catered for, which was why Felicity had telephoned her for the booking last night.

Over the years Jane had made a point of not getting too close to clients; she was employed by them, and so she never, ever made the mistake of thinking she was anything else. But somehow yesterday had been different. Felicity had obviously been deeply worried, had desperately needed someone she could talk to. And she had chosen Jane as that confidante, probably because she realised, with the delicacy of Jane's position working in other people's homes, that she had to be discreet, that the things Felicity talked to her about would go no further.

Jane never had been a gossip, but now there was a very good reason why what Felicity had told her would go no further: she simply had no one she could possibly tell!

Her life was a busy one, and she met lots of people

in the course of her work, but friends, good friends, were something she had necessarily moved away from in recent years. It was an unspoken part of her contract that she never discussed the people she worked for, and Jane guarded her own privacy even more jealously!

Her life had taken a dramatic turn three years ago, but determination and hard work meant she now ran her own life, and her own business. Successfully.

That success meant she could afford to rent this apartment; it was completely open-plan, with polished wood floors, scatter rugs, antique furniture, and no television, because not only did she not have the time to watch it, but she didn't like it either, her relaxation time spent listening to her extensive music collection, and reading the library of books that took up the whole of one wall. It was all completely, uniquely her own, and her idea of heaven on an evening off wasn't to go out partying as she would once have done, but to sit and listen to one of her favourite classical music tapes while rereading one of her many books.

But somehow those last three messages on her answer machine seemed even to have invaded the peace and tranquillity of her home...

Much as she liked Felicity and felt sorry for the other woman, she simply couldn't return that beseeching telephone call.

She just couldn't...!

SHE was tired by the time she returned to her apartment at one o'clock the following morning. The dinner party had been a success, but the reason for her weariness was the disturbance in her personal life over the last twenty-four hours.

The answer machine was flashing repeatedly—one, two, three, four, five, six, she counted warily. How many of those calls would be from Gabriel Vaughan?

Or was she becoming paranoid? The man she had met the evening before did not look as if he had to chase after any woman, least of all one who cooked for other people for a living! And yet on the second of those last recorded messages he had said he would "try again later"!

Jane sighed. She was tired. It was late. And she wanted to go to bed. But would she be able to sleep, knowing that there were six messages on her machine that hadn't been listened to?

Probably not, she conceded with impatient anger. She didn't like this. Not one little bit. She deeply resented Gabriel Vaughan's intrusion, but at the same time she was annoyed at her own reaction to it. She was not about to live in fear ever again. This was her home, damn it, her space, and Gabriel Vaughan was not welcome in it. He certainly wasn't going to invade it.

She reached out and firmly pushed the "play" button on the answermachine.

"Hello, Jane, Richard Warner here. Felicity wanted me to call you. She's been taken into hospital. The doctor thinks she may lose the baby. I—she— Thank you for all your help last night." The message came to an abrupt end, Richard Warner obviously not knowing what else to say.

Because there was nothing else to say, Jane realised numbly. What had Gabriel Vaughan said to Richard, what had he done, to have created such—?

No!

She couldn't become involved. She dared not risk— dared not risk— She just didn't dare!

But Felicity had called her earlier today, feeling that in some way she needed Jane. And, from Richard's call just now, the other woman had been proved right! Could Jane now just ignore this call for help? Or was it already too late...?

She couldn't change anything even if she did return Richard's call. What could she do? She would be the last person Gabriel Vaughan would listen to—even if she reversed her own decision about never wanting to speak to him again.

But what about Felicity...?

It was almost one-thirty in the morning now—too late to call either Richard or the hospital; she doubted the nurses on duty at the latter would volunteer any information about Felicity, anyway. She would go to bed, get a good night's sleep, and try calling Richard in the morning. Maybe Felicity's condition would be a little more positive by then.

Or maybe it wouldn't.

She absently listened to the rest of her messages, curious now about the other five calls.

They were all business calls, not a single one in the transatlantic drawl she had quickly come to recognise—and dread—as being that of Gabriel Vaughan. And after those two calls this morning within an hour of each other his silence this evening did not reassure her. It unnerved her!

"She's—stable—that's how the doctor described her condition to me this morning," Richard Warner told Jane in answer to her early morning telephone query about Felicity. "Whatever that means," he added disgustedly.

"What happened, Richard?" Jane prompted abruptly.

This call was against her better judgement; it came completely from the softness of emotions that she must never allow to rule her a second time. But she couldn't, she had decided in the clear light of day, simply ignore Felicity's and Richard's telephone calls.

"What do you think? Gabriel Vaughan is what happened!" Richard told her bitterly—and predictably!

Gabriel Vaughan seemed to just sail through life, sweeping away anything and anyone who should happen to stand in his way. And at the moment Richard Warner was in his way. Tomorrow, next week, next month, it would be someone else completely, any consequences that might follow Gabe's actions either ignored or simply unknown to him.

"I would really rather not talk about it, Jane," Richard added agitatedly. "At the moment my company is in chaos, my wife is in hospital—and just talking about Gabriel Vaughan makes my blood-pressure rise! I'll tell Felicity you rang," he added wearily. "And once again, thank you for all your help." He rang off.

And a lot of good her help had done them, Jane sighed as she replaced her own receiver. Gabriel Vaughan had happened—who else...? What else? He was a man totally without—

Jane almost fell off her chair as the telephone beside her began to ring. Eight-fifteen. It was only eight-fifteen in the morning; she had deliberately telephoned Richard Warner this early so that she could speak to him before he either left for the office or the hospital. But she wasn't even dressed yet herself, let alone taken her run; who on earth—?

Suddenly she knew exactly who. And, after her recent calls from the Warners, and her conversation with

Richard just now, she was in exactly the right frame of mind to talk to him!

She snatched up the receiver. "Yes?" she snapped, all of her impatience evident in that single word.

"I didn't get you out of bed, did I, Jane Smith?" Gabriel Vaughan returned in his mocking drawl.

Her hand tightened about the receiver. She had known it was him—it couldn't have been anyone else, in the circumstances!—but even so she couldn't help her instant recoil just at the sound of his voice.

She drew in a steadying breath. "No, Mr Vaughan," she answered calmly, "you didn't get me out of bed." And, remembering what she had once been told about this man, she knew that he had probably already been up for hours, that he only needed three or four hours' sleep a night.

"I didn't—interrupt anything, did I?" he continued derisively.

"Only my first coffee of the morning," she bit out tersely.

"How do you take it?"

"My coffee?" she returned, frowning.

"Your coffee," he confirmed, laughter evident in his voice now.

"Black, no sugar," she came back tautly—and then wished she hadn't. In retrospect, she could think of only one reason why he would be interested in how she liked her first cup of coffee of the morning!

"I'll make sure I remember that," Gabriel Vaughan assured her huskily.

"I'm sure you didn't call me to find out how I take my coffee," Jane snapped, sure that he remembered most things.

Except that other her, it seemed.

But how long would that last? Three years on, and not only did she look different, she *was* different, but Gabriel Vaughan had a very good reason for remembering everything that had happened three years ago, leading her to believe that his memory lapse where she was concerned would not continue. She had no doubt there would be no flirtatious early morning telephone calls then!

"You're wrong there, Jane Smith," he murmured throatily now. "You see, I want to know everything about you that there is to know—including how you take your coffee!"

Jane's breath left her in a shaky sigh, her hand tightening painfully about the receiver. "I'm an extremely boring individual, I can assure you, Mr Vaughan," she told him abruptly.

"Gabe," he put in smoothly. "And I very much doubt *that*, Jane," he added teasingly.

She didn't care what he doubted. She worked, she went to bed, she ran, she shopped, she read, she worked, she went to bed Her life was structured, deliberately so. Routine, safe, uncomplicated. This man threatened complications she didn't even want to think about!

"Are you aware that Felicity Warner is in hospital, in danger of losing her baby?" she attacked accusingly.

There was a slight pause on the other end of the telephone line. Very short, only a second or two, but Jane picked up on it anyway. To her surprise. Three years ago nothing had deterred this man. And she couldn't really believe that had changed in any way.

"I wasn't aware that Felicity was pregnant," he finally rasped harshly.

"Would it have made any difference if you had

known?" Jane scorned disgustedly, already knowing the answer to that question. Nothing distracted this man away from his purpose. And she couldn't help feeling that he had been playing with the Warners by accepting their dinner invitation two evenings ago...!

"Any difference to what?" he returned in a silkily soft voice.

"Let's not play games, Mr Vaughan." She continued to be deliberately formal, despite his earlier invitation for her not to be. "You have business with Richard Warner, and that business appears to be affecting his wife's health. And that of their unborn child," she added shakily. "Don't you think—?"

"I'm not sure you would like to hear what I think, Jane Smith," Gabriel Vaughan bit out coldly.

"You're right—I don't," she snapped tersely. "But I think it's way past time someone told you about your lack of thought for the people lives you walk into and instantly dismantle! Your method of dealing with people leaves a lot to be desired, and—" She broke off abruptly, feeling the icy silence at the other end of the telephone line as it blasted its way in her direction. And at the same time she realised she had said too much...

"And just what do you know about my 'method of dealing with people', Jane Smith?" he prompted mildly— too mildly for comfort!

Too much. She had said too much! "You're a public figure, Mr Vaughan." She attempted to cover up her lapse.

"Not in England," he rasped. "Not for several years," he added harshly, all his previous lazy charm obliterated in cold anger.

"Strange; I'm sure I saw your photograph in my daily

newspaper yesterday morning…" she came back point-edly; she had to try and salvage this conversation as best she could; she'd already been far too outspoken.

The last thing she wanted to do was increase this man's interest in her! Ideally, she would like him to forget he had ever met someone called Jane Smith, but she would settle for disinterest—which wasn't going to be achieved if she kept challenging him!

"Of course, that was a social thing," she added lightly. "You were a guest at a party."

"I'm a sociable person, Jane," he drawled dryly. "Which was actually the reason for this call…"

He was going to ask her to cater a dinner party for him! There was no way she could work for or with this man. Absolutely no way!

"I'm very heavily booked at this time of year, Mr Vaughan," she told him stiffly: Christmas was now only two weeks away. "My diary has been full for weeks, some of those bookings made months ago. However, I could recommend another catering firm who I'm sure would be only too pleased to—"

Gabriel Vaughan's husky laugh cut in on her business-like refusal. "You misunderstood me, Jane," he mur-mured, that laugh still evident in his voice. "I was asking you to have dinner with me, not trying to book your services as a cook—impressive as they might be!"

Now it was Jane's turn to fall silent. Not because she was angry, as Gabriel Vaughan had been minutes ago—where had that anger gone…? No, she was stunned. Ga-briel Vaughan was asking her for a date. Impossible. He just didn't realise how impossible that was.

"No," she said abruptly.

"Just—no?" he said slowly, musingly. "You don't even want a little time to think about it?"

She doubted too many women had to do that where this man was concerned; he was handsome, single, undoubtedly rich, sophisticated, witty—what more could any woman want?

All Jane knew was that she did not want Gabriel Vaughan!

"No," she repeated sharply.

"Then I take it I was right earlier in assuming there's someone else in your life," he dismissed hardly, a chill edging his tone.

Jane frowned. When earlier in this conversation had he assumed there was already someone else in her life? They hadn't even touched on the subject.

"I have no idea what you're talking about," she snapped.

"It's occurred to me, Jane, that you have an unhealthy interest—as far as Felicity goes—in Richard Warner's affairs. And I don't just mean his business ones!" he added harshly.

"You're disgusting, Mr Vaughan," Jane told him angrily. "Other women's husbands have never held any appeal for me, either!" She deliberately threw his words to Felicity two evenings ago back in his face, then slammed down the receiver, immediately switching on the answer machine.

She didn't think Gabriel Vaughan was the sort of man to ring a woman back when she had angrily terminated their telephone conversation, but on the off chance that he just might she had no intention of answering that call herself.

He had just implied she was having an affair with Richard Warner!

How dared he?

CHAPTER FOUR

"WE MEET again, my dear Jane Smith."

Jane froze in the act of placing the freshly baked meringues onto the cooling tray, closing her eyes briefly, hoping this was only a nightmare. One that she would wake up from at any second!

But closing her eyes achieved nothing, because she could smell his aftershave now, and knew that when she turned Gabriel Vaughan was going to be standing only feet behind her. Could it only be coincidence that this was the second dinner party in a week that she had catered for where Gabriel Vaughan was a guest…?

She opened her eyes, straightening her shoulders before turning sharply to face him, her heart missing a beat as the total masculinity of him suddenly dominated the kitchen in which she had worked so harmoniously for the last four hours.

She was realising that he was a man who wore a black evening suit and white shirt with a nonchalance that totally belied the exclusive cut of the expensive material. He was vibrantly attractive, in a way that stated he didn't give a damn how he looked, that he was totally confident of his own masculinity, the challenging glitter of those aqua-blue eyes daring anyone to question it.

To her dismay, Jane realised that was probably exactly

what she had done two days ago when she had turned down his invitation to dinner!

She gave a cool inclination of her head. "You mentioned that you're a sociable person," she dismissed coldly.

"And you," Gabe returned mockingly, "mentioned how busy you were for the next few weeks." He shrugged. "The mountain came to Mohammed!"

Her eyes narrowed warily. Could this man possibly have—? No, she couldn't believe he would go to the extreme of having himself invited to a dinner party she was catering simply so that he— Couldn't she...? Hadn't the hostess this evening telephoned her earlier this morning and apologetically explained that, if it wasn't going to be too much of a problem for her, there would be two extra guests for dinner this evening. Was Gabriel Vaughan one of those guests...?

"I see," she murmured noncommittally. "I hope you're enjoying the meal, Mr Vaughan," she added dismissively.

But Gabe wasn't to be dismissed, leaning back against one of the kitchen units, totally relaxed—at least, on the surface; he must have been as aware as she was that the last time the two of them had spoken she had slammed the telephone down on him!

"I am now," he assured her huskily, looking at her admiringly. "That's quite a temper you have there, Jane Smith." There was an edge of admiration in his mocking tone as he too recalled the abrupt end of their telephone conversation two days ago.

Jane returned his gaze unblinkingly. "That was quite an accusation you made—Gabriel Vaughan," she returned, undaunted.

He smiled. More of a grin really, deep grooves beside his mouth, teeth white against his tanned skin. "Richard wasn't too happy about it, either," he murmured with amusement.

Her eyes widened, the colour of rich sherry. "You repeated that—that ridiculous accusation to him?" she gasped disbelievingly.

"Mmm," Gabe acknowledged ruefully, his gaze lightly mocking. "Tell me," he continued consideringly, "what *do* you do for exercise?"

She shook her head, totally amazed at this man's insulting conversation; he didn't even try to be polite!

"I run, Mr Vaughan," she snapped angrily. "And I really can't believe you were so insensitive as to have repeated such an accusation to Richard, at a time like this—"

"Felicity is out of hospital, you know." Gabe straightened, not as relaxed as he had been; in fact he looked slightly defensive, the challenging look back in his eyes.

As it happened, Jane did know—but she was surprised he did. She hadn't actually gone in to see Felicity when she was in hospital, but she had telephoned the hospital to pass on her well wishes, and she had called Richard every day to check on his wife's condition, relieved when she'd spoken to him this morning and heard that the doctor considered Felicity well enough to go home, the miscarriage in abeyance. For the moment. But surely if this man continued his hounding of Richard—and throwing out obscene accusations—that may not last...!

"How long for?" Jane scorned. "When do you intend making your next assault on Richard's company?" she added disgustedly.

"I don't assault, Jane," Gabe drawled derisively. "I acquire companies—"

"By going for the jugular of the owner!" she accused heatedly. "Look for the weakness, and then go for it!"

Gabe looked completely unmoved by her accusation. But those aqua-blue eyes had narrowed and a pulse was beating in his clenched jaw. Maybe he wasn't as completely lacking in compassion as she had believed...

No, she couldn't believe that. Three years ago he had been completely ruthless, totally without compassion. It had been his behaviour then that had turned an unbearable situation into a living hell. It was the very reason she had reacted so strongly to Felicity and Richard's situation. For all the good that had done her—Gabriel Vaughan had taken her emotional response and immediately jumped to the conclusion that she must be having an affair with Richard!

"Every company has its weak spot, Jane," Gabe mocked now. "But I only acquire the ones that are of interest to me." He pursed his lips thoughtfully. "I don't wish to alarm you, Jane, but there appears to be smoke coming from—"

Her second batch of meringues!

Ruined. Burned, she discovered as she quickly opened the oven door and black smoke belched out into the kitchen.

"Don't be a fool!" Gabe rasped harshly, pushing her none too gently out of the way as she would have pulled the tray from inside the oven. "You open the kitchen door, and I'll throw the tray out into the garden." He took the oven-glove from her unresisting fingers. "The door, Jane," he prompted again firmly as she still didn't move.

Damn the man, she muttered to herself as she finally went to open the door. She couldn't remember the last time she had burnt anything, let alone in the middle of a dinner party. But this man had disturbed her so badly that he had achieved it quite easily. She was losing it, damn it. Damn him!

"Out of my way, Jane," Gabe instructed grimly, going past her to throw the blackened meringues, and the tray, out into the garden.

Jane watched wordlessly as the burnt mess landed outside in the snow. Yes, snow. Somewhere, in the midst of what was turning out to be a terrible evening—the second in a week—it had begun to snow, a layer of white already dusting everything, the overheated tray sizzling and crackling in the coldness.

"Where do you run?"

She turned back to look at Gabriel Vaughan, dismayed at how close he was to her as they both stood in the open doorway, blinking up at him dazedly, the coldness of their breath intertwining. "The park near my apartment. Why?" She frowned her sudden suspicion at the question.

His gaze remained unblinkingly on her own. "Just curious."

She shook her head, outwardly unmoved by his closeness, but inwardly…! But if she moved away he would merely realise how disturbing she found it to be standing this close to him. And as far as she was concerned he already had enough of an advantage—even if he wasn't aware of it!

And he could keep his damned curiosity to himself! Not that it really mattered; he had no idea where she lived, and so consequently he wouldn't know which park it was, either!

"By the look of this snow—" she looked up into a sky that seemed full of the heavy whiteness "—I won't be running anywhere tomorrow morning." Her morning run in the nearby park cleared her head and set the tone for the rest of her day, and finding Gabriel Vaughan there, accidentally or otherwise, would totally nullify the exercise!

"A fair-weather runner, hmm?" Gabe drawled derisively.

Her brows rose indignantly over wide sherry-brown eyes. "I don't—"

"Ah, Gabriel, this is where you've been hiding yourself," murmured a husky female voice. "What on earth is that dreadful smell?" Celia Barnaby, the hostess of the evening, a tall, elegant blonde, wrinkled her nose at the smell of the burnt meringues that still lingered in the kitchen.

Gabe looked down at Jane, winking conspiratorially before turning to stroll across the kitchen to join his hostess. "I believe it was dessert, Celia," he drawled laughingly, taking a light hold of her arm as he guided her back out of the kitchen. "I think we should leave Jane alone so that she can do her best to salvage it in peace!"

"But—"

"I believe you were going to tell me about the skiing holiday you're taking in the New Year?" Gabe prompted lightly, continuing to steer the obviously reluctant Celia away from the disaster area. "Aspen, wasn't it?" He glanced back at Jane over the top of the other woman's head, his smile one of intimate collusion.

"Damn the man," Jane muttered to herself as she set about "salvaging"; and she didn't have a lot of time to do it. Her two helpers for the evening were now returning with the empty vegetable dishes, as the main course had just been served.

By the time she had finished arranging the meringues and fruit on the plates, lightly covering the latter with a raspberry sauce, no one would ever have guessed that there should actually have been two meringues on each plate.

Except Gabriel Vaughan, of course. But then, he was the reason for the omission; if she hadn't been busy fending off his questions then this disaster wouldn't have happened. She was just too professional, too organised, for this to happen under normal circumstances. But with Gabriel Vaughan once again present it was far from normal!

In fact, she was slightly on edge for the rest of the evening, kept half expecting Gabriel Vaughan to stroll back into the kitchen unannounced; it just didn't seem to occur to him that the dinner guests weren't supposed to just stroll about the homes of their host or hostess, let alone go into the kitchen and chat to the hired help! That was his inborn arrogance, Jane decided derisively; Gabriel Vaughan would go where he wanted, when he wanted.

And he would also say exactly what he pleased, even if it was insulting!

She couldn't even imagine what Richard Warner must be thinking about the other man's accusations concerning the two of them. It was so ludicrous it would be laughable in other circumstances. As it was, she could imagine that Gabe's words that Richard "wasn't too happy" about it were definitely an understatement where Richard was concerned!

It was extremely late by the time she had tidied away the last of the dishes from the meal, and she had to admit she was exhausted. But not from physical work; it was due entirely to tension. Unfortunately, she didn't manage to make her escape before Celia Barnaby came through to the kitchen, the last of her guests having finally left.

And it was unfortunate, because Celia wasn't one of Jane's favourite people. She was a beautiful divorcee, who had obviously only married her weak husband for the millions she had been able to take off him as part of their divorce settlement. Jane found her brittle and condescending, altogether too jaded.

Nevertheless she smiled politely at the other woman; she didn't have to like the people she worked for; it certainly wasn't conditional to her supplying the superb food she was known for. If that condition had applied two years ago, when she'd first begun this exclusive service, then she would have been out of work within a month!

Celia arched shaped brows. "Have you and Gabriel known each other long?" she enquired lightly.

Jane gave her a startled look. This woman certainly didn't believe in the "lead up to" approach! "Known each other long...?" she repeated dazedly. The two of them didn't know each other at all!

"Mmm," Celia drawled. "Gabriel explained to me that the two of you are old friends."

"He—!" Jane broke off, swallowing hard. "He said that?" She frowned darkly.

"Don't be so coy, Jane." The other woman gave her a knowing smile. "I always thought you were a bit of a dark horse, anyway. And I've never understood why you became a brunette; did no one ever tell you blondes have more fun?" she drawled suggestively, looking disparagingly at Jane's hair.

Jane was totally stunned. By all that this woman had just said. For one thing, she was surprised this woman had ever spared her a second thought. And she was rendered speechless by that comment about blondes.

The change of colour and style to her hair, she had felt two and a half years ago, had been an important part of the new her. It wasn't only Gabriel Vaughan she didn't want recognising her; it wouldn't do for any of the people she worked for to realise she had once led a similar lifestyle to their own, either, and so the change in her appearance had served a double purpose. Until this moment she had thought the disguise worked, always took care to have her hair coloured once a month. Before now no one had ever told her they knew she was really a blonde!

On top of that Gabriel Vaughan's claim that the two of them were "old friends" was just too much. Almost a week's acquaintance did not make them old friends—and she wouldn't term them as friends anyway!

Unless Gabriel Vaughan did remember her from three years ago, after all, and he was just playing with her...?

"Not very long, no." She woodenly answered Celia's original question.

"Pity." Celia grimaced her disappointment at her answer. "I wondered what his wife had been like. You did know he's been married, didn't you?" She looked at Jane fron beneath lowered lashes.

Oh, yes, she knew he had been married, Jane acknowledged with an inward shiver. The death of Gabriel

Vaughan's wife had only added to the spiralling out of control of her own life!

"Yes," Jane confirmed abruptly. "And surely you saw her photograph in the newspapers at the time of the accident?" She seemed to be having trouble articulating; her lips felt stiff and unmoving. It was so long since anyone had talked about these things...!

"Didn't everyone? Such a scandal, my dear," Celia said with obvious relish. "Jennifer Vaughan was so beautiful it made every other woman want to weep!" she added disgustedly. "No, I know what she looked like, Jane; I just wondered what she was really like. I never actually met her, you see; I didn't know Gabriel in those days."

Jane had never met Jennifer Vaughan either. But she had come to fear her, and the effect of her beauty.

"I can't be of any help to you there, I'm afraid, Celia," she dismissed coolly, wanting to make good her escape now, and it had little to do with the lateness of the hour. All this talk of Jennifer Vaughan; it was unnerving! "I've only met Gabriel since the death of his wife, too." She was deliberately economical with the facts.

For herself she didn't care if Celia knew she and Gabriel Vaughan had only spoken for the first time a few days ago, but to tell the other woman that, in the face of Gabe's contradictory claim, would only arouse the other woman's curiosity even more. And that she didn't want!

"Oh, well." Celia straightened, obviously realising she wasn't going to get much information out of Jane. "It was a marvellous meal this evening, Jane," she added offhandedly. "You'll send your bill through, as usual?"

"Of course," she nodded, and, as usual, Celia would

delay paying it for as long as possible; for a woman with millions, she was very loath to pay her bills.

In fact, Jane had thought long and hard before agreeing to cater this dinner party. Celia could be extremely difficult to work for, and with the added problem of her reluctance to pay...

In view of the fact that Gabriel Vaughan had turned out to be one of the guests, she wished she had followed her instincts and said no, Jane told herself as she left the house, a blast of icy snow hitting her in the face. It was—

"Here, let me take that for you." The box of personal utensils was plucked out of her hands, Gabriel Vaughan grinning at her unconcernedly over the top of it. "Hurry up, Jane," he encouraged as she stood rooted to the spot, stunned into immobility by his presence. "It's still snowing!" he pointed out dryly, his mouth twisting derisively as he stated the obvious.

In actual fact, it was snowing heavier than ever, everywhere covered with it now, although luckily the roads looked to be clear. But it wasn't the snow or the conditions of the road that bothered her. What was Gabriel Vaughan still doing here? She'd thought he'd left some time ago.

She hoped Celia, inside the brightly lit house, didn't see the two of them outside together! Although, having spoken to Jane, and realising how little she actually knew about Gabriel Vaughan, the other woman had seemed to lose interest. Jane just hoped that Celia hadn't questioned Gabe in the way she had her—or mentioned the curious fact of Jane's dyed hair!

"Come on, Jane," he urged impatiently, both of them

having snowflakes in their hair now. "Open up your van, where it's at least dry!"

She moved automatically to unlock the door and climbed inside, only to turn and find Gabe sitting in the passenger seat beside her. And looking very pleased with himself, too, his smile one of satisfaction now.

"What are you doing here?" Jane snapped irritably; she really had had enough for one night.

His mouth twisted derisively. "That's a pretty blunt question, Jane," he drawled.

"I'm a pretty blunt person—Mr Vaughan," she bit out caustically. "You see, I thought we had said all we have to say to each other earlier."

He leant his head back against the seat as he gave her a considering look. The snow had melted on his hair, making it look darker than ever in the light blazing out from the house. "What have I ever done to you, Jane, to provoke such animosity? Oh, I'll accept you don't like my business practices," he continued unhurriedly before she could make a reply. "But you said yourself—and Richard confirmed it—that you aren't involved with him, and Felicity didn't give me the impression the two of you are big buddies either, so what is the problem you have concerning my business dealings with Richard? You don't give the impression of someone who takes up a campaign against injustice on someone else's part—in fact, just the opposite!" He looked at her through narrowed lids.

Jane stiffened at this last statement. "Meaning?" she prompted tautly.

He shrugged. "Meaning you don't seem to me to be a person that likes to draw attention to yourself. That, like me, you prefer to shun the limelight."

Her mouth twisted at the latter description. "That sounds a little odd coming from someone whose photograph recently appeared in the daily newspapers!" There had been yet another mention of him yesterday after he'd attended a charity dinner. Thankfully, she hadn't reacted to it in the way she had the other morning, and she had managed not to spill any of her coffee, either! "But then, you did mention that you're a sociable person!" she added mockingly.

Again he gave her that considering look, very still as he sat beside her. "Believe it or not, Jane, I hate parties," he finally drawled. "And dinner parties are even more boring; whoever your dinner companion for the evening turns out to be, you're stuck with them! And this evening I was stuck between Celia and a woman old enough to be my grandmother!"

In fact, Jane knew, the elderly lady he was referring to was actually Celia's grandmother, a titled lady that Celia considered of social value. But as she was aged in her seventies, and slightly deaf, it was only too easy to guess why Celia had seated Gabe as she had; given the choice between talking to an elderly, slightly deaf lady and the beautiful Celia, Gabe would be sure to spend the majority of the evening talking to Celia herself. Except for those ten minutes or so when Gabe had joined Jane in the kitchen.

"You hide your aversion to dinner parties very well," Jane told him dryly.

"You know exactly why I was at Richard and Felicity's that evening," Gabe rasped. "Would you like to hear why I was here tonight?" He quirked dark brows challengingly.

She looked at him, recognising that challenge, and

suddenly she knew, in view of Celia's call this morning concerning two extra guests, that Gabe's reason for being here tonight was the last thing she wanted to hear!

"It's late, Mr Vaughan." She straightened in her seat, putting the key in the ignition in preparation for leaving. "And I would very much like to go home now," she added pointedly.

Gabe nodded. "And exactly where is home?" he prompted softly.

She glanced at him sharply. "London, of course," she answered warily.

Gabe's mouth twisted wryly. "It's a big place," he drawled. "Close to one of the parks, I imagine— Your running, Jane," he explained at her sharp look. "But couldn't you be a little more specific?" he coaxed softly.

No, she couldn't; her privacy was something she guarded with the ferocity of a lioness over her den! And her apartment was her final point of refuge.

"You're a very difficult woman to pin down, Jane Smith," he murmured at her continued silence. "No one I've spoken to about you seems to have any idea where you live. Clients contact you by telephone, bills are paid to a post office box number, there's none of the usual advertising on the side of your van—in fact, it's unmarked." He shook his head. "Why all the secrecy, Jane?"

Jane stared at him with wide sherry-coloured eyes. He had talked to people about her? Tried to find out where she lived? Why?

"Why?" he repeated questioningly—making her aware that she had spoken the word out loud. "Do you have any idea how beautiful you are, Jane Smith?" he asked her huskily, suddenly much closer in the confines of the van. "And your damned elusiveness only makes you all the more intriguing!" He was so close now, the warmth of his breath stirred the wispy strands of her fringe.

She couldn't move, was held mesmerised by the intensity of those aqua-blue eyes, was transfixed by the sudden intimacy that had sprung up between them.

"Jane—"

"I don't think so, Mr Vaughan." She flinched away from the caressing hand he laid against the nerve pulsing in her throat, straightening again in her seat, moving away from him as she did so. "Now, would you please get out of my van?" she said angrily—not sure if that anger was directed at him or herself.

Had she really almost felt tempted to let him kiss her, as his warm gaze had promised he wanted to do as he'd moved closer to her? That would have been madness. Not only for her personally, but it would have threatened every vestige of peace she had built for herself over the last two years.

Gabe didn't move, frowning across at her. "Was I wrong, and you are involved with someone? Is that why you protect your privacy so fiercely?" he rasped.

And why she flinched away from letting him kiss her? He didn't say the words, but the question was there anyway. Jane realised that, to him, a man used to getting what he wanted, and having any woman he wanted, her aversion to him had to have some explanation. Whereas the real reason for her aversion to him would probably send him into shock—before another emotion entirely took over!

"No," she assured him dryly.

Blue eyes narrowed. "No man," he mused. "How

about a woman?" he added as if the thought had just occurred to him.

Jane gave a slight laugh. "Or woman," she added, with a derisive shake of her head.

He shrugged. "You never can tell." He excused his own grasping at straws. "Look, Jane, I've been completely open with you from the first. I like you. I was drawn to you from the moment—"

"Please don't go on," she cut in coldly. "You're only going to embarrass me—as well as yourself!"

Anger flashed briefly across his face, his jaw hardening, and then he had himself under control again, relaxing as he smiled that slow, charming smile. "I'm rarely embarrassed, Jane. And you don't get anywhere without asking," he added huskily.

She shot him a chilling look. "Most men would be gracious enough to accept what is definitely no for an answer!"

"Most men," Gabe nodded. "But I've invariably found that it's the things worth persisting for that are worth having," he teased lightly, before glancing out of the van window. "The snow appears to be getting heavier, so perhaps you should be getting home." He reached for the door handle. "Take care driving home, won't you?" came his parting shot.

She always took care, in everything that she did. And one of the biggest things she had taken care over was avoiding any possibility of meeting this man over the last three years. But now what she had always dreaded had happened; he had found her. And, for some inexplicable reason, he believed he was attracted to her!

He had tried to find her three years ago. He had pursued her until she had felt she couldn't run any longer, when the only answer had seemed to be to shake off all that she was, all that she had been. And with those changes—her name, her appearance—she had finally been able to make the life for herself that she had been searching for. How ironic, after all that had happened, that she should have Gabriel Vaughan to thank for making that possible!

But how long would it be, Jane wondered with a sinking heart as she drove home through the treacherous snow conditions, before Gabe saw through what was, after all, only a superficial disguise, and that attraction he believed he felt towards her turned into something much more ugly...?

CHAPTER FIVE

"I HAVE no idea what you said to him, Jane," Felicity announced happily, "but whatever it was I thank you for it!"

Jane had called in to see Felicity two days after Celia Barnaby's dinner party, having no bookings for that day and, having decided long ago that, no matter how good it was for business to have so many bookings in the run up to Christmas, she also needed a certain amount of time off. It would do business absolutely no good whatsoever if she should collapse under the strain.

There were plenty of other things she could have done with her day off, but she was very conscious of the fact that she hadn't actually visited the other woman since her discharge from hospital, and so she had called in after lunch.

But she couldn't actually say she liked the turn the conversation had taken once the two women were sitting down with a cup of tea. "I'm sorry, Felicity." She shook her head. "I have no idea what you're talking about." She gave a vaguely dismissive smile, appearing outwardly puzzled—she hoped. Inwardly she had an idea she knew exactly who "him" was, even if she wasn't too sure what Gabriel Vaughan had done now. The one thing she was absolutely sure of was that whatever it was, she didn't come into it!

Felicity gave her a teasing smile, still taking things easy after the scare earlier in the week, although she certainly looked glowing enough this afternoon. "From what Richard told me," Felicity grinned, "I got the impression you had told Gabe exactly what you thought of him!"

Jane could feel the warm colour in her cheeks. "Only from a business point of view," she confirmed reluctantly.

Felicity raised auburn brows. "Is there another point of view?"

"Not as far as I'm concerned, no," Jane told the other woman flatly.

"Whatever," Felicity accepted, giving Jane's arm an understanding squeeze. "I'm not going to pry," she assured her huskily. "All I know is that instead of buying Richard out, and basically taking over the company, Gabe has agreed to financially back Richard until the company is back on its feet again."

"Why?" Jane frowned; it sounded too good to be true to her. There had to be something in it for Gabriel Vaughan.

"Richard asked him the same question." The other woman nodded knowingly. "And do you know what his answer was?"

She couldn't even begin to guess. Didn't really want to know. But she had a feeling Felicity was going to tell her anyway!

"I have no idea," she shrugged.

The other woman smiled. "Gabe said it was because of something someone had said to him. And the only 'someone' we could think of was you!"

Jane didn't believe that anything she could have said

to Gabriel Vaughan could possibly have made any difference to his sudden change of plans where Richard's company was concerned. There had to be another reason for it. Although she very much doubted Gabe would decide to let any of them in on what it actually was. Until he was ready to, of course!

"I don't think so, Felicity," she said dryly. "Although I'm glad, for both your sakes, that he's decided to back off." And she sincerely hoped, for Felicity's sake, that he didn't as quickly change his mind back again! "But if I were Richard I would make the agreement legally binding as soon as possible," she added derisively.

"Already done," the other woman assured her happily. "Gabe has his own legal team, and between them and Richard's lawyer they tied the deal up very neatly yesterday afternoon. I can't tell you how much better I feel, Jane." Felicity sighed contentedly.

Jane could see how much more relaxed the other woman was; she just wished she felt the same way!

Unfortunately she didn't. As she drove back to her own apartment she was filled with disquieting feelings. Why had Gabriel Vaughan, when he had seemed so set on taking over Richard Warner's company, suddenly done an about-face and come to a much less aggressive agreement with the other man?

Jane refused point-blank to believe it had anything to do with what she had said to him! The man was simply too hardened, too ruthless to be swayed by such things as human frailty in Felicity's case, and emotional accusations in hers. She should know!

So it wasn't the best time in the world, with her thoughts confused and worried, for her to arrive back outside her apartment, her arms full of the food shopping she had done on the way home, to find a huge bouquet of flowers lying outside her apartment front door!

For one thing the flowers, whoever they were from—and she had an uneasy feeling she knew exactly who that might be!—were completely unwelcome. She had made a decision, after the pain and disillusionment she had suffered three years ago, that no man, apparently nice or otherwise, would ever get close enough to her again to cause the complete destruction of her life that she had known then.

For a second thing, how had the flowers got all the way up here to her apartment in the first place? This was supposed to be a secure building, and her apartment on the fourth floor—laughingly called the penthouse apartment—could only be reached by the lift and fire-stairs. In which case, any flowers that had been delivered to the building should have been left downstairs in the vestibule between the outside door and the security door, a door that could only be unlocked by one of the four residents.

So just how had this bouquet of flowers arrived up here outside her door...?

"The lady in apartment number three let me in." Gabriel Vaughan rose to his feet from the shadows of the hallway where he had obviously been sitting on the carpeted floor, walking slowly towards her. "A very romantic lady," he explained as he drew level with an open-mouthed Jane, dressed casually in denims and a black shirt, the latter worn beneath a grey jacket. "She was only too happy to let me in when I explained I was your fiancée from America, and that I had come over to surprise you!"

Jane was still stunned at actually seeing him standing

here in the hallway, let alone able to take in what he was actually saying.

But the words finally did penetrate her numbed brain, and with that comprehension came anger at the way he'd managed to trick his way in. And she was already angry enough that he was here at all! This was her home, her private sanctuary, and no one invaded it. And certainly not Gabriel Vaughan.

Never Gabriel Vaughan…!

She looked at him with coldly glittering eyes. "Take your flowers, Mr Vaughan," she bit out in a heavily controlled voice, "and—"

"I hope you aren't about to say something rude, Jane," he cut in mockingly.

"And yourself," she finished hardly, breathing deeply in her agitation, two spots of angry colour in her cheeks. "And leave. Before I call the police and have you thrown out!" she added warningly as he would have spoken. "I have no idea how you found out where I actually live, but—"

"I've hired a car for my stay over here; the weather was so bad the other evening, I decided to follow you home, to make sure you got back okay," he explained softly, his eyes narrowed on her as he saw all too easily how angry and upset she was.

He might be able to see it, but he was also going to hear it! "Your behaviour, Mr Vaughan, is bordering on harassment," she bit out tartly. "And if it continues I certainly will make a complaint to the police." Even as she repeated that threat, she knew that she would do no such thing.

The police had been involved three years ago, calling at her home, poking and prying into her personal life, into Paul's life— There was no way she would willingly open herself up to that sort of turmoil again, and certainly not with Gabriel Vaughan once again at its centre!

Gabe gave a pained grimace. "I only wanted to make sure you got home safely in that awful weather," he excused challengingly.

Jane glared at him. "I don't believe you! And after I've explained your other behaviour I don't think the police would either!"

"Aren't you taking this all a little too seriously, Jane?" He attempted to cajole her, shaking his head teasingly.

He had followed her home the other evening so that he knew where she lived, had tricked his way into her apartment building today on the pretext of bringing her flowers but actually so that he could be here waiting for her when she got home; no, she didn't think she was overreacting at all!

"Evie—the lady in the apartment below," she explained impatiently at his puzzled look, "may have found your actions romantic, Mr Vaughan..." The other woman had been trying to find out from Jane for months if there was a man in her life; Evie was involved with a married man herself, which was how she was able to live in the apartment she did. "I, on the other hand," Jane added hardly, "find them completely intrusive. If I had wanted you to know where I lived then I would have told you!"

His mouth twisted ruefully. "Don't you have any sympathy at all for a lone male in a foreign country?"

Jane gave him a disgusted look. "Not when that 'lone male' could have women queuing up outside his door to keep him company!"

He raised dark brows. "I prefer to choose my own female company," he drawled.

"Me?" Jane sighed scathingly.

"In a word—yes," Gabe nodded. "Jane, you're bright, funny, independent, run your own very successful business, and you're very, very beautiful," he added huskily.

She swallowed hard. It was so long since any man had spoken to her like this, had told her she was beautiful. It had been her decision, she accepted that, but why, oh, why did that man now have to be Gabriel Vaughan?

"As opposed to?" she prompted dryly, sure she couldn't be that unique in his acquaintance.

He grimaced. "Oh, undoubtedly beautiful," he conceded. "But also vacuous, self-oriented, self-centred, and usually having no other thought in their head other than marrying a rich man. So that they can continue to be vacuous, self-oriented, et cetera, et cetera," he concluded harshly.

He had just, from what little Jane knew of the other woman, exactly described the woman who had been his wife—Jennifer Vaughan, she'd been tall, beautiful, elegant—and totally selfish!

Jane sighed, closing her eyes briefly before looking at him once again. "Gabe—"

"That's the first time you've dropped the Mr Vaughan." He pounced, sensing some sort of victory. "Do you have the makings of dinner in here?" He took the two bags of shopping out of her arms before she could stop him, looking in at the contents. "Spaghetti bolognese," he guessed accurately seconds later. "I could make the sauce while you see to the pasta," he offered lightly.

"You—"

"Let someone else cook for you for a change, Jane," he prompted determinedly. "I make a mean bolognese sauce," he promised her.

She did a mental inventory of her apartment as she had left it a couple of hours ago: tidy, comfortably so, but also impersonal, no incriminating photographs, absolutely nothing to show the woman she had once been...

And then she brought herself up with a start. She wasn't seriously contemplating taking Gabriel Vaughan into her home, was she?

That was exactly what she was thinking!

What magic had this man worked on her that she could even be considering such an idea? Perhaps it was that "lone male" remark, after all...? She, of all people, knew just how miserable, how desolate loneliness could be...

"No standing around just watching me work once we're inside," she warned as she picked up the flowers before unlocking the door and going inside.

She strode through, giving him little time to look around her open-plan lounge. The large kitchen was wood-panelled, with herbs and spices hanging from the ceiling, pots and pans shining brightly as they hung from hooks placed over the table in the centre of the room— an old oak table that she had bought in an auction at a manor house, its years of constant use meaning it was scored with cuts and scratches, some of which Jane had added herself in the last year.

"Exactly as I imagined it," Gabe said slowly as he looked around admiringly.

How he had "imagined it"...? Since when had he started imagining what her home looked like?

"Since that first night at Felicity and Richard's." He lightly answered the accusing question in her eyes. "You can tell a lot about a person from their home."

Which was probably the reason why she never brought anyone here! She didn't want anyone to be able to "tell" anything about her—

"This is the kitchen of a chef," Gabe announced happily, starting to unpack the shopping bags. "Everything you could possibly need to cook." He indicated the numerous pots and pans. "The knives all sharp." He pulled one neatly from the kniferack. "And a bottle of red wine—room temperature, of course!—to sip and enjoy while we cook." He looked at her enquiringly as he held up the bottle that already stood on the table.

He was right; she had left the wine out so that it would be exactly the right temperature for drinking when she returned home to prepare her meal. But this to "enjoy while we cook" sounded a little too—cosy, intimate. Everything she was hoping to avoid where this man was concerned.

"Lighten up, Jane," Gabe advised laughingly as he read the indecision in her expression, deftly removing the cork from the bottle of wine as Jane busied herself putting the flowers in water. "I was suggesting we share a bottle of wine—not a bed!" He slipped off his jacket, placing it on the back of one of the kitchen chairs.

Jane put the vase of flowers down on the window-ledge with a thump. "You'll find the glasses in the cupboard over there." She nodded abruptly across the kitchen.

Share a bed, indeed! She hadn't shared a bed with

any man since— She shuddered just at the thought of having once shared a bed with Paul!

Luckily she was concentrating on preparing the pasta by the time Gabe came back with the wine glasses, her shudder of revulsion unseen by him. Otherwise he might have wanted to know just why a woman of twenty-eight, obviously healthy, and not unattractive, should shudder at the mere thought of such intimacy...!

Gabe sliced up the onion with one of her sharp knives, and Jane couldn't help but admire the way he diced it into small pieces, ready for sautéing in the butter he had gently melting in a frying pan on top of the Aga. And he was obviously enjoying himself too, perfectly relaxed, humming softly to himself as he worked.

Strange; she had always thought of Gabriel Vaughan as an over-tall man, powerfully built, his face set into grimly angry lines. And this man, grinning to himself as he fried onions, didn't fit into that picture at all...!

He turned to take a sip from the nearest of the two glasses of wine he had poured out for them. "This is fun, isn't it?" He smiled widely at her.

Jane's smile was much more cautious; she had a feeling a little like having been swept over by a tornado, not even sure how the two of them had come to be in her kitchen cooking a meal together. He was the very last man she would have thought she would spend any time with!

"Jane?" he prompted softly at her silence, no longer smiling, frowning at her lack of response.

It was the disappearance of that smile that affected her the most; it had been a completely natural smile, without cynicism or innuendo. He really had been enjoying himself a moment ago as he'd cooked the onions!

And now she felt guilty for upsetting his pleasure...

"You dealt with that onion very professionally," she told him lightly, taking a break to sip her own wine. "At a guess, I would say it's something you've done before!" she added teasingly.

"Dozens of times," he nodded, that light note back in his voice as he turned to toss the onions in the butter. "I've always liked to cook at home," he shrugged. "Although I have to admit I haven't done so for some time." He frowned at the realisation. "Jennifer—my wife— didn't think it was worth bothering to eat at all if there was no one to see her doing it," he added ruefully.

His wife. Jennifer. How the very sound of that name had once hurt her! But now she'd heard it, from the man who had been her husband, and she felt nothing, not even the numbness that had once been so necessary to her.

"There was you," she told Gabe dismissively, suddenly busy with the pasta once again.

"There was me," he echoed self-derisively, tipping in the minced steak to cook with the onions. "Unfortunately, Jennifer was the type of woman who was more interested in what other women's husbands thought of her rather than what interested her own husband!"

Jane hadn't even been aware of holding the knife in her hand, let alone how she came to slice her finger with it, but suddenly there was blood on the work surface in front of her, and, she realised belatedly, a stinging pain on the index finger of her left hand.

How ironic, she thought even through the pain, that it should be her left hand that she had cut. The hand that had once worn her wedding ring...

"It was something I— Hell, Jane!" Gabe suddenly saw the blood too, taking the frying-pan off the heat before rushing over to her side, pressing her finger to stop the flow of blood. "What the hell happened?" He barked his concern. "Do you think it's bad enough to need stitches? Perhaps I should call—"

"Gabe," Jane cut in soothingly—she was the one with the cut finger, but he was definitely the one who was panicking! "It's only a tiny cut. A hazard of the trade," she added lightly, deliberately playing down the problem this cut would give her over the next busy few weeks. Preparing food, having her hands constantly in and out of water—this cut, even though it really wasn't very serious, would cause her deep discomfort for some time to come.

Damn; she couldn't remember the last time she had done anything this silly. Of course, it had been Gabe's comments about his wife that had caused her lapse in concentration...

"You'll find some plasters in the cupboard over the dishwasher," she told him abruptly, moving to wash the cut under cold water as he went to get the plasters, the stinging pain in her hand helping to relieve some of the shock she had felt at hearing him discuss his wife so casually.

Gabe deftly applied the plaster once her finger had been dried. "I don't have a wife any more, Jane," he told her softly, his gaze searching as he looked down into her face.

He believed it was the thought of having dinner with a potentially married man that had caused her to have this accident! Perhaps it was better that he should continue to think that was the reason...

"I'm glad to hear it," she dismissed lightly. "Because if you did," she added as she saw the light of triumph in his eyes, "Evie—the woman downstairs—" she reminded him who had let him into the building—and why "—would be devastated. It would blow all her romantic illusions out of the window!"

"I see," he sighed, nodding abruptly, before turning his attention back to his bolognese sauce. "My wife died," he rasped harshly, no longer looking at Jane.

Because the memory of Jennifer's death must still be a painful one for him, Jane acknowledged. She should know, better than most people, that a person didn't necessarily have to be nice to have someone fall in love with them.

And Jennifer Vaughan had not been a nice woman: tall, beautiful, vivacious, and ultimately dangerous, with a need inside her to bewitch every man she came into contact with, while at the same time eluding any ownership of herself. Only one man had succeeded in taming her even a little. Gabriel Vaughan. And from the little he had so far said about Jennifer, and from what Jane already knew from her own experience, that ownership had been bitter-sweet—and probably more bitter than sweet!

But there could be no doubting that, despite all her faults, Gabe had loved his wife—

"Jennifer was a bitch," he bit out suddenly, those aqua-blue eyes piercing in their intensity now as he turned back to hold Jane's gaze. "Beautiful, immoral, whose only pleasure in life seemed to be to destroy what others had built," he told Jane grimly. "Like a child with a pile of building bricks another child may have taken time and care to put in place; Jennifer would knock it all down, with an impish grin and a flash of her wicked green eyes!"

Jane swallowed hard. She didn't want to hear any of this! "Gabe—"

"Don't worry, Jane," he bit out derisively. "The only reason I'm telling you this is so that you know I'm not about to launch into some sorrowful tale about how wonderful my marriage was—"

"But you loved her—"

"Of course I loved her!" he rasped, reaching out to grasp the tops of Jane's arms, his gaze burning with intensity now. "I married her. Maybe that was my mistake, I don't know." He shook his head impotently. "The excitement was all in the chase to Jennifer." His mouth twisted. "A loving captive was not what she wanted!"

"Gabe, I really—"

"Don't want to hear?" He easily guessed her cry of protest. "Well, that's just too bad, because I intend telling you whether you want to know or not!" he told her savagely.

"But why?" Jane choked, looking up at him imploringly, her face pale, eyes dark brown. "I've asked you for nothing, want nothing from you. I don't want anyone—"

"You don't want anyone disturbing the life you've made for yourself in your ivory tower," he acknowledged grimly. "Oh, I'll grant you, it's comfortable enough, Jane." He looked about him appreciatively. "But, nevertheless, it's still an ivory tower. And I'm giving you notice that I intend knocking down the walls—"

"Doesn't that make you as destructive as you just described your wife?" Jane cut in scornfully, her whole body rigid now, standing as far away from him as his grasp on her arms would allow.

Because those fingers were like steel bands on her

flesh, not hurting, but at the same time totally unmoveable. The only way to distance herself from him was verbally, to hurt him as his words were hurting her.

"Late wife, Jane," he corrected her harshly. "Past tense. And no, it doesn't make me like Jennifer at all. I'm not out to destroy for destruction's sake. I want to build—"

"For the couple of months or so you claim you're going to be in England?" she came back disgustedly, shaking her head. "I don't think so, thank you, Gabe. Why don't you try Celia Barnaby?" she scorned. "I'm sure she would be more than happy to—"

Her words were cut off abruptly as Gabe's mouth came crashing down on hers, pulling her into the hardness of his body, knocking the breath from her lungs as he did so, rendering her momentarily helpless.

And Gabe took full advantage of that helplessness, his mouth plundering, taking what he wanted, sipping, tasting the nectar to be found there. And then finally the onslaught ceased, Gabe having sensed her lack of response.

He began to kiss her gently now, his hands moving to cradle either side of her face as his lips moved caressingly against her own, that gentleness Jane's undoing.

She began to respond…!

Something deep, deep inside her began to break free at the softly caressing movement of Gabe's lips against hers, a yearning for something she had denied herself for the last three years, a warming to an emotion she hadn't allowed in her life for three years.

But Gabe didn't love her. And she certainly didn't love him. And anything else they might be able to give each other would be totally destroyed the moment he discovered who she really was…!

Gabe raised his head slightly, his hands still cradling each side of her face, his eyes glittering down into hers, but not with anger now—with another emotion entirely. "I'm not interested in Celia Barnaby, Jane," he told her huskily. "In any way. The only reason I was anywhere near her home at all the other evening was because I knew you would be there," he admitted self-derisively.

It was as she had guessed, but hoped wasn't true. Gabe had to have been one of those extra guests Celia had telephoned her about—and it had been by his own design.

"I want you, Jane—"

She pulled sharply away from him, breathing easier once she was free. "You can't have me, Gabe," she told him dully. "Because I don't want you," she added as he would have protested, his expression grim now. "I realise it must be difficult for the eligible Gabriel Vaughan to accept that a woman may not want him, but—"

"Cut the insults, Jane," he put in scathingly. "I heard what you said the first time around! What is it about you, Jane?" he added with a shake of his head as he took in her appearance from head to toe, her hair slightly dishevelled now from his caressing fingers, her eyes twin pools of sherry-brown in the paleness of her face. "I've wanted you since the moment I first set eyes on you! Not only that," he continued harshly, "but I've found myself thinking more—and now talking, too—about the wife I've tried to put from my mind for three years. Why is that, do you think, Jane?" His eyes glittered with anger once again, but it was impossible to tell whether that anger was directed at Jane or himself.

She knew exactly why she had thought more of the past, of Paul, her own dead husband, this last week. Gabriel Vaughan, with his own involvement in that death, had brought back all the unwanted memories she had mainly succeeded in pushing to the very back of her mind. And part of Gabe, Jane was beginning to realise—although it was only subconsciously in him at the moment—recognised something in her, evoking his own thoughts and memories of the past.

How long before those subconscious memories became full awareness…?

"I really have no interest in learning why, Gabe," she told him dismissively. "And that's something I do know the answer to—I'm not interested in you!" She looked across at him with cold challenge, her heart pounding loudly in her chest as she waited for his reaction.

He predictably met that challenge, his gaze unwavering. "You know damn well that isn't true—and so do I!" he bit out harshly. "Whoever he was, Jane—" he shook his head "—he certainly isn't worth hiding yourself away—"

"In my ivory tower?" she finished scornfully, angry with herself and him—for the tell-tale colour that had appeared in her cheeks when he had challenged her denial of being interested in him. Because he had breached the barriers she had erected around her emotions, no matter how briefly… "Was Jennifer worth it?" she returned pointedly.

His brows arched, his mouth twisting ruefully. "Neatly turned, Jane," he drawled admiringly. "But completely ineffective; Jennifer, and anything she may have done while she was alive, lost the power to hurt me long ago," he assured her disgustedly.

"How about the pain she caused when she died?" Jane returned harshly.

And then wished she hadn't as she saw Gabe's gaze narrow speculatively. She was becoming careless in her own agitation with this situation...!

"She died in a car accident, Jane," Gabe said softly. "And there's nothing more final than death," he added harshly. "Dead people can't hurt you."

"Can't they?" she breathed huskily.

He gave a firm shake of his head. "If Jennifer hadn't died when she did, I think I would one day have ended up strangling her myself! So you see," he added scathingly, "the only thing Jennifer did when she died was save me the trouble of doing the job myself!"

It wasn't. Jane knew it wasn't. And, no matter how bitter he might now have become about his wife's past behaviour, so did Gabe. Because three years ago, after the car accident in which Jennifer died, Gabe had been like a man demented, had needed to blame someone, and with the death of the only person he could blame he had turned his anger and humiliation onto the only person left in the whole sorry mess that he could still reach...!

Gabe was right when he guessed a man was responsible for her living in an emotional fortress, what he chose to call her "ivory tower".

It was the same man who was partly responsible for her becoming plain Jane Smith.

The same man she had been hiding her real self away from for the past three years.

And that man was Gabriel Vaughan himself!

CHAPTER SIX

"Don't look so worried, Jane," he taunted now. "Those murderous feelings were only directed towards my wife; I actually abhor violence!"

So did she. Oh, God, so did she. But, nevertheless, she was no stranger to it...

"It's said there's a very fine line between love and hate," she said dully.

And she knew that too. She had been so in love with Paul when she'd married him, but at the end of four years she had hated him. For what he had done to her family. And for what he had taken from her.

But she also knew, no matter how difficult to live with, how selfish Jennifer had been, that Gabe had loved his wife. That he had loved her enough to seek out the people he felt were involved in her death...

"Shouldn't we finish cooking this meal?" Gabe suddenly suggested with bright efficiency, placing the frying-pan back on top of the Aga.

Jane continued to look at him dazedly for several long seconds. She had no interest in cooking the meal, let alone eating it, not after what had been said. Or the way Gabe had kissed her minutes ago... She wasn't even sure she could eat after that!

"Come on, Jane," Gabe said briskly. "The food will do us both good." He turned away again, as if what he had just said settled the matter; they would eat dinner together.

Because he was a man used to giving orders. And having them carried out.

But Jane didn't finish cooking the spaghetti for either of those reasons. Quite simply, when she cooked, created, she could forget all that was going on around her. And, after thinking of her marriage to Paul, it was very necessary that she do that at this moment.

"Excellent!" Gabe pronounced with satisfaction a short time later, having almost finished eating the spaghetti bolognese on his plate. The two of them were seated at the huge oak dining table, their glasses replenished with the red wine, the remaining food still steaming hot on their plates. "Maybe the two of us should go into business together," he added in a challengingly soft voice.

Jane gave him a sharp look, knowing by the teasing glitter in his eyes that he was looking for a reaction from her. "I don't think so," she came back dismissively. "Somehow I don't see you working for anyone!"

Dark brows rose. "I was thinking more along the lines of a partnership," he drawled.

She gave an acknowledging inclination of her head—she was well aware of exactly what he had meant! "And I was thinking more along the lines of the clients I work for!"

Gabe laughed softly, forking up some more of his food. "Why a personal chef, Jane, as opposed to the restaurant Felicity suggested the other evening?" he asked interestedly. "Surely a restaurant would mean more customers, more—"

"Overheads," she finished for him. "More people

working for me. Just more complications altogether," she shrugged dismissively.

Although she had to admit that, at the time she'd begun her business it hadn't been for those reasons that she had chosen to go alone. There had been no money to invest in such a risky venture as opening up her own restaurant. Three years ago she had been left with only one commodity she could use—herself. And her talent at cooking had seemed by far the best course for her to take! Even then it had been a painful year of indecision before that option had occurred to her.

"And you're a person that likes to avoid complications, aren't you?" Gabe said shrewdly.

She returned his narrow-eyed gaze unblinkingly. "With only myself to rely on, I felt I stood a better chance of success." She deliberately didn't answer his question.

"But what about now?" Gabe continued conversationally. "You've already effectively built up your clientele; it wouldn't take too much to—"

"Not everyone is as ambitious as you are, Gabe," she cut in firmly. "Three years ago I didn't even have my business—"

"What happened three years ago?" he interrupted softly. "Just curiosity, Jane," he assured her as she gave him a startled look. "Maybe I phrased the question badly," he conceded ruefully as she still didn't answer. "Perhaps I should have asked what it was you did *before* three years ago?"

Until the age of eighteen she had been at school. And at eighteen, instead of going to university, she had chosen to go to France, where she had taken an advanced cookery course. At twenty, a few months after her return home, she had met Paul and they'd become engaged. At twenty-one she was married. And at twenty-five she was widowed. The details of those four years as Paul's wife she preferred not to think about!

And she intended telling Gabriel Vaughan none of those things, wished now that she hadn't mentioned "three years ago" at all. Because it was exactly that length of time since his wife had died...

"I kept busy." She was deliberately noncommittal, studiously avoiding that searching aqua-blue gaze. "But I had always wanted to run my own business." Instead of living in someone else's shadow, always having to tell them how wonderful they were, how successful, how— How *deceitful*!

"And now you have it," Gabe acknowledged lightly. "Is it as much fun as you thought it would be?"

Fun? She hadn't ever expected it to be "fun". She had wanted independence, freedom, hadn't looked for anything else. And her business had certainly given her those things; she answered to no one!

"There's more to life than success, Jane," Gabe added at her lack of reply.

"Such as?" she challenged scornfully; he wasn't exactly unsuccessful himself, so how could he be a judge of that?

He shrugged. "Love," he suggested huskily.

Jane gave a derisive laugh. "I don't see how you can possibly say that when you obviously had a love/hate relationship with your own wife!"

His mouth tightened. "Jennifer did not make me happy," he conceded. "But I thought I'd found the perfect woman," he rasped, his thoughts all inwards now. "And then she just evaporated, disappeared before my eyes."

He looked across at Jane with pained eyes. "I haven't been able to look at another woman since without seeing her image imprinted there. At least," he added gruffly, "I hadn't. Until six days ago."

"What happened—? Oh, no, Gabe," she dismissed scathingly as she realised he was talking of his initial meeting with her. "Does this chat-up line usually work?" she added disgustedly.

"It isn't a chat-up line," he told her steadily. "You know that. And so do I," he added evenly, keeping his gaze fixed on hers.

It was that steady gaze that made her realise he meant every word he was saying!

"You're being ridiculous, Gabe," she bit out agitatedly. "You can't be attracted to me!"

He tilted his head thoughtfully to one side. "That's a very interesting way of putting it."

Again she realised her mistake too late; it was an "interesting way of putting it". And she knew exactly why she had said it that way. But the last thing she wanted was for Gabe to know that reason!

"I'm just not your type," she said impatiently.

Those dark brows rose again. "Do I have a type?" he drawled in amusement.

Jane sighed. "Of course you do," she snapped irritably. "You've always been attracted to tall, elegant blondes. You married a tall, elegant blonde! Whereas I—" She broke off, having realised by the widening of his eyes that she had once again said too much.

She just couldn't seem to help it where this man was concerned. She simply wasn't any good at playing the sophisticated games that people like Gabe—and Paul— liked to play. It was one of the reasons Paul had become so bored with her; he had been sure that the doting daughter and equally doting fiancée were an act, had been furious after their marriage to learn that that was exactly what she was. Her shyness annoyed him, her total love irritated him, and as for the doting daughter—!

It had become a marriage made in hell, her shyness turning to coldness as a way of protecting herself from Paul's taunts; her total love had deteriorated to pity that he obviously wasn't able to feel such emotion himself. And the "doting daughter" had kept all her pain and misery to herself, in an effort to spare her parents the heartache of knowing she had made a terrible mistake in marrying Paul!

"You're a short brunette," Gabe conceded dryly. "Which makes a mockery of the tall blonde." His eyes narrowed. "How did you know my wife was blonde? I'm sure I didn't mention it…"

There was an underlying edge of steel to his tone that hadn't been there before, and Jane realised that a lot depended on her next answer. "Celia Barnaby insisted on talking to me about you the other evening," she told him truthfully, relieved to see some of the tension ease out of his stiffly held shoulders. And it was the truth—except Celia hadn't told her his wife was a blonde either! But if what he had told her about Celia was true, then he was never likely to find that out from the other woman, was he? "I believe the implication was that, being tall and blonde herself, she was worthy of your interest," Jane added mockingly.

He shrugged, relaxed once more. "I seem to have lost my appetite for tall blondes," he returned dryly.

Then it was a pity her hair wasn't its natural honey-blonde; it would have nullified her attraction on one count, at least! But if her hair had still been blonde Gabe would probably have instantly recognised her, anyway. And that would never do!

"Celia assures me that blondes have more fun," Jane derided, having no intention of explaining to him the circumstances under which the other woman had made that remark! She was still unnerved herself at the other woman's realisation of her real hair colour...

"If you like that sort of fun." Gabe's mouth twisted scornfully. "I don't. How old are you, Jane?" He abruptly changed the subject.

She blinked, seeming to have averted one catastrophe—but unsure whether or not she was heading for another one! "Twenty-eight," she supplied with a frown.

He nodded, as if it was about what he had already guessed. "And I'm thirty-nine."

She shook her head. "I don't see—"

"Because I hadn't finished," he told her with mild rebuke. "I'm thirty-nine years old, was married, and now I'm not. I'm a wealthy man, can do what I like, when I like—pretty much as you can, I imagine," he acknowledged ruefully. "The difference being," he continued as she would have spoken, "that for me it isn't enough. When my wife died three years ago— Strange that your life seems to have changed around that time too...?" he added thoughtfully.

Jane held her breath as she waited for him to continue. If he did. Oh, please, God, don't let him pursue that subject!

He shrugged, as if it was something he would go back to another time; right now he was talking about something completely different. "When Jennifer died all

my illusions died along with her," he continued harshly.
"And that illusion of perfection disappeared too."

Not surprising, in the circumstances! He must have
really loved Jennifer to have ever thought she was perfect! But then, hadn't Jane made the same mistake about
Paul...? Love, it appeared, made fools of them all!

"Or so it seemed," Gabe added softly, looking pointedly at Jane.

He didn't seem the type of man who fell victim to
infatuations, and yet the way he was looking at her...!
Maybe she had formed completely the wrong impression
of this man, because at this moment that was exactly how
he was behaving!

"I can assure you, I'm far from perfect," she told him
firmly, standing up to clear away her plate, the food
only half eaten, but the evening over as far as she was
concerned. "I wish you luck in your search for this perfection, Gabe," she added dismissively. "But count me
out. I don't meet the criteria, and, even more important,
I happen to like my life exactly the way it is." Her eyes
flashed a warning.

Because she did like her life the way it was. She was
her own boss, both privately and professionally, could
pick and choose now what she would and wouldn't do.
And she had deliberately planned for it to be that way.
And it was how she intended it to stay.

Gabe clearly saw that warning in her eyes, standing
up too. "Don't you ever long for anything different, Jane?
Marriage? Children?" he persisted.

Jane felt the pain only briefly, bringing a shutter down
over her emotions, her gaze impenetrable as she looked
at him coldly. "Like you, Gabe, I've tried the former,"
she bit out between stiff lips. "And I also know it isn't

necessary for the latter," she added flatly. "And no, I don't long for either of those things." Not again. Not ever again. She belonged to herself, would never be owned by anyone ever again.

Gabe looked at her through narrowed lids. "You've been married?"

Once again this man had provoked her into saying too much. Far, far too much. She seemed to head him off from one direction, only to find he was going in another one that was just as intrusive.

"Hasn't everyone?" she dismissed with deliberate carelessness. "With the divorce rate as high as it is, surely it's inevitable!" she added scathingly.

That aqua-blue gaze remained narrowed on her thoughtfully. And Jane hadn't missed that glance he had briefly given her left hand. But he would find no tell-tale signs of a ring having been worn there, no indentation, no paler skin from a summer tan; her ring had been consigned to a river long ago. Along with all the painful memories that went with it.

"You're divorced?" Gabe probed softly now.

Oh, no, he wasn't going to get any more information out of her that way!

"My father told me you should try everything once," she answered mockingly. "And if you don't like it the first time then don't repeat the experience!" Once again she didn't actually answer his question, and she knew by the rueful expression on his face that he was well aware of the fact, that it was yet another subject he would store away for the moment to be returned to on another occasion.

And he would be wasting his time, now and in the

future; she had no intention of answering any of his questions about her marriage!

"Do your parents live in London?"

She drew in a gasping breath—this man just didn't give up, did he!

"No," she answered unhelpfully. "Do yours live in America?"

His mouth twisted in acknowledgement of her having turned the question back to him. "They do," he drawled dryly, the two of them having cleared the table now. "In Washington DC. My dad was in politics, but he's retired now."

If he thought that by appearing open about his own family she would return the compliment, then he was mistaken! "Do politicians ever retire?"

"Not really." Gabe smiled at the question. "But it's what he likes to tell people. He and Mom have been married for forty years."

And her own parents had been married for thirty. In fact, tomorrow was their wedding anniversary, and she intended going to see them for a few hours on Saturday. Sadly a few hours was all she could bear nowadays.

It used to be so different, her parents doting on their only child. But what Paul had done three years ago had affected them all, and now her father was a mere shadow of his former self, and her mother desperately tried to keep up a pretence for Jane's benefit that everything was normal whenever she went to see them. But Jane wasn't fooled for a minute, and her visits, few and far between nowadays, were as much of a strain for her as they were for her parents.

"Someone should give them a medal," she told

Gabe cynically. "A lasting marriage seems to be a dying art!"

"That isn't true," he defended. "There are lots of happily married couples. Look at Felicity and Richard," he pointed out triumphantly.

"You didn't," Jane reminded him dryly. "You accused me of having an affair with Richard!"

Gabe grimaced. "A natural mistake, in the circumstances."

Jane gave him a look of exasperation. "And just what 'circumstances' would they be?"

He shrugged uncomfortably. "You were very strong in your defence of him."

Because of her past knowledge of Gabe, not because she was actually close to the other couple. Although she did like Felicity and Richard, admired their happy marriage and beautiful daughters. And it had been the destruction she knew this man could wreak that had made her defend them so fiercely. It seemed that defence had succeeded in arousing Gabe's suspicions, but in completely the wrong direction—thank goodness!

"It's an English trait," she answered dryly. "We always root for the underdog," she explained at Gabe's puzzled expression.

His mouth twisted ruefully. "I doubt Felicity and Richard think of themselves as such!"

"I visited Felicity today." Jane looked at him pointedly.

He gave that mocking inclination of his head. "And she told you about my business deal with Richard," he guessed wryly. "And now part of you—a very big part if I know anything about you at all—is wondering what I'm up to now! Will it make any difference if I tell you nothing; it's a straightforward business arrangement, with no hidden agenda?"

Jane still looked at him sceptically. "And what's in it for you?" Because from what Felicity had told her about that deal, he had gained absolutely nothing. And that didn't sound like the Gabriel Vaughan she knew at all!

"It means I can sleep nights," he muttered harshly.

Her eyes widened. "Don't tell me you have a conscience, Gabe?" she said disbelievingly.

"Is that so hard to believe?" he rasped.

She shrugged; three years ago she wouldn't have believed he had a conscience to bother—and she didn't want to start changing her opinion of him now! "I find it so, yes," she answered truthfully.

"Oh, it's there, I can assure you," he bit out. "And I've just realised you very neatly changed the subject again a few minutes ago," he added mockingly.

Jane looked at him with innocently wide sherry-brown eyes. She wasn't actually sure which subject he meant; there seemed to be so many of them that she didn't wish to discuss with this man!

Gabe threw back his head and laughed. "Does that innocent-little-girl expression usually work?" he finally sobered enough to ask.

"Usually—yes." Jane grinned back at him in spite of herself.

"God, Jane, you're beautiful when you smile!" he said with husky admiration. "You're also trying to change the subject—again!" he added chidingly.

She arched her brows. "Am I?"

"Oh, yes," he acknowledged without rancour. "Tell me, do you play bridge?"

"As a matter of fact, I do," she admitted dryly.

"And chess?"

She smiled again, knowing exactly what he was getting at. "Yes," she confirmed wryly.

"Unfortunately—for you—so do I!" Gabe drawled teasingly. "Tell me, Jane, do you believe in love at first sight?" he added softly, his gaze suddenly intense once again.

"No," she answered without hesitation. "Not at second, third, or fourth, either!" she bit out tautly.

He frowned at her answer. "Was your marriage that awful?"

"In its own way. Wasn't yours?" she challenged, once again avoiding talking about her marriage to Paul. "Awful" didn't even begin to describe it! "Even loving your wife as you did?"

He sighed heavily. "Let me tell you about my feelings for Jennifer—"

"Gabe, I don't want to know about your marriage or your wife," Jane cut in agitatedly; she already knew all she needed to know about both those things. "If you're still having trouble coming to terms with what happened, and need someone to talk to about it, then I suggest you try a marriage guidance counsellor—or a priest!" she added insultingly, eyes gleaming darkly.

He drew in a sharp breath. "What the hell do you mean by that?"

"I have no idea," she sighed wearily. "But that's my whole point really, Gabe; I have no idea because I don't want to know. How many times do I have to keep saying that?" she added with deliberate scorn.

"I'm obviously a slow learner," he murmured thoughtfully, picking up his jacket from the back of the chair. "I thought you were different, Jane." He frowned. "I still think that," he added firmly. "I also don't think you're as indifferent to me as you would like to think you are." He shrugged into his jacket. "Thanks for the meal, Jane. And the conversation. Believe it or not, I enjoyed both!"

She did find that hard to believe. Oh, parts of the evening—very small parts!—had been pleasant, but his kisses had had a devastating effect on the emotional barriers she had succeeded in putting up over the last three years, and the conversation about his wife was something she hadn't enjoyed at all, and she couldn't believe Gabe had enjoyed talking about Jennifer either. And Jane certainly regretted having revealed so much about her own life...

"Thank you for the flowers," she said stiffly. "But please don't try and use Evie again to get in here," she added hardly, eyes glittering warningly. "She may be a romantic—but I'm not!"

"And you intend putting her straight about your American fiancée," Gabe guessed easily. "Next time I come here, Jane, it will be at your invitation," he promised.

That day would never come, she inwardly assured herself as she walked him to the door.

Gabe turned in the doorway, gently touching one of her pale cheeks. "I really mean you no harm, Jane," he told her huskily.

He might not mean to harm her, but he had already shaken the foundations of her new life. "I wouldn't allow you to," she assured him firmly.

He gave a wry smile. "Look after yourself, Jane Smith," he told her softly. "Because I very much doubt you would allow anyone else to do so!" came his parting shot.

Jane closed and locked the door before he had even walked down the carpeted hallway to the lift, leaning back against it with a sigh, closing her eyes wearily.

But the action had little effect in closing out the image of Gabe in her apartment, of Gabe kissing her until she responded...

CHAPTER SEVEN

THE house looked the same as it always had as Jane drove down the long driveway. There was snow still on the grass verge and trees, but it had mainly melted on the gravel driveway—evidence that one or both of her parents had driven down it in the last few days.

Jane had always loved this house set in the Berkshire countryside. She'd grown up here from child to teenager in the surrounding grounds and woods. This was her parents' home, where she had only ever known love and the closeness of a happy family.

Although she felt none of that warmth now as she parked her van outside the house. It was no longer the grand house it had once been; the paintwork outside was in need of redoing, and inside only the main parts of the house were kept in liveable order now. The once gracious wings on either side of this were closed up now, being too expensive to heat, let alone keep clean and tidy. There was only Mrs Weaver in the kitchen now to cook and tend the house, a young girl from the village coming in at weekends to help with the heavy housework. Once the house had had a full-time staff of five, and three gardeners to tend the grounds. But not any more. Not for three years now...

Jane got out of her van, taking with her the cake she had made for her parents' anniversary and the bunch of flowers she had bought to signify the occasion. She let herself in through the oak front door, knowing Mrs Weaver had enough to keep her busy without having to answer the door to the daughter of the house.

Jane paused in the grand hallway, putting down the box containing the cake on the round table there, before looking up at the wide sweep of the staircase, briefly recalling the ball that had been held here for her eighteenth birthday—her walking down that staircase in the beautiful black gown her mother had helped her to choose, with her honey-coloured waist-length hair swinging loosely down her slender back.

At the time it had seemed to Jane she had the whole world at her feet, little dreaming that ten years later her perfect world would have been totally destroyed. And as for her youthful dreams that night of Mr Right and happy-ever-after...! As she had told Gabriel Vaughan two evenings ago, she no longer believed in them, either!

Gabriel Vaughan...

She had tried not to think of him for the last two days, and as she had been particularly busy, catering for a lunch as well as a dinner yesterday, she had managed to do that quite successfully. Although she had to admit she had felt slightly apprehensive about the dinner party the evening before, in case Gabe should once again be one of the guests!

But it had been a trouble-free evening. As the last two days had been Gabriel Vaughan-free. And strangely enough, after his initial bombardment of her privacy and emotions, she found his complete silence now almost as unnerving. What was he up to now...?

"Janette, darling!" her mother greeted warmly as Jane entered the comfortable sitting-room, a fire blazing in the hearth—the only form of heating they had in the house now that central heating was an unaffordable luxury. Fires were lit each day in this sitting-room and in the master bedroom.

Her mother looked as elegantly beautiful as ever as she rose to kiss Jane, tall and stately, blonde hair perfectly styled, make-up enhancing the beauty of her face. And despite her fifty-one years, and the birth of her daughter, Daphne Smythe-Roberts was still as gracefully thin as she had been in her youth.

It took Jane a little longer to turn and greet her father, schooling her features not to reveal the shock she felt whenever she looked at his now stooped and dispirited body. Ten years older than her mother, her father looked much older than that, no longer the vibrantly fit man he had once been, a force to be reckoned with in business.

Jane forced a bright smile to her face as he too rose to kiss and hug her, over six feet in height, but his stooped shoulders somehow making him appear shorter, the thickness of his hair no longer salt-and-pepper but completely salt, his handsome face also lined with age.

Guilt.

Jane felt overwhelmed with it every time she visited her parents nowadays. If she hadn't fallen in love with Paul, if she hadn't married him, if her father hadn't decided to groom his son-in-law to take over the business from him one day, handing more and more of the responsibility for the day-to-day running of the company to the younger man, at the same time trusting Paul more and more on the financial side of things too... If only. If only!

Because it had been a trust Paul had abused. And as

his wife, as his widow, Jane could only feel guilt and despair for the duplicity on Paul's part that had robbed her parents of the comfortable retirement years they had expected to enjoy together.

"You're looking wonderful, darling." Her father held her at arm's length as he looked at her proudly with eyes as brown as her own.

"So are you," she answered, more with affection than truth.

Her father had lost more than his business three years ago, he had also lost the self-respect that had made his electronics company into one of the largest privately owned companies in the country. And at fifty-eight he had felt too old—too defeated!—to want to start all over again. And so her parents lived out their years in genteel poverty, instead of travelling the world together as they had once planned to do when her father finally retired.

Guilt.

God, yes, Jane felt guilty!

"I think you're looking a little pale, Janette," her mother put in concernedly. "You aren't working too hard, are you, darling?"

Guilt.

Yes, her parents felt that guilt too, but for a different reason. The life Jane had now, catering for other peoples' dinner parties, was not the one they had envisaged for their only and much beloved child. But none of them had been in a financial position three years ago to do more than offer each other emotional support.

Things were slightly better for Jane now, and she did what she could, without their knowledge, to help them in the ways that she was able. Before she left later this afternoon she would deliver to the kitchen such things as the smoked salmon that her mother loved, several bottles of her father's favourite Scotch, and many other things that simply could not be bought in the normal budget of the household as it now was. Her mother, Jane felt, probably was aware of the extras that Jane supplied them with—after all, her mother had always managed the household budget—but by tacit agreement neither of them ever mentioned the luxuries that would appear after one of Jane's visits.

"Not at all, Mummy," Janette Smythe-Roberts assured her mother. She'd once been Janette Granger, before she'd thrown that life away along with her wedding ring—Jane Smith, personal chef, taking her place. "The business is doing marvellously," she told her. "It's just a busy time of year. But I'm not here to talk about me." She smiled, holding out the flowers to her mother. "Happy Anniversary!"

"Oh, darling, how lovely!" Her mother blinked back the tears as she looked at her favourite lilies and orchids that Jane had picked out for her.

"And this is for you, Daddy." She handed her father a bottle of the whisky that she wouldn't have to sneak to Mrs Weaver in the kitchen later, her eyes widening appreciatively as she saw for the first time the display of roses on the table in the bay window. "My goodness, Daddy," she said admiringly, the deep yellow and white roses absolutely beautiful. "Did you grow these in your greenhouse?" Rose-growing had become her father's hobby in the last few years, and whenever he couldn't be found in the house he was out in the greenhouse tending his beloved roses.

In years gone by, the house would have been full of flowers, a huge display on the table in the hallway, smaller vases in the sitting-room and dining-room, posies of scented flowers in the bedrooms. But not any more; there were no gardeners now to tend the numerous blooms her mother had needed to make such colourful arrangements.

"I'm afraid not." Her father grimaced ruefully. "Would that I had. Beautiful specimens, aren't they?" he said admiringly.

Beautiful. But if her father hadn't grown them, where had they come from...?

Her parents' circle of friends had narrowed down to several couples they had known from when they were first married, and Jane couldn't imagine any of them had sent these wonderful roses either. There were at least fifty blooms there, and they must have cost a small fortune to buy.

Her parents' sudden change of financial circumstances had had a strange effect on the majority of people they had been friendly with three years ago, most of them suddenly avoiding the other couple, almost as if they were frightened the collapse and financial take-over of David Smythe-Roberts' company might be catching!

So who had given them the roses?

"We had a visitor yesterday, darling." Her mother's tone was light, but her gaze avoided actually meeting Jane's suddenly sharp one. "Of course, he didn't realise it was our anniversary yesterday." Daphne laughed dismissively. "But the roses are absolutely lovely, aren't they?" she continued brightly.

He? A sense of foreboding began to spread through Jane. He! Which he?

Her hands began to shake, and she suddenly felt short of breath, sure she could actually feel the blood starting to drain out of her cheeks as she continued to stare at her mother.

"Oh, Janette, don't look like that!" Her mother moved forward, clasping both of Jane's hands in her own. "It was perfectly all right," she assured her. "Mr Vaughan didn't stay very long—well, just long enough for a cup of tea," she admitted awkwardly. "Talking of tea," she added desperately as Jane looked even more distressed, "I think I'll ring for Mrs Weaver to bring us all—"

"No!" Jane at last found her voice again.

Mr Vaughan! Her worst fear had come true; it was Gabe who had come here, to her parents' home, bringing those beautiful roses with him.

Why? It was three years ago now; why couldn't he just leave them all alone? Or had he come here to see the results of what he and Paul, between them if not together, had done to her family?

The man she had spent time with this last week didn't seem to be that cruel, and his actions towards Felicity and Richard Warner didn't imply deliberate cruelty either. But if it wasn't for that reason, why had he come here...?

"I'll take these flowers through to the kitchen and put them in a vase," she told her parents desperately. "And I'll ask Mrs Weaver for the tea at the same time." She had to escape for a few minutes, had to try and make some sense out of what was happening. And she needed to be away from her parents to be able to do that.

"Janie—"

"I won't be long, Daddy," she assured him quickly, his use of his childhood name for her making her want to sit down and cry. Instead she fled from the sitting-room, much to the dismay of her parents, but necessarily for her own well-being.

She drew a deep breath into her lungs once she was out in the hallway, desperately trying to come to terms with what her mother had just said.

Gabe had been here! To her family home. In the house where she had spent her childhood and teenage years.

Why? she inwardly cried again.

She could hear the concerned murmur of her parents' voices in the room behind her, knew that her reaction had disturbed them. Ordinarily she kept her feelings to herself, felt her parents already had enough to cope with. But hearing of Gabe's visit here had just been too much of a shock, so completely unexpected that this time it had been impossible to hide her emotions from her parents.

But she had to calm herself now, put the flowers in a vase, ask Mrs Weaver to serve tea, and take in to her parents the cake that she had made to celebrate their anniversary. She had to keep everything as normal as possible. After all, her parents had no idea she had met "Mr Vaughan" again too...

The housekeeper was, as usual, pleased to see Jane, having worked in the house since Jane was a child. The two of them chatted amiably together as Jane arranged the orchids and lilies in the vase, the very normality of it helping her to put things into perspective. Her family would have their tea and cake, and then they could return to the disturbing subject of Gabriel Vaughan; she felt she had to know what Gabe had found to talk to her parents about during his visit. More to the point, she needed to know what her parents had talked to him about!

Her parents seemed relieved at her relaxed mood

when she rejoined them, thrilled with the cake she had made them, all of them having a slice of it with the tea the housekeeper brought in a few minutes later.

But they were all just biding their time, Jane knew; she could feel her parents' tension as well as her own.

"You'll stay and have dinner with us, of course, darling?" her mother prompted expectantly a short time later.

Jane grimaced her regret. "I'm afraid I won't be able to," she said.

"Another dinner party, Janie?" her father guessed mildly, the regret in his eyes saying she should be attending the dinner party, not cooking it for other people.

"It's almost Christmas, Daddy," she reminded him, looking pointedly at the festive decorations they had already put up. "It's my busiest time."

He sighed heavily. "You'll never meet anyone stuck in other people's kitchens!"

She didn't want to meet anyone! Besides, she had met someone. She had met Gabriel Vaughan...

"Always the bridesmaid, never the bride, that's me," she dismissed teasingly. "But tell me," she added lightly, "besides bringing you the roses, what did Gabriel Vaughan come here for?"

Jane had taken a good look around the sitting-room when she'd returned from the kitchen, looking for any incriminating photographs. There were no recent ones of her in here, only ones of her when she was very young, and then at gymkhanas as she went up to collect one of the rosettes she'd often won. And in those she was a round-faced teenager, with long blonde hair, smiling widely into the camera, a brace on her teeth that she had worn until shortly before her sixteenth birthday.

No, there was nothing in this room to indicate that Jane Smith had once been Janette Smythe-Roberts. And not a single thing in the house, she knew, to say she had ever been Janette Granger, Paul Granger's wife. As Jane had done herself, her parents had destroyed anything that would remind them she had ever been married to Paul Granger, and that included disposing of any photographs of them together. Including their wedding photographs.

"I really couldn't say, dear," her mother answered vaguely. "He didn't really seem to want anything, did he, David?" She looked at her husband for support.

"No, he didn't." Jane's father seemed to answer a little too readily for Jane's comfort. "He just spent a rather pleasant hour here, chatting about this and that, and then he left again." He shrugged his shoulders.

From the little she had come to know about Gabe, he didn't have "pleasant hours" to waste chatting! "Daddy, the man sat back and watched as your company floundered and almost fell, and then he stepped in with an offer you couldn't refuse—literally!" she said exasperatedly. "How on earth could you have just sat there and taken tea with the man?"

"What happened in the past was business, Janette," her father answered firmly, showing some of his old spirit. "And you have to give the man some credit for keeping on most of the original staff and turning the company around."

She didn't have to give Gabriel Vaughan credit for anything! But then, her parents had no idea of the way the man had tried so relentlessly to hound her down three years ago. Oh, Gabe had asked her parents for her whereabouts too, and in the circumstances her parents had decided she had already been through enough heart-ache, and had refused to tell him where she was.

That was when the lies had begun, on Jane's part, her guilt taking on the form of protectiveness from any more emotional pain for her parents. They had already suffered enough.

And so her parents simply had no idea of how Gabe had gone to each of her friends in turn with the same question, how for three months she hadn't been able to contact anyone she knew for fear Gabriel Vaughan would get to hear about it and somehow manage to find her.

Her parents weren't even aware that Gabe was part of the reason she had chosen to open her business under the name Jane Smith. They'd believed her when she'd told them it was because she would prefer it that no one realised she had once been Janette Smythe-Roberts. They'd been through too many humiliations themselves concerning their change of financial circumstances not to believe her!

But now Gabe had been here, to their home, and there was just no way that Jane, having come to know him a little better this last week, believed he had simply come here for tea and a pleasant chat!

"You could have done all that yourself if he had backed you financially rather than taken over the company," she reasoned tautly. He had just done that for Richard Warner; he could have done the same for her father three years ago!

Her father shook his head, smiling sadly. "Gabriel Vaughan is not a charitable institution, Janette, he's a businessman. Besides, I was almost sixty then—far too old to dredge up the youthful enthusiasm needed to turn the company around."

Jane bit back her angry retort, knowing that in a way her father was right about Gabe; he hadn't been the one responsible for breaking her father's spirit. The person who had done that was dead, and beyond anyone's retribution.

Paul, her own husband, was responsible for what had happened to her father's company, for all that had happened three years ago.

And now she was back full circle to those feelings of guilt that always assailed her whenever she visited her parents.

"I still think it's very odd for Gabriel Vaughan to have come here," she muttered.

It was so odd, she decided later on the slow drive home, that she intended, at the first opportunity, to find out exactly what he had thought he was doing by going to see Daphne and David Smythe-Roberts!

"JANE!" Felicity greeted her warmly as she recognised her voice on the other end of the telephone line. "How marvellous! I was just about to call you."

"You were?" Jane prompted warily.

It had taken her twenty-four hours of thought, of trying to sit back from the problem, to try and work out how best to approach solving it. And her problem was Gabriel Vaughan. Wasn't it always?

But the problem this time wasn't how to avoid him, but how to meet him again without it appearing as if she had deliberately set out to do so. Not knowing where his rented apartment was, or where he had set up his office for his stay in England, she had been left with only one line of attack: Felicity and Richard Warner.

She had telephoned the other woman with the intention

of calling in to see her, and at the same time casually bringing the conversation round to Gabriel Vaughan.

"I was." Felicity laughed happily. "I'm feeling so much better now, and Richard and I did so much want to say thank you for all your help—"

"There's no need—"

"So you've already said," the other woman dismissed lightly. "We happen to disagree with you. I suggested we invite you out to dinner, but Richard said that was like taking coals to Newcastle! But being a woman I don't think that's the case at all; I know just how nice it is to let someone else do the cooking for a change!"

Felicity was right, of course. Because Jane cooked for a living, most people seemed to think she just threw meals together for herself like the ones she served to them. She didn't, of course, and one of the few luxuries she allowed herself was to occasionally order a take-out pizza!

"It's a lovely thought, Felicity." She answered the other woman politely. "But there really is no need. And I have no wish to play gooseberry—"

"Oh, but you won't be; we're going to invite Gabe to make up the foursome!" Felicity announced triumphantly.

Jane wanted to see Gabe, needed to see him—wasn't that the reason for her call in the first place?—but did she really want to sit down and have dinner with the man?

The answer to that was definitely no; the last time the two of them had had dinner together Gabe had kissed her until her legs felt weak! But the other side of the argument was that they wouldn't be alone this time, so there would be no occasion for him to take such liberties.

Another positive thing about accepting this invitation was that she wouldn't have organised meeting Gabe again; Felicity and Richard would be their hosts for the evening...

"Jane?" Felicity prompted uncertainly at her continued silence.

She quickly flicked through her business diary that always sat beside the telephone. With only a week to go to Christmas, she really was heavily booked. But she also appreciated she wasn't going to find a better opportunity for meeting Gabe on more neutral ground than this.

Not that she had any idea how she was possibly going to broach the subject of his visit to her parents— or, rather, the Smythe-Robertses—all she could hope was that an opportunity would present itself some time during the evening.

"I only have a cocktail party to cater for on Tuesday evening," she told Felicity thoughtfully. "I just may be able to make dinner for eight-thirty that evening, if that's any good for you and Richard...?" And, of course, Gabriel Vaughan. Because if he wasn't there, the whole evening would, as far as she was concerned, be a complete waste of time.

It wasn't that she didn't appreciate the Warners' invitation, or the reason behind it; it was just that ordinarily there were so many other things she could have done on Tuesday evening—like taking a rest for a few hours.

"Lovely." Felicity accepted instantly. "We'll book Antonio's. Shall we call for you? Or perhaps Gabe would—"

"I'll meet you all at the restaurant," Jane put in quickly, well acquainted with the popular Italian restaurant. "I can't leave until the people at the cocktail party have gone on to the theatre, so I can't guarantee it will be exactly eight-thirty when I get there."

She had no intention—no matter how Felicity might still think she was trying to matchmake!—of going to the dinner party as Gabe's partner for the evening, and she didn't want to give that impression by arriving at the restaurant with him.

"As long as you get there eventually," Felicity said lightly. "See you Tuesday." She rang off.

Jane replaced her own receiver much more slowly. She had her wish—she was going to see Gabriel Vaughan again...

She had never thought a time would come when she would willingly place herself in his company!

She only hoped she didn't live to regret it!

CHAPTER EIGHT

"JANE!" Antonio himself came out of his kitchen to greet her when she arrived at the restaurant shortly after eight-thirty on Tuesday evening.

She wasn't deliberately late: she'd been delayed clearing up from the cocktail party. And then she'd had to change before coming here. Luckily she had taken her black dress and shoes with her, and had been able to drive straight to the resturant once she had finished tidying up.

She and Antonio were old friends. Pasta hadn't been something she was too familiar with preparing two years ago, and so she had gone to the expert so that she might learn before opening up her own business. She had spent a month here at the restaurant working in the kitchen at Antonio's side, and despite what she had heard about temperamental Italian chefs—and Antonio was definitely an example of that!—her month here had been highly enjoyable, and by the end of that time she and Antonio were firm friends.

They kissed each other on both cheeks in greeting, Jane grinning up at the handsome Italian. "I'm meeting Mr and Mrs Warner," she explained.

Dark brows rose over teasing brown eyes. "And Mr Gabriel Vaughan," he added pointedly.

Gabe was here! She hadn't spoken to either Felicity or Richard since the telephone call on Sunday, so she'd had no idea whether or not Gabe had accepted their invitation. Antonio's speculative teasing assured her that not only had he accepted, but he was obviously already here!

"And Mr Gabriel Vaughan." She dryly echoed Antonio's words. "Stop grinning like that, Antonio; this is business." Which wasn't strictly true, but it certainly wasn't pleasure either, not in the way Antonio thought it was!

"Always business with you, Jane." He held up his hands exasperatedly. "Although you never came to work in my kitchen dressed like that!" He looked at her admiringly, the black fitted dress showing the slender perfection of her figure, its short length revealing long, shapely legs. She had brushed her hair loosely about her shoulders, having applied some light make-up, and a peach gloss to her lips.

No, she had to admit, she had never come to work in Antonio's kitchen dressed like this...!

And she had delayed going to the table long enough! "Point me in the right direction, Antonio," she requested.

"I will do better than that." He took a firm hold of her elbow. "Tonight you are the customer, Jane; I will personally show you to your table."

Having the extremely tall, incredibly handsome proprietor of the restaurant guide her through the dining-room to her table wasn't conducive to the low-profile life she liked to lead, with all eyes turning in their direction. And Jane couldn't even bring herself to look at the three people already seated at the table he took her to, aware that the two men stood up when Antonio pulled back her chair with a flourish for her to sit down.

Antonio paused to pick up one of her hands, bending to kiss the back of it lightly. "It's wonderful to see you again, Jane," he told her huskily, devilment gleaming in those dark brown eyes before he turned and walked arrogantly back to his kitchen.

Devil just about described him, Jane decided with affectionate irritation, her cheeks burning with embarrassment. Antonio had deliberately—

"Mutual admiration society?" rasped an all-too-familiar voice.

Jane turned calmly to meet the hard mockery in those aqua-blue eyes, hopefully revealing none of the nervousness she felt at meeting this man again. Nervous, because the last time they had met he had kissed her. And, worse than that, this man had visited her family home, had talked with her parents, and she still had no idea why, or what he had learnt by going there.

"As it happens, Gabe, yes," she answered him lightly. "I admire Antonio as a chef immensely. And I believe he respects my ability too," she added challengingly.

Heavens, Gabe looked so handsome in his black evening suit and snowy white shirt, the dark thickness of his hair lightly brushing the shirt collar. Jane's breath caught in her throat as she returned the steadiness of his gaze.

She had to thrust her trembling hands beneath the table, on the pretext of placing her napkin across her knees, but in reality so that he shouldn't see that shaking of her hands, and speculate as to the reason for it.

Meeting Gabe again, she decided, under any circumstances, was a mistake!

"Good evening, Felicity, Richard." She turned warmly to the other couple. "And once again thank you for inviting me."

"Our pleasure," Richard assured her warmly, much more relaxed than when Jane had last seen him.

"I had no idea you knew Antonio?" Felicity teased interestedly.

Jane ruefully returned the other woman's smile. But even as she did so she could feel that aqua-blue gaze still on her. Had no one ever told Gabe it was rude to stare? Probably, she acknowledged ruefully, but, as she knew only too well, Gabe was a law unto himself, and would do exactly as he pleased. And at the moment, despite how uncomfortable it might make her feel, it pleased him to stare at her!

"I worked here for a while," she explained to Felicity; what was the point in doing anything other than telling the truth? She worked for a living, and, no matter how much her parents might hate the fact that she had to do so, it was an irreversible fact! "It was where I learnt to avoid the flying kitchen utensils," she recalled ruefully; Antonio's patience was non-existent when it came to his cooking staff!

"Temperamental, is he?" Gabe drawled dismissively.

Once again she calmly returned his gaze. "Most men are, I've found," she told him softly.

"You meant in the kitchen, of course," Gabe returned challengingly.

She gave a slight inclination of her head. "Of course," she agreed dryly.

Gabe chuckled, shaking his head. "You meant no such thing," he acknowledged, visibly relaxing as he sat forward, elbows resting on the table-top. "It's good to see you again, Jane Smith," he told her huskily.

She wasn't quite sure how she felt about seeing him again! Her pulse rate had definitely quickened at how handsome he looked in his evening suit, so powerfully male. And yet deep inside her was still that fear of what he might, or might not, have learnt on his visit to her parents' home. And at the moment she wasn't sure which emotion was the dominant one!

"How are the flowers?" he prompted softly at her continued silence. "Or did you give them away to the first person you saw after I left the other evening?" he added self-derisively.

Jane gave Felicity and Richard a self-conscious glance, but they both gave every impression of being engrossed in their menus. Although Jane was sure that Felicity, for one, romantic that she was, was listening avidly to their exchange.

As for the flowers, Jane hadn't been sure initially whether he meant the flowers he had given her or the roses he had given to her parents! Thankfully, his second question had clarified that for her.

"That would have been the height of bad manners, Gabe," she returned coolly. "Especially considering all the trouble you went to to give them to me," she added pointedly.

"Oh, it was no trouble at all, Jane," Gabe returned huskily, eyes glowing with laughter—at her expense. "And you did give me dinner afterwards."

Devil!

She had thought she was meeting him challenge for

challenge, but from the grin Felicity shot her way she knew Gabe had definitely won this particular round. "As I recall," she said derisively, "you had to help cook it!"

"It's such fun cooking together, isn't it?" The effervescent Felicity simply couldn't stay out of the conversation any longer. "We used to do it all the time, didn't we, Richard?" She turned warmly to her handsome husband.

Richard looked up from his menu. "We still do, if your condition is anything to go by!" he drawled teasingly.

Felicity blushed prettily. "I was actually talking about cooking together, darling," she rebuked laughingly.

Jane couldn't help but admire the obvious happiness of this married couple. Felicity was the same age as her, and yet the other woman had a marvellous husband who obviously adored her, two lovely daughters, and a third child on the way.

Jane had longed for those things too once; for a while she'd even thought that she actually had them. Her expression was wistful now as she realised how fleeting that dream had been.

Then she realised Gabe was watching her, dark brows raised questioningly as he saw the different emotions flitting across her face!

She deliberately schooled her features into their usual inscrutable expression. "Time to order, I think," she murmured pointedly, smiling up at Vincenzo as he gave her a friendly wink of recognition.

But her own smile wavered and faded as she turned back and found Gabe was still watching her, the harsh expression on his face saying he didn't appreciate her friendly exchange with the waiter one little bit.

Well, what had he expected? She was twenty-eight

years old, and just because she was disillusioned with the opposite sex that did not mean that men didn't still flirt with her! Besides, hadn't Gabe himself been doing that since the moment the two of them were introduced?

His scowling expression seemed to say it was okay for him to do it, but not any other man!

Which wasn't very realistic on his part; most men liked to flirt, but that didn't mean they wanted it to go any further than that. And Vincenzo was a prime example of that. Jane knew for a fact that he adored his wife. Besides which, Anna would probably beat her husband to a pulp if he went any further than flirting with another woman!

Gabe's scowl lightened slightly as he saw that Vincenzo spoke to Felicity with the same warmth he had to Jane seconds earlier, Gabe's expression becoming rueful as he turned and saw Jane's mocking one. He shrugged, as if to say, Okay, my mistake.

It wasn't the only mistake he had made, Jane decided irritably. He had no right to feel jealous of the other man in the first place! One bunch of flowers and a home-cooked meal did not give him any rights where she was concerned!

But as the evening progressed, with Felicity and Richard's presence ensuring that it went smoothly, it became more and more obvious to Jane that she still had no idea how to introduce the subject of his visit to her parents. It was impossible to introduce such a delicate subject casually into the conversation. Even Felicity's questions to Gabe on how his work in England was going only elicited a dismissive reply that he was keeping himself busy.

By the end of the evening Jane felt thoroughly

frustrated at not being able to find out what she really wanted to know: why Gabe had visited her parents on Friday!

"Did you drive here, Gabe?" Richard asked as they prepared to leave the restaurant. "Or can Felicity and I offer you a lift home?"

"I was hoping Jane might offer to drive me." Gabe answered the younger man, but his aqua-blue gaze was fixed compellingly on Jane at she looked up at him sharply. "I noticed you only drank half a glass of wine with your meal," he drawled. "So I guessed you must have driven here yourself." He added, "I came by cab."

With satisfaction, it seemed to Jane. And he noticed too damn much!

But if she did drive him home maybe then she would find the opportunity—? Who was she kidding? There was no way that she could think of to casually introduce the subject of his visit to the Smythe-Robertses' home!

"I'll drive you home," she offered flatly. After all, with the other couple present, what choice did she have? "Thank you both for dinner." She turned to Felicity and Richard. "I've enjoyed it."

And she had. The food had been superb, as usual, and with the other couple present the conversation had flowed smoothly too. Even Gabe's annoying presence hadn't jarred too much as, after his initial terseness, he seemed set to be charming for the rest of the evening. And so Jane's only irritation with the evening was that question regarding her parents. And the way things stood she might just have to let that go. If it wasn't repeated, then perhaps it wasn't a problem...?

"Jane!" Antonio left his kitchen for the second time that evening as he came out to hug her goodnight, smiling down at her as he still held her in his arms. "I have two wonderful new recipes that you would love," he told her huskily. "Come in and see me when you have the time, hmm?"

She answered Antonio positively, explaining that it would have to wait until after the New Year now, as she was so busy, all the time aware that Gabe was listening to their conversation with a sceptical glitter in his eyes and a mocking twist to those firm lips.

"Sorry about that," she apologised dismissively as they walked out to her van, having parted from the other couple, Gabe's hand light on her elbow. "Antonio and I are old friends."

"So you explained earlier." He nodded tersely as she unlocked the doors. "'Come and try my recipes' is certainly a twist on 'etchings'!"

Jane turned to give him a cold look once they were seated inside her van. "Antonio is a married man!" she told him disgustedly.

"And you have no interest in other women's husbands," Gabe remembered dryly.

"None whatsoever," she acknowledged stiffly as she turned on the ignition, warming the engine, as well as themselves. The weather outside was still icy cold, although the snow of last week had now disappeared. "I would never cause another woman that sort of pain!"

Gabe sat back, perfectly relaxed. "Then it's as well I'm not still married, isn't it?" he said with satisfaction.

Jane made no reply, not quite sure what he meant by that remark—and not sure she wanted to be, either! This man had so many other minuses against her ever becoming involved with him that his being married would have come last on her list of dislikes where he was concerned!

"Perhaps you would care to tell me where I'm to drive you?" she prompted distantly.

"Mayfair."

Where else? Only the best for this man. After all, he didn't like hotels, did he? Too impersonal—

"I telephoned you over the weekend."

Jane glanced sharply across at Gabe before instantly returning her attention to the road. She had received no call from him, no more cryptic messages left on her machine from him, either. But then, as she very well knew, he hated those "damned things"!

She shrugged. "I did tell you I was very busy in this time leading up to Christmas."

"It was Saturday afternoon," he told her evenly. "I decided that if I waited for you to contact me I would be dead in my coffin and you might—only might, you understand!—turn up for my funeral!" he bit out disgustedly.

A long shot, concerning his funeral, she had to agree!

And Saturday afternoon she had been visiting her parents...

"I was out of town," she told him lightly, her heart once again thudding in her chest. But it was probably the only chance she was ever going to have... "A thirtieth wedding anniversary," she told him truthfully. "In Berkshire. A couple called Smythe-Roberts." The last was added breathlessly.

Ordinarily she would never have dreamt of talking of her clients to a third party, but as her parents weren't actually clients… This was too good an opportunity to be missed!

"I've met them," he nodded dismissively. "Working on a Saturday afternoon, too." He shook his head. "You do keep busy," he teased. "Turn left here," he advised softly. "It's the apartment block on the right."

Was that it—"I've met them"? She had finally got around to the subject she was really interested in, and he'd dismissed it with just three words!

And it wasn't true that he had only "met them". He had visited them only the day before she had, had taken them roses; wasn't the coincidence of that worth mentioning?

Jane was so agitated by his casual dismissal that she only narrowly avoided hitting a Jaguar coming the other way as she drove the van over to the other side of the road and parked outside the building Gabe had indicated.

Well, she wasn't going to give up now, not when they had come so close. "What a coincidence," she said lightly.

Gabe's expression was completely blank in the light given off by the street lamp outside. "My renting an apartment in Mayfair?" He frowned. "Do you know someone else who lives here?"

Hardly! Maybe once upon a time her friends might have moved in these sorts of circles, as she had herself, but, as with her parents' friends, most of her own had drifted away too with her own change of circumstances.

Besides, was this man being deliberately obtuse? Probably not, she conceded grudgingly as she saw he still looked baffled by her remark.

"I meant that you know the Smythe-Robertses' too," she explained patiently.

"I think 'know' them is probably putting it too strongly," Gabe dismissed uninterestedly. "I knew their daughter much better!"

Jane stared at him, her whole body stiffening in reaction. They hadn't even met three years ago, so how on earth could he claim to have known her?

"Daughter?" She forced herself to sound only casually interested—although it was definitely a strain on her nerves. "I didn't see their daughter when I was there on Saturday." Well, she hadn't looked in any of the mirrors there, had she?

She was a person who hated lies—being told them and telling them herself—but she was aware she was stretching the truth now, no matter what she might tell herself to the contrary!

"That doesn't surprise me," Gabe said disgustedly, glancing up at his apartment building. "Would you like to come in for a nightcap?"

Would she? Not really. And yet if she wanted to continue this conversation with him...

"Just a coffee would be nice," she accepted. She got out, and locked the van behind them before following Gabe into the building, the man in the lobby ensuring there could be no incidents like the one where Gabe had tricked Evie into letting him go up to her own apartment.

She didn't really want the coffee, found that it kept her awake if she drank it last thing at night. But she wanted to know why Gabe wasn't surprised that Janette Smythe-Roberts hadn't been present at her own parents' thirtieth wedding anniversary...

"Decaffeinated?" Gabe questioned as they entered the plush apartment, switching on the soft glow of lights as he made his way over to the kitchen.

"Thanks," Jane accepted vaguely, following slowly.

The apartment was gorgeous, with antique furnishings, the brocade paper on the walls looking genuine too. Only the best, Jane thought again.

"Do I take it that you had an involvement with the Smythe-Robertses' daughter?" she prompted teasingly as she joined Gabe in the ultra-modern kitchen.

She knew damn well he hadn't been involved with Janette Smythe-Roberts, but she needed to keep on this subject if she were to get anywhere at all.

"Hardly." Gabe barely glanced at her as he moved economically about the kitchen, preparing the coffee. "Spoilt little rich girls have never appealed to me, either!"

Spoilt little—! Jane glared across the room at the powerful width of his back. She might have been over-indulged by her loving parents when she was younger, but marriage to Paul had obliterated any of that. And there was no money now for her to be "spoilt" with!

And this man, after his visit to her parents' home last week, must be aware of that...

"The Smythe-Robertses didn't appear overly wealthy to me." She spoke lightly as Gabe joined her at the breakfast-bar with the coffee.

"Nor me," he acknowledged tightly. "But there was plenty of money there three years ago—and I should know, because I bought David Smythe-Roberts's company from him!—so I can only assume the daughter has it all!"

Jane stared at him. Was that really what he thought?

That she would have gone off with the money and left her parents living in what was, in comparison to how they had once lived, near poverty?

Didn't this man know of the debts there had been to pay three years ago, of Paul Granger's gambling, of the way he had siphoned money out of the company to supplement his habit?

But even that hadn't been enough for Paul in the end, and he had begun to sign IOUs he hadn't a hope of paying. IOUs that on his death had passed on to his widow. IOUs that, because of Janette's own ill health at the time, her father had paid out of the money he had received for his much depleted company, her parents having decided she had already suffered enough at Paul Granger's hands.

By the time Jane had felt well enough to deal with any of it, it was already too late; her father had already sorted it all out.

Only Gabriel Vaughan's need for vengeance had survived that sorry mess, and the only person left alive to answer that need had been Janette Granger, Paul Granger's widow. So Janette had been the one to come under his vengeful gaze.

Because, at the time of her death, Gabe's wife, Jennifer, had been leaving him. And the man she had been leaving him for had been Paul Granger, Jane/Janette's own husband...!

CHAPTER NINE

JANE licked suddenly dry lips, frowning darkly. "You mean that the daughter—"

"Janette Smythe-Roberts, or rather Janette Granger—her married name," Gabe supplied scornfully.

"Are you saying her parents gave her all their money and left themselves—left themselves—?" How to describe her parents' present financial position? Genteel poverty probably best described it. But "spoilt little rich girl" did not best describe her!

"Almost penniless, from what I saw last week," Gabe said much more bluntly. "According to the parents their daughter now lives abroad." The disgust was back in his voice. "Admittedly, she was beautiful—the most beautiful woman I've ever seen—present company excepted, of course—"

"Please, Gabe," Jane protested weakly in rebuke, still totally stunned by his summing-up of Janette Smythe-Roberts. As for living "abroad", there was more than one meaning to that word, and she lived in freedom now, not in another country, as Gabe believed!

And beauty was no good, no good at all, if the person who possessed that beauty was as unhappy as she had been married to Paul. Gabe didn't know, couldn't even begin to guess at the hell her marriage had been. Or the pain that had quickly followed his death...

Gabe grinned now in acknowledgement of her rebuke. "Okay, I'll cut the compliments. But Janette Smythe-Roberts had the perfect face, the perfect body, the most glorious golden hair I've ever set eyes on," he told her grimly. "And all that perfection only acted as a shield to the selfishness within. Do you have any idea what she did three years ago, after her husband died, and her father's company was in trouble? No, of course you don't." He shook his head as he scathingly answered his own question. "There was simply no sign of the grieving widow, the supportive daughter, because Janette disappeared. Just disappeared!" he repeated disbelievingly.

Jane stared at him, taken aback by the interpretation he had obviously put on that disappearance.

But there had been a very good reason why she hadn't been on show, why she couldn't face the barrage of publicity that accompanied the death of her husband in the company of Gabe's wife; why her parents had shielded her from the worst of their financial ruin.

For, like Felicity Warner now, with her husband Richard in difficulties with his own company, Janette had been pregnant three years ago. And upon learning of Paul's duplicity, of how he had taken money from her father's company to back up his gambling, of his intention of walking out on her, and leaving her father's business in ruins and herself pregnant with their child, she had lost the baby that she had so wanted, her own life also hanging in the balance.

Was that the selfishness of Janette Smythe-Roberts that Gabe referred to...?

Because she hadn't "disappeared" at all. She'd been in a private nursing home, under the protection of her parents and doctor, until the danger had passed and she had been well enough to go home—not to the home she had shared with Paul, or even her parents' home, but a rented cottage in Devon, far away from prying eyes.

Gabe had simply chosen to put his own interpretation on how he perceived her disappearance... But he was wrong, so very wrong.

Jane looked at him now. "Is it still possible to disappear in this day and age?" she derided lightly.

"Thousands do it every year, so I'm told." Gabe shrugged dismissively. "And Janette Smythe-Roberts did it so well, no one seems to have seen her since!"

She shook her head. "I find that hard to believe."

He shrugged again. "Nevertheless, that appears to be the case."

"Appears to be" was certainly correct! "Has anyone ever tried to find her?" Jane asked.

Gabe grimaced. "I had some sort of mistaken idea of helping her myself three years ago—"

"You did?" Her surprise wasn't in the least feigned. Help? Gabe hadn't come bearing gifts three years ago, but something else completely! "I thought you said you weren't involved with her?" She tried to sound teasing, but somehow it came out accusingly...

"I wasn't." Gabe grimaced again, his gaze warm now as he reached out and lightly touched her hand. "Do I detect a note of jealousy in your voice, Jane?"

How could she possibly be jealous of herself?

She snatched her hand away as if he had burnt her. "Don't be ridiculous," she snapped, standing up. "I think it's time I was going—"

"I was only teasing you, Jane." Gabe laughed softly as he too stood up. "For some reason that's beyond me, we seem to have spent the latter part of this evening discussing a woman you don't even know—and who I haven't set eyes on for three years!" He frowned. "And we were doing so well until then, too!" he added cajolingly.

That was his interpretation of the evening; until these last few minutes she hadn't even been able to approach the subject that really interested her!

But in a way he was right; talking of Janette Smythe-Roberts and her parents had certainly caused friction in what had, until then, been a lightly enjoyable evening. Surprisingly so, Jane realised. But then, Felicity and Richard had been understandably relaxed after the end of their recent worries, and Gabe had been charming to all of them.

But as she looked up at Gabe now and saw the teasing light in his gaze turn to something much more dangerous she knew it was definitely time she left...

She knew, as Gabe's head lowered and his mouth claimed hers, that she had left it far too late to reach that conclusion...

She wrenched her mouth away from his. "No, Gabe—"

"Yes, Jane!" he groaned, cradling either side of her face with his hands as he kissed her gently—first her eyes, then her nose, then her cheeks, and finally her mouth again.

It was that gentleness that was her undoing. If he had been demanding, or even passionate, she would have resisted, but he just kissed her again and again with those gently caressing lips.

"That wasn't so bad, was it?" he finally murmured, resting his forehead against hers.

"No..." she confirmed huskily. "Not bad." In fact, it

had felt too good. And yet she wished he would kiss her again!

He smiled at her, aqua-blue eyes so close to her own as he gazed into those sherry-brown depths. "How long did you think you could go on hiding, Jane?" he murmured affectionately.

Every alarm bell she possessed went off inside her at the same time, her eyes widening, her breath catching in her throat, every muscle and sinew in her body seeming to stiffen into immobility. "I wasn't hiding from you," she snapped angrily, moving sharply away from him.

Gabe gave her a deeply considering look. "I didn't say you were hiding from me," he pointed out softly.

Jane swallowed hard, thinking back to what he had said. No, he hadn't said that exactly, but— "Or from anyone else, either!" she bit out tautly, glaring at him accusingly.

He shook his head in gentle rebuke. "You've misunderstood me totally."

Had she? Minutes ago he had been telling her about Janette Smythe-Roberts, about the fact that she had disappeared three years ago without apparent trace, and now he was asking her how long she'd expected to go on hiding! What conclusion was she supposed to draw from that?

With her own knowledge that she was Janette Smythe-Roberts—his supposed "perfect" woman he had once seen—there could only be one conclusion to draw. But as Gabe had given no indication, either now or in the past, that he realised she was Janette, perhaps she had jumped to the wrong conclusion...?

She swallowed hard, looking at him with narrowed

eyes. "Kindly explain what you did mean," she invited stiffly.

He shrugged, a smile playing about those sensuous lips. "I was referring to your role in the kitchen—always keeping in the background."

"Always the bridesmaid, never the bride." She came back with the same comment she had made to her father at the weekend, warning bells still ringing inside her, but a little more quietly now.

"Exactly," Gabe nodded, grinning openly now. "While you hide away in other women's kitchens, you're never likely to have one of your own."

His reply was much like her father's had been too!

"But I already have a kitchen of my own," she reminded him mockingly. "You've seen it for yourself."

"You're being deliberately obtuse now," he drawled impatiently. "I meant—"

"I know what you meant, Gabe," she cut in with dismissive derision. "And your remarks are presupposing that I want a kitchen of my own." She shuddered at the thought of it, her experience of marriage definitely not a happy one. "I'm happy the way I am, Gabe," she assured him lightly, picking up her evening bag. "Thank you for the coffee," she added with finality.

"And goodbye. Again," he added wryly.

Jane glanced back at him, not unmoved by how ruggedly handsome he was, or that teasing light in his eyes as he looked across at her with raised brows. But he was dangerous—very much so.

"Exactly." She ruefully acknowledged his last remark. "That word doesn't seem to have worked too well on you so far!"

"Are you sure you really want it to?" he prompted softly.

"Of course I want it to!" she replied sharply. "You—"

"Jane, I have a confession to make..." he cut in reluctantly.

She looked at him warily; he already seemed to have said so much tonight! "Such as?" she challenged brittlely.

He sighed. "Well, I'm not sure just how close you and Felicity are—"

"I've already told you, I'm not especially close to either of the Warners! I just don't like to see injustice." She looked at him pointedly.

He gave a mocking inclination of his head. "Your views were duly noted on that subject," he drawled self-derisively. "But I think you should know—just in case Felicity feels duty-bound to mention it at some stage—that I—well, I sort of mentioned to Richard at the weekend that it might be nice if the four of us had dinner together some time!" he admitted, with a pained wince for what her reaction to that was going to be.

Ordinarily she would have been furious at the machinations behind this evening's dinner invitation, but in the circumstances it was difficult to stop herself smiling. There she had been, racking her brain trying to think of some way of seeing him again, albeit so that she could question him about his visit to her parents, and all the time he had been nefariously arranging such a meeting himself!

But Gabe wasn't to know that!

"You really are a man that likes his own way, aren't you?" she said disgustedly. "So okay, Gabe, we've all had dinner—but I still have to go now," she added firmly.

"Could we say goodnight rather than goodbye?" he prompted huskily. "Goodbye is so final, and goodnight leaves a little hope—for me—that we'll meet again."

Jane couldn't help herself; she did laugh this time, shaking her head ruefully. This man really was impossible.

"Goodnight, Gabe," she told him dryly.

"There, that wasn't so difficult, was it?" he said with light satisfaction as he walked with her to the door, his arm resting lightly about her shoulders. "Drive home carefully," he told her softly.

And, unlike Jane when he had visited her at her apartment last week, Gabe watched her as she walked over to the lift and stepped inside, pressing the button for the ground floor, Gabe still standing in the doorway to his apartment as the lift doors closed.

Gabe had had no need to tell her to drive carefully; she never drove any other way. She was all too aware of how fragile metal and glass could be, the glass smashing, the metal twisting out of all recognition. As fragile as the people inside the vehicle...

She hadn't been the one to go and identify Paul after the accident three years ago; that onerous task had fallen to her father. Jane had been admitted to a private nursing home almost as soon as she'd learnt of the accident, delirious with pain as she lost the baby she had only carried for nine weeks.

It was a time in her life she tried very hard not to think about—Paul's death, his betrayal nothing in comparison with the loss of her baby.

The pregnancy couldn't have happened at a worse time in their marriage: Paul was rarely at home any more, and Jane was no longer bothered by his long absences; in fact she felt relieved by them.

But when she'd found out about the pregnancy she had known that she wanted her baby, wanted it very much, and had thought that perhaps there was something to be salvaged from their marriage after all. But Paul had easily disabused her of that fairy tale, laughingly informing her that he was leaving her to be with Jennifer Vaughan.

Which was what he had been doing at the time of the accident...

The scandal that had followed the two of them being killed together in Paul's BMW had been too much for Jane on top of what she had already suffered. The newspapers had been full of it, her own photograph, as Paul's wife, and that of Gabriel Vaughan, as Jennifer's husband, appearing side by side together in a stream of speculation that had gone on for days on end.

Jane had been too emotionally broken to deal with any of it, and it had been weeks before she was even aware enough to realise that Gabriel Vaughan was looking for her. And as far as she was concerned there had been only one conclusion to draw from his search: somehow he blamed her for the fact that her husband had been involved in an affair with his wife!

That was when she had decided Janette Granger had to disappear, not just for the months she had already been secluded away because of her ill health, but for always if she were ever to make a life for herself.

And so she had disappeared.

But her fear of Gabriel Vaughan had not! Oh, not the Gabe who teased and kissed her; that Gabe was all too easy to like. But the Gabe who had been to visit

Daphne and David Smythe-Roberts last week, the Gabe who could still talk so contemptuously of his believed selfishness of Janette Granger; he was definitely a man still to be feared!

And, while Janette Granger might have been able to disappear without apparent trace, Jane Smith knew better than not to heed that fear...

"GOOD MORNING, Jane. Lovely morning for a run, isn't it," Gabe said conversationally as he fell into stride beside her.

Jane faltered only slightly at the unexpected appearance of her running companion, continuing her measured pace.

And Gabe was right about the morning being lovely; it was one of those crisp, clear days so often to be found in England in mid-December, and with the snow now melted it was perfect for her early morning run. Although its perfection had now been marred somewhat by the advent of Gabe at her side! Gabe was the last person she had expected to see running in *her* park at seven o'clock in the morning...!

They ran on in silence, Jane determined not to have her routine disrupted. She enjoyed these early morning runs, putting her brain in neutral, just concentrating on the physical exercise, unhindered by cares or worries.

And this morning was no different as she continued her run round the park. Gabe, at her side, seemed to have no trouble at all keeping pace with her, for all that he must spend most of his time sitting behind a desk.

"I run too when I'm at home." He seemed to read her thoughts. "And when I'm not at home I usually find a gym where I can work out."

She should have known, by the width of his shoulders and the hard muscles of his stomach and legs. "I'm honoured," she shot back dryly, looking to neither right nor left as she continued her run.

She didn't believe for a moment that his presence here, at this time, was a coincidence. She had told him last week that she ran in the park near her apartment, and now that he knew the location of that apartment it couldn't have been too difficult for him to work out where it was that she ran. It was the fact that he was here, obviously waiting for her, at seven o'clock in the morning, that had surprised her. And still did.

Gabe glanced sideways noting her concentrated expression. "I've had some very strange looks while I've been waiting for you!" Again he seemed able to read her thoughts.

Jane could well imagine he had! The only people here at this time of the morning were the homeless who had managed to find—and keep—one of the benches on which to spend the night, and other dedicated runners like herself, exercising before they prepared to go to work. Gabe, in his expensive, obviously new trainers, designer-logo shorts and sweatshirt top, did not fit into either of those categories.

"I'm not surprised," she drawled, continuing her pounding on the tarmacked pathway.

It was beautiful here at this time of the morning. The birds were singing in the treetops, the sounds of the early morning traffic muted. Ordinarily Jane enjoyed this time of day, but with Gabe for a companion her enjoyment was as muted as the traffic noise!

She stopped once she reached the gate through which she had made her entrance earlier, having worked up a healthy sheen of perspiration, her breasts heaving slightly beneath her white vest-top. Gabe's breathing was much heavier, his chest moving as he took in long gulps of air. Not so untroubled by the exercise as she had assumed!

He looked up at her with a rueful frown. "Okay, so I haven't managed to find a gym since I arrived two weeks ago; I've been too busy chasing after the most elusive woman I've ever known!" he said irritably as there was no change in her mockingly knowing expression.

Jane stiffened. "Janette Granger?" she said warily.

"You!" he corrected impatiently. "Give me a break, Jane. Haven't I proved to you yet that I'm not as ruthless as you initially thought I was?"

Her eyes narrowed, still slightly shaken by his earlier remark. "Is that what it was all about? Your change of heart where Richard Warner's company was concerned," she explained scathingly. "Was it done to impress me?"

Gabe became suddenly still, aqua-blue eyes narrowed angrily. "You know something, you really are the most—" He broke off abruptly, his mouth a thin, straight line. "Do you mean to be insulting, Jane, or does it just come naturally to you?" he grated harshly.

She had been thrown by what she had thought was a reference to her past self, and in retrospect she had just been incredibly insulting. After all, it had been three years; she had changed, so why shouldn't he...?

"I'm sorry," she told him tersely, not quite meeting his own suddenly mocking gaze.

Gabe relaxed slowly, a rueful smile finally curving his lips. "So what happens now?" He lightly changed the subject. "Do you go home and take a shower? Or do you have some other form of physical torture—exercise," he amended dryly, "in mind first?"

Jane smiled—as she knew she was supposed to do—at his deliberate slip. "Coffee, croissants, and the newspapers," she reassured him teasingly.

"Now you're talking!" He lightly grasped her elbow as they turned towards the road. "I could do with a coffee and a sit down."

"Oh, we aren't going to sit down yet," Jane turned to tell him smilingly. "I pick up the croissants and news-papers, and then I run home for the coffee. Usually," she added mockingly as she saw his instantly disap-pointed expression. "As you've obviously had enough running for one day, I'll make an exception today," she conceded, leading the way to the little patisserie down one of the side streets away from the park where she usu-ally stopped to buy her croissants on the way home.

As usual the door to the patisserie was already open and the smell of percolating coffee was wafting tempt-ingly out into the street. Several people were already seated at tables as they entered, sipping their coffee, and indulging themselves with the best croissants Jane had ever tasted—her own included.

It wasn't much of a place to look at from the outside, and Jane could see Gabe's eyes widen questioningly as she led the way through the serviceable tables and chairs to the counter beyond.

"Trust me," she told him softly.

"Without question," he conceded as softly.

The man behind the counter glanced up from his newspapers as he heard their approach, his handsome face lighting up with pleasure as he saw Jane was his customer. "Jane, *chérie*," he greeted in heavily accented

English, moving around the counter to kiss her on both cheeks. "Your usual?" he prompted huskily.

"Usual?" Gabe murmured beside her with dry derision.

She gave him a scathing glance. "I've brought a friend with me this morning, François." She spoke warmly to the other man as he looked speculatively at Gabe. "Two 'usuals', to eat in this morning, and two cups of your delicious coffee," she requested before leading Gabe firmly away to sit at a table by the window.

"First an Italian and now a Frenchman," Gabe muttered, with a resentful glance towards the handsome François.

Jane looked across the table at him with laughing, sherry-coloured eyes. "Multinational Jane, that's what they call me!" she returned laughingly. "Although I'm having more than a little trouble with a certain American I know!"

Gabe returned her gaze with too innocent aqua-blue eyes. "Me?"

She laughed softly at his disbelieving expression. "The part of the injured innocent doesn't suit you in the least, Gabe!"

"I—" He broke off as François arrived at their table, expertly carrying the two cups of coffee, two plates containing croissants, and the butter and honey to accompany them. "That looks wonderful, François." Gabe spoke lightly to the other man. "I'm Gabe Vaughan, by the way." He held out his hand.

François returned the gesture once he had divested himself of the plates and cups. "Any friend of Jane's is a friend of mine," he returned a little more coolly.

A coolness that Gabe had obviously picked up on as

he gazed speculatively across the table at Jane once the other man had returned to the counter to continue reading his newspaper. "Exactly how well do—"

"He's a married man, too, Gabe," she put in curtly. "Now eat your croissants!" she advised him exasperatedly, already spreading honey on one of her own.

"Yes, ma'am!" he returned tauntingly, turning his attention to the plate of food in front of him.

"At last," Jane breathed softly seconds later. "I've found a way to shut you up!" she explained as she watched the expression of first wonder, and then bliss, as it spread across his face after the first mouthful of croissant. As she knew from experience, the pastry would simply melt in his mouth, in an ecstasy of delicacy and taste.

"This guy could make a fortune in the States!" Gabe gasped wonderingly when he could speak again.

"This 'guy' is doing very nicely exactly where he is, thank you very much," Jane told him warningly. "Tempt him away from here at your peril!" She simply couldn't envisage a morning now without François's croissants to start her on her way!

Gabe took another bite of the croissant, as if he couldn't quite believe the first one could have been quite that delicious. "I'd marry him myself if he weren't already married," he murmured seconds later. "How are you on croissants, Jane?" he added, brows arched hopefully.

"Not as good as François," she answered abruptly. She didn't find any talk of marriage, even jokingly, in the least bit funny!

"Pity," Gabe shrugged, spreading more honey on what

was left of his first croissant. "I guess I'll just have to stick to François!"

He most certainly would!

Not that she didn't realise he had meant the remark to be a teasing one; it just wasn't a subject she could joke about. And certainly not with Gabriel Vaughan.

Of all people, never with him...!

CHAPTER TEN

"TELL me," Jane prompted derisively as they lingered over their second cup of coffee, "what would you have done if I hadn't turned up for a run in the park this morning?" She looked mockingly across at Gabe.

He shrugged. "I have faith in your determination, Jane, no matter what I may have said to the contrary the other evening!"

She put her cup down slowly, her expression wary. "My determination…?"

"You don't look in the least like a fair-weather runner to me." He looked admiringly at her slender figure.

And Jane didn't in the least care for that look.

"After that wonderful meal we had last night, I thought I ought to join you this morning," he added ruefully. "I just wasn't sure of your starting time, although I didn't think it would be too late, not with your work schedule," he added teasingly.

"You're certainly a persistent man," she said distractedly.

Gabe looked unperturbed. "Something I inherited from my father—"

"The politician," Jane recalled dryly.

"Retired," Gabe acknowledged ruefully, although he looked pleased that she had remembered.

"So he claims." Jane remembered that conversation

only too well. In fact, she remembered all of her conversations with Gabe. "I usually take a break from running at the weekends," she explained, still distracted by his persistence. "It tends to be my busiest time anyway. Although, as it happens, I do usually run later in the morning than this; today I'm up and about early because I'm catering for a lunch."

"To my good." He huskily acknowledged the breakfast they had just shared together. "It would have been even more pleasurable if we hadn't parted at all last night—but I realise I can't have everything!" He looked across at her with teasing eyes.

"You certainly can't where I'm concerned!" Jane dismissed laughingly as she stood up; she had virtually given up trying to stop Gabe coming out with such intimate remarks about the two of them—he took little or no notice of her protests, anyway! "Time I was going," she told him briskly. "I have work to do," she added pointedly.

"So do I, madam, so do I," he drawled in rebuke as he followed her back to the counter. "Let me—"

"My treat," she insisted firmly, handing over the correct money to François. "Gabe thinks you should go to the States and make your fortune, François," she told the other man lightly.

"And deprive myself of the pleasure of paying all these English taxes every year?" François returned with a Gallic shrug. "Besides, I have an English mother-in-law," he confided to Gabe with a pointed roll of warm brown eyes. "And an English mother-in-law has to be the most formidable in the world!" he added heavily.

"All the more reason to leave the country, I would

have thought," Gabe returned sympathetically, his eyes twinkling with his enjoyment of the conversation.

"There is no way she would let me take her two grandchildren with me, let alone her daughter!" François shook his head with certainty. "Not that my wife would be agreeable to such an idea, either," he added frowningly. "You know, ten years ago, when I first met her, she was very sweet and very beautiful, always agreeable. But with the passing of time she grows very like her mother…!" He gave another expressive Gallic shrug.

"Did no one ever warn you to look at the mother before marrying the daughter?" Gabe drawled mockingly.

"Er—excuse me?" Jane cut in pointedly on this man-to-man exchange. Did Gabe get on with everybody? It seemed that he was able to put most people at their ease, was able to adapt to any situation. Strange; three years ago she had had an impression of him being a much more rigid individual… "When the two of you have quite finished…?" she added ruefully.

Gabe looked down at her with mocking eyes. "Perhaps it would be a good idea for me to meet your mother…!" he murmured tauntingly.

But he had already done so! And, from the comments he had made to her after that meeting with the Smythe-Robertses, he had obviously liked both her parents.

"Sorry to disappoint you," Jane derided. "But I'm nothing like my mother! She's sweet and kind, and has been completely devoted to my father from the day she first met him!" She didn't think she was necessarily unsweet, or unkind, but she had one failed marriage behind her, and no intention of ever repeating the experience!

The two men laughed at her levity, although Gabe's smile faded once they were once again outside in the street, his hand light on her elbow. "You know, Jane, we can't all be as lucky with our first choice of partner as our parents have been," he told her gruffly. "In fact, I've often thought that my own parents' happy marriage gave me the mistaken idea they were all like that!" He shook his head in self-derision.

He could be right in that surmise, Jane allowed. She knew that she had viewed her own marriage, at age only twenty-one, to be a lifetime commitment to love and happiness. It had taken only a matter of months for her to realise that with Paul that was going to be hard work, if not impossible. But she had made the commitment, and so she had worked at the marriage. Unfortunately, Paul hadn't felt that same need...

"With hindsight, I'm sure our parents' marriages are the exception, not the rule," she said tightly.

"Probably." Gabe nodded thoughtfully, glancing at his wristwatch. "Now that's dinner and breakfast I owe you." He quirked dark brows. "Any chance we could start with the dinner?"

And end up having breakfast together the next morning...!

Gabe certainly had to be given marks for trying. After all, he had waited at the park for her this morning in the hope she would turn up. And she hadn't thought that a man like Gabe—rich, handsome, and available—would chase after any woman so persistently, let alone one who was obviously so reluctant to be chased! But perhaps that was the appeal...?

"I did tell you this is my busy time—"

"Even Santa Claus has some time off before the big day," Gabe reasoned persuasively.

"But as it happens," she continued firmly, "I'm free

this evening. It's very rare for me to organise a lunch and a dinner on the same day," she explained dismissively.

"And today you have a lunch," Gabe said with satisfaction. "My lucky evening!"

It could be. But then again, it might not be, not if all he was after was a conquest...

"And how do you know Father Christmas takes time off?" she asked inconsequentially.

Gabe burst out laughing. "I wondered if you would pick me up on that one!"

She would pick him up on anything she felt she should. But as she glanced at him she saw he was looking at his watch once again. "Am I keeping you from something? Or possibly someone?" she added dryly.

His mouth quirked. "As it happens—both those things! I have an appointment at ten o'clock, and after our run I need a shower before going to the office."

Jane's returning smile lacked humour. "Some other unlucky person whose business is in trouble?"

Gabe shook his head, looking at her with narrowed eyes. "I would like to know who gave you this detrimental version of my business dealings," he drawled irritably. "I could thank them personally!"

Not really! It was Paul who had told her all about Gabriel Vaughan and the way he did business, and he had been out of Gabe's—and anyone else's—reach for three years...

She shrugged. "It isn't important—"

"Maybe not to you," Gabe bit out tersely. "But it sure as hell is to me! I may have stepped in and taken a business over when it was in danger of failing— If I hadn't done it then someone else would have!" he defended harshly at her sceptical expression. "And at least with me the original workforce, and often the management too, would be kept on if they weren't the reason for the problem."

As he had with her father's company...except for her father, of course! "Somehow, Gabe, you don't strike me as a knight in shining armour—"

"I'm well aware of how I strike you, Jane," he rasped tautly. "And I'm doing my damnedest to show you how wrong you are!"

And in part, she realised with a worried frown, he was succeeding. Because several times in their new acquaintance she had been surprised by his actions, found them difficult to place with the ruthless shark she had originally thought him to be...

"Oh, to hell with this," he suddenly snapped impatiently. "Just tell me when and where this evening, and I'll meet you there. And try not to make it in yet another establishment where the male proprietor greets you like a long-lost lover, hmm?" he added grimly.

He was jealous! Of Antonio and François. He had been pleasant to both men; in fact, this morning she had noted how easy he found it to get along with people and put them, as well as himself, at their ease. And yet that continued show of relaxation hid another emotion completely.

"Caroline's," she told him, adding the address of her favourite French restaurant. "Hopefully we'll be able to get a table for eight o'clock," she added dryly. "Although that may be difficult this close to Christmas."

"Do I take it that Caroline is a female?" Gabe muttered warily.

"You do," Jane nodded. "But it's her husband Pierre who does the cooking," she added with a grin.

"I give up!" Gabe sighed disgustedly, glancing at his watch once again. "And I'm sure you'll have no trouble getting us a table—even if it is Christmas!" he dismissed exasperatedly. "I'll meet you there at eight o'clock. Now I really do have to go!" He bent and kissed her briefly on the lips before turning and running off towards the main road where, hopefully, he would be able to flag down a taxi to take him home.

Jane watched him go, ruefully shaking her head as she did so. The man had a way of first bursting in and then bursting out of her life!

And of kissing her whenever he felt like it!

He had dropped that kiss lightly on her lips just now, as if they were two lovers parting briefly to be reunited later in the day. Which was exactly what they were going to do. But they certainly weren't lovers!

Nor ever likely to be either...!

JANE sat at the table waiting, a frown marring her brow as she remembered the telephone message that had been left on her answer machine when she'd got in earlier.

"Janette, darling," her mother had greeted excitedly. "Such fun, darling! Daddy and I have decided to come up to London for the day, and we thought it would be marvellous if we could all have tea at the Waldorf like we used to. Daddy and I will be there at four-thirty. But don't worry if you aren't able to make it," she'd added doubtfully. "If that's the case I'll give you a ring in a few days' time."

A few days' time...! There was no way Jane could wait a few days before finding out what had prompted her parents to come up to London.

The London house had been sold three years earlier

along with the rest of their surplus needs, and with it most of their London friends had disappeared too. Besides, Jane knew there was little cash to spend on a day in London, let alone tea at the Waldorf...

Tea at the Waldorf had always been a first-day-home-from-boarding-school treat that she and her mother had indulged in, her father usually too busy to join them.

But that wasn't the case today, and luckily Jane had returned from catering the lunch to receive her mother's recorded message in time for her to get to the Waldorf.

A day in London...

Her parents rarely came to London nowadays, and when they did it wasn't done spontaneously, as this visit appeared to have been. And it was never just for the day; the two of them usually stayed with Jane for several days.

So here she sat, the troubled frown still marring her brow, the time one minute to four-thirty...

Her mother looked transformed as she entered the hotel, radiant in a fine woollen rose-pink suit, her hair newly coloured and styled, her smile graciously lovely as she greeted several other people she knew at the tables as she and Jane's father approached their own reserved table.

Jane's father looked the tall, handsome man she had known when she was a child and teenager, his smiles of greeting as warm as her mother's.

But Jane's feelings of pleasure at the change in her parents were tinged with trepidation as she wondered at the reason for that change...

"Darling!" Her mother kissed her warmly on the cheek as Jane stood up on their arrival at the table.

"Janette." Her father greeted her more sedately, but there was a teasing glitter in the warmth of his eyes.

"This was a lovely idea," Jane smiled as they all sat down. "Thank you both for inviting me."

But still her feelings of trepidation wouldn't be pushed aside. Although it wouldn't do to just blurt out her curiosity concerning their spontaneity. Besides, she didn't want to wipe out that happy light in the two faces she loved best in the world.

"Have you had an enjoyable day?" she asked casually once their sandwiches and tea had been placed on the table, the latter in front of her mother so that she could pour the Earl Grey into the three china cups. "It's a little late for Christmas shopping, and the weather hasn't exactly been brilliant for walking around the shops." There had been flurries of snow and rain most of the day, and the wind was bitterly cold.

"Everywhere looks so festive we didn't notice." Her mother smiled her pleasure. "I had forgotten how wonderful everywhere looks at this time of the year," she added wistfully.

Jane had barely noticed the decorations, she had to admit, not because she didn't like Christmas, but because until the evening of the twenty-fourth of December she would be worked off her feet providing other people's food for the festive season. Christmas Day she would spend with her parents, and on Boxing Day the round of parties and dinners would all begin again. But, yes, everywhere did look rather splendid, and, without her being aware of it until this moment, she was feeling lightened by some of the Christmas spirit herself.

And part of her now wondered just how much of

that was due to the presence of Gabriel Vaughan in her life...

She quickly pushed the question to the back of her mind, not wanting to know the answer. He couldn't be coming to mean anything to her; he just couldn't!

"Was there a special reason for your coming up to town today?" she queried as she took her cup of tea from her mother.

Her parents looked briefly at each other before her father answered her. "Actually, Janette, I had a business meeting. Don't look so surprised." He laughed at her shocked response to his statement. "I do still have some contacts in the business world, you know," he chided teasingly.

And most of those contacts hadn't wanted to know when he'd run into financial difficulty and had to relinquish his company. To Gabriel Vaughan...

But, whatever had transpired earlier today at this "business meeting", her father was transformed from that man already grown old at only sixty-one, his shoulders no longer stooped and defeated, that playful twinkle back in his eyes.

"I know you do, Daddy," she soothed apologetically. "I just thought—I believed—"

"That I had turned my back on all that," he finished lightly. "As most of them turned their back on me," he added tightly, the first time he—or her mother—had ever indicated the pain they had suffered over the last three years because of the defection of their so-called friends. "Retirement isn't all it's cracked up to be, you know," he added wryly, stirring sugar into his tea.

Especially when it had been forced on him!

But, nevertheless, her father was now sixty-one; he

couldn't seriously be considering fighting his way back into the business arena at this stage of his life...

Jane looked across at her mother, but her mother only had eyes for her husband: proud and infinitely loving. That love and pride in her mother for her father had never changed.

As it hadn't in Jane. It was just that she could see something else in her mother's gaze today, something she couldn't quite put a name to...

"Well, don't keep me in suspense, Daddy." She turned back to her father. "Tell me what you've been up to!"

"I haven't been 'up to' anything," he smiled at her frustration. "And I'm not sure I should actually tell you anything just yet," he added less assuredly. "Not until things are a little more settled. What do you think, Daphne?" A little of the hesitancy that had been with him so much over the last three years crept back into his face as he looked at Jane's mother for guidance.

"I think everything is going to work out splendidly," Daphne answered him firmly, one of her hands reaching out to rest briefly on his. "But I'm sure it can all wait until after Christmas," she added briskly. "You are still coming to us for Christmas Day, aren't you, Janette?" She looked across at her encouragingly.

Where else could she possibly be going for Christmas? Besides, she always spent Christmas with her parents. Even during the really bad times with Paul, Christmas had been a family time, when they had all been together, happily or not.

And she couldn't say she was particularly happy now with the way the conversation had been turned away from her father's business meeting earlier today. She never had been able to stand mysteries, and that dislike had been heightened during her marriage to Paul, when everything he did and said had become questionable. Until it had got to the stage where she'd stopped asking and he'd stopped telling!

"Of course I am," she assured them brightly. "But are you really not going to tell me anything else about what is obviously good news?"

Her father laughed. "Do you know, Janie, I haven't seen you pout like this since you were a little girl?" he explained affectionately at her hurt look.

Jane gave a rueful grin; maybe she had been trying a little too hard! "Did it work?" She quirked mischievous brows.

"Maybe back then," her father conceded warmly. "But you're twenty-eight now; it doesn't have the same impact."

She laughed. It was a long time since she had heard her father being quite this jovial. But she liked it. Whatever the reason for the change in him, and her mother, she could only thank whoever was responsible.

"Drink your tea, Janette," her mother encouraged briskly. "Your father and I have a train to catch in a couple of hours."

She sipped obediently at her tea; her mother was certainly starting to sound like her old self again too. In fact, it felt as if all of them were emerging from a long, dark tunnel...

"Why aren't you staying with me as you usually do?" she prompted lightly. "Do you have to rush back?"

"You're so busy, darling." Her mother smiled understandingly. "We don't want to intrude on what little time you do have for yourself. I know you never mention any young men in your life, but you're so beautiful, darling—more beautiful with your blonde hair, of course," she sighed, "but—"

"Now let's not start that, Daphne," her husband rebuked gently. "I agree with you, of course, but young women of today seem to change the colour of their hair depending on which outfit they're wearing! Janette may decide to be a flaming redhead by next week!"

"I don't think so, Daddy," she assured him dryly—although she was glad to have the subject changed from "young men" in her life! Until Gabe had forced himself into her life just under two weeks ago, there had been no man in her private life at all in the last three years. And she didn't think Gabe was at all the sort of "young man" her mother was talking about!

"Neither do I, really." Her father gave an answering smile. "And your mother is right, Janie—you are beautiful. And one bad experience shouldn't sour you for any future—"

"It did, Daddy," she cut in firmly. "There have been no young men, there is no young man, and there will be no young men, either!" She didn't consider Gabe a young man at all, and he wasn't in her life—instead he kept trying to pull her into his!

"And just how do you think I'm ever going to become a grandfather if you stick to that decision?" her father chided softly.

"Adoption?" she suggested helpfully.

"Now stop it, you two." Her mother tutted. "It's been a wonderful day, it's nearly Christmas, and I won't have the two of you indulging in one of your silly going-nowhere conversations. More tea, David?" she added pointedly.

It was wonderful to see her parents looking, and

being, so positive once again. And, Jane realised on her
way back to her apartment an hour later, it was the first
time for a very long time—three years, in fact!—that she
had spent time with her parents without those feelings
of guilt that had been like a brick wall between them.

Their lives were changing.

All of them.

Her own because of Gabriel Vaughan, she realised.

But if her parents were to realise, were to know that
Gabe was the "man in her life" at the moment, albeit
by his own invitation, how would that affect their own
new-found happiness?

Not very well, she accepted frowningly. And nothing,
absolutely nothing, must happen to affect her parents'
mood of anticipation for the future.

Which meant, she decided firmly, that tonight had
to be the last time, the very last time, that she ever saw
Gabe...

CHAPTER ELEVEN

"I FIND it very difficult to believe, with the catering connections you seem to have, that you couldn't book a table at a restaurant for us anywhere!" Gabe didn't even pause to say hello as he strolled into her apartment. "So we're eating at home again, hmm?" He turned in the hallway and grinned at her.

Jane's mouth had dropped open indignantly at his initial bombardment as he came through the open doorway, but his second remark, and that grin—!

"What can I say?" she shrugged. "It's Christmas!"

Heavens, he looked gorgeous!

She had spent the last two hours telling herself that Gabe meant nothing to her, that they would have dinner together, and then she would tell him this was goodbye. And this time she intended making sure he knew she meant it!

But he did look so handsome in the casual blue shirt worn beneath a grey jacket, and black trousers.

It wasn't true that she couldn't get a table at the restaurant: Caroline and Pierre were old friends; they would have found a table for her even if they'd had to bring another one into the restaurant for her! But a restaurant wasn't the best place for her to say goodbye to him, especially if he should prove difficult—as he had done in the past... And so she had acquired his telephone number from Felicity and called to tell him they were eating at her apartment instead.

"I brought the wine." Gabe held up a marvellously exclusive—and expensive—bottle of red wine. "You didn't say what we were eating, but I guessed it wouldn't be beans on toast!" he said with satisfaction.

"You guessed it was eggs, hmm?" she came back derisively.

Gabe gave her a chiding look. "I've had a good day, Jane; don't spoil it by serving me eggs!"

She grimaced as she took the bottle of wine and went back into the kitchen where she had been when he'd rung the bell. "Everyone seems to be having a good day today," she murmured as she uncorked the wine, remembering her parents' happiness earlier. "Stay away from those pots, Gabe," she warned sharply as he would have lifted one of the saucepan lids. "Anticipation is half the fun!"

"I know, Jane."

She became very still, turning slowly to look at him. And then wished she hadn't. Gabe was looking at her as if he would like to make her his main course!

And she'd deliberately dressed down this evening, wearing a green cashmere sweater she had bought several years ago when she was still blonde, and a black fitted skirt, knee-length, not so short as to look inviting.

What she didn't realise was how much more the green colour of her sweater suited the new darkness of her hair, picking out those red highlights—she almost appeared the "flaming redhead" her father had referred to this afternoon!

"Glasses, Gabe," she told him through stiff lips.

"Certainly, Jane." He gave a mocking inclination of

his head before strolling across the kitchen, opening the correct cupboard and taking out two glasses.

Maybe having dinner at her apartment wasn't such a good idea, after all! Gabe was too comfortable, too relaxed, altogether too familiar with her home. And not just with her home, either…!

"What shall we drink to?"

While she had been lost in thought, Gabe had poured the wine into the two glasses, holding one out to her now.

"Good days?" he suggested huskily.

That had to be better than "us"!

This had not been a good idea. She could only hope the time would pass quickly.

"Why don't you go through to the sitting-room and pick out some music to play while I serve our first course?" she suggested abruptly, her usual calm having momentarily deserted her.

But then, when didn't it when she was around this man? It was past time to say goodbye to him!

"So why did you have a good day?" she prompted conversationally as they sat down to their garlic prawns with fresh mayonnaise, an old John Denver CD of hers playing softly in the background.

Gabe's gaze met hers laughingly. "Well, this morning I went for a run for the first time in two weeks—"

"Shame on you, Gabe!"

"Mmm, this tastes wonderful, Jane." He had just tasted his first prawn dipped in the mayonnaise. "I can hardly wait to see what we have for the main course!"

With any luck, his enjoyment of the food would stop him talking too much.

She could live in hope!

The wine, as she had already guessed when she'd seen the label, was beautiful—rich and silky smooth. Only the best for Gabriel Vaughan.

"Did you have a good day too?" Gabe looked up from his food to ask her, frowning at her derisive smile. "What...?" he prompted warily.

She gave a mocking shake of her head. "We don't have to play those sorts of games, Gabe," she told him dryly. "We're having dinner, not spending the rest of our lives together!" she explained scornfully at his puzzled expression.

"It starts with conversation, Jane, eating dinner together, finding out about each other, likes and dislikes, things like that. People don't leap straight into marriage—"

"I don't believe I mentioned the word marriage, Gabe." She stood up abruptly, their first course at an end as far as she was concerned.

"As I've already said," Gabe murmured, turning in his chair to watch her departure into the kitchen, "he must have been some bastard."

She didn't remember him saying any such thing! But, nevertheless, he was right; that was exactly what Paul had been.

Their used plates landed with a clatter on the kitchen worktop, her hands shaking so badly she'd had trouble carrying them at all.

What was wrong with her?

She had made a conscious decision this afternoon to tell Gabe this was definitely the last time they would see each other. One look at him and she knew her resolve had weakened. One smile from him, and she began to tremble. If he should actually touch her—

"Anything wrong—? Hell, Jane, I only touched your arm!" Gabe frowned down at her darkly as Jane had literally jumped away from the touch of his hand on her arm. "What the hell is wrong with you tonight?"

She had asked herself the same question only seconds ago!

And, looking at him, she was beginning to realise what the answer was…

No!

She couldn't have those sorts of feelings towards Gabe, couldn't actually want him to touch her, to make love to her?

But she did; she knew she did! And she hadn't felt this way since— But no—she hadn't ever felt quite this way towards Paul. She'd never trembled at the thought of him touching her, had never ached for his lips on hers.

But she'd loved Paul. She wasn't in love with Gabe. If she was anything, she was in lust with him!

Oh, God…!

"What is it, Jane?" he prompted again, his frown having deepened to a scowl at her continued silence.

She had to pull herself together, finish the meal—she doubted he would consider leaving before then!—and then she must make it absolutely plain to him that she did not want him appearing in her life whenever he felt like it; that there would be no more runs together in the park, no more turning up at her apartment, and no more impatient messages left on her answer machine.

And, most important of all, there would be no further occasion for him to kiss her!

"Sorry," she dismissed lightly. "My thoughts were miles away when you came into the kitchen, and I'm a little tired too, I'm afraid." She gave him a bright, meaningless smile as she voiced these excuses for her extraordinary behaviour, at the same time totally distancing herself from him as she crossed the kitchen to check on the food simmering on the hob. "If you would like to go back to the dining area, I'll serve our main course and bring it through in a few minutes."

She deliberately didn't look up at him again before she began to do exactly that, but all the time she busied herself with the food she was aware of him still standing across the other side of the kitchen, watching her with narrowed, puzzled eyes. And then, with a frustrated shake of his head, he turned and impatiently left the room.

Jane leant weakly against the table in the middle of the kitchen. She had never wanted any man the way she wanted Gabe!

And there was no way, simply no way, she could ever assuage this sudden hunger she felt for his kisses and his touch.

She had always thought of him—when she'd allowed herself to think of him at all—as a man who took his pleasure where he found it, and then moved on. But the one thing she had learnt about him since his reappearance into her life was that if Gabe wanted something, then he didn't relinquish his right to it easily. And she didn't doubt for a moment that, physically at least, Gabe wanted her as much as she wanted him.

And she also didn't doubt that to give him what he wanted wouldn't mean it would end there…

Goodbye was the word she had to say to him. Not angrily; it had to be said in such a way that he would never want to come back.

The ache inside her would go away, she assured

herself as she served the noisettes of lamb with tarragon sauce and the still crunchy vegetables from the steamer, and then everything could go back to the way she liked it—untroubled, and uncomplicated.

Why did that realisation suddenly hold no appeal for her?

Ridiculous. That was what this whole situation was—ridiculous! Thank you. And goodbye. Four words. Very easy to say.

But could she say them as if she meant them?

Her heart skipped a beat when Gabe turned to smile at her as she came in with the food.

Thank you. And goodbye, she repeated firmly to herself. She would say them. And mean them!

"Cooking dinner for us this evening has been too much for you," Gabe told her apologetically as she sat down opposite him. "I should have thought of that when you telephoned me earlier. You've already been at work today; the last thing you needed this evening was to cook another meal." He shook his head self-disgustedly. "The least I could have done was offer to cook for you." He sighed ruefully.

Jane knew from watching him the other evening that he was more than capable of doing it, too. But spend the evening at his apartment…? She didn't think so!

"Don't give it another thought, Gabe," she dismissed—knowing that he'd been thinking about it ever since he'd left the kitchen a few minutes ago. And the reason he had come up with for her skittishness was obviously that she had been working too hard. "Cooking for two people, and in the comfort of my own home, isn't work at all," she assured him.

"But the whole point of this evening was that I would take you out," he protested.

"You know, Gabe," she said softly, "I'm one of those chefs that's inclined to turn nasty if my food isn't eaten while it's still hot!"

He seemed on the point of protesting again for several seconds, and then he grinned, relaxing once again as he picked up his knife and fork in preparation for eating. "Never let it be said...!"

Jane ate sparingly, her appetite having deserted her with the realisation that after a couple of hours' time she would never see this man again.

How had he crept into her emotions like this—even lustful ones? *When* had he?

"—parents arrive in the country tomorrow, and I wondered if you could join us all for dinner tomorrow evening?"

Jane blinked across at him, having been lost in her own thoughts, and slowly took in what he had just said to her. His parents were arriving in London tomorrow? And why not? It was Christmas, and, from what he had said, he was an only child, too. But as for the suggestion of her having dinner with them...!

"I've told you, Gabe," she replied lightly. "This is my busy time of year. I'm catering for a party of thirty people tomorrow evening," she said thankfully.

"You work too damned hard," he bit out disapprovingly.

"I like to eat myself occasionally." She wryly pointed out the necessity for her to work. Maybe Gabe had forgotten what that was like; he was certainly in a financial position not to have to work any more, but she certainly wasn't!

He scowled heavily. "You shouldn't have to—"

"Now, now, Gabe," she cut in tauntingly. "Don't let your chauvinism show!"

"This isn't funny, Jane." He frowned across at her. "When I think—"

"I often think that the mere act of thinking only complicates things at times," she dismissed calmly, putting down her knife and fork, the food only half eaten on her plate, although Gabe seemed to have enjoyed his, his plate now empty. "Would you like your cheese or dessert next? People seem to vary in their preference nowadays, I've noticed."

"Actually—" he sat forward, leaning his elbows on the table as he looked straight at her "—I'd like an answer to my original question."

She raised dark brows. "Which question was that, Gabe?" But she knew which one it was. She also knew that she had no intention of meeting his parents, now or ever! After this evening she wouldn't be seeing him again, either...

His mouth quirked, and he gave a slight shake of his head. "It isn't going to work this time, Jane. I would very much like you to meet my parents," he told her bluntly. "And for them to meet you."

"Why?" she came back just as bluntly.

"Because they're nice people." He shrugged.

His parents wouldn't be the ones under inspection at such a meeting; she would. And she had been through all this once before in her life, eight years ago. She'd tried so hard at the time to win the approval of Paul's parents, little knowing that she needn't have bothered. The fact that she was the only child of very rich parents was the only asset she had needed in the eyes of Paul's parents!

It had never occurred to the elder Grangers that money could be lost more easily than it had been made...

Jane hadn't seen or heard from Paul's parents since just before Paul's death. On the one occasion she had attempted to telephone them they had claimed they would never forgive her for not even being at their son's funeral. The fact that she had been in a clinic at the time, having just lost her baby—their own grandchild—and that Paul had been in the company of another woman at the time of his accident, hadn't seemed to occur to them...

"Do you introduce all your friends to them, Gabe?" The derision could be heard in her voice.

He didn't even blink, his gaze remaining steady on hers. "The ones that matter, yes!"

She gave a humourless smile. "We barely know each other, Gabe. Did you introduce Jennifer to them before you married her?" she couldn't resist adding.

And then wished she hadn't! Jennifer had been his wife; their own relationship wasn't in the same category.

"As it happens, yes, I did." He relaxed back in his chair, smiling lazily. "My father was bowled over by the way she looked; my mother hated her on sight." He gave a wry chuckle. "I'm sure I don't have to tell you which one proved to be right!"

From what Jane knew of Jennifer Vaughan, men had always been "bowled over" by the way she looked. And the majority of women seemed to have disliked her intensely. Herself included.

"That can't have been easy for you," Jane sympathised.

"Nothing about that relationship was easy for me," he

acknowledged grimly. "And you're changing the subject again, Jane—"

"Because I don't want to meet your parents, Gabe," she sighed, becoming impatient with his persistence.

"Why not?" he came back as bluntly as she had minutes ago.

"Several reasons—"

"Name them," he put in forcefully, no longer relaxed, sitting upright in his chair, his gaze narrowed on her.

"I was about to," she rebuked softly; she did not want to get into an argument about this; she disliked arguments intensely. There had been too many of them with Paul. "Firstly, it puts a completely erroneous light on our friendship." She deliberately used the casual term, knowing he had registered that fact by the way his mouth tightened ominously. "And secondly," she added less confidently, knowing she was going to have that argument whether she wanted it or not, "I don't think the two of us should see each other again after tonight!" It all came out in a rush, so desperate was she to get it over with as quickly as possible.

Gabe raised those expressive dark brows. "And exactly what brought this on?" he questioned mildly.

"Nothing 'brought this on', Gabe," she returned exasperatedly. "I've been telling you to go away, one way or another, since the night we first met!" For all the good it had done her!

"Exactly," he nodded. "But this time you seem to mean it…" he said thoughtfully.

"I meant it all the other times too!" Jane claimed scathingly, wondering, in the light of the fact that she had now, inwardly at least, acknowledged her attraction towards him, whether she *had* really meant all those other refusals she had given him...

"Did you?" Gabe seemed to doubt it too!

Of course she had meant them, she told herself strongly. Gabriel Vaughan was a man for her to avoid, not encourage. Besides, she was sure she hadn't encouraged him. Not consciously, at least...

But subconsciously? Had she been forceful enough in telling him to go away? She had thought so at the time. But—

Enough of this! It was just confusing her.

She stood up abruptly, intending to clear their plates. And there would be no cheese or dessert. After this conversation, a little earlier in the meal than she had anticipated, she acknowledged, it was time for Gabe to leave!

"I meant it, Gabe," she told him forcefully. "I don't want to have dinner with you. I don't want to meet your parents. And, most important of all, I don't want to see you again! There, I can't be any plainer than that." She looked down at him with challenging brown eyes.

He coolly returned her furious gaze. "And what about the Christmas present I got for you today?" he said softly.

Present? He had bought her a Christmas present? "I think you were a little premature in buying me anything!" she told him impatiently. "But with any luck you'll have found someone else before Christmas that you can give it to instead—after all, there are still a few days to go!"

"Hmm, so we're back to the insults, are we?" Gabe murmured thoughtfully as he stood up. "The present was meant for you, Jane, not someone else," he bit out harshly, reaching out to clasp her arms.

Jane suddenly had trouble breathing, knowing it was due to Gabe's close proximity. "I don't—"

"Want it," he completed harshly. "You know, Jane, determination, and a certain independence of spirit, is to be admired in a woman. But not," he added dismissively as she would have made an angry reply, "when they are taken to the extreme of pigheaded rudeness! You went past that point several minutes ago," he added tightly.

"I—"

"Shut up, Jane," he rasped, pulling her effortlessly towards him.

"You can't—"

"Please!" he added with a groan, his head bending and his lips claiming hers.

Jane melted.

It was as if she had been waiting for this moment since he had kissed her so lightly this morning. And there was nothing light or distracted about this kiss; all Gabe's attention was focused on the passion that flared up between them so easily. Like tinder awaiting the flame. And it seemed they were that flame for each other...

Her arms moved up about his neck, one hand clinging to the broad width of his shoulder, the other becoming entangled in the dark thickness of his hair, her body held tightly against his, moulded to each muscle and sinew.

Without removing his lips from hers Gabe swung her up into his arms and carried her over to the soft gold-coloured sofa, laying her down on it before joining her there, their bodies even closer now, their breath mingling, Gabe's hands moving restlessly over the slenderness of her back and thighs.

Jane gasped softly as one of those hands moved to cup her breast, the gently sloping curve fitting perfectly against his own flesh, the nipple responding instantly to the gentle caress of his thumb, the tip hardening to his touch, a pleasurable warmth spreading through her thighs all the way to the tips of her toes.

She wanted this man!

Not like this, with their clothes between them, she wanted the naked warmth of his body next to hers, wanted to feel his hard possession, wanted to give him the same pleasure he was undoubtedly giving her.

His hand was beneath the woollen cashmere of her jumper now, and he was groaning low in his throat at his discovery that she wasn't wearing a bra, her breast naked to his touch.

Her breasts had always been firm and uplifting, definitely one of her better assets, and she rarely saw the necessity to wear a bra.

She groaned low in her own throat now as Gabe pushed aside the woollen garment, his head bending as his lips claimed possession of that fiery tip, his tongue rasping with slow, moist pleasure across her sensitive flesh.

She was on fire, offered no protest when, hindered by its presence, Gabe pulled the jumper up over her head and discarded it completely. Her gaze was shy as she looked up at him and he looked at her with such pleasurable intensity.

"You're beautiful, Jane," he murmured huskily. "But then, I always knew you would be!" he groaned before his head lowered, his mouth capturing hers with fierce intensity, passion flaring uncontrollably now, carrying them both on a tide that was going to be impossible to stop.

Not that Jane had any thought of bringing this to an end. She wanted Gabe as badly as he appeared to want her. She had never known such need, such desire, trembling with anticipation, knowing—

"Oh, Janie, Janie!" Gabe groaned as he buried his face in the warmth of her neck, breathing in deeply of her perfume. "If you only knew how I've wanted this, how long I've needed to hold and kiss you like this." His arms tightened about her as his lips travelled the length of her throat.

Jane felt cold. Icy.

Janie…

He had called her *Janie*. Only her father had ever called her by that pet name.

It could be coincidence, of course, Gabe's own arousal making him unaware of what he had just said.

Or just carelessness…?

Gabe tensed beside her, suddenly seeming to become aware of the way she had moved as far away from him as she was able on the confines of the sofa, slowly lifting his head so that he could look down at her, his expression—wary!

She wasn't mistaken.

It wasn't coincidence!

She moistened suddenly dry lips. "How long, Gabe?" she demanded coldly.

He frowned. "How long…?" he repeated, that wariness having increased.

She nodded, more certain with every second that passed that she wasn't mistaken in the conclusion she had just come to. "How long have you known exactly who I am?" she said plainly.

Because he did know.

She was sure now that he did.

So why hadn't he told her that days ago...?

CHAPTER TWELVE

"How long have you known, Gabe?" she repeated in a steady voice, fully clothed again now, standing across the room looking over to where Gabe still sat on the couch.

He drew in a ragged breath, running agitated fingers through the darkness of his hair. "I—"

"Don't even attempt to avoid answering me, Gabe," she warned harshly. "We both know—now—that you realise I was once Janette Smythe-Roberts!"

How long had he known? she asked herself again. And why hadn't he said so as soon as he made the discovery?

She literally went cold at the only explanation she could think of!

"You still are Janette Smythe-Roberts, damn it!" he rasped, standing up himself now, instantly dwarfing what had already seemed to her to be a space too small to hold them both.

She felt sick, had perhaps cherished some small hope inside her that he really didn't know. But his words confirmed that he did!

"Don't come near me." Jane cringed away from him as he would have reached out and touched her. "You still haven't told me exactly how long you've known," she prompted woodenly.

Or what he was going to do about it! He hadn't been behaving like a man still out to wreak vengeance, but perhaps making her want him was his way of exacting retribution...?

Gabe gave a weary sigh, shrugging wide shoulders. "I realised who you were about thirty seconds after I came into the kitchen with Felicity last week," he admitted quietly.

Jane drew in a shaky breath, her arms wrapped about herself protectively. "That long? How on earth—?"

"Your hair may be a different colour, Jane," he rasped. "And your face has taken on a certain maturity it didn't once have. But it's still the same face I remember," he added huskily. "A face I'll never forget."

She shook her head disbelievingly. "But I never even saw you face to face until last week—"

"But I saw you," Gabe cut in firmly. "We were never actually introduced to each other, but I saw you at a party one evening with your husband."

Her husband. Gabe's wife's lover. The man Jennifer had left him for.

She sighed. "I don't remember that evening." She shook her head; a lot of the time before the accident was a blank to her, her misery as Paul's wife already well established.

"You looked beautiful that night," Gabe recalled softly. "You were wearing a brown dress, the same colour as your eyes, little make-up that I could see—but then, you don't need make-up to enhance your beauty. And your hair—! I had never seen hair quite that colour before, or that long; it reached down to your waist like a curtain of gold! I didn't need to be introduced to you to remember you, Jane—you stood out in that crowd like a golden light in darkness!"

Her mouth twisted scornfully. "Please stop waxing lyrical about me, Gabe; I was very unhappy at that time; I probably didn't even want to be there. I no longer loved my husband but felt trapped in the marriage—"

"Until he walked out of it!"

"Until Paul walked out of it," she acknowledged shakily. "To be with your wife," she added hardly.

Gabe shrugged. "So the fairy story goes," he said dryly.

Jane gave him a sharp look. "There was no fairy-tale ending to that particular story—for any of us! And you've been playing with me for the last twelve days—"

"To what end?" he challenged harshly.

"I have no idea." She sighed wearily. "I presume for the same reason you tried to find me after the accident." She shrugged.

"The same reason. But not the one you think! And I backed off then when I heard the rumour that you had lost your baby," he rasped.

"Did you?" she said heavily, no longer looking at him but staring sightlessly at her music centre. The CD had long since finished playing. But neither of them had noticed that fact; they'd been too engrossed in each other at the time. Which brought her back to Gabe's kisses and caresses. Was he still trying to make someone pay for what happened three years ago? "Then you know that if anyone was a victim of my husband's relationship with your wife, Gabe," she bit out evenly, "it was my unborn baby!"

"Jane—"

"I told you not to come near me!" she flared as he

made a move towards her, her eyes flashing in warning. "What did you think when you met me again last week, Gabe?" She looked at him challengingly. "Did you see I had nothing left to lose and decide to hurt me in another way?"

He became suddenly still. "What way?"

"You tell me!" She smiled humourlessly. "Those conversations we had about Janette Smythe-Roberts." She shook her head disgustedly. "You were playing with me all the time!" she realised self-derisively. And all the time she had thought she was the one not being completely honest!

"I was trying to get you to defend yourself!" Gabe returned impatiently. "But you didn't do it," he added disappointedly.

"Didn't defend myself against being thought a cold-blooded, manipulative gold-digger? Someone who would take money from my parents and leave them almost penniless?" Jane looked at him scathingly. "As I told you once before, Gabe, you sweep through people's lives, uncaring of the chaos and pain you leave behind you—"

"That isn't true!" His hands were clenched angrily.

"Perhaps uncaring is the wrong word to use," she conceded disgustedly. "You're simply unaware of it! Which is perhaps even worse. What do you think happens to people when you've stepped in and bought their company, possibly their life's work, out from under them? Do you think they simply shrug their shoulders and start all over again?" she challenged.

"It's business, Jane—"

"So my father said when he tried to explain your behaviour to me!" she scorned. "But I call it something else completely!"

Gabe drew in a harsh breath. "Let's not lose sight of the real villain here, Jane," he rasped. "And it wasn't me!"

Paul... It always came back to Paul. And with thoughts of Paul came ones of Gabe's wife Jennifer...

"If you're going to blame Paul for this then let's include your wife in it too," Jane said with distaste. "Who do you think he was trying to impress with his gambling and high living?"

Gabe became suddenly still. "I accept Jennifer's blame—"

"Do you?" Jane gave another mirthless smile. "She was beautiful, immoral, utterly uncaring of anyone but herself. She knew of my pregnancy, too, because Paul had told her, but it made no difference when she decided she wanted my husband—"

"Jennifer couldn't have children herself," Gabe put in softly. "She'd had tests. She was infertile. Pregnant women represented a threat to her."

Jane felt the momentary sadness that she would for any woman unable to have children of her own. But it was only momentary where Jennifer Vaughan was concerned. "That didn't give her the right to entice away the husbands of those women!"

"I agree." Gabe sighed heavily. "But it's an inescapable fact that that's exactly what she did. With dire results in your particular case."

Jane stared at him as she fully registered all that he had just said. "Are you telling me that that wasn't the first time Jennifer had done something like that?" It seemed incredible, but that was exactly what it sounded like he was saying!

He ran a weary hand across his brow. "Jennifer was

a very troubled woman. The fact that she couldn't have children—"

"I asked you a question, Gabe," Jane cut in tautly.

He looked at her steadily. "I believe I've already told you that Jennifer was much more interested in other women's husbands than she was in her own—"

"But pregnant women in particular?" Jane persisted.

"Yes!" he acknowledged harshly, turning away. "To Jennifer there was nothing more beautiful than a pregnant woman. To her they seemed to glow. More importantly, they carried life inside them. A pregnant woman became the ultimate in beauty to her."

"That's ridiculous!" Jane snapped. "Most pregnant women don't feel that way at all. Oh, there's a certain magic in creating life, in feeling that life growing inside you," she remembered emotionally. "But for the most part you feel nauseous, and in the beginning it's a nausea that never seems to stop. And, added to that, you feel fat and unattractive—"

"Pregnant women aren't fat," Gabe cut in softly. "They're blossoming."

"That's a word only used by people who aren't pregnant," Jane put in dismissively. "Believe me, most of us just feel fat!" And that feeling hadn't been helped, in her case, by the fact that Paul had obviously found her condition most unattractive!

"Maybe," Gabe conceded with a sigh. "But to a woman who has never been pregnant, and who never can be, that isn't how pregnancy appears at all. Oh, I'm not excusing Jennifer's behaviour—"

"I hope not," Jane told him tightly. "Because it isn't a good enough excuse as far as I'm concerned!" She had lost her baby—the only good thing to come out of her marriage—because her husband had left her for Jennifer Vaughan, and the two of them had subsequently died together in a car crash. There was no excuse for that!

"It isn't a good enough excuse for any woman," Gabe accepted heavily. "But it's what Jennifer did."

"Then why didn't you leave her?" Jane frowned. "Why did you stay with her, and in doing so condone her behaviour?"

A nerve pulsed in his tightly clenched jaw. "I didn't condone it, Jane. I would never condone such behaviour. But I thought that by staying with her I could—" He shook his head. "I don't believe in divorce, Jane," he told her abruptly. "And neither did Jennifer," he added softly.

She became suddenly still, her frown deepening. Jennifer didn't believe in divorce...? "But she left you..."

Gabe sighed. "No. She didn't."

"But—"

"I know that's what Paul told you three years ago, and it's what everyone else thought at the time too, but I can assure you, Jennifer was not leaving me." He shook his head. "There were so many times I wished she would," he admitted harshly. "But I was her safety net, the let-out when any of her little affairs became too serious. As Paul did..."

Jane was having trouble absorbing all of this now. Was Gabe really saying what she thought he was?

Paul had said he was leaving her, that he and Jennifer were going to be together.

"Are you telling me—?" She ran her tongue over suddenly dry lips. "Are you saying that Paul and Jennifer weren't going away together?"

"That's exactly what I'm saying." Gabe nodded grimly. "Jennifer was furious the day of the accident. Paul had telephoned her to say he'd left you, and now he expected her to do the same to me. She met him that day only so that she could tell him what a fool he was, that she had no intention of leaving me, that he had better hurry home and make it up with his wife before she decided his leaving had been the best thing that ever happened to her! Her words, Jane, not mine," Gabe told her bleakly.

But it had already been too late for Paul to do that. She might not already have realised that Paul's leaving "had been the best thing that ever happened to her", but Paul had been in too deeply in other ways to backtrack on his decision. As her father's assistant, he had stolen money from the company, and in doing so had brought that company almost to the point of ruin.

"I've often wondered if it was an accident," Gabe murmured softly, as if partly reading her thoughts.

Jane looked at him dazedly. Not an accident? What was he saying, suggesting? But hadn't she just told herself there had been no way back for Paul, that he had already burnt his bridges, both professionally and privately? But could he have thought that there was no reason to carry on? No, she wouldn't believe that! Paul had been too selfish, too self-motivated, to take his own and Jennifer's lives.

"It's something we'll never know the answer to," Gabe continued gently. "Probably something best not known."

Jane agreed with him. That sort of soul-searching could do neither of them any good. No matter what the reason for doing so…

"Love is a very strange emotion," she said dully. "It appears to grow and exist for people who really don't deserve it." And Jennifer Vaughan certainly hadn't deserved Gabe's, or any other man's, love. And yet who but a man in love could ever have thought her the "perfection" he had once called her?

"Death is rather final," Gabe muttered. "But you're still well rid of Paul Granger!"

"I've never—" She shook her head. "We're getting away from the point here—"

"Maybe I caught that from you." Gabe attempted to tease, although he couldn't even bring himself to smile, let alone encourage her to do so. "What is the point here, Jane? You tell me." He shook his head. "Because I've certainly lost it!"

For the main part, so had she! Except that Gabe had known exactly who she was for the last twelve days. And for reasons of his own he had chosen to keep that fact to himself!

She looked at him coldly. "The point is that for me the past is as dead and buried as Paul himself is. Why do you think I've been asking you to go away for the last twelve days? Because you remind me of a time I would rather forget," she told him bluntly.

Gabe looked pale now. "I didn't imagine what happened between us a short time ago—"

"It's been a long time for me, Gabe," she said scornfully. "My marriage may have been a mistake, but despite all that I'm still a normal woman, with normal desires, and you—"

"Just happened to be here!" he finished disgustedly. "Is that it, Jane?"

No, that wasn't it! She had met plenty of other men

over the last three years, much more suitable men, men just as handsome as he was, just as interested in a relationship with her. And she hadn't responded to any of them, hadn't allowed any of them as close to her as this man had got in a matter of days.

But to find the reason for that she would have to delve into her own emotions. And she had already done enough of that where Gabriel Vaughan was concerned.

"That just about sums it up, yes!" she confirmed hardly. "It probably has something to do with the time of year, too," she added insultingly. "Let's face it, no one likes to be on their own at Christmas!"

And strangely, despite the fact that this Christmas was actually going to be no different from the last three she had spent with her parents, she had a feeling she was going to feel very much alone...

What had Gabe done to her? What was it that she felt towards him? Because it was no longer that mixture of fear and apprehension she had felt before .

Gabe gave a pained wince at her deliberate bluntness. "I had better make myself scarce, then, hadn't I?" He picked up his jacket, but didn't put it on. "That way you still have time to meet someone else before the big day!"

Although his words hurt—as they were meant to do!—Jane offered no defence. Nor did she try to stop him as he walked out of the door, closing it softly behind him.

There would have been no point in stopping him. They had said all that needed to be said. Probably more than needed to be said!

And she still had no idea why Gabe had pursued her so relentlessly for the last twelve days. She felt he had offered no real explanation for such extraordinary behaviour when he had known all the time she was Janette Smythe-Roberts.

Two things she did know only too clearly, though.

One; Gabe must have loved his wife very much; he must have done to have tolerated her behaviour. Secondly—and this was against all that she had tried to do for herself for the last three years—she didn't need to delve into her own emotions to find out why she had responded to Gabe in the way that she had. She had known the answer to that question as soon as he had closed the door behind him...

Somehow—and she wasn't sure how such a thing could have happened—she had fallen in love with Gabe!

Stupidly.

Irrevocably!

CHAPTER THIRTEEN

JANE made the drive to her parents' home on Christmas morning with more than her usual reluctance. The last few days, since Gabe had walked out of her life for good, had been such a strain to get through, and as a consequence she looked paler than usual, despite the application of blusher.

And even in those few days she had lost enough weight for it to be noticeable. She had put on a baggy thigh-length jumper, burnt orange in colour, and styled black trousers, in an effort to hide this fact from her parents. But there was nothing she could do to hide the gauntness of her face, or the dull pain in her eyes that wouldn't go away.

She had let Gabriel Vaughan get to her. Not only that, she had allowed herself to fall in love with him.

Maybe that was what he had hoped for, she had told herself over and over again in the last few days, when not even her work could blot him from her mind and senses. If it was, then he had succeeded, even if he wasn't aware of it.

At least, she hoped he wasn't aware of it. That would be the ultimate pain in this whole sorry business!

Jane drew in a deep breath after parking her van, forcing a bright smile to her lips as she got out and walked towards the house. It was only a few hours of forced gaiety; surely she could handle that? After all, it was Christmas Day!

"You're looking very pale, darling," her mother said, sounding concerned, kissing her in greeting as she did so.

"And you've lost weight, too," her father added reprovingly after giving her a hug.

So much for her efforts at camouflage!

"You're both looking well too," she returned teasingly. "And one of your Christmas lunches, Mummy, should take care of both those things!" she assured them lightly.

"I hope so," her father said sternly. "But first things first—a glass of my Christmas punch?"

"Guaranteed to put us all to sleep this afternoon!" Jane laughed, finding she was, after all, glad to be home with her parents on this special day.

"I sincerely hope not." Her mother smiled. "We have guests arriving after lunch!"

It was the first Jane had heard of anyone joining them on Christmas Day, but even if company was the last thing she felt in need of she was glad for her parents' sake. Whatever it was her father had become involved with on a business level, it had obviously given their social life a jolt too; it was years since they had spent Christmas with the house full of people.

Besides, company would take the pressure off her.

"In that case, I suggest we drink our punch and open our presents." She had brought her parents' presents with her. "And then I can help you cook lunch, Mummy," she offered—Mrs Weaver always spent Christmas with her sister in Brighton. "Windy, cold place this time of year", the housekeeper invariably complained, but

Jane's parents insisted she must be with her family at Christmas-time.

"Busman's holiday, Janie?" her father teased.

Her smile wavered for only a fraction of a second. The last person to call her Janie had been Gabe. No, she wouldn't think of him any more today! Her parents were in very good spirits, and she would allow none of her own unhappiness to spill over and ruin their day for them.

Which proved more than a little difficult later that afternoon when the "guests" turned out to be Gabe and his parents!

It hadn't even occurred to Jane to ask who the guests were going to be, having assumed it was friends of her parents whom she had known herself since childhood, friends she could feel perfectly relaxed with.

A tall, handsome man, dark hair showing grey at his temples, entered the room first with her mother, her parents having gone together to answer the ring of the doorbell. Her father entered the room seconds later with a tall, blonde-haired woman, elegantly beautiful, her soft American drawl as she spoke softly sending warning bells through Jane even before Gabe entered the room behind the foursome.

Jane was dumbstruck. Never in her worst nightmare could she have imagined her parents inviting Gabe and his parents here on Christmas Day! They barely knew Gabe, let alone his parents, so why on earth—?

But even as she stared disbelievingly across at Gabe, his own gaze coolly challenging as he met hers, Jane knew exactly what Gabe and his parents were doing here. That day, when her mother and father had come to London so unexpectedly, had also been the day Gabe

had told her he had an important business meeting he
had to get to for ten o'clock…!

Gabe was the person who had offered her father some
sort of business opening, was the reason why her father
looked so much younger, and her mother looked so much
more buoyant!

He couldn't! He couldn't be going to hurt her parents
all over again? He—

No, she answered herself confidently even as the idea
came into her head. The man she had come to know
over the last two weeks, the man she loved, wouldn't do
that.

Then why? What was it all about? What did it all
mean?

"Think about it a while, Jane." Gabe had strolled
casually across the room to stand at her side, his tone
pleasant, but those aqua-blue eyes were as cold as ice.

Like the blue of an iceberg Jane had once seen in a
photograph…

"Really think about it, Jane," he muttered harshly. "But
in the meantime come and say hello to my parents."

The trouble was, she couldn't think at all; she wasn't
even aware that she was being introduced to his father,
although she did note that he was an older version of his
son, the only difference being that on the older man the
aqua-blue eyes were warm and friendly as he shook her
hand.

Marisa Vaughn, although aged in her early sixties,
was undoubtedly a beautiful woman, possessed of an
air of complete satisfaction with her life.

Jane found she couldn't help but like and feel drawn
to both the older Vaughns.

"Janette is such a pretty name," Marisa Vaughn murmured huskily. "It suits you, my dear." She squeezed

Jane's arm warmly before turning away to accept the glass of punch being poured to warm them all.

"Janette has just suggested the two of us go for a walk," Gabe put in loudly enough that the four older people could hear him over their own murmur of conversation. "Would any of you care to join us?"

"Excellent idea." His father nodded approvingly. "But after the drive this fire—" he held out his hands to the blazing warmth of the coal fire "—has much more appeal!" He grinned at his son.

"Take my coat from the hallway, Janette," her mother told her. "We don't want you to catch cold."

She didn't want to go for a walk, had made no such suggestion in the first place, but with the four older people looking at her so expectantly she didn't seem to have a lot of choice in the matter. Not without appearing incredibly rude.

"I thought it best that you say what you have to say to me away from our parents," Gabe bit out once they were outside in the crisp December air, walking over to the paddock where Jane had once kept her horse stabled.

She wasn't sure she could say anything to him, wasn't sure she could speak at all. She was still stunned by the fact that he was here at all. She had thought she would never see him again...

And how she had ached these last few days with that realisation!

How she ached now. But with quite a different emotion.

"Why, Gabe?" she finally managed to say.

He had been staring across at the bleak December landscape, a little snow having fallen in the night, leaving a crisp whiteness on everything. "Why did I come here today with my parents?" he ground out. "Because we were invited, Jane," he responded harshly. "It would have been rude not to have accepted." He turned back to look over the paddock.

Jane looked up at his grim profile, his cheeks hollow, his jaw clenched. As if waiting for a blow...

She swallowed hard. "I didn't mean that." She shook her head. "Why did you try to find me three years ago?" She felt that if she had the answer to that she might, just might, have the answer to the whole puzzle...

He looked down at her again, frowning slightly now. "I thought you already knew the answer to that one," he rasped scathingly. "I was out to wreak vengeance, wasn't I? On a woman who had not only been deserted by her husband because of my wife, but had also been bombarded with reporters because of the scandal when the two of them died together in a car crash. Not only that, that woman had also lost her baby! That's the way it happened, isn't it, Jane?" he challenged disgustedly. "You see, I've been doing some thinking of my own!" He shook his head. "My conclusions aren't exactly pretty!"

She still stared up at him, couldn't seem to look away. She loved this man.

"I—" She moistened dry lips, swallowing hard. "I could have been wrong—"

"Could have been?" Gabe turned fully towards her now, grasping her arms painfully. "There's no 'could have been' about it, Jane; if that's what you thought, you were wrong!" His eyes glittered dangerously, a nerve pulsing in his cheek. "In fact, you're so damned far from the truth it's laughable. If I felt like laughing, that is," he muttered grimly. "Which I don't!"

She had done a lot of thinking herself over the last few days, and knew that somehow, some way, there was something wrong with what she had believed until two weeks ago, when she'd actually met Gabe for the first time. Maybe Gabe had been devastated by Jennifer's death, but the man she had come to know wouldn't blame anyone else for that death; he'd known the destructive streak that had motivated his wife better than anyone.

So if he hadn't wanted retribution all those years ago, what had he wanted...? It was that Jane wanted— needed—to know.

"Gabe, I was wrong," she told him chokingly, putting her hand on his arm, refusing to remove it even when she felt him flinch. "I know that now. I know *you* now."

He shook his head. "No, you don't, Jane. Not really."

And now she never would? Was that what he was saying?

She didn't want that, couldn't bear it if she were never to see him again after today. The past few days had been bad enough, but to go through that pain all over again...!

"Gabe, I'm trying to apologise. For what I thought," she explained abruptly.

"Accepted." He nodded tersely, his expression still hard. "Can we go back inside now?" he added gratingly.

"Why are you helping my father, Gabe?" She refused to move, knowing that once they were back inside the house Gabe would become a remote stranger to her. And after telling him for days that that was what she wanted him to be it was now the last thing she wanted.

He gave a rueful grimace. "So you know about that

too now, hmm?" He nodded dismissively. "Well, obviously I'm up to something underhand and malicious, entangling your father in some sort of plot—"

"Gabe!" Jane groaned her distress at his bitterness. "I was wrong! I know I was wrong! I'm sorry. What else can I say?" She looked at him pleadingly.

He became very still now, looking down at her warily. "What else do you want to say?"

So many things, but most of all, that she loved him. But how cautious she had, by necessity, been over the last three years of her life held her back from being quite that daring. What if he should throw that love back in her face?

She chewed on her bottom lip. "I think your mother likes me," she told him lightly, remembering what his mother's opinion of Jennifer had been.

His expression softened. "You're right, she does," he acknowledged dryly. "But then, I knew she would," he added enigmatically.

"Gabe, tell me why you tried to find me three years ago!" She tried again, because she was still sure this was the key to everything. "Please, Gabe," she pleaded as he looked grim once again.

"Do you have any idea what it's like to love someone so badly you can't even see straight?" he attacked viciously. "So that you think of nothing else but that person, until they fill your whole world? Do you have any idea what it's like to love someone like that?" he groaned harshly. "And then to have them disappear from your life as if they had never been, almost as if you had imagined them ever being there at all?" His hands were clenched at his sides, his face pale.

She was beginning to. Oh, yes, she was beginning to!

And if he could still talk about his dead wife like this, still felt that way about her, then her own love for him was as worthless as ashes.

She drew in a deep breath. "I'm sorry Jennifer died—"

"Jennifer? I'm not talking about Jennifer!" he dismissed incredulously. "She was my wife, and as such I cared what happened to her, and could never actually bring myself to hate her—I felt pity for her more than anything. I hadn't loved her for years before she died. If I ever did," he added bleakly. "Compared with what I now know of love I believe I was initially fascinated by Jennifer, and then, after we were married, that fascination quickly turned to a rather sad affection. Beneath that surface selfishness was a very vulnerable woman, a woman who saw herself as being less than other women—I've already explained to you why that was. So you see, Jane, I felt sorry for Jennifer, I cared for her, but I was not in love with her. Before or after she died," he said grimly.

"But—" Jane looked at him with puzzled eyes. If it wasn't Jennifer, then who was this mysterious woman he loved...? "That perfect woman—the woman who evaporated, disappeared before your eyes." She painfully recalled what he had told her of the woman he loved. The woman she had for so long assumed was Jennifer...

"What about her?" he echoed harshly.

Jane shook her head. "Where is she? *Who* is she?"

Gabe looked down at her with narrowed eyes, his expression softening as he saw the look of complete bewilderment in her face. "You really don't know, do you?" He shook his head self-derisively, moving away from her to lean back against the fence, the collar of his jacket turned up to keep out the worst of the cold. "I was at a party one night—one of those endless parties that are impossible to enjoy, but you simply can't get away from. And then I looked across the crowded room—that well-worn cliché!—and there she was."

Jane couldn't move, could barely breathe now.

Gabe was no longer looking at her, his thoughts all inwards as he recalled the past. "I told myself not to be so stupid," he continued harshly. "Love didn't happen like that, in a moment—"

"At first sight." Jane spoke hoarsely, remembering he had once asked her if she believed in the emotion. She had said a definite no!

"At first sight," he echoed scornfully. "But I couldn't stop watching this woman, couldn't seem to look anywhere else. And as I watched her I realised she wasn't just beautiful, she was gracious and warm too. She spoke to everybody there in the same warm way, and there was an elderly man there, who had been slightly drunk when he arrived, but instead of shying away from him as everyone else was she sat next to him, talking to him quietly, for over an hour. And by the time he left he was slightly less drunk and even managed to smile a little."

"His wife had died the previous month," Jane put in softly. "That evening was the first time he had been out in company since her death. And people weren't shying away from him because he'd had slightly too much to drink; it was because they didn't know what to say to him, how to deal with his loss, and so they simply ignored him." She remembered that night so well—it had been the last time she had gone anywhere with Paul, because, ironically enough, a few days later *he* had been dead.

Gabe nodded abruptly. "I know that. I asked around who he was. Who you were. You were another man's wife!"

She was that perfect woman, the woman who had seemed to disappear, evaporate. And after the accident, after losing the baby, that was exactly what she had done!

Gabe had been in love with her three years ago! Not a man on a quest for vengeance, but a man on a quest for the woman he had fallen in love with at first sight at a party one night!

"You were another woman's husband," she reminded him gruffly.

"Not by the time I came looking for you." He shook his head firmly. "The first time I saw you, I accept we were both married to other people, and in those circumstances I would never have come near you. I didn't come near you. And maybe I did act with indecent haste by trying to find you after our respective partners were killed," he acknowledged grimly. "But, as it happened, my worst nightmare came true." He looked bleak. "You had disappeared. And, no matter how I tried to find you, someone would put a wall up to block my way. After three months of coming up against those brick walls, of finally discovering that you had lost your baby because of what happened—"

"That was the reason you did a deal with Richard Warner rather than buy him out, wasn't it?" Jane said with certainty.

"A horror of history repeating itself?" Gabe nodded. "It was too close to what happened to you three years ago."

Jane gasped. "You weren't responsible for my miscarriage—"

"Maybe I could have done something to stop Jennifer." He shook his head. "Who knows? I certainly didn't. So I tried to convince myself I had imagined you." He sighed. "I went back to the States, buried myself in my work, and told myself that Janette Granger was a myth, that even if I had finally got to meet you, speak to you, you would have hated me; that it was best to leave you as a dream, a mirage. The only trouble with dreams and mirages is that they transpose themselves over reality." He grimaced.

"No normal woman can possibly live up to a dream one. And for me no woman ever has."

He turned away abruptly, staring out across the empty paddock. "When I met you again so suddenly two weeks ago. You were everything I had ever thought you were. And I was sure that you knew me too, but I thought— stupidly, I realise now—that if you could just get to know me, realise I wasn't a cold-hearted ogre, you might come to— Oh, never mind what I thought, Jane," he rasped. "I was wrong, so very wrong."

"My name is Janette," she put in softly, pointedly. "Janie, if you prefer; it's always been my father's pet name for me."

Gabe loved her. At least, he had loved her three years ago... Had the reality lived up to that dream?

He turned back to look at her. "That night, at your apartment, I called you Janie..." he realised softly.

"You did," she nodded. "And I don't know what you're trying to do to help my father—"

"I'm putting him into Richard's company as his senior manager," Gabe told her gently. "Richard is good at PR work, and your father is good at the management level; together they should turn that company around in six months." He swallowed hard. "You were right about me; I had no idea of the financial difficulties your father had three years ago, of the debts he had to pay—"

"Paul's debts," Jane put in hardly. "My father did that for me. And what you're doing for him now has transformed his life—his and Mummy's. I could love you for just that alone," she added shyly.

"Don't, Jane—"

"But I don't love you for that alone," she continued determinedly, eyes very big in the paleness of her face as she looked up at him. "I love you because you're warm and funny, caring and loving. And when you kiss me…!" She gave a self-conscious laugh.

"When I kiss you," Gabe agreed throatily, "I'm back to that first night I saw you; I can't think straight, can't see straight, all I know is you. With every part of me. Oh, Janie!"

She needed no further encouragement, flinging herself into his arms, both of them losing themselves in the sheer beauty of loving and being loved.

How long they remained like that Jane didn't know, finally laughing gently against the warmth of his chest, where he had cradled her as if he would never let her go again.

"All we have to do now is find a way to explain to our respective parents that we're going to be married." She chuckled softly. "Considering my parents don't even realise we know each other—"

"Marriage, Janie?" Gabe looked down at her searchingly. "You love me that much?"

And more. Marriage to Paul had been possession and pain; with Gabe it would be sharing and love. With Gabe, she had no doubts about making such a commitment. No doubts whatsoever.

"If you'll have me." She nodded shyly, suddenly wondering if he was prepared to make such a commitment again after his disastrous marriage to Jennifer.

He let out a whoop of delight, picking her up to swing her round in the snow. "Oh, I'll have you, Janette Smythe-Roberts, Janette Granger, Jane Smith. All of you! I love you, Janie, so very much." He slowly lowered her to the snow-covered ground. "And my parents already know how I feel about you, have known for some time that I left my heart behind in England three years ago," he acknowledged ruefully. "As for your own parents, they only want for you what will make you happy. And I certainly intend doing that! So will you marry me, Jane? Soon!" His arms tightened about her. "It has to be soon!"

He had already waited long enough, his pleading expression told her. And so had she, she realised weakly. "As soon as it can be arranged," she assured him huskily. "I can't wait for us to belong to each other. And my father was asking me only the other day when I was going to give him grandchildren...!" She looked up at Gabe hopefully.

"Children... *Our* children, Janie," he groaned, his hands trembling as he held her. "*Soon*, Janie. Oh, yes, very soon!"

CHAPTER FOURTEEN

Gold.

Bright, shiny, *warm* gold.

Her hair, returned to its natural colour for almost a year now, flowed like liquid gold over Gabe's fingers as he played with the silky tresses, his attention so intense he hadn't realised Jane had woken beside him in the bed and lay looking up at him.

It had been a good year—a year in which they had married and moved into a house of their own in London. Initially Jane's time had been filled with choosing the décor and furnishings, and soon—very soon!—her time was going to be filled with their son or daughter.

Being with Gabe, as his wife, was the deepest happiness Jane had ever known—falling asleep in his arms every night, waking still held in those strong arms, and spending their days busy in each other's company. Both sets of parents were constant visitors, eager for the birth of their first grandchild. As Jane and Gabe were.

"Good morning, my love." She greeted her husband huskily, warmed by the pleasure that lit his face as he realised she was awake.

He kissed her lingeringly on the lips. "I've just been wondering what I ever found to do with my time before I had you to look at and love," he admitted ruefully. "You're so beautiful, Jane," he told her shakily.

She laughed softly, reaching up to gently touch his cheek. "At the moment I look like a baby whale!"

His hand moved to rest possessively on the swell of her body that was their unborn child. "To me you're beautiful."

And she knew he meant it, that he had enjoyed every aspect of her pregnancy, been a part of all of it, as far as he was able. And since Felicity and Richard's son Thom had been born six months ago, the other couple now close friends who visited often, Gabe had been practising changing nappies, much to baby Thom's disgust.

"You were very restless last night, darling." Gabe frowned down at her concernedly now. "Do you feel okay?"

Jane grinned up at him. "As okay as I can be in the early stages of labour," she informed him lightly, knowing that the slight cramps she had had in her stomach the evening before had deepened during the night, although not seriously enough yet for her to need to go to hospital, which was why she had been napping on and off during the night, preparing herself for the much heavier labour she was positive was imminent.

Gabe shot out of bed so quickly Jane could only lie and stare at him, moving up to lean on one elbow to watch him as he raced around the bedroom, throwing on his own clothes, before puling her own out of the adjoining wardrobe and laying them down on the bed.

"Gabe…?" She finally stopped his rushing about. "It's going to be hours yet—"

He came to an abrupt halt, sitting down on the side of the bed, gently clasping her shoulders. "I'm not taking any chances with you, Jane," he told her emotionally. "If anything should happen to you—"

Jane placed her fingertips lightly against his lips. "Nothing is going to happen to me," she assured him confidently. "We fell in love with each other against all the odds; nothing could possibly happen to part us now," she said with conviction, sure in her own heart that they were meant to be together. Always.

"I love you so much, Jane," he choked. "My life would be empty without you!"

"And mine without you. But that isn't going to happen, Gabe." She was absolutely positive about this, felt sure they were going to grow old together. "Nothing is going to happen in the next few hours except we're going to have our own darling little baby." She gave him a glowing smile. "But perhaps you're right about going to the hospital now." She began her breathing exercises as a much stronger contraction took her breath away. "I think the baby has decided that today would be a good time to be born!"

And six hours later, when their daughter Ami was born, with Jane's golden hair and Gabe's aqua-blue eyes, they knew that their world was complete.

"She's gorgeous, Jane." Gabe gazed down wonderingly at their tiny daughter, each tiny feature perfect. "I can't believe you're both mine." He shook his head.

"Believe it, Gabe," Jane told him emotionally.

As she believed.

In Gabe.

In their marriage.

In their for ever…

* * * * *

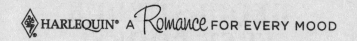

HARLEQUIN® A *Romance* FOR EVERY MOOD

If you enjoyed these passionate reads, then you will love other stories from

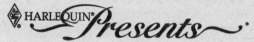

HARLEQUIN® *Presents*

Glamorous international settings...
unforgettable men...passionate romances—
Harlequin Presents promises you the world!

HARLEQUIN® *Blaze*

Fun, flirtatious and steamy books that tell it
like it is, inside and outside the bedroom.

Silhouette® *Desire*

Always Powerful, Passionate and Provocative

Six new titles are available every month from each of these lines

Available wherever books are sold

REQUEST YOUR FREE BOOKS!

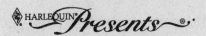

2 FREE NOVELS PLUS
2 FREE GIFTS!

YES! Please send me 2 FREE Harlequin Presents® novels and my 2 FREE gifts (gifts are worth about $10). After receiving them, if I don't wish to receive any more books, I can return the shipping statement marked "cancel." If I don't cancel, I will receive 6 brand-new novels every month and be billed just $4.05 per book in the U.S. or $4.74 per book in Canada. That's a saving of at least 15% off the cover price! It's quite a bargain! Shipping and handling is just 50¢ per book.* I understand that accepting the 2 free books and gifts places me under no obligation to buy anything. I can always return a shipment and cancel at any time. Even if I never buy another book, the two free books and gifts are mine to keep forever.

106/306 HDN E5M4

Name	(PLEASE PRINT)	
Address		Apt. #
City	State/Prov.	Zip/Postal Code

Signature (if under 18, a parent or guardian must sign)

Mail to the **Harlequin Reader Service:**
IN U.S.A.: P.O. Box 1867, Buffalo, NY 14240-1867
IN CANADA: P.O. Box 609, Fort Erie, Ontario L2A 5X3

Not valid for current subscribers to Harlequin Presents books.

Are you a current subscriber to Harlequin Presents books and want to receive the larger-print edition? Call 1-800-873-8635 today!

* Terms and prices subject to change without notice. Prices do not include applicable taxes. N.Y. residents add applicable sales tax. Canadian residents will be charged applicable provincial taxes and GST. Offer not valid in Quebec. This offer is limited to one order per household. All orders subject to approval. Credit or debit balances in a customer's account(s) may be offset by any other outstanding balance owed by or to the customer. Please allow 4 to 6 weeks for delivery. Offer available while quantities last.

Your Privacy: Harlequin Books is committed to protecting your privacy. Our Privacy Policy is available online at www.eHarlequin.com or upon request from the Reader Service. From time to time we make our lists of customers available to reputable third parties who may have a product or service of interest to you. If you would prefer we not share your name and address, please check here. ☐

Help us get it right—We strive for accurate, respectful and relevant communications. To clarify or modify your communication preferences, visit us at www.ReaderService.com/consumerchoice.

HP10R

HARLEQUIN *Presents*

USA TODAY bestselling author

Carole Mortimer

is back with her most scandalously
entertaining romance yet!

ANNIE AND THE RED-HOT ITALIAN

When single mother Annie is forced back into the world of
Luca de Salvatore, the gorgeous father of her child, sparks fly!
Can Annie find a way to make Luca understand why she kept
her pregnancy secret—and let her little boy know his father?

Part of the exciting
Harlequin Presents® miniseries

The Balfour Brides

Available January 2011 from Harlequin Presents®.

www.eHarlequin.com

HP12964

If you enjoyed this story from
USA TODAY *bestselling author*
Carole Mortimer,
here is an exclusive excerpt from her upcoming book
ANNIE AND THE RED-HOT ITALIAN
Available January 2011 from Harlequin Presents®.

THE MAN GRINNED DOWN AT HER. "I have finished skiing for today and now it is my intention to return to my chalet for a glass of wine. Perhaps you would care to join me?" he asked.

"I would?" She blinked up at him owlishly. "I mean... yes, I would." She gave a firm nod.

"Luc." He removed his ski glove before proffering his hand.

She returned the gesture, her hand small and warm in his much larger one. "Annie."

Luc had kept to himself since his arrival at the resort two days ago, but nevertheless he had seen the group of university students intent on having a good time. He had noticed this young woman in particular, as she seemed to stand slightly apart from the antics of her friends. She was certainly worth noticing, with her long, rich chestnut hair, the vibrant blue of her eyes flashing whenever she laughed and the way her blue ski suit outlined the lush, feminine curves of her body. He'd been consumed by a curiosity to see the lushness of those curves without the ski suit....

If nothing else, her joining him for a few glasses of wine might succeed in a temporary banishment of the mess Luc had left behind him in Rome.

"I will wait here for you if you wish to tell your friends where you are going." He glanced across to where her friends were seated outside the cafeteria, chatting and laughing together as they enjoyed warming drinks.

"I... Yes." Color warmed her cheeks. "How thoughtful of you."

Not thoughtful at all, Luc acknowledged cynically, but merely an effort on his part to make sure that the night he was now contemplating enjoying with this young woman was not interrupted by her friends if they came looking for her.

He reached up and gently touched the creaminess of her cheek, instantly aware of the darkening of those wide blue eyes and the way her breath caught and held in her throat. "Do not keep me waiting long, hmm?" he murmured.

Once again Annie felt that thrill of awareness down the length of her spine. Dear God, this man was lethal. Absolutely, 100 percent lethal. And for once in her so-far-practical life, Annie was going to be daring. Reckless.

And to hell with the consequences.

But Annie could never have imagined how far-reaching the consequences of her outrageously pleasurable night with Luc were going to be! Now she has a secret, one that will change Luc's life forever when he discovers it....

Be seduced, scandalized and utterly swept away
by Carole Mortimer's latest romance!
ANNIE AND THE RED-HOT ITALIAN
Available January 2011 from Harlequin Presents®.